T0190717

THE
KILLING
PLACE

KATE ELLIS

THE KILLING PLACE

PIATKUS

PIATKUS

First published in Great Britain in 2023 by Piatkus
This paperback edition published in Great Britain in 2024 by Piatkus

1 3 5 7 9 10 8 6 4 2

Copyright © Kate Ellis 2023

The moral right of the author has been asserted.

*All characters and events in this publication, other than those
clearly in the public domain, are fictitious and any resemblance
to real persons, living or dead, is purely coincidental.*

All rights reserved.
No part of this publication may be reproduced, stored in a
retrieval system, or transmitted, in any form or by any means, without
the prior permission in writing of the publisher, nor be otherwise circulated
in any form of binding or cover other than that in which it is published
and without a similar condition including this condition being
imposed on the subsequent purchaser.

A CIP catalogue record for this book is available from the British Library.

ISBN 978-0-349-43315-8

Typeset in New Baskerville by M Rules
Printed and bound in Great Britain by Clays Ltd, Elcograf S.p.A

Papers used by Piatkus are from well-managed forests
and other responsible sources.

Piatkus
An imprint of
Little, Brown Book Group
Carmelite House
50 Victoria Embankment
London EC4Y 0DZ

An Hachette UK Company
www.hachette.co.uk

www.littlebrown.co.uk

For the next generation;
Eloise, Ivy, Alex and Orla

1

5 *November*

The woman in the sedan chair had been wearing a powdered wig and a fine gown of blue satin, low-necked and edged with yellowing lace. She could easily have been mistaken for the restless ghost who was said to inhabit the place. But Patrick North knew that she was no ghost. She was a corpse.

Patrick had never experienced real terror before. But this was the first time he'd ever come face to face with death.

He forced himself to keep moving, trying to ignore the sharp stitch in his side and the aching heaviness in his legs. He needed to reach safety and tell someone what he'd seen. But the woodland around him seemed endless, and as he ran, his trainers slipped on the damp brown foliage covering the ground. He could smell decay, the musty rot of dying things. An omen perhaps; a sign that his life was about to end.

He could hear explosions in the distance, loud as gunfire, and he saw faraway cascades of light brighten the sky. It was Bonfire Night, and not too far away, people were enjoying themselves, oblivious to his fear.

He stopped to catch his breath and listened. When the noise of the fireworks stopped, he could hear faint taunting laughter getting closer, as though his tormentor was confident of victory – however long it took.

Patrick took his phone from his pocket. There'd been no signal when he'd tried before, but now maybe ... But the thing was as dead as the leaves on the ground. Any chance of escape was fading fast.

He knew he was somewhere on the estate, but he wasn't sure where. All he knew was that if he didn't reach the road soon, he was a dead man. His pursuer was closing in on him, crashing through the undergrowth. Patrick flattened his body against a thick tree trunk. Perhaps if he kept very still ...

'Come out, come out, wherever you are. You can't get away. You might as well give up now.'

His tormentor's voice disturbed the crows in the treetops, and their raucous cries mocked him too, as though the birds were enjoying the game of cat and mouse happening below their nests. Then Patrick heard a twig snap nearby. Someone was creeping towards his chosen tree. This was it. Fight or flight. Life or death.

He broke cover, and when he twisted round, he saw his tormentor walking steadily towards him. He backed up, but found his way blocked by a thick tree trunk.

'Not much good at this, are you?' The taunting voice sounded completely calm as Patrick saw the rifle pointing straight at his chest.

Instinctively he raised both his hands, something he'd seen people do in films, but the eyes staring at him were cold and pitiless, as though this was nothing – just a game to pass the time.

Patrick had always thought himself too young to imagine how he'd face death when the time came. But to his surprise, he felt numb and detached, as though he was in the middle of a nightmare, and he'd soon wake and find everything as it should be.

He closed his eyes. A few seconds later, he was lying on the ground. Dead.

2

As an archaeologist, it wasn't unknown for Neil Watson to come across human remains in the course of his job, but he hadn't expected any to turn up in this particular location.

The developer, Jason Fonsby, was anxious to get the archaeological report on the site completed as soon as possible so the building work could begin. Twelve luxury executive homes, each with four bedrooms, the same number of bathrooms, and kitchens double the size of Neil's Exeter flat. Neil didn't think anyone he knew personally could afford to live in such luxury. But then most of his social circle were impecunious fellow archaeologists – apart from his old friend from university days, Wesley Peterson, who was a detective inspector.

As soon as he'd arrived that morning, Neil had stood at the entrance to the field, staring at the copse at its centre: a small patch of trees, their branches almost bare now that autumn had stripped them of their foliage. The field had once belonged to a big house nearby, but it had been sold to a local farmer fifteen years ago. The farmer had used it to graze his herd of Devon red cattle until Jason Fonsby made him an offer for the field that was difficult for a cash-strapped farmer to refuse. The place was within easy reach of Neston, and so ideal for housing. Exclusive housing, of course. There wasn't sufficient profit in affordable homes for local people.

Prior to planning permission being granted, Neil had carried out a routine desk-based archaeological assessment of the site and found vague hints in a Victorian history of the area that strange activities had taken place there in the eighteenth century, although this might have been the product of the nineteenth-century author's lurid imagination. People love a good story, the more ghoulish the better. However, during his investigations he'd made a surprising discovery: a map of the area dating back to the eighteenth century showing an unexpected feature in the middle of the copse with one intriguing word. *Grotto*.

Most people associated the word with Santa Claus, but not Neil. Because the land had once formed part of the large estate connected to Nesbarton Hall, a modestly sized but perfectly designed Palladian mansion dating back to the reign of George II, he wondered whether this particular grotto might be a decorative folly, the kind popular with fashionable gentry at that time. In those days a folly was a status symbol to impress the neighbours – like a hot tub or a swimming pool today.

When he'd alerted Jason Fonsby to this possibility, the man hadn't bothered to hide his irritation. Time was money and he needed the bulldozers on site as soon as possible. But Neil stood his ground. He needed to investigate the feature on the map, and that was that. The County Archaeological Unit didn't cut corners. And Dr Neil Watson, in his capacity as Heritage Manager, Archaeology and Historic Environment, intended to do a thorough job whether the developer liked it or not.

Neil had decided to make this site visit with his second in command, Dave, who always wore an Indiana Jones hat like a badge of office. Dave was a taciturn man, a good archaeologist, conscientious and reliable, and as the crows cawed from their scruffy nests in the copse, Neil was glad of his company. The dark tunnel of trees ahead of them had the look of a sinister wood from a fairy tale, and both men hesitated a few moments before marching in.

'Creepy place,' said Dave, and Neil was relieved that the atmosphere hadn't just been his imagination.

At first they saw nothing out of the ordinary; just tree trunks, and dank fallen leaves carpeting the ground. If there was anything like a grotto here, it was well hidden.

'What's that?'

They'd reached a small clearing, and Dave was pointing to a pile of rocks rearing up from the earth; around eight feet high and covered with moss. Neil walked slowly round them until he saw a round gap in the stones. An entrance into the unknown.

'Think it's safe?' Dave had always been keen on health and safety.

'Only one way to find out.'

Neil had to stoop a little to gain access. Once inside, he called to Dave. 'Come and have a look.'

He took his torch from one of the many pockets of his combat jacket and flashed it around the circular chamber. The stones had been worked by a mason and were covered with faded images he couldn't quite make out in the weak torchlight.

'What is it? An ice house?' Dave suggested.

'It's too far from the big house. I think it's some kind of folly; a decorative grotto like it says on that old map. We'll need to get the team over here to record it properly. With any luck we'll be able to persuade the developer to preserve it – make it a feature of the development.'

Dave looked sceptical, as though he thought Neil was being over-optimistic.

Neil swept his torch beam around the earth floor. The structure, whatever it was, seemed watertight, because there were no puddles to show that the Devon rain had seeped through. As he did another, slower sweep, the beam caught something at the far end of the cave-like room. The shadow of another entrance. Without another word, he walked towards it.

'Shouldn't we be wearing hard hats?' said Dave behind him.

'Looks solid enough to me,' said Neil, his eyes focused on the gap in the stones, a narrow doorway just large enough for a man to get through.

Once he'd squeezed through the entrance, he found himself in a second, smaller room. He pointed his torch at the roof just in case Dave's misgivings were justified. When he was satisfied that the structure was safe, he flashed the beam round the floor and walls. This room was rectangular, and at the far end he saw what looked like an altar, carved from stone like the rest of the little building. There were words etched on the wall above it, but he couldn't make them out in the dim light. Cobweb-draped remnants of candles stood in small niches around the walls, and Neil's first thought was that the place had been used as some sort of chapel.

Then he saw the thing on the altar. A human figure, naked, with unnaturally pale limbs. He backed away, his eyes fixed on the altar as though he hoped the body would get up and tell them it was all a joke. He squeezed back through the entrance and joined Dave in the outer room.

'Well?' Dave said as soon as he emerged. 'What's in there?'

Neil didn't answer. He took Dave's arm and steered him outside into the damp autumn air before taking his phone from his pocket. 'I've got to call the police. There's a dead body in there and it looks as though it hasn't been there long.'

He pressed the key to dial Wesley Peterson's number. Wes would know exactly what to do.

April 1787

A GENTLEMAN IS DESIROUS OF AN ACTOR TO
ASSUME A MOST IMPORTANT ROLE FOR THE
AMUSEMENT AND ENTERTAINMENT OF CERTAIN
PERSONS OF QUALITY IN THE COUNTY OF
DEVONSHIRE.
THE ACTOR IN QUESTION SHOULD BE YOUNG AND
PERSONABLE WITH THE ABILITY TO PERFORM
CONVINCINGLY ANY ROLE GIVEN TO HIM.
A GENEROUS REWARD AWAITS THE SUCCESSFUL
APPLICANT.
CONTACT NATHANIEL NESCOTE AT THE MOON
AND STARS TAVERN ON FLEET STREET AT ONE OF
THE CLOCK THIS SATURDAY.

When this request for an actor to perform for persons of quality was brought to my attention by Mr Bruce, I wavered at first.

I had nursed such hopes of acquiring a leading role at our theatre, but since Mr Bruce's nephew joined the company, I have had to be contented with taking minor roles in each production.

I carried a spear in the play of Macbeth *but did not speak,* and I was a servant in Mr Wycherley's play The Country Wife. It seems that each role I am offered requires me to be dumb, and yet I have been told I have a fine speaking voice.

I fear that my dearest hopes are destined to be thwarted while Mr Bruce's relative plays the hero. He is a handsome young man – more handsome than myself, I confess. I do not like his haughty manner, but as Mr Bruce is manager of the theatre as well as the leading actor, I see no future for me here.

I shall attend the Moon and Stars tavern at one of the clock this Saturday. They say Devonshire is a fine county.

3

The Anglo-Saxon name for November was Blotmonath –
Blood Month, when fattened animals were slaughtered to
save the expense of keeping them alive through winter.
The second of the month is All Souls' Day, when people
traditionally remember the souls of the departed, and
more recently, it has become the month when the nation
commemorates the war dead. Spring might herald
hope and rebirth, but November has always been the
time of death.

Geoff Haynes loved the old country lore and he liked
to think he was quite an expert, having lived in the Devon
countryside for seventy-nine years. He'd even written a
book about it – more of a booklet really – which still sold
in small quantities in the tourist shops of Tradmouth
and Neston.

Geoff pulled on his sturdy black wellingtons, spattered
with mud after years of service in the landscape around
Gorfleet Farm. He'd seen the incomers in their posh green
wellies getting out of their massive SUVs. All show; playing
at being country folk like that French queen who had her
head chopped off used to play at being a shepherdess even
though she wouldn't have known one end of a sheep from

the other. Geoff had no time for people like that – and there were so many of them about these days.

Bessy, his black and white Border collie, who was a veteran of many a sheep dog trial, hurried to her master's side. Walk time. Even dogs who were well past retirement enjoyed their daily exercise.

It wasn't raining, which made a change at that time of year. As Geoff walked across the cobbles in front of his cottage with Bessy trotting by his side, he glanced back at the recently renovated building. It had once housed a labourer and his family – up to eight kids in those days – but Geoff lived there alone. He'd never married, unlike his nephew, Peter, whose son, Nigel, now ran the farm. Geoff had always been the odd one out in the Haynes family, the impractical dreamer among a tribe of down-to-earth farmers. He'd done his bit on the farm in his time, but now it was just him and Bessy. And his recently arrived unexpected guest.

Geoff had considered it his Christian duty to offer the stranger shelter in his spare bedroom. He'd been raised to be kind to his fellow creatures, so when he'd found the man who called himself Ben wandering in a nearby lane, confused and obviously in need of help, he'd brought him back to the cottage. He'd asked gentle questions, but the man's replies were evasive, so he still knew nothing about Ben or his background. When he'd tentatively asked him whether he'd like someone to take him to hospital for a check-up, the answer had been no; all he needed was rest and time to recover.

Geoff knew that if his nephew or great-nephew found out about Ben, they'd warn him to be careful. Nigel was married to a policewoman – a detective sergeant – so maybe she had taught him to be suspicious. Perhaps Rachel came home from work each night with tales of robbery and murder, and no doubt she'd say that any stranger who turned up out of the blue might be a threat to his safety. However, at his age, Geoff preferred to use his own judgement.

Geoff trudged across the fields. It was Nigel's land now, much of it pasture for the dairy herd. Cows stared at him curiously as he passed by, but Bessy dutifully ignored them; she was a farm dog who knew how to behave around livestock. When he reached the thick hedgerow that formed the field boundary, he paused. Beyond that, the land belonged to the place they'd always called the Big House, although its proper name was Nesbarton Hall. Many years ago, Gorfleet Farm had belonged to the hall, and the Haynes family had been tenant farmers until Geoff's great-grandfather had bought the farm from the then owner of the hall, who'd run up tremendous gambling debts and been forced to sell his assets at a knock-down price. The Nescote family, who'd owned Nesbarton Hall back then, had been a terrible lot, according to Geoff's grandad, but the last of them had passed away in the 1960s, leaving no heirs. Since then the hall had been used as a convent, a convalescent hospital and a boarding school. Then for years it had lain unused until the present owner had bought it. Rumour had it that he was a billionaire, but few people in the area had ever seen him.

Geoff opened the big metal gate and Bessy walked through ahead of him before he shut it again. Although he'd never seen the billionaire, he imagined it would be no skin off his nose if one of his neighbours walked his dog on a distant piece of his extensive estate. More than likely he'd never even realise. From where Geoff stood, he could see the Big House nestling in a hollow almost a mile away. Its white facade reminded him of a doll's house. With a classical portico at the centre and a wing either side, it was pleasingly symmetrical, with a compact practicality that made it feasible as a family home – providing the family could afford that sort of thing.

He walked on, keeping close to the hedgerow, making for the area of woodland where Bessy loved sniffing for foxes and squirrels. As he walked in among the trees, he could see tattered nests dotted around in the bare branches. The crows were making more of a racket than usual, and he wondered fleetingly what had disturbed them. He hoped the landowner hadn't chosen that moment to take a stroll around his estate, but if he encountered him – or her – he'd plead ignorance; play the village idiot. It was what some incomers expected after all.

Bessy ran ahead into the undergrowth and started to bark urgently, which wasn't like her at all.

'Here, Bessy. Come here, girl.'

She came bounding back, looking up at him, still barking loudly. Geoff knew she was trying to tell him something important, and as he followed her, she stopped every now and then to check that he was still behind her.

'All right, girl. What is it? What have you found?'

When she stopped, tail still wagging, he saw that she was standing beside a human body. A young man, fully clothed and lying face down.

'Come away, girl. Leave it.'

Bessy sloped to his side as though he'd just ruined her moment of triumph. Geoff didn't have a mobile phone. He didn't believe in them. He retraced his steps to the cottage and rang the farmhouse on his landline.

'Is that you, Nigel? It's Uncle Geoff. Is your Rachel there? There's something she might want to know.'

4

'What's all the fuss about? Your mate Neil's always finding skeletons. That's his job, isn't it?'

Detective Inspector Wesley Peterson smiled indulgently at his boss. He'd learned long ago never to take DCI Gerry Heffernan's comments too seriously – unless they were about a case they were working on. Wesley and Neil had studied archaeology together at Exeter University, but Wesley had joined the police while Neil pursued a career in archaeology. The two had remained friends despite their very different backgrounds. Wesley was the son of two doctors from Trinidad who'd sent their academically bright children to expensive schools and steered them towards what they considered to be suitable paths, while Neil's parents had favoured a more relaxed approach. Eventually both men had found their respective niches in life – although Wesley sometimes wondered whether his career choice had disappointed his ambitious parents.

'If Neil had unearthed a skeleton during a dig, he'd hardly be in such a panic. He says he's found a body and suggests we send the crime-scene team to have a look – and Dr Bowman.'

DCI Heffernan scratched his head. He was a big man,

with grizzled hair and a Liverpool accent he'd never lost even though he'd lived in Devon for decades. 'What else did he say? Is it a man or a woman? Any sign of a cause of death – or a murder weapon?'

'He said it was a woman and he thought she might be naked.'

'Surely he knows what a naked woman looks like by now. Didn't know he'd led such a sheltered life.' Wesley saw Gerry's lips twitch upwards in a smile, then he swiftly became serious. Gerry's mischievous sense of humour meant that he made a joke of many things, but untimely death was no laughing matter.

'He only had a small torch, so there was hardly any light. And he didn't want to hang around and contaminate the scene. He knows the procedure as well as we do.'

Gerry made the call – the whole circus, as he called it, would be converging on the location Neil had specified. And he and Wesley would be joining them.

The CID office was quiet. The tourist season with its accompanying troubles was well and truly behind them for another year, but there'd been reports of pickpockets operating at the fireworks display on the riverfront the previous Saturday. Crowds always attracted crime. They were also dealing with a spate of distraction burglaries, stolen quad bikes, the theft of kayaks that had been locked up for the winter, and an assault outside a pub over the river in Queenswear. Gerry tried to look on the bright side, saying that if crime stopped, they'd all be out of a job.

But now it looked as though they had something more serious to deal with. A suspicious death between Tradmouth and Neston, not far from Gorfleet Farm, where Rachel lived with her farmer husband, Nigel Haynes. DS

Rachel Tracey – she still used her maiden name at work – was on maternity leave following the birth of her first baby in August, a son called Freddie. Wesley was surprised at how much he missed his detective sergeant, and he wondered whether to pay her a visit while they were in the area. He was sure she'd want to know what was happening in the CID office in her absence. On the other hand, he remembered how his wife, Pam, had felt after their own first child was born. With the relentless demands of a new infant, she didn't have the head space to think about work. That came later, once things had settled down into a manageable routine. However, it was possible that by now Rachel had started to see things differently; that she might even be longing for a glimpse of the outside world.

He was surprised when Gerry seemed to read his mind.

'The place isn't far from Rach's farm, so maybe we can pop in to say hello after we've seen what's going on. We're bound to have half an hour or so twiddling our thumbs while the crime-scene people do their bit, and if I know Rach, she'll want to be kept up to date with all the station gossip.' He tapped the side of his nose. 'Plus it'll give her a break from dirty nappies.' Gerry chuckled. He might put the fear of God into new recruits to CID, but Wesley had learned long ago that underneath the bluster he was a big softie, and he guessed his boss was looking forward to a cuddle with the new baby.

Gerry said little more as they drove to the site of Neil's discovery. When they arrived, the first thing Wesley noticed was a large sign standing at the field entrance. *Fonsby Executive Homes – an exclusive development of twelve luxury homes.* There was a phone number and a website address beneath the announcement.

'Bet they won't come cheap,' Gerry observed as he climbed out of the passenger seat. 'What was Neil doing here anyway?'

'It's a condition of planning permission that there has to be an archaeological assessment. You can't have developers digging just anywhere. If there's an Anglo-Saxon cemetery, for instance . . .'

'Is that what he thinks is here?' Gerry stood at the gate to the field.

'No. I'm just using that as an example. He spotted a feature on an old map and he wanted to investigate. A grotto.'

'That reminds me, it'll be Christmas soon.' Gerry grinned, showing the gap in his front teeth, something he'd always claimed was a sign of good luck. 'Maybe we should make the CID Christmas do fancy dress this year. I bags being Santa.' He chuckled. 'Can you imagine our DCs dressed as elves?'

Wesley couldn't resist a smile at the mental image of the team wearing green tights and pointed ears. 'It isn't that kind of grotto, Gerry. He thinks it might be a folly connected with the big house nearby – Nesbarton Hall.'

'I stand corrected. Field looks muddy – we'll need our wellies.'

Without another word, Wesley opened the car boot and both men pulled on their wellington boots. Wesley could see activity about a hundred yards away centred round a copse of trees. It had been raining for the past few days and the water had softened the earth, so as they made their way across the field, their feet sank into the ground. He hoped the new luxury homes would have good foundations.

A barrier of blue and white police tape was draped around the trees at the entrance to the copse, and two

CSIs in white crime-scene suits were strolling through the trees towards them. Wesley was surprised to see that they were grinning.

'Well?' Gerry shouted to them. 'What have we got?'

'False alarm. It's some kind of dummy. Someone must have put it there as a joke. We've called the pathologist to let him know. Didn't want him to have a wasted journey.'

Standing there in the cold and damp, Wesley found himself wishing that his friend hadn't been so fastidious about preserving a potential crime scene and had at least bothered to make a cursory examination of the 'body'. On the other hand, he knew that Neil had done the right thing. Archaeologists were as good as crime-scene teams at preserving vital evidence.

'At least it's got us out into the fresh air,' said Gerry with a sigh. 'We might as well have a look now we're here.'

The CSI turned and pointed. 'It's in a weird sort of cave in the middle of the trees. 'Keep going and you'll see it straight ahead.'

Wesley followed his directions with Gerry following behind. By good fortune they arrived just as the floodlights were about to be dismantled, and Gerry asked if they could hang on a few minutes while they took a look.

As they walked through the first chamber, Wesley felt a sudden surge of panic, as though the rough stone walls were closing in on him. He'd suffered from claustrophobia most of his life and he found the place oppressive, with its painted symbols and sinister images. Some of the paintings and carvings were hard to make out, but others appeared to be depictions of the devil, along with upside-down crosses and other signs of black magic. He'd been raised by strictly God-fearing parents and his brother-in-law was a vicar, and he sensed the presence of evil. There was a motto painted on the stone above the entrance. *We are masters of all and our will is law.* He shuddered. The paint was old and faded, suggesting that whatever had gone on in there had happened a long time ago in the past.

Scanning the earth floor, he noticed discarded drinks cans and crisp packets. The litter didn't surprise him; it was the sort of place that might attract local youths with time on their hands. He could see a gap in the wall, a narrow entrance into a brightly lit inner chamber, and it was with a sense of trepidation that he stepped through it, his heart pounding and his palms tingling.

The floodlights were focused on the stone altar at the far end, and in the bright light it was obvious that the thing lying there was a dummy of some kind. But if Neil had seen it in the weak beam of a small torch, he couldn't be blamed for assuming the worst.

'What do you reckon, Wes? Kids messing about?'

Wesley took another deep breath, determined to overcome what he knew was his irrational fear of enclosed spaces, and walked over to the figure on the altar. When the word 'dummy' was first mentioned, he'd imagined a shop dummy, hard plastic with generic features and long limbs. But the life-sized figure before him was no mass-produced mannequin. Its pale limbs were made of some soft material, possibly linen, stuffed with horsehair or straw perhaps. The face and hands were finely modelled, and when Wesley touched the cheek, he guessed it was made of painted papier mâché. There was no hair on the head, and the features were those of a beautiful woman, with rouged cheeks and wide blue eyes. The thing was old; possibly rare. He glanced up and saw the same words carved on the wall above the altar as he'd seen at the grotto's entrance. *We are masters of all and our will is law.*

'Well? What do you think?'

Wesley gave his verdict. 'It looks very old, but I don't think it's been here long because it's in remarkable condition. We ought to take it back to the station with us. It could be part of someone's antique collection.'

'I can't recall anyone reporting anything like this missing.'

'Perhaps the owners are away and they don't realise they've been burgled yet.'

'I suppose we can give her a home in our exhibits store until we find out,' said Gerry.

He helped Wesley pick up the figure, which seemed to weigh almost as much as a human body, and they carried it between them, manoeuvring it carefully through the narrow doorway.

'Who's your friend?' said the CSI who was busy clearing up in the outer chamber, chuckling at his own joke.

Wesley looked at the DCI and rolled his eyes. They'd probably be on the receiving end of more wisecracks before they eventually got her into the car.

They carried the model carefully, keeping it away from the damp ground, and when they reached the car, Gerry suggested putting it in the boot with the wellingtons. But Wesley insisted on installing her on the back seat, duly strapped in. If she was a rare antique as he suspected, the last thing he wanted was to cause any damage.

As Wesley was about to get into the driver's seat, his phone rang. He was surprised to see Rachel's name on the caller display. She began to speak before he could even say hello.

'Wes, it's Rachel. I've just had a strange call from Nigel's uncle – well, great-uncle actually. He says he's found a body. It was all a bit vague, but he said he told me first because I'd know what to do. He's only got a landline, so he must be at home in his cottage.'

'We're not far from you; we can be there in ten minutes or so.'

'Uncle Geoff's a bit … eccentric and Nigel thinks he could be losing his marbles, so perhaps he's been seeing things. But it's best to make sure, don't you think?'

'Absolutely.' Wesley glanced at Gerry, who was waiting impatiently in the front seat while their passenger sat in the back with an inscrutable half-smile on her painted face. 'We're going to Rachel's,' he said. 'Her great-uncle-in-law's claiming he's found a body.'

'It might be her,' Gerry said, gesturing towards their silent companion. 'He could have been exploring that cave place.'

'According to Rachel, he's a bit eccentric, and I remember her saying he's into local history and folklore, so I wouldn't rule it out. But we still need to check.'

Gerry nodded slowly as Wesley started the engine.

5

Wesley knew the way to Gorfleet Farm. A few years ago, he'd got to know the Haynes family during an investigation at a nearby property, though he'd never come across Great-Uncle Geoff before. Presumably he'd been at Rachel's wedding, but Wesley didn't remember him amongst the crowd of relatives and friends.

He parked in the yard in front of the farmhouse and Rachel hurried out of the front door to meet them. Gone were her smart working clothes; she was wearing old jeans and hugging a chunky cardigan around her body for warmth.

As Wesley emerged from the car, she bent down to peer at the mannequin in the back seat. 'Made an arrest, have you?' she asked with a grin. 'Who or what is that?'

'I'll explain inside.'

'Hello, Rach love. You'll be pleased to know we're missing you like mad,' said Gerry as he hauled himself out of the passenger seat.

'Likewise,' said Rachel, leading the way to the front door. 'Freddie's asleep, so keep your voices down.'

A look of disappointment passed across Gerry's face. 'I was hoping to see him. How is the little chap?' he asked once they'd reached the warmth of the farmhouse kitchen.

'He's fine. But I reckon Nigel can't wait until he's big enough to help around the farm. He's gone up to Uncle Geoff's cottage – Nigel, that is, not Freddie.' She smiled again, and Wesley thought that motherhood suited her. 'To be honest, I couldn't make much sense of what Geoff said on the phone.'

'He told you he'd found a body?'

'I think that's what he said. Mind you, knowing Geoff, it could have been a dead sheep. Go on then, what's the story with your passenger?'

'Neil found it in a field nearby that's being developed for housing.'

Rachel rolled her eyes. 'Do you mean the one on the main road? Big sign for Fonsby Homes.'

'That's it. There's some kind of folly in the middle of a copse, and Neil was doing a routine investigation; a condition of the planning permission. The inside of the folly was too dark to see properly, so when he spotted our friend, he thought it was a body. He didn't want to look too closely in case he disturbed a crime scene, so he called me – along with the whole CSI team. It caused some amusement.'

'I can imagine.'

'It's some kind of dummy, but it looks very old, so I thought we should make sure it didn't get damaged.'

Rachel shrugged. Wesley had once served in the Met's Art and Antiques Unit, and she was used to him being distracted by antiquities. But a life-size naked female figure was a first.

Her mobile phone started to ring, and she picked it up from the kitchen table. Wesley listened intently to the one-sided conversation and saw that she was looking troubled.

She turned to face them as she ended the call. 'That was

Nigel. Uncle Geoff's sticking to his story. He says he found a body in woodland on the Nesbarton Hall estate, swears he wasn't imagining it. We've told him time and time again not to walk there; we've heard on the local grapevine that the owner's a billionaire businessman, and people like that don't usually take kindly to trespassers.' She rolled her eyes in exasperation. 'Not that Uncle Geoff ever takes any notice of anything we say. He's a law unto himself.'

'Maybe we should have a word with him,' said Gerry. 'You OK to come with us, Rach? Is the nipper . . .?'

'That's no problem. I'll ask Nigel's mum to keep an eye on him. She enjoys playing the doting granny.'

She left the room for a few minutes, and returned wearing an old waxed coat and wellies. 'We can walk,' she said, looking with approval at her colleagues' footwear. They hadn't removed their wellingtons because the kitchen floor was stone-flagged, traipsed across by generations of the Haynes family in muddy boots.

It had been warm in the kitchen because the AGA had been going full pelt, but as the chilly November air hit his face, Wesley shivered. Rachel marched ahead across the farmyard, past a barn full of farm equipment, and the milking parlour, cleaned and awaiting its bovine clients, who would be on parade there later that afternoon.

Great-Uncle Geoff's cottage was further from the main farmhouse than Wesley had expected. The air was damp, and it started to drizzle as they trudged across a field, watched by a group of bored-looking cows.

The cottage looked well kept, with tubs of bare earth beside the front door waiting to be planted with colourful flowers once spring arrived. The rendered walls were painted cream and the double-glazed windows looked new.

The Haynes family made sure that their elderly relative lived in comfort.

Wesley, Rachel and Gerry didn't glance upwards, so they didn't see the man standing behind the cottage's upper window, watching them intently from the shadows.

April 1787

As I stood outside the tavern, I saw other young men entering and wondered whether they too hoped to be appointed to the position. I recognised one of them as my fellow actor, John Hampton, who was working at a theatre that had recently closed. Most of the men looked thin and hungry, their clothing shabby and worn. Perhaps they had been without employment for a while.

I nodded to Hampton, who smiled sadly in return. As he approached me, he looked over his shoulder as though he feared we would be overheard.

'How now, Charles? What brings you here?' he said.

'The same as you, I wager.'

'Some person has posted a bill at all the stage doors in London offering a most lucrative post to some fortunate fellow. Do you know what the work is?'

'No,' I answered, for this was the truth. 'But they say Devonshire is a goodly place and I have a fancy to get out of London. Shall we go in?'

We entered the tavern side by side, and the landlord showed us to a private chamber at the back. He told John to wait outside and opened the door to admit me.

I tried my best to assume the bold confidence of a man who considers himself to be a success on the stage. It would have angered my late father greatly if he'd witnessed my defiance of Our Lord's assurance that the meek would inherit the earth. In my experience, the meek go hungry while the bold and arrogant prosper.

The young man in fine clothes and a powdered wig looked me up and down in the manner of a farmer assessing a beast at market and then ordered me to sit.

His first question concerned my family. Did I have a father and mother? When I replied that they were both dead, he asked about brothers and sisters. I told him that I was the youngest of three brothers and that the elder two lived in the north. I said I had come to London to become an actor and he said that he wagered I made a fine one.

He then asked me whether I had ever played a madman.

6

According to Rachel, Great-Uncle Geoff's eccentricity had become more marked in recent years. Wesley, however, saw little evidence of odd behaviour as the man led them towards the place where he claimed to have found the body. His dog, Bessy, walked at his heels, glancing up adoringly at her master every now and then. Man and dog seemed inseparable, which was hardly surprising if Bessy was his sole companion in the cottage.

When Rachel had introduced them, Geoff had studied Wesley with interest for a while. Wesley understood that in the world the old farmer had grown up in, people with his skin colour were a rare and exotic novelty. There was no malice in his curiosity; in fact he seemed to attach himself to Wesley as they walked, asking him questions about where he was from and how long he'd been in Devon. Wesley answered simply. His parents were from the Caribbean, and he'd been born in London. He'd met a Devon girl at university, and when they'd married he'd moved here because Pam's widowed mother had been on her own. Geoff nodded with approval, satisfied once he'd learned Wesley's story.

'How far is it, Uncle Geoff?' Rachel asked.

'Just over yonder, maid.' Geoff always used the old Devon address for any young woman. Rachel found it quaint, but secretly rather liked it. He pointed to an area of woodland about a hundred yards away where the land began to dip down.

'Nigel worries about you going onto Nesbarton Hall land, you know. He says they could accuse you of trespassing.'

'That husband of yours is a right fusspot. I've been walking on this land since I was a lad, and no one's ever said anything. Besides, there's no gamekeeper there now, so who's to stop me.'

Nesbarton Hall had just come into view, sitting in a hollow in the undulating landscape, pristine white against its green surroundings. Wesley could see that the house was surrounded by formal gardens that must need a lot of maintenance. 'Who owns the estate?' he asked.

Geoff hesitated for a few moments before replying. 'I don't bother him and he doesn't bother me. We mind our own business, me and him.'

'Do you know his name?'

It was Rachel who answered. 'Smithson. Silas Smithson. They say he's a billionaire. Must be to buy Nesbarton Hall. Although I don't know how he made his money.'

Gerry was walking behind her, and Wesley heard him grunt in agreement. 'Must be flaming loaded. The upkeep of a place like that . . .'

'He's not in the habit of calling on the neighbours to borrow a cup of sugar, so I've never met him,' said Rachel. 'But I've heard it's not his only property. He has a place in London and another in the south of France.'

'How do you know that?' Wesley asked.

Rachel grinned. 'Word gets round. I've also heard he has

31

a glamorous Russian wife, and I think there are a couple of kids, although they don't have anything to do with the locals. They keep themselves to themselves.'

They were nearing the trees. Unlike the small copse where Neil had discovered the mannequin, this was serious woodland, probably covering a couple of acres or more. But in common with the copse, the trees here were bare and crows were keeping their noisy watch from the treetops.

Geoff hesitated, as though he was reluctant to venture any further.

'Can you show us the way?' Wesley asked gently. So far the elderly man had seemed undaunted by his grim discovery, but the true horror of the situation was probably beginning to sink in.

'It's this way,' Geoff said, glancing at Rachel, who gave him an encouraging smile.

He didn't say another word until they reached a spot around thirty yards into the trees. The sun had just emerged from behind the clouds, and weak wintry light dappled the woodland ground as they walked.

Wesley had been wondering whether, like Neil, Geoff had been mistaken about what he'd found. But he soon discovered that this was no false alarm. The man's body, lying prone on the damp ground with his right arm stretched above his head, was real enough.

Geoff moved forward, but Rachel put a warning hand on his arm. 'We mustn't disturb the scene, Uncle Geoff. They'll want to do tests. Forensic science and all that.'

Geoff nodded and backed away, Bessy following like his shadow, while Gerry took out his phone to call out the team, assuring them that this time their journey wouldn't be wasted.

'Bet you didn't think when you got up this morning that you'd be involved in the investigation of a suspicious death,' Gerry said to Rachel as the three of them stood back and studied the scene.

'I'd been hoping for a bit of a rest. Trust you two to turn up and spoil it.'

One look at her expression told Wesley that she wasn't being serious.

'Don't blame us,' said Gerry. He hesitated as though he wasn't sure whether his next question would be welcome. 'I know you're meant to be on maternity leave, but what do you make of it? Any first thoughts?'

Rachel's eyes shone, as though she was glad they weren't leaving her out. 'At this distance it's hard to tell,' she said. She peered at the body. 'His coat's dark, but I think that patch might be blood. An exit wound or stab wound maybe.' She frowned. 'He doesn't look that old; probably late twenties or early thirties. I don't think I've seen him around, but I can't be sure until he's turned over and we can see his face. He's well dressed, and those trainers look clean and expensive, so he probably hasn't been living rough. But we mustn't speculate yet. It could be a heart attack. Or a drug overdose. We'll have to wait for Colin and the CSIs.'

Patience had never been one of Gerry Heffernan's virtues, but he acknowledged that Rachel was right. The three of them left the shelter of the trees and joined Geoff, who was waiting with Bessy.

'OK for me to go now, maid?'

Rachel reassured him that it was fine, although her colleagues would need a statement from him later. Just routine. Nothing to worry about.

It seemed an age before a pair of patrol cars arrived, followed by the CSIs, the same team Wesley had met a couple of hours before in the grotto. No wonder they looked sceptical.

'Found another dummy, have we?' Wesley knew from experience that this particular CSI had always been a joker.

'Not this time, I'm afraid,' he said. 'It's a body – male. Definitely dead.'

Wesley took the team to the body. A uniformed constable busied himself erecting a barrier of police tape while the CSIs went about their work. On Gerry's orders, a sergeant had taken on the role of crime-scene manager, recording the comings and goings on a clipboard. Then the pathologist arrived, greeting everyone pleasantly. Dr Colin Bowman was a genial man, with years of experience. Wesley knew Gerry would be relieved that he was the one dealing with the case.

'Hello, Wesley. I've just seen Rachel with Gerry. Surely her maternity leave's not over yet?'

'No. Her farm's next door and it was her husband's great-uncle who found the body, while he was out walking.'

'Fancy that,' said Colin, before squatting down to begin his initial examination. 'Small world.'

He turned the body over gently as the crime-scene photographer snapped away. Wesley heard a sound behind him, and turned his head to see that Rachel and Gerry had joined him.

'Well, Colin, what have we got?' said Gerry.

Wesley watched Colin unzip the dead man's coat and make a close examination of a wound in the region of his heart. There was a patch of blood on the abdomen, and he moved the shirt the man was wearing to look at the flesh beneath. Then a swift inspection of the back confirmed that Rachel had been right about the exit wound.

'Well, well.' The doctor looked up at Gerry. 'I'll need to get him to the mortuary to confirm it, but I think this chap's been shot. Twice. Although I can definitely rule out a shotgun, the usual weapon of choice in rural areas like this.'

'Not an irate farmer after a trespasser, then?' Gerry glanced at Rachel.

'Doubtful. As I said, I'll be able to tell you more at the post-mortem.'

'Any ID on him?' Wesley asked. If this was going to be a murder investigation, it would help to know who the victim was.

Colin went through the pockets of the man's coat; the sort of waxed jacket that was virtually a uniform in the countryside. Only this one looked fairly new, as though it had been bought by a town dweller to fit in with his new environment.

Wesley saw Rachel studying the dead man's face intently. 'Do you recognise him?'

She shook her head. 'I think I might have seen him, but for the life of me I can't remember where or when.'

Colin was removing items from the man's pockets and placing them in plastic evidence bags. 'Here's your ID,' he said. 'A driving licence in the name of Patrick North. Address in Manchester. He's a long way from home.'

'That's a good start, Colin,' Gerry said with inappropriate cheerfulness. 'Anything else?'

'A key. Tissues. Throat sweets – it's that time of year.' He searched another pocket. 'Wallet with a couple of ten-pound notes and three ... no, four credit cards. Motive wasn't robbery.'

'You don't get many muggers round these parts,' said Rachel, catching Wesley's eye and giving him a small smile.

'Any sign of a phone?' Wesley's question was addressed to the CSIs who were conducting an examination of the surrounding area.

It was another ten minutes before someone found the dead man's phone at the foot of a tree about twenty feet further into the woods.

'Now we might get somewhere,' said Gerry with satisfaction as the CSI handed him the phone in an evidence bag. He dangled the bag in his fingers for a moment, staring at the phone as though he was willing it to give up its secrets. 'Better get this examined by the techies sooner rather than later. Hopefully it'll give us everything we need.'

But Wesley didn't share the DCI's optimism. 'We need to find out where the victim was staying. Let's start at Nesbarton Hall. This is their land.'

Rachel shrugged. 'True enough. But there's hardly a security fence around these woods, so anyone can gain access. I'd better get back. Freddie'll need feeding.'

As Wesley watched her walk away, he felt Gerry's large hand on his shoulder. 'Come on, Wes. Let's pay a call on the gentry. You do the talking. Your manners are better than mine.'

7

Wesley drove to Nesbarton Hall, aware that his strange passenger was still sitting in the back. He planned to take her to the police station's evidence store as soon as they returned to Tradmouth, but in the meantime, at least she wasn't going to complain about the wait while they conducted their enquiries.

They passed a lodge next to an impressive set of gates topped with carved stone pineapples, and the tyres crunched on pristine gravel as Wesley steered the car down the long, winding drive, eventually coming to a stately halt at the hall's front entrance. Gerry hung back with his hands thrust in his pockets, leaving it to Wesley to press the bell; a posh polished brass affair, large to match the house.

'There might be a butler,' Gerry whispered. 'He'll probably order us round to the tradesman's entrance.'

'If he does, he's going to be disappointed,' Wesley said as he pulled his ID from his pocket.

'Know anything about the person who owns this place?'

'I looked him up on my phone. Silas Smithson founded a tech company and sold it a few years later for seventy-five million pounds. Now he has fingers in a number of pies and invests in start-up companies. Like Rach said, he owns several houses, and he's got a yacht moored on the river – the kind of vessel you'd call a gin palace.'

'Nice work if you can get it,' said Gerry, with what sounded like envy, although Wesley knew his boss had never been the materialistic type.

Wesley rang the bell again. It was a big house and there was a chance the occupants hadn't heard.

After his third attempt, he heard a sound from the interior of the house, sharp footsteps coming nearer, heels tapping on a hard floor.

The door opened slowly to reveal a middle-aged woman dressed in black. She was tall and thin, with a long face, and brown hair cut in a neat bob. She wore glasses and a calm, neutral expression.

'Can I help you?' The question was businesslike, like a receptionist used to fending off unwanted demands on her employer's time.

Wesley and Gerry showed her their ID and introduced themselves. They could have left the visit to one of the detective constables, or even to uniform, but Wesley knew it was a lot harder to send away a couple of senior officers by pulling social rank.

'May we come in?' said Wesley, at his most polite. His years at an expensive private school had endowed him with charm and excellent manners. Gerry was the grandson of a Liverpool docker, and he always left it to Wesley to deal with the moneyed classes.

The woman stood aside to admit them. 'Of course. If you'd like to come this way.'

As she led them through the house, Wesley seized the opportunity to take in his surroundings. The proportions of the grand entrance hall were perfect, and the walls were painted in a tasteful duck-egg blue. The room was hung with portraits, original oils of ancestors such as he'd seen in many a stately home. Considering the new owner of the house was an entrepreneur, he wondered whether the people in the paintings were related to him in any way, or whether they were there simply to give the impression that his family had owned the place for generations. He suspected the latter.

A portrait at the top of the staircase caught his eye, a picture of a beautiful seated woman in a blue satin gown and a powdered wig, the height of fashion in the eighteenth century. It was in the style of Gainsborough, although from that distance he couldn't be sure of the true attribution. The house was filled with antiques: furniture and tastefully displayed *objets d'art*. The contents of the place alone were worth a fortune.

The woman led them into a well-proportioned room with yellow walls and two large windows overlooking the garden. She waved the two detectives to a comfortable-looking sofa, and sat down opposite them, looking perfectly at home, as though this was her private domain.

'Your name, madam?' Wesley asked tentatively. He was pretty sure she was staff, albeit high-up staff, but he still wasn't sure and he didn't want to commit a social faux pas if she turned out to be the owner's wife.

'Karensa Carlton. I'm Mr Smithson's personal assistant.'

'Do you live here?'

'Yes.'

'Are Mr and Mrs Smithson at home?'

'They're in Scotland at the moment. You haven't told me what this is about.'

'Forgive me,' said Wesley. 'We should have said right

away. We're investigating a suspicious death in the grounds of this property.'

Ms Carlton gave a puzzled frown. 'What on earth do you mean?'

'A man's body was found in an area of woodland a mile away, near a narrow lane that leads to the village. It's adjacent to fields belonging to Gorfleet Farm and we've been informed that the location is part of Mr Smithson's estate.'

There was no mistaking the relief on her face. 'The estate is very extensive, Inspector, and I'm afraid the days of loyal gamekeepers patrolling the boundaries of a property are long gone. A lot of local people use the grounds for walking and goodness knows what else. But in the absence of high security fencing and guards, it's not easy to keep them out.'

'We have a name for the dead man. Patrick North. Have you heard of him?'

The atmosphere in the room changed abruptly. The woman's mouth dropped open, and she remained silent for a few seconds, clearly in shock. Then she spoke. 'I know Patrick. He lives here.'

'You mean he's on the staff?'

She swallowed hard and nodded. 'He's Darius's tutor. He's been here since the start of term in September.'

'Who's Darius?' It was the first time Gerry had spoken, and Ms Carlton looked at him with undisguised curiosity.

'Darius is Mr Smithson's son,' she replied as though this was obvious.

'How old is he?' Wesley asked.

'Thirteen. Almost fourteen.'

'Why does he need a tutor?' Gerry asked bluntly. 'Shouldn't he be at school?'

There was a lengthy pause, as though she was trying to think of the best way to explain. 'Darius was at boarding school, but it didn't suit him. He's a very sensitive boy, so Mr and Mrs Smithson decided that it would be best to hire a private tutor to teach him at home.'

Gerry glanced at Wesley, then back at Karensa Carlton. 'Where's Darius now? We'd like to speak to him.'

'He's with his parents. They left for Scotland last Tuesday and they won't be back for at least another week, possibly longer.'

'We'd be grateful for their contact details. We need to let them know what's happened on their property,' said Wesley. 'They may have to cut their trip short, I'm afraid.'

'That won't be possible, Inspector.'

Gerry sat forward. 'This is a murder inquiry, love. I'm sure the Smithsons will want to co-operate.'

'No, Chief Inspector, you don't understand. They're travelling around the Highlands in their mobile home, and I have no way of contacting them. Mr Smithson likes to get away from civilisation every so often, with no phone signal and no internet. A complete detox, he calls it.'

'But you must be able to get in touch in case of an emergency.'

'I'm afraid not.'

'Darius was happy to go with them?' Wesley asked, curious.

'Of course.'

Wesley's own son, Michael, was around the same age, and he couldn't imagine him taking kindly to a digital detox in the middle of the Scottish Highlands in a cold, damp November. One look at Gerry's face told him he was thinking exactly the same.

'Do Mr and Mrs Smithson have any other children?'

41

'Yes. Their daughter, Tatiana's staying with her aunt at the moment. She's ten.' Ms Carlton looked away, as though the subject of Tatiana and the aunt was distasteful. In contrast, there had been a fond look in her eyes when Darius's name was mentioned.

'Is Tatiana not at boarding school?' Gerry asked.

'She's at Lowton Grange, the day school on the other side of Neston. As I said, she's staying with Mr Smithson's sister, Betina, who runs a writers' retreat in the lodge by the gates to the estate. You probably passed it on your way in.'

Wesley added Aunt Betina to his list of people he wanted to speak to, and was reminded that Della, Pam's mother, had been going on for some time about escaping to a writers' retreat for some peace and quiet. She claimed she was writing a book, although Pam, having studied English at university, was sceptical about her literary abilities. Della was notorious for her sudden enthusiasms, which lasted a few months before something new came along, and the book was her latest project. A couple of days ago, Pam had mentioned that Della's visit to her retreat was imminent, although Wesley had taken little interest in the details. Now, however, he wondered whether she might have chosen the lodge. He hoped not. The last thing he needed was his mother-in-law turning up during a murder investigation.

'Tatiana's an unusual name,' said Gerry.

'Mrs Smithson is Russian. I believe Tatiana was her late mother's name.'

'What's Mrs Smithson's first name?'

'Natalia.'

'Who else works here, Ms Carlton?'

'A couple of local women come in three times a week to clean, but they've been given time off while the family are away. And a firm from Tradmouth see to the formal garden every Tuesday and Friday in the spring and summer months, but not at this time of year, of course. I'm the only person who lives in.' She hesitated. 'Apart from Mr North, that is . . .' She took a tissue from her pocket and dabbed her eyes. 'He seemed such a nice young man. I can't believe anyone would want to harm him. Surely it must have been a tragic accident?'

'We think he's been dead a couple of days. Where were you over the weekend?'

'I've been here.'

'Any witnesses to that?' Gerry asked.

'I'm afraid not. I never thought I'd need any. And before you ask, as far as I can remember I've never been near that part of the estate, and I certainly haven't been aware of anything suspicious.'

'When did you last see Mr North?'

She closed her eyes as though she was making a great effort to remember. 'He was given time off when the family went to Scotland, of course, and he left on the afternoon of October the thirty-first. Mr and Mrs Smithson set off the following morning. I believe Mr North went to stay with his girlfriend. I didn't see him again after that.'

'Did he have a car?'

'Yes, a blue Ford Ka. It's parked at the back of the stables. I assumed he'd arranged to meet his girlfriend at the end of the drive and left the car here because she was picking him up.'

'Do you know anything about his girlfriend?'

'I think she lives in Dukesbridge, but I'm afraid that's all I know.'

'What about his family?'

'They live up north. Manchester, I think, although I don't have an address for them.'

'We need to look at his room.'

'Of course. I'm sure there's a spare key somewhere, although it might take me a while to lay my hands on it.'

'We found a key on the body,' said Wesley. 'That might save you the trouble of searching. If you can show us to his accommodation, we can find out.'

'Of course, Inspector. It's on the top floor.'

'Did he use any other part of the house?'

'Only the old schoolroom, on the same floor as his apartment. He had no cause to venture anywhere else.'

She rose from her seat and Wesley caught Gerry's eye. It was time to ask the difficult question. 'Would you be willing to identify the body?'

For a second she looked horrified. Then she nodded. 'If there's no one else.'

Rachel would have been his first choice to go with her to the hospital, but as she was unavailable, he would call on DC Trish Walton to perform the task instead. Trish was reassuringly sensible; a good person to have around at a time of crisis.

'If you and Patrick North were the only two members of staff who lived here, you must have got to know him well,' said Wesley as Ms Carlton walked ahead of them up the grand staircase.

'Oh no, I wouldn't say that at all,' she said quickly. 'Patrick kept himself to himself. And so did I. Our accommodation is in different wings of the house, so we never had much to do with each other.'

'What was he like?'

'As I say, I didn't know him well, but he seemed pleasant

enough. Quiet. When he was off duty, he spent most of his time away from the house, presumably with his girlfriend.'

'Do you know her name?'

'I'm afraid not. He didn't confide in me.'

'You must have formed an impression of him.'

She stopped walking and swung round. 'If I'm being honest, I found him a little . . . evasive. When he first came here, I asked him about himself, but he kept changing the subject. If you want to know what I really think, I reckon he was hiding something. But before you ask, I've no idea what that might have been.'

Wesley looked at Gerry. This was something they hadn't expected. And if Patrick North had a secret, it might provide a motive for his murder. All they had to do was to find out what that secret was.

At the top of the main staircase, Ms Carlton led them off to the left, towards a door beyond which lay a second, narrower staircase. The old servants' quarters.

Like downstairs, the paint here was fresh, and when Wesley tried the key from the dead man's pocket in the lock of the nearest door, it opened smoothly. He was pleasantly surprised by what he saw. Several of the attic rooms had been knocked together to make a spacious flat – an airy sitting room with a small, modern kitchen at one end, a bedroom and a pleasant en suite bathroom, all bathed in what light there was on a dull November afternoon. The furniture was modern, pale wood in the Scandinavian style, and there was a well-stocked bookcase. He walked over and studied the titles, surprised to see a lot of volumes about local history – and the history of Nesbarton Hall in particular.

But this was no time in indulge his curiosity. He was

there to do a job. He made the call to Trish Walton and told Ms Carlton that an officer would be there in half an hour to take her to the hospital in Tradmouth. She said she'd wait for DC Walton downstairs.

Once she'd left, Wesley and Gerry went in search of the schoolroom. They found it down the corridor; a light, spacious room with bars at the windows, which must once have served as a nursery. There was a large table in the centre of the room and shelves of modern educational books around the walls. The whiteboard at the far end was filled with mathematical equations. This had been Patrick North's domain.

'Once the identification's been made, we'll get the team over here to carry out a proper search,' said Gerry as they left the room. 'And hopefully the tech team will have unravelled the secrets of his phone for us by the time we get back to the station. We also need to find the girlfriend. In the meantime, let's have a nose around his flat.'

Wesley didn't argue, He was curious as to why a young man would choose to hide himself away in the countryside tutoring a sensitive thirteen-year-old boy. Perhaps it was just a case of the boy's billionaire father making a penniless teacher a financial offer he couldn't refuse. Although he couldn't help wondering whether he'd been running away from something; something that had ultimately led to his death.

Patrick North had been an organised man. He'd kept lesson plans and teaching materials in neat box files, and there was a folder filled with correspondence. When Wesley looked through it, he saw that there were a number of printed-out emails from Silas Smithson, outlining his duties and the terms of his employment. Wesley noticed that the salary was extremely generous, but he wondered whether there was anything the correspondence didn't say; for instance what Darius was really like.

As he continued to look through North's paperwork, he was a little puzzled by the lack of evidence of any life outside the four walls of Nesbarton Hall. Or any clue to the dead man's past.

8

Wesley and Gerry hoped that Silas Smithson's sister would be able to throw some light on the life of her nephew's tutor, but when they called at the lodge on their way out of the estate, there was nobody at home, so they returned to Tradmouth police station.

An hour later DC Trish Walton reported that Karensa Carlton had identified the dead man as Darius Smithson's tutor, Patrick North. According to Trish, the woman hadn't seemed particularly upset, giving a businesslike nod when the sheet was pulled back to reveal the corpse's face. Wesley told her not to read too much into the lack of emotion. Even though they'd lived in the same house for a couple of months, the pair hadn't had much to do with each other. And they almost certainly hadn't been friends.

A search team had been sent over to Nesbarton Hall to go through the dead man's apartment and the schoolroom. Gerry had made impatient phone calls to the tech team, ordering them to hurry up with the examination of the victim's phone, and they'd promised to have the job done by the following morning. First thing.

On Wesley's suggestion, a couple of uniformed constables took the mannequin to the evidence store. He'd pointed out that it was probably very old and should be treated with care, and as the officers walked through the police station with their mysterious burden, he could hear them running the gauntlet of clever comments.

'I'd like to set up an incident room near the scene,' Gerry announced. 'That hall's got big stables. If we can get permission ...'

'According to Karensa Carlton, Mr and Mrs Smithson can't be contacted,' Wesley pointed out. 'And we can hardly use his premises without his permission.'

Gerry grunted. 'There's the aunt – his sister. Maybe we can ask her when we see her.'

'It's worth a try,' said Wesley.

Gerry's phone rang and after a short conversation he looked at Wesley. 'I asked the search team to keep a look out for any vehicles at the lodge and it looks like we're in luck,' said Gerry, rubbing his hands together in anticipation. 'Let's pay Auntie Betina a call. Hopefully she'll be able to tell us more about the Smithsons and the set-up at the hall.'

Before they left for Nesbarton, Wesley called Pam to warn her that he'd probably be late home. Before he ended the call, he asked her a question. 'This writers' retreat your mum says she's going to – do you know if it's at Nesbarton Hall Lodge, between Tradmouth and Neston? The one I'm thinking of is run by a woman called Betina.'

'I confess I wasn't taking much notice when she told me – you know what she's like. But the name Betina does ring a bell. I tried to call her earlier, but her phone's switched off.'

'Can you try her again?' he said before promising to be home as soon as he could.

As they set off for Betina's, Gerry reminded him that Colin had booked the post-mortem for 4.30. 'Let's hope he has some decent biscuits in for afterwards,' he added.

'He hasn't failed us yet,' Wesley replied.

Twenty minutes later, they drew up at the white house set beside the gates to the Nesbarton estate. It had once served as a lodge for the main house, but in recent times it had been extended to more than double its original size. The extension was at the back of the property and was unashamedly modern, with plenty of glass to let in the light. Next to the entrance at the rear was a tasteful sign saying *Nesbarton Lodge Retreat*.

They parked beside a vehicle that hadn't been there when they'd first called and Wesley quickly realised that it was a hearse, painted in lurid purple swirls. 'Not a good advert for any establishment, having a hearse parked outside, even if it is purple.'

'If they took me away in that thing, I'd come back and haunt 'em,' said Gerry with a laugh.

Wesley pushed the glass door open and they found themselves in an airy reception area. The walls were covered in quotes written in flowing purple letters. *Be kind to yourself. You are beautiful. You are special. You are talented. You are the most wonderful star in the universe.*

'I knew that already,' Gerry whispered.

Wesley pressed a button on the wall bearing the legend *Welcome dearest guest. Press this and we'll meet as friends.*

'Or suspects,' Gerry quipped while Wesley did his best to look serious. It was obvious that this particular writers' retreat had a New Age edge. The small, pretty town of Neston had over the years become a hub for that sort of thing, and some of the activities on offer provided a source of amusement for the more traditional inhabitants of the area.

The woman who emerged from a door behind the reception desk was plump, with long purple hair and a flowing dress to match. It was hard to guess her age, which might have been anywhere between thirty and fifty.

'Welcome,' she simpered as she left the counter to greet them. 'You come as strangers now, but strangers are only friends we haven't yet met. Welcome, friends. Dear friends.' She grabbed Wesley's hand and looked as though she was about to embrace him until Gerry held out his warrant card.

'Police, love. Are you Betina? Silas Smithson's sister?'

The woman's manner changed abruptly. She stepped back and regarded them with suspicion.

'I'm Betina Smithson. Why?' She looked as though she was racking her brains, trying to remember whether she'd broken any law. In Wesley's experience, this was a perfectly normal reaction amongst members of the public when the police came calling.

'I don't know whether you've heard that a man's body was found in woodland at the other side of the estate earlier today. We're treating his death as suspicious.'

'That's terrible, but I don't see how I can help you. I've been here all day and I haven't seen anyone apart from my guest. Anybody can access the estate, so it's unlikely that this dead man has anything to do with us,' she added hopefully.

'We've spoken to Ms Carlton up at the hall. She told us your niece is staying with you while her parents are away.'

'That's right.' Betina glanced at the clock on the wall. 'She'll be home from school soon, but I can tell you for certain that she won't know anything. And I don't want her upset.'

'I understand,' said Wesley. 'But we will need to ask you some questions, I'm afraid. Do you know Patrick North? Your nephew Darius's tutor.'

'My niece, Tatiana, has mentioned him a few times, but I've never actually met him. Why do you ask?'

'I'm afraid the dead man has been identified as Mr North.'

Betina looked genuinely shaken. 'Poor Silas and Natalia will be so shocked when they get back,' she said in a whisper.

'Not Darius?'

'Oh . . . of course. He'll be devastated, poor child. What a dreadful thing to happen. I expect it was an accident. I can't imagine anyone . . .'

'Did Mr Smithson speak to you about hiring a tutor for Darius?'

Betina sniffed. 'He mentioned it, but he didn't ask my opinion.'

'Which is?'

There was a long pause. 'I didn't think it was a good idea at all. Darius needs to be with children of his own age, and I told Silas he was bound to resent having his teacher living in the same house. There was no escape for the poor boy, you understand.'

'Are you saying Darius didn't get on with Mr North?'

'I didn't mean that. It's just that Darius is . . . rather highly strung. I don't think he had a problem with Mr North, just the situation.'

'How did Mr North get the job?' Gerry asked.

'Natalia put an advert online. He seemed to have the relevant experience, so she invited him to the hall for an interview. She met him at Neston station and brought him home to meet Darius. According to Natalia, he was very pleasant – very suitable.' There was something guarded in the way she said it, as though she had a low opinion of her sister-in-law's judgement.

'What do you know about North's background?'

'Natalia said that he'd taught at a number of schools in Manchester, and that he left his last one after a difference of opinion about teaching methods. He told her he'd decided to take a year's sabbatical but now he felt ready to get back into teaching again.'

'I expect your sister-in-law contacted his past schools for references?'

'Natalia's very . . . independent-minded,' Betina said with a hint of disapproval. 'She took a liking to Mr North and that was enough for her.'

'Do you know anything else about him?'

'I'm sorry. My brother might know more, but he's away in the wilds of Scotland on one of his detox trips and he can't be contacted. Everyone needs that sort of thing from time to time, don't you think? That's what I try to provide here. Refreshment for the mind and soul. Electronic devices are strictly forbidden.'

'Nice,' Gerry muttered. He wasn't a lover of technology.

'You said you had a guest staying here at the moment?' Wesley asked.

'That's right. Georgina. November's always a quiet month. We'll be a lot busier after Christmas – and in the summer months, of course. But I do have another lady arriving soon to work on her novel.'

'Her name wouldn't be Della Stannard, by any chance?'

Betina looked at Wesley as though he'd just performed a spectacular magic trick. 'How did you . . .?'

'She's my mother-in-law. She told my wife that she'd booked into a writers' retreat.' He caught Gerry's eye. He would have preferred Della to cancel her booking, but he knew that if he suggested this, it would make her even more determined to go ahead. Pam claimed that her late father had kept Della on the straight and narrow during their marriage, but since his death, she'd almost reverted to her teenage self, entering into short-term relationships with unsuitable men and getting into any fashionable fad that came along. Pam seemed to be the adult in their relationship, and her mother was a constant source of worry to her.

'We need to talk to Georgina in case she saw anything.'

Betina looked as though she was about to object. 'Very well, if you must.' She glanced at the clock on the wall. 'But I need to go out and meet my niece. She likes to think she's grown up, but I do worry about her walking back from the bus stop on her own. I'm going to have to be very careful how I break the news to her. She didn't have much to do with Mr North, but I don't want to upset her.'

'Of course,' said Wesley with some sympathy. Breaking news like that was never easy, especially to a child.

'You'll find Georgina in her room,' said Betina. 'Second door on your right. Knock first. She's meditating.'

'Wouldn't dream of doing otherwise,' said Gerry. 'Before you go, we need to set up an incident room. Would it be possible to use the stables at the hall? We'd have asked Mr and Mrs Smithson, but as they can't be contacted ...'

Betina thought for a moment. 'I don't see why not. My brother usually keeps the mobile home in there, but as he's away in it at the moment, I'm sure it'll be fine. And if Karensa Carlton raises any objection, tell her you've asked me. I think Silas would be more than happy to help the police, and if there's a killer on the loose, I for one would find it reassuring to have officers around.'

'Thank you, Ms Smithson. That's a great help,' said Wesley. It had been a lot easier than he'd expected.

April 1787

I said that I had never played the role of King Lear, being too tender in years for the part, but that I hoped to one day, should the gods of theatre smile upon me.

The young man laughed and told me that I'd spoken well. I still had not been told his name, and I wondered whether he was the Nathaniel Nescote named in the notice I had seen. Before my companion could say more, mine host entered the room with more ale, though I was not given any.

'Is there aught else you require, Master Nescote?' the landlord asked with a bow as he reached the door. This confirmed that Nescote was indeed the man's name. I knew that about him at least.

'Leave us,' he said with a dismissive wave of his hand. As the landlord scuttled out, Nescote addressed me in a low voice.

'Are you a blabbermouth, Charles Burbage?'

'I am not, sir,' I replied.

'Will you perform any task requested of you?'

I should have said no there and then. But the prospect of an empty belly makes a man desperate.

Nescote dismissed me, and I was about to take my leave when he called me back, saying, 'Wait.'

I turned to look at him, and it was difficult to read the

expression on his face. He ordered me to stand before him while he sat in silence, staring at me as though he would see into my very soul.

'I think you are well suited to the position my cousin has in mind,' he said. 'It would amuse him greatly if you would dress in rags and feign madness. You will live in a grotto he has ordered to be built in the grounds of his fine mansion, and his orders must be obeyed to the letter. He will brook no dissent or disobedience. Do you understand?'

I said that I did. Then he asked where I could be found. I told him I lodged at the sign of the fighting bear in Soho, and he said that I would hear word from him in due course.

I was about to take my leave, thinking that I would tell John Hampton of my good fortune, when Nescote spoke again.

'Tell nobody of the matters we have discussed. Remain silent on pain of death.'

9

Betina hurried off, and Wesley watched her walk towards the gates past the parked purple hearse.

'Let's have a word with Georgina,' Gerry said.

Georgina Selby, a stick-thin woman in her sixties with tanned skin and bright blue eyes, told them she lived in London and that she'd decided to come to the retreat to work on her novel. She didn't seem at all bothered about her meditation period being disturbed. In fact she looked quite relieved about it. She said she hadn't seen anything. For the past few days it had been far too cold and damp to venture out, so she'd used the time to make progress with her novel. Next year she planned to spend the winter at a retreat in Spain, she added as though she held them personally responsible for the Devon climate. She'd never heard of Patrick North, although she was aware of the Smithsons at the hall. Anyone who read the newspapers couldn't fail to have heard of Silas Smithson, she said. He featured a lot in the financial press, she added, which made Wesley wonder whether the woman was more astute than he'd given her credit for.

They thanked her for her time and were just about to leave when she spoke again.

'I expect it was someone from that place in the village.'

Wesley turned to face her. 'What place?'

'I've heard it's a house for ex-convicts. Surely you know about it.'

Wesley saw Gerry raise his eyebrows. This was something that wasn't on their radar. But it would have to wait, because they had an appointment with Colin Bowman at the mortuary.

As they were approaching the hospital, Gerry received a call from the CSI team. Two bullets had been retrieved from the crime scene and had been sent off to ballistics for examination.

They made straight for the mortuary, where Colin began the post-mortem at 4.30 exactly. His initial observation was that the subject was a healthy male, with no sign of liver damage and good muscle tone due to plenty of exercise. Gerry commented that all that clean living hadn't done him much good in the long run.

After observing that there was recent bruising and lacerations on the dead man's face, as though he'd been in a fight, Colin made a close examination of the torso.

'You say they found the bullets?' he said as he delved into the gunshot wounds on Patrick North's chest.

'Yes. The CSIs said they looked as though they'd come from a .22 rifle. They've been sent off to ballistics for examination.'

'Well, one of the nasty little chaps ricocheted inside the chest cavity and hit the aorta. Made a terrible mess. The other hit the lungs. Poor man didn't stand a chance.'

'How far away do you think the killer was from the victim?' Wesley asked, trying not to look at the body on the stainless-steel table.

Colin considered the question for a few moments. 'From the wound, I'd say he was shot at fairly close range. Two or three feet maybe.'

'What about time of death?' said Gerry. 'Can I pin you down?'

'Now don't be naughty, Gerry. Haven't I taught you anything?' Colin and Gerry were old friends, and the pathologist's refusal to give an exact time of death had become a standing joke over the years. 'All I can say is that he probably died between twenty-four and thirty-six hours before he was found.'

'Saturday night was Guy Fawkes Night. Lots of fireworks means lots of bangs and crashes,' said Wesley. 'Ideal for concealing the sound of a gunshot.'

Colin agreed. 'He could well have been killed then, but don't take that as gospel.'

Once Colin had dictated his final conclusions into the microphone dangling over the table, he removed his protective clothing and left his assistant to finish off before leading Wesley and Gerry to his office for refreshments. This was a familiar and welcome ritual, the sweet after the bitter. While he was pouring the tea, he turned to Wesley. 'Did you ever solve the mystery of that other body you found this morning – the one they called me out to? I was halfway there when I got a message saying it was a false alarm.'

'It was a dummy – a mannequin. From the look of it, it was probably over a hundred years old. Although how it ended up where it did is a mystery.'

'Somebody probably put it there as a joke,' said Gerry.

'You could be right,' said Colin. 'As long as it has nothing to do with our corpse in there.'

'I don't think that's likely,' said Gerry. 'Do you, Wes?'

Wesley shrugged his shoulders. 'Probably not. But I'd still like to find out where it came from. It could be a rarity; something of interest to a museum. I'll ask Neil to try and discover more about it.'

Gerry rolled his eyes and Wesley thought it wise to change the subject. A man was lying dead in the room across the corridor, and finding out who put him there was their priority. Historical curiosity would have to wait.

When they left the hospital, they made their way back to the police station along Tradmouth's waterfront. The grey river was churning angrily; a storm was forecast for the following day, and the only activity apart from the toing and froing of the ferries was a pair of fishing boats chugging out to sea, hoping to finish their work ahead of the bad weather. The chill wind blowing off the water made Wesley hug his coat closer to his body as they walked.

'Our first job when we get back is to find out about this ex-offenders' place Betina's guest mentioned,' said Gerry as the police station came into sight.

'I'm surprised we don't already know about it.'

'Unless it isn't official.'

When they returned to the CID office they made a few calls but nobody at Neston or Tradmouth police stations could tell them anything about a refuge for ex-offenders in Nesbarton. Georgina might have been mistaken. But they needed to find out.

10

Geoff Haynes made dinner for two that evening. Sausages and mashed potato with baked beans. Bessy had already eaten two of the sausages. It had given Geoff great pleasure to see her wolfing them down with such enjoyment.

He covered his own plate and left it on top of a pan of hot water to keep warm before climbing the stairs. He knocked on the door opposite his own before going in. Everyone was entitled to their privacy – even a man with no memory.

Ben was sitting on the bed, on top of the old eiderdown Geoff had given him.

'Are you sure you won't come downstairs by the fire?' Geoff said softly. 'I feel bad about leaving you up here on your own.'

'I'm all right here, thanks,' was the reply. 'I don't want to put you to any trouble.'

Geoff handed the plate to his guest and watched him shovelling the food into his mouth as though he hadn't eaten for a while.

'Have you remembered anything yet?' The question was tentative. The last thing he wanted was to cause any distress.

'Not a thing,' the man said with his mouth full, as though he was too hungry to stop eating even for a moment.

'When I found you wandering about in the lane, you said you didn't know who you were. Or where you'd come from.'

Ben didn't answer. He just shook his head and continued eating. When he'd finished, he said thank you.

Geoff had found Ben the previous Wednesday night, trudging down the lane wet through and apparently in shock. The man was well spoken, and as far as Geoff could tell, his clothing was good quality, which made his predicament all the more puzzling. He'd said that he thought his name might be Ben, although he couldn't be sure, and he had no idea of his surname. He claimed that he couldn't remember how he came to be there, and Geoff had taken pity on him, unable to allow a fellow creature to wander about in the darkness on a damp November night.

Geoff had contemplated telling Rachel about him, but he felt protective about the stranger he'd taken under his wing. He knew Rachel would insist on reporting him to the authorities, but Ben had said he didn't want any fuss, so involving the police would seem like a betrayal. It had always been one of Geoff's most dearly held beliefs that everyone had the right to live as they pleased without interference. And Ben was no exception.

The following morning in the Peterson household, Pam made porridge for breakfast. She'd decided to embark on a new health regime in the run-up to Christmas, much to the children's dismay. Michael left half his breakfast, but his sister, Amelia, ate hers after a token protest. Wesley, however, consumed his bowlful enthusiastically; after all, it was a father's role to set a good example. Because they'd worked late on the new case the previous night, Pam had been asleep by the time he got in, exhausted after a day's teaching. Today, however, was her day off, and after their late night, Gerry wasn't due to give his daily briefing until 9.30.

Once the children had left to catch the ferry across the river to the grammar school, Pam began to clear the breakfast table while Wesley packed the dishwasher automatically. Detectives in crime dramas were never burdened by such mundane domestic chores, he thought, but real life was different. When he'd finished, they both sat down at the table, glad of a few minutes to catch up.

'Ever heard of a billionaire called Silas Smithson?' Wesley asked. 'That writers' retreat your mum's going to is run by his sister.'

'I know. She told me.'

'Know anything about him?'

'Only that he and his wife used to appear in a lot of magazines and Sunday supplements at one time. So-and-so shows you round their gracious home – that sort of thing.'

'Nesbarton Hall. I went there yesterday.'

Pam looked impressed. 'Makes a change to be mixing with the great and the good rather than the usual lowlifes you consort with at work.'

'We didn't get to meet the Smithsons. They're away in Scotland at the moment. We spoke to Smithson's PA, but she didn't give us the guided tour.'

'Pity,' said Pam, glancing at the clock.

'The murder we're investigating took place on the Smithsons' land and the victim was their son's private tutor.'

'I've always told you that teaching's a dangerous occupation, but you never believed me,' she said with a laugh. 'So how did he end up murdered?'

'That's what we're trying to find out. Preferably today. I'll probably be late again, so don't wait up.'

'Don't worry. I've got better things to do,' she said before giving him an absent-minded peck on the cheek and telling him to take care.

He walked to the police station down the steep, narrow streets that led from his modern house at the top of the hill into the ancient medieval port. Tradmouth had once been a prosperous centre of maritime trade, considerably more important during the Middle Ages than Gerry's native Liverpool, which had been little more than a fishing village during that period. But times had changed, and now, because of Tradmouth's picturesque appeal, its main industry was tourism.

His route took him down cobbled streets between higgledy-piggledy houses painted in pastel colours, many with names redolent of their seafaring past, until eventually he reached flatter ground, reclaimed from the sea in centuries gone by. The police station stood next to the new arts centre and library, and when the automatic door swished open, the civilian officer on the reception desk gave him a welcoming nod.

The CID office on the first floor was already buzzing with activity, and Gerry was in his glass-fronted office making a phone call. Wesley joined him and sat down, waiting for him to finish. Someone was getting what Gerry referred to as 'a rocket up the backside'. Eventually he slammed the phone down.

'Hi, Wes. The incident room's being set up in the stables at Nesbarton Hall, but the tech people are saying the computers won't be in till later this morning. They came out with a load of technobabble; couldn't understand a word they said, but I told them to pull their finger out.'

Wesley thought it best not to comment. He was only

too familiar with Gerry's frustration regarding anything remotely technical. 'Anything come in about the victim's phone?' he asked after a few moments.

The grin on the DCI's face told him the answer was yes. 'The techies found a load of texts.' He picked up a sheet of paper and handed it to Wesley. 'Here's a transcript. There's nothing earlier than September. Looks like he only bought the phone recently.'

Wesley read, scanning the conversations quickly. 'This Gemma's obviously his girlfriend. Lots of kisses underneath the first messages. On the tenth of September she wrote, "Missing you. Are you free this weekend? Call me. Now that you're so nearby I thought we could make a go of it again."'

'She sounds keen, doesn't she?'

'Yes and he seems keen at first too, but later on a lot of his replies sound like excuses. "So sorry, can't make it tonight." "Work. I'll call you." Two weeks ago she sent this one: "I really need to see you." He didn't reply. Sounds to me as though she's getting desperate.'

'I agree.'

Wesley continued to read the messages aloud. "Sorry, something's come up." Short and sweet. Then there's "Sorry, can't make it. Too much work on."'

'Either Smithson expects his pound of flesh or North's cooling off.'

'You could be right.' Wesley paused. 'Have you seen this one Gemma sent ten days ago? "Sorry, I tried to stop him but he wouldn't listen."'

'That one interested me too,' said Gerry. 'I wonder who the *him* is?'

'Doesn't say but it goes on, "I haven't heard from you.

What's happening? We need to sort things out. Please." Then on the thirty-first of October North seems to change his tune. "Smithsons going away tomorrow morning. Don't want to stay here alone. Mind if I come to yours???" Three question marks. She says, "Yes, I'll tell him. I'm going to sort it. Promise." Whatever that means.'

'I looked for mentions of his job,' said Gerry. 'There's an interesting one he sent her in early September when he first started working at the hall.' He took the transcript from Wesley and searched through it until he found what he was looking for. '"Don't like the set-up here. Kid's strange and woman reminds me of Mrs Danvers. But needs must and it pays well." Mrs Danvers. That's from that film, isn't it? The creepy housekeeper from hell?'

'That's right. *Rebecca*, by Daphne du Maurier. I presume he means Karensa Carlton.'

'Probably. But I didn't think she was as bad as that, did you? Mind you, she might have been turning on the charm for our benefit.'

Wesley agreed. People tended to be on the best behaviour when the police came calling.

Gerry consulted the printout again. 'The very last message North sent was at eight fifteen on Saturday night. It says, "Things to do. See you in an hour. Just make sure he's not around." She replies, "OK. Call me before you set off."' He consulted another sheet of paper. 'According to his phone records, he never made that call.'

'Which gives us a probable time of death between eight fifteen when he sent the message and nine fifteen when he was supposed to meet her and didn't turn up,' said Wesley. 'We need to speak to this Gemma. I take it someone's tried her number?'

'Of course, but she's not answering. They're trying to get an address for her, but you know how slow these phone providers can be. And I've asked Traffic to see if any of North's car journeys have been caught on camera.'

After Gerry's briefing to the team, Wesley spent the rest of the morning making a further study of the victim's calls and text messages and sorting through the various reports that had come in. At 11.30, he received a call to say that the incident room was up and running, so he went over to Gerry's office to tell him the welcome news.

A couple of minutes later, there was a knock on Gerry's glass door. When Wesley looked round, he saw DC Rob Carter waiting outside, fist raised ready to knock again. Rob looked worried; he'd been looking that way for the past week. The young DC had always been keen and ambitious, but recently his confidence appeared to have vanished, and Wesley wondered whether something was wrong. Rob never discussed his life outside work and Wesley didn't even know whether he lived alone or was in a relationship. They'd worked together for the past couple of years, so perhaps he should have taken more interest.

Gerry signalled to him to come in.

'You OK, Rob?' Wesley asked as soon as Rob had stepped into the boss's office.

Rob ignored the question and took a deep breath. 'I've contacted the schools in Manchester named on the victim's CV and they all confirm that he worked there, but no one knew anything about a difference of opinion. They said he left voluntarily with good references.'

'So he lied to Natalia Smithson?' said Wesley. 'There's a one-year gap in his CV, so we don't know what he was doing immediately before he came to Devon.'

'You think he might have been hiding something?' said Gerry.

'It strikes me as a bit odd that a young man like that would want to shut himself away in the middle of nowhere,' Wesley replied.

'To teach a rich spoiled brat.'

Wesley laughed. 'Now, Gerry, you're letting your prejudices show. We have to keep an open mind. The child might be perfectly charming; Little Lord Fauntleroy himself. And we have to remember Patrick had a girlfriend in the area – not to mention the fact that the money was good.'

Rob had been standing by the door in subdued silence, but now he spoke again. 'I rang round some other schools just in case he did take a teaching job during the missing year.'

'Good.' Wesley was impressed that he had used his initiative.

'I didn't think it likely that he'd worked in the state sector, so I tried some private schools, in the Manchester area and elsewhere in the north-west.' He paused as though he was about to make a dramatic revelation. 'One of the schools was in Cumbria – Falsham Place. Last summer term, a member of staff was dismissed because one of the sixth form girls had accused him of sexually assaulting her. His name was Patrick North.'

11

Wesley and Gerry fell silent for a few moments as they took in the news.

'I presume the police were involved?' said Wesley.

'Apparently not,' said Rob. 'I spoke to the school administrator. She didn't want to discuss it at first, but when I told her it was in connection with a murder inquiry, her manner changed. She said the girl was very quick to drop the allegation, insisting that she'd made a mistake and that she wanted to forget the whole thing. Even so, the head obviously believed in the old saying "there's no smoke without fire" and told North to leave.'

'What about the girl?'

'She's no longer at the school.'

'What was her name?'

'The woman I spoke to wouldn't tell me at first, pleading confidentiality, but eventually I got the information out of her. The girl's name is Lisa Lowe.'

'This explains why North decided to go to ground at Nesbarton Hall and leave that particular school off his CV,' said Gerry.

'We need to speak to the girl who made the accusation.' Wesley turned to Rob. 'Can you email Falsham Place a photo of the dead man and ask them to confirm that he's the Patrick North who taught there. And if he is, get the girl's details and an address for her family. If they plead confidentiality again, tell them that obstructing a murder inquiry is an offence.'

Normally Rob would have set about his task with eager efficiency; he'd always reminded Wesley of a sheep dog, ready to round up a flock on his master's orders. But today his natural enthusiasm appeared to have deserted him.

'Is something up with Rob?' Gerry asked once he and Wesley were alone.

'He's not been his usual self for the past few weeks, that's for sure.'

'Maybe he's having trouble with his love life,' said Gerry. 'Let's get over to the new incident room. Trish and Paul are already there setting things up.'

Gerry rose slowly from his seat. He was a big man who kept claiming he wasn't getting any younger. But Wesley dreaded the day he'd eventually retire. They'd worked together for so long now they'd become a double act, a close-knit team. He was still adjusting to working without Rachel. Although Paul Johnson, her temporary replacement, was a competent officer, he lacked Rachel's insight. He missed her; seeing her at the farm the previous day had made him realise just how much.

As they drove out to Nesbarton Hall in amicable silence, Wesley concentrated on steering through the narrow Devon lanes, fearing at each bend that he'd be confronted by a tractor – or worse still, a car taking the blind corner far too fast. Rachel had been driving these byways since she passed her test at the age of seventeen and they held no terror for her. Whenever possible, Wesley left the driving to her, but today that wasn't an option.

They were pleased to see that heaters had been brought in to the old stables and that officers were already at work at their newly erected desks. Some, he knew, were out making house-to-house enquiries on Gerry's orders; there was always a chance that someone might have seen something on Bonfire Night. Wesley found a note waiting on his desk saying that the search of the victim's car had revealed nothing, apart from a lipstick that had rolled under the front passenger seat. He wondered whether it was Gemma's – or someone else's.

His phone rang and the caller display told him it was Neil. He'd almost forgotten about the strange discovery in the grotto. Once he'd found he had a real corpse to deal with, he'd put the incident out of his mind.

Neil came straight to the point. 'Wes. What's happened to the mannequin?'

'Don't worry. It's safe in our evidence store.'

'I need to have a proper look at it.' With Neil, history took priority over everything else. 'Something's come up.'

'What?'

'I've been back to the grotto with some decent lighting. I tried to persuade your CSIs to let us use their floodlights, but they said no, so I borrowed some from the storeroom at the archaeology department.'

'Good. Look, Neil—'

'I'm meeting a local historian there this afternoon. He's been researching the history of the Nesbarton estate and he wants me to show him the grotto. Join us if you like.'

'I'm a bit busy with this murder at the moment,' Wesley said with studied patience.

'But this might be connected with your murder. According to the man I'm meeting, it's not the first violent

72

death at Nesbarton Hall. There was a double murder there in the eighteenth century.'

'Sorry, but like I said, I'm otherwise occupied.' Intrigued as he was, Wesley had to turn down Neil's offer. He'd heard the disappointment in his friend's voice, but the investigation into the death of Patrick North was at a crucial stage. If they didn't act fast, the trail would go cold.

A couple of seconds after Neil's call ended, Wesley's phone rang again. It was Rob Carter this time. He'd emailed the dead man's photograph over to Falsham Place and the administrator had called him back straight away. She recognised the man at once. He was definitely the same Patrick North who'd taught there; the man who'd left under a cloud of suspicion.

Rachel wished she knew what was going on at Nesbarton Hall. She felt like a child excluded from an exciting party who could only watch from outside with her nose pressed against the window. She was reluctant to mention this to Nigel or her in-laws in case they thought she was a neglectful mother. They'd be wrong, of course. She adored Freddie, but that didn't mean that she didn't miss the challenge of police work. And she missed Wesley, although this was something she didn't want to admit even to herself.

Freddie was restless, so she decided to take him to see Great-Uncle Geoff. The Haynes family considered Geoff eccentric, but Rachel liked him. He was a gentle man, at one with nature and the old ways, and besides, when she'd taken Freddie over to see him before, his presence had had a calming effect on the baby. She was sure Geoff enjoyed their visits too, and she reckoned it did him good to have contact with the next generation of the family.

She put Freddie in his sling, the terrain being too uneven for the expensive pram her parents had bought just before he was born; a gift from proud new grandparents. She wrapped herself and the baby up against the cold and donned her wellies. Nigel was out on the farm, although she wasn't sure where. It was time to think of bringing the cattle in for the winter, and some tracks and ditches needed attention. She was used to the relentless work. It had been part of her life since birth.

As she walked to Geoff's cottage, the sky was an ominous grey, but at least it wasn't raining. When she reached his front door, she noticed that Freddie had fallen asleep against her chest, and as she knocked and waited for Geoff to answer, she could hear shots in the distance. Someone was out with their shotgun, a common sound in the countryside. It reminded her of the man who'd been shot dead nearby, and she wished again that she knew how the investigation was progressing. It was hard being shut out from the job that had been her world for so many years.

There was no answer, so she knocked again. Then she heard faint voices coming from inside the cottage. Geoff had company. She called out his name and waited. When there was still no answer, she assumed she hadn't been heard, so she pushed the door open.

'Uncle Geoff? Are you there? It's Rachel. I've brought Freddie to see you.' With perfect timing the baby's eyes opened and when she stepped inside the cottage, she saw Geoff sitting in the battered armchair by the fire with Bessy lying contentedly by his feet.

He seemed surprised to see her. 'Rachel, I wasn't expecting you.'

'I heard voices. Got a visitor?'

'No, maid. Just me.' He glanced at the old radio on the windowsill, stained with the dirt and grease of decades. 'You must have heard the wireless.'

He seemed nervous, but Rachel told herself that he'd recently discovered a murder victim, an experience that would make anyone jumpy.

He began to make a fuss of the baby, clearly delighted when Freddie treated him to a wide, gummy smile. But in spite of this, Rachel sensed that he was on edge; certainly not his usual self.

'Are you all right, Uncle Geoff?' she asked. 'Is something wrong?'

'No, maid, I'm still a bit shaken by finding that dead man, that's all.'

'Of course. It must have been a terrible shock.'

She was about to sit down when a smell that had become all too familiar in recent months hit her nostrils. She began to search in her bag for a fresh nappy but she couldn't find one. Cursing her lack of preparedness, she knew she needed to cut the visit short.

'Sorry, Uncle Geoff. I'll have to go and change Freddie's nappy. I'll call again soon, I promise.'

Freddie started to grizzle with the discomfort and as Rachel made for the front door, she was sure she could hear a noise from upstairs; footsteps padding quietly across the bedroom floor above. She took her leave, and when she turned to wave, she thought she saw a look of relief on Geoff's face.

April 1787

John Hampton was waiting for me in the tavern, and he rose from his stool when he saw me.

'Well, Charles? Am I to go in now? The landlord says the others have been sent away.'

He looked anxious and I felt for him. I could not tell him what the employment entailed, but I could tell him that it was useless to wait in hope.

'It seems I have won the post, John. I am sorry for your disappointment, but the gentleman's mind is quite made up.'

I glanced towards the door of the private chamber, fearing Nescote would emerge and see me talking to my friend. I did not want him to think that I'd broken my promise of silence, so I told John that we should repair to another inn, one where the ale was cheaper. If he enquired further about my interview with Master Nescote, I would tell him that I had not yet been informed about the work I was to do.

As I wandered back to my lodgings that night, the initial feeling of triumph I experienced after being told the job was mine began to fade. Things Nescote had said worried me a little. And yet work was work. And I had been assured that his cousin would pay me well.

I had not been told the cousin's name, and the only thing

I knew about him was that he lived in Devonshire and had a fine mansion. Also that it seemed he trusted Nathaniel Nescote sufficiently to allow him to use his judgement regarding my employment.

I wondered whether Nescote's cousin was reclusive – or perhaps mad. Perhaps it would be my task to be his companion in madness in the grotto Nathaniel had spoken of. My feelings of unease remained, but I told myself that my journey into the unknown would be a great adventure.

What did I have to lose but my poverty?

My lodgings at the sign of the fighting bear were poor, and I shared a room with two of my fellow would-be actors, country boys come to London to seek their fortune. We also shared our accommodation with fleas and lice and the mice that scuttled across our straw-filled beds. We all had dreams of greatness, but those dreams remained distant. From time to time one of us won a role, and that triumph was celebrated with ale in the nearest low tavern, so it pained me to keep silent about my new work. But I am a man of my word.

After my meeting with Nescote, I heard nothing for a week, and I began to wonder whether the whole thing had been a jest. Rich young gentlemen have been known to mock the poor and desperate, and I feared I had become the victim of such trickery. I was about to abandon hope when a letter arrived at my lodgings containing instructions.

I was to return to the Moon and Stars two days hence and await Master Nescote, who had a coach to convey me to Devonshire. I was to tell nobody.

12

The developer, Jason Fonsby, had called Neil earlier that morning to ask when the archaeological assessment of the site would be completed, but Neil's answer had been evasive. He said there was a feature that needed to be investigated more closely, but he didn't go into detail, because he was playing for time. He couldn't bear the thought of the grotto being flattened by Fonsby's bulldozers before he'd had a chance to discover more about it. The developer would have to be patient.

Neil was pinning his hopes on the man he'd arranged to meet that afternoon. He'd asked his friend Annabel, who worked in the Exeter archives, to search for anything connected with the Nesbarton estate, and she had told him about Edward Hawk, local amateur historian and author.

At that time of year, most of Neil's work was carried out indoors, so it was good to escape the paperwork and reports that had been on his to-do list since the end of the digging season. He parked his car on the road and trudged across the field, thrusting his hands in his pockets. As he made for the copse, he heard shots in the distance – some farmer out after vermin, no doubt. Then a more sinister explanation flashed into his mind, rapidly dismissed.

There'd already been one fatal shooting in the vicinity. Surely it was unlikely there'd be another so soon. But from experience, he knew it wasn't impossible.

He'd arranged to meet Edward Hawk at the copse, and he waited for him outside the trees, stamping his feet on the damp grass to keep warm and hoping the man wouldn't be late. According to Annabel, Hawk was writing a book on the history of the area, and the Nesbarton estate in particular. When Neil had spoken to the man on the phone, he'd sounded as though he was holding something back. Neil hoped he'd be more forthcoming in the flesh.

He looked at his phone. Hawk was ten minutes late, and he was about to try his number when he spotted a car driving slowly down the lane. It stopped by the huge sign at the entrance bearing the artist's impression of Jason Fonsby's finished development, and the driver got out and let himself into the field through the metal five-barred gate.

The newcomer was dressed in a beige anorak with beige trousers and a matching bobble hat. His wellingtons were green and he carried a briefcase, hugging it to his chest as though it contained something very valuable.

'Mr Hawk, I presume.'

'Dr Hawk. You're Dr Watson?'

'Neil, please.' The man didn't invite him to use his first name in return, and Neil recognised a stickler for formalities when he saw one. 'So what have you found out about our grotto?'

'If I could see the grotto first, Dr Watson. I've been waiting for this moment ever since I began my research for the book.'

'Is it finished, or is it a work in progress?' Neil asked.

'I prefer not to say.'

The man had a strange, pedantic way of speaking, and Neil wondered why he was being so cagey. Surely he didn't imagine that Neil would steal his ideas and write a volume of his own on the same subject. Even if he did fancy indulging in a spot of plagiarism, with his workload as head of the County Archaeological Unit, he wouldn't have time.

'But you don't mind telling me what you've discovered?' he asked. It was time to be honest. 'I'd like to persuade the developer to preserve the grotto, as I suspect it's of historical significance, but first I need to know more about it.' He hoped this explanation would do the trick.

Hawk considered Neil's words for a few moments before replying. 'Of course, Dr Watson. I suppose the information is available to any competent researcher.'

Neil led him through the trees to the grotto. Hawk stopped and stared at the structure. 'I hadn't expected it to be so substantial. I imagine Dionisio Nescote had it built by his estate workers. There would have been a lot of men working on the Nesbarton estate in those days.'

'Dionisio? Unusual name.'

'He was probably called after Dionysus, the Greek god of wine.'

'Together with feasting and general debauchery,' said Neil with a grin, hoping to lighten the mood.

But Hawk's face remained solemn. 'Quite. Perhaps Dionisio was aptly named.'

Neil led the way inside. The floodlights had been erected, and when he switched them on, the space was bathed in light. He'd cleared up the litter, grateful that the youths who must have used it as a meeting place hadn't done any real damage.

'The graffiti is intriguing,' he said, pointing to the stone walls. 'Those moon symbols are repeated a lot, along with naked men and demons. And that strange thing that looks like an axe.'

'That was the symbol of the Wildfire Society.'

This caught Neil's attention. 'The Wildfire Society?'

'It began in the reign of George III, around 1786, give or take a year or so. Like many young men of his class, Dionisio had been on the Grand Tour, but when he returned, he founded the society for the purpose of getting closer to man's true nature. The story goes that he found a wild man and brought him here to live in the grotto. Decorative hermits were fashionable at the time amongst the higher echelons of society, all part of the craze for romanticism and the appreciation of nature in all its forms. Nobody knew where this wild man came from, and he appeared to have no name. One document I came across said that he acted as the society's high priest. There was a suggestion that he kept some sort of record or journal, but I found no trace of such a thing in the archives.'

'If he was wild, how come he could read and write?'

'Good question. All we really have is unsubstantiated rumours about what went on. One thing is on record, though.'

'What's that?'

'The so-called wild man was hanged in Exeter in 1787 for the brutal murder of Dionisio's mother and father.'

Hawk continued speaking as though he was giving a lecture, hardly aware that Neil was standing beside him. 'There was talk in the district of a secret society; of fashionable young men coming from as far as London to stay at Nesbarton Hall and take part in rituals. Some thought it was just local gossip, but now that I've seen this place . . .

81

Those words above the entrance – "We are masters of all and our will is law" – that was the society's motto.'

'There's another room,' said Neil. 'It's through here. Bit of a squeeze.' He manoeuvred himself through the narrow entrance into the inner chamber, and Hawk followed. Lights had been set up here too, focused on the altar where he'd found the strange dummy.

'This must be the place of sacrifice,' said Hawk, awe-struck. 'The holy of holies.'

'More like the unholy of unholies,' said Neil quickly. He regarded himself as a scientist, a professional, and he wasn't overimaginative as far as historical locations were concerned, but he had a bad feeling about this particular place. 'Let's go back into the other room.'

Hawk followed him out reluctantly.

'What exactly do you think Dionisio Nescote got up to in here?' Neil asked.

'There were several similar societies at the time fre-quented by so-called persons of quality, the most famous being the Hellfire Club – or the Order of the Friars of St Francis of Wycombe, as it was first known. Francis Dashwood and his fellow high-society rakes conducted obscene pagan rituals in a series of tunnels and caves in the grounds of his stately home. It's my guess that Dionisio Nescote set up a society of his own modelled on Dashwood's and built this grotto as its headquarters. You say it was featured on an old map?'

'Yes, the map was dated 1790, but the grotto doesn't appear on any earlier or later maps, which puzzled me.'

'Not if Dionisio or his family wanted it obliterated from local memory.'

'It isn't on the hall's land any more,' said Neil. 'It hasn't been for a while, because this part of the estate changed hands years ago. This field was sold recently to a developer, so if the grotto does have historical significance, I want to make sure it isn't flattened to make way for executive homes. But I'm not too hopeful.'

A horrified look appeared on Hawk's face. 'They can't destroy such a unique feature, surely.'

'They can and they will, unless I manage to negotiate some sort of preservation order. I told you about the mannequin on the altar, didn't I?'

'Could it date from Dionisio's time?'

'It looks old, but it was in good condition. We found evidence that someone's been in here recently – probably kids – so it may have been put it here as a joke. But I'd love to know where it came from. It's in the police exhibit store at the moment and I've asked if I can examine it. So far I've had no luck.'

Hawk began to circle the chamber, running his fingers lovingly over the carvings on the walls. Each time Neil looked at them, he saw something new; something even more disturbing and obscene. The interior of the grotto was becoming oppressive. Or perhaps it was because he could imagine the kind of things that had once gone on in there. He experienced a sudden urge to escape into the fresh air, but Hawk showed no sign of moving.

'Where did the Nescotes get the money to build a place like Nesbarton Hall?' Neil asked, hoping his question would return the man's attention to more mundane matters.

Hawk turned to him. 'Dionisio's father made his fortune as a privateer. Many Tradmouth ships were involved in such activities at the time, and by all accounts, Samuel Nescote was extremely successful. His ships regularly captured

French, Spanish and Dutch vessels and brought them back to Tradmouth to be sold, along with their valuable cargoes.'

Neil knew about Tradmouth's seafaring history, and that some of it hadn't always involved honest trade, but even so, Hawk's words surprised him. 'So he became wealthy?'

'Very wealthy. And respectable. He was a rough sailor who clawed his way up the social ladder and became a prosperous country gentleman with all the trappings, including a beautiful Italian wife who was said to have had several lovers. By all accounts Samuel had lots of mistresses too, so they were hardly a devoted couple. Samuel didn't get on with his only son. He considered Dionisio a wastrel and didn't approve of his friends.'

'So Samuel was a ruthless pirate whose ambition was to attain respectability to match his wealth. It sounds like Dionisio was a chip off the old block.'

Hawk's face clouded. 'Whatever Samuel may have done, I suspect Dionisio did far worse.'

13

Karensa Carlton was cleaning Silas Smithson's study, a task only she was trusted to perform. The cleaners from the village weren't allowed in there because the room contained confidential files and Smithson didn't want strangers to have access to such sensitive information. Not only that, but the mahogany shelves held his collection of valuable old books. Smithson hoarded precious volumes, particularly first editions, gloating over them in the evenings like a miser over his gold. He was a man who valued the sanctity of his private domain, and Karensa was gratified that he put so much trust in her. But then their relationship went back a long way.

Her final job was polishing the huge oak partners' desk standing in the centre of the room on a fine Turkish rug. She set to work and moved the blotter in the middle of the desk; she always did a thorough job. As she pushed it aside, she saw a folded sheet of paper underneath.

She unfolded it and began to read. The message was typed, or rather it had been generated by a laser printer. The bold block capitals were large, as though they were screaming at the reader:

WE'RE GOING TO GET DARIUS YOUR PRECIOUS
SON AND WHEN WE DO YOU WILL OBEY OUR
INSTRUCTIONS TO THE LETTER OR WE'LL KILL
HIM. DON'T TELL THE POLICE. WE WILL BE IN
TOUCH SOON.

The incident room was up and running and Gerry, as Senior
Investigating Officer, had assured Karensa Carlton that the
disruption would be kept to a minimum. Police Scotland had
been contacted and were trying to trace the whereabouts of
Silas and Natalia Smithson, but as yet they'd had no luck.
A resident of Nesbarton had spotted the Smithsons' mobile
home driving very fast through the village towards Neston
on the morning of 1 November, the day of their departure.
There'd been no sightings of the vehicle since, but according to Ms Carlton, Silas always preferred to use back roads,
which probably explained why his vehicle hadn't been
caught on traffic cameras. Scotland contained vast swathes
of wild, mountainous country, and it might take some time
to track down a family in a mobile home, however luxurious,
who'd chosen to stay far away from civilisation.

It was three o'clock on the day after Patrick North's body
had been found, and they still didn't know much about
him, apart from the incident at the school. But he had been
shot twice at fairly close range, and it was no countryside
accident. It was a deliberate murder, which meant that
someone had wanted him dead.

Wesley's temporary desk was situated next to Gerry's,
and he leaned over to ask a question.

'Anything else come in on Patrick North's background yet?'

Before Gerry could reply, Paul Johnson came rushing
up. He was a tall, athletic man, a keen runner. He was also

sharing a house with DC Trish Walton. Gerry joked that he was hoping for an invitation to their wedding – and the free booze that went with it – but so far there'd been no mention of any approaching nuptials.

'I've found some more information, sir,' said Paul eagerly. 'Patrick North was thirty years old and born in Manchester. His family are still up there. Divorced mother and a sister. No sign of the father. He studied English at Liverpool University and did his postgrad teacher training in Manchester. He worked in various comprehensive schools in the Manchester area, leaving the last one at the end of the summer term the year before last. That's when he must have taken the job at Falsham Place. The Manchester schools he taught at reported no problems.'

'Thanks, Paul,' said Wesley. 'Have the relatives been informed?'

'Greater Manchester's seeing to it. I'm waiting to hear from them.'

Wesley looked at Gerry. 'It looks as though North's career was running on pretty conventional lines until the incident at Falsham Place.'

'He kept changing jobs,' said Gerry. 'Was he hoping to move to something better or did he jump before he was pushed?'

'I'll get someone to contact the schools again. See if we can dig a little deeper,' said Paul. 'Surely this alleged sexual assault can't have come out of the blue.'

'You do that, Paul. And we need to speak to Lisa Lowe, the girl who made the accusations against him up in Cumbria.'

'The school hasn't come back yet with the details I requested. I'll chivvy them along.'

Wesley watched him return to his desk. Rob Carter was sitting next to Paul, apparently deep in concentration as he studied a witness statement. He didn't look up until Paul said something to him. Even then he seemed lost in his own thoughts.

Gerry spoke. 'They said the girl retracted her allegation against North and that's why the authorities weren't alerted. I'm wondering whether pressure was put on Lisa Lowe. Something like that could wreck a school's reputation if it got into the public domain. What parent is going to send their precious daughter to a school where she's not safe from predatory teachers? No parents, no school fees. No fees, the school goes under. I don't like the idea, but it can't be ruled out.'

Wesley nodded in agreement. 'We need to establish exactly what happened.'

The incident room buzzed with activity as officers spoke on the phone or tapped at their computer keyboards, and half an hour passed before Ellie Taylor, one of the DCs who'd only recently joined the team, approached Wesley's desk, glancing nervously at Gerry. She hadn't been there long enough to learn that he seldom lived up to his fierce reputation.

'Sir, the phone provider still hasn't got back to me with a full name and address for the victim's girlfriend.'

'Keep nagging them. Sometimes they need a bomb up their backsides,' said Gerry, who'd been listening in. 'As soon as we find Gemma, we need to speak to her.' He smiled, as though he was a favourite uncle about to dole out a special treat. 'Would you like to go along with DI Peterson here and pay her a visit?'

Ellie glanced at Wesley and nodded. Wesley approved.

She'd shown a lot of promise, and it was time she took a more active part in a major investigation.

Gerry's phone began to ring, and Wesley watched his face as he answered, hoping it was something that was going to move the case forward. The DCI's expression was serious at first, then he frowned as though he couldn't quite believe what he was hearing. When the call ended, he looked Wesley in the eye.

'New development, Wes. That was Karensa Carlton.'

'She's heard from the Smithsons?'

'No, but she was tidying Silas Smithson's study when she came across an anonymous letter threatening to kidnap Smithson's son. It said not to involve the police, but she thought as the Smithsons were away and probably out of danger ...'

'What if the tutor was killed because he stumbled on the plot and was trying to stop the boy being taken?'

'Indeed, Wes. This changes everything.'

14

A wild man: the phrase conjured up all sorts of strange images in Neil's mind. Who was he? And what had led to his hanging for the murder of Samuel Nescote and his wife? Had he really been guilty, or had he been the victim of prejudice against somebody with mental health problems? The eighteenth century was notorious for its brutal justice system and its unenlightened attitudes.

With so many unanswered questions, Neil knew that he was in danger of becoming distracted from the reason he'd been keen to investigate the grotto in the first place. He needed to prevent Jason Fonsby wantonly destroying anything of historic or archaeological importance. Anything more than this he'd have to pursue in his own time.

Once Edward Hawk had left, Neil walked back to the car with the man's last words ringing in his head. Whatever Samuel Nescote had done during his lucrative career as a pirate – or privateer, if you wished to give it a veneer of respectability – his son, Dionisio, had probably done far worse. He hadn't explained what he meant, and Neil suspected that he might have said it for dramatic effect – or to make sure that Neil bought his book when it was finally published.

What exactly had Dionisio done all those years ago? Neil knew his curiosity wouldn't allow him to let the matter drop. Besides, any discoveries he made might help him to protect the grotto. Perhaps Jason Fonsby might even be able to use the story as a selling point. Although he had a nagging suspicion that its history might appeal only to those with a taste for the lurid or Gothic.

Now that the team were settled in the stable block at Nesbarton Hall, Wesley and Gerry didn't have to walk far to investigate the latest development in the case. Karensa Carlton was waiting for them by the side door across the cobbled yard; the door the servants would have used in times gone by.

She walked ahead of them in silence, leading them through the green-painted utilitarian corridors below stairs until they reached the swing door that gave access to the world of privilege and luxury. This time they were shown into a spacious room at the front of the house with a view over the drive. Wesley guessed that at one time it would have been a library, but now it was a study, with a magnificently proportioned desk, comfortable leather chairs and sofa, and bookshelves stocked with antique volumes. There were photographs on the desk, framed in silver. A beautiful woman with luxuriant dark hair and a feline face. There was a noticeable mole or beauty spot on her cheek, the kind that was the height of fashion in the eighteenth century, and she stood arm in arm with a distinguished middle-aged man with thick grey hair and a well-trimmed beard. The Smithsons, no doubt. There were other pictures of the same couple with their children, a well-built, handsome dark-haired boy who was as tall as his father and a plump little girl with her hair in plaits who resembled her mother but lacked her good looks.

Wesley couldn't resist examining the shelves, and he saw amongst the leather spines first editions of famous books – an eclectic mix ranging from H. G. Wells to James Bond novels in their original dust jackets. Collecting such books was a rich man's hobby.

A computer sat on a second desk along with an array of printers and other technology he only vaguely recognised. A massive flat-screen TV had been placed on the wall over the Adam fireplace where an elegant mirror might once have hung. It was a masculine room and Wesley guessed it was Silas Smithson's private domain.

'I'm the only person allowed in here,' said Karensa with a hint of pride. 'Silas won't let the cleaners in because there are a lot of valuable books and sensitive documents.'

She walked over to the desk and picked up a sheet of paper. 'I was tidying up when I noticed this underneath the blotter.'

Gerry caught Wesley's eye and winked. Wesley could read his mind. She'd been having a nose round in the boss's absence. Probably couldn't resist it.

'I've touched it, so if you want to take my fingerprints for elimination ...'

'Thanks, love,' said Gerry, pulling on his crime-scene gloves. He took the sheet from Karensa and read the message out to Wesley.

'When did it arrive?' Wesley asked as he produced an evidence bag from his pocket.

'It must have been before the family left for Scotland on the first of this month.' She paused. 'Do you think that's why they left so suddenly? Mr Smithson arranged the trip rather quickly, but then he does like to act on impulse sometimes.'

'We'll need to take the letter for examination,' said Gerry as he dropped it into Wesley's bag. 'There've been no other notes since? No phone calls demanding a ransom?'

'No, and as far as I know, Darius is safely with his parents.'

'The Scottish police are still trying to locate the family,' said Wesley. 'They didn't give you any clue as to where they were heading?'

'No. But they've done this before – gone off grid for a couple of weeks. They lead stressful lives.' She paused. 'But this time they might have decided to take Darius away from any potential danger. Perhaps Silas didn't tell me about it because he thought it was safer that way, although he's always trusted me in the past.' She sounded a little hurt by the possibility.

'I'm surprised they left their daughter behind.'

'The threat was against Darius, and Tatiana has school. Besides, she loves staying with her aunt.'

'I think we should inform Betina Smithson about this new development as soon as possible,' said Wesley. 'If there's been a threat against Darius, his sister might be in danger too.'

'I wouldn't want you upsetting her.'

Wesley knew that if his own daughter was anything to go by, she'd probably enjoy feeling important while the police hung on her every word. He knew every child was different, but he found it hard to believe that a girl brought up with such privilege wouldn't match his Amelia in the confidence stakes. Unless she was troubled; unless there were things they didn't know about Nesbarton Hall and its inhabitants.

They left with the letter and the suspicion that all might not be well in the Smithsons' earthly paradise.

April 1787

The coach awaited me, but the blinds were down so I could not see inside. Nescote had met me at the tavern but had offered me no refreshment. I was led straight to the conveyance in silence.

As I climbed into the gloomy interior, I experienced a sudden surge of fear. I was bound for the unknown. But Devonshire was not reputed to be a dangerous county, and I told myself that it was merely my imagination that made me fearful. I was a lucky man, luckier than my fellow actors. My late father would have said I should be grateful to the Lord for my good fortune.

Nathaniel Nescote said we would stay at an inn that night and he would pay for my room and victuals, for which I was thankful, as I had very little money. He asked me many questions during our journey. What roles had I played, and who were my friends? His main interest, however, seemed to be my family. Had I told them of the work I was about to undertake? Did they know I was bound for Devonshire?

I told him I was not on good terms with my brothers and it was no business of theirs what I did or where I was. This seemed to please him greatly. Then he said that I would find many friends when we reached our destination, and laughed. When I asked the meaning of his words, he would not say.

The journey was long and arduous, and I know not where we spent that night. When we reached the inn, Nathaniel Nescote retired into a private room at the back for his repast, and our coachman, who had so far said not a word to me, vanished, leaving me in the tap room where, as a stranger, I was stared at. However, the ale was pleasing and the stew appetising. That night I shared a room above the stables with a taciturn young man lately returned from France and a groom in the employ of a gentleman bound for Somerset. My companions said little and I felt alone and in need of reassurance as I began to wonder what awaited me in Devonshire.

15

Patrick North's girlfriend still wasn't answering her phone and Ellie was still waiting to learn her address. In the end, Gerry tried the service provider himself, infuriated by the recorded message telling him that his call was important to them. In the end he slammed the phone down and said he'd leave it to scientific support to sort out. It was their job after all, and pulling rank had done no good whatsoever.

Gerry said he wanted to make an early start in the morning, so Wesley left the incident room at six. Just as he reached home, he received a call from Neil – did he fancy a swift drink at the Tradmouth Arms later? He accepted the invitation, adding that he couldn't stay long because Pam hadn't been seeing much of him and he felt guilty. When Neil said she was invited too, Wesley had to smile to himself – it was obvious that Neil had no children to consider.

Pam was pleased to see him. She'd had a tough day at work because the head teacher had just heard that an inspection was imminent. Wesley knew the stress of an inspection always affected Pam badly, so the timing of his murder investigation couldn't have been worse. She'd need his support. But unless they caught Patrick North's killer quickly, he couldn't guarantee that he'd be around to give it.

After feeding Moriarty, the cat, and the Petersons' recently acquired rescue dog, Sherlock, Wesley started cooking supper while Pam helped herself to a glass of wine. As soon as they'd eaten, the children vanished up to their bedrooms, and when Wesley offered to postpone his drink with Neil, Pam shook her head. 'You go. I've got loads of marking to do, so I won't be very good company – and with this case of yours you might not get another chance for a while. Give Neil my love, won't you?'

'Of course.'

Pam and Neil had gone out together briefly at university, until she'd abandoned him for Wesley. Neil, with his obsessive passion for archaeology, had never had much luck with long-term relationships. He'd even let his once-blossoming relationship with fellow archaeologist Lucy lapse in recent months. He was married to his job as much as any fictional hard-drinking policeman. Undoubtedly more so than Wesley.

Wesley decided to take Sherlock with him because Pam hadn't had a chance to give him his walk that day. He clipped on the dog's lead and checked the time If he didn't leave the house soon, he'd be late for his appointment with Neil.

A fine mist was rolling in off the river as he walked down the steep hill, stopping every now and then so Sherlock could sniff at walls and lamp posts. As he neared the centre of town, he could only see a few yards ahead of him, and his footsteps echoed eerily on the pavement. When he reached the waterfront, the river became a sea of shifting white spectres as a gentle breeze blew the mist to and fro. Luckily the terrain was so familiar he had no difficulty finding the welcoming brightness of the Tradmouth Arms. In summer the quayside teemed with drinkers, tourists enjoying the view over the river. Gerry lived a few yards away, in a small house at the end of Baynards Quay, and the visitors drinking outside irritated him in the warmer months. But there was nobody outside the pub that evening.

The lights in Gerry's house were on and Wesley wondered whether to invite him for a drink, but the boss had Joyce to keep him company, and she might not approve of his colleagues interfering with their evening. Wesley still had his reservations about whether Joyce and the DCI made the perfect pair.

He was about to enter the pub when he saw two people approaching along the quayside. Like him, they had a dog on a lead, and as they emerged from the mist, Wesley recognised one of them as DC Rob Carter. But Rob didn't notice him, because his attention was focused on his companion, a young man around his own age who looked painfully thin and fragile. Wesley had always thought of Rob as ambitious, possibly even insensitive, but the concerned expression on his face told a different story; one of worry and compassion. Rob had been uncharacteristically quiet at work in recent weeks – perhaps Wesley had just discovered the reason.

In spite of Sherlock pulling on his lead, eager to greet a fellow canine, some instinct made Wesley decide not to speak to his colleague. Instead he slipped into the pub, where Neil was sitting in a far corner, nursing his pint.

16

The following morning Wesley decided not to mention that he'd seen Rob near the pub. But he couldn't help feeling concerned about the change the young DC had undergone over the past weeks. It was obviously something he didn't want to discuss at work, so unless it was affecting the case, Wesley told himself it was none of his business.

Ten minutes after Wesley's arrival, Gerry walked in, discarding his coat and asking whether anything new had come in overnight – in particular, had Police Scotland got back to them yet? The answer was no. There was no fresh information – but the day was young.

Once Gerry had settled at his desk, Wesley was about to join him when the phone on his desk began to ring. When he answered, a female voice asked who was dealing with the shooting on the Nesbarton estate. The woman sounded confident, as though she was used to taking charge.

'This is Detective Inspector Peterson speaking. I'm dealing with the case. Can you give me your name, please?'

'It's Elspeth Bell. I have information regarding the murder.'

Wesley signalled to Gerry, who rose from his seat and ambled to Wesley's desk, giving Wesley a chance to put the instrument on speakerphone.

'What do you have to tell us, Ms Bell?'

'*Mrs* Bell,' she said firmly. 'I'm co-ordinator of the Nesbarton Village Watch and I'll tell you where you should be looking.'

'Where's that, madam?'

'A house on the edge of the village is being rented by a woman who claims she's a reverend.' The disapproval in her voice was unmistakable. 'She takes in ... well, I can only describe them as criminals. I wouldn't be surprised if some of them have convictions for violence.' She lowered her voice. 'Even murder.'

Wesley glanced at Gerry, who raised his eyebrows.

'How do you know they're criminals?'

'It's common knowledge that the men who stay there have recently been released from prison. Surely you're aware of the establishment.'

Georgina Selby had mentioned such a place, but all their enquiries had drawn a blank. If Mrs Bell was right, this particular place must have slipped under their radar.

'If you can give us the address of this ... house, we can make further enquiries,' said Wesley, not wanting to admit to ignorance.

The woman sounded impatient as she gave the details. Then, just as Wesley was about to end the call, she spoke again. 'I saw one of them while I was out walking near those woods where all the police tape's been set up. It's private land and I believe the family at the hall are away. I wondered whether to report him. Perhaps I should have done.'

'When was this?'

'At the weekend. Bonfire Night, around half past five. I made a note of it.'

'And you're sure it was one of the men from this hostel?'

'Er . . . I can't be sure, but I've often seen them hanging round in the village. Smoking,' she added, as though this was the worst sin she could think of. 'And I'm sure one of them's been watching my house.'

'That must be very worrying, madam. Would you be willing to give a statement?'

'Of course. Anything to help the police,' she said righteously.

'Don't worry, madam. We'll look into it. '

'Make sure you do.' With that, she ended the call.

Gerry straightened himself up and addressed the room in a booming voice. 'During the house-to-house enquiries in the village did anyone come across a female vicar?'

One of the DCs stood up like a nervous schoolboy who'd been hauled in front of the head. He had a shock of ginger hair and freckles and was one of those officers people meant when they said that policemen were getting younger. 'I called at a house on the edge of the village and a vicar answered the door, sir. She said he had guests staying there but none of them had seen anything.'

'A vicar? Are you sure?'

The DC consulted his notebook. 'The Reverend Becky Selkirk.'

'Did you speak to any of her guests?' Wesley asked.

'The reverend said she could vouch for them all,' the DC said. 'I had no reason to disbelieve her, sir.' He hung his head as though he was expecting to be the focus of one of Gerry's barbed remarks.

Wesley took pity on him and got in first, thanking the lad, who sank into his chair, relieved.

Gerry took Wesley by the elbow and led him out of ear-shot. 'I can't help wondering whether Mrs Bell has her own agenda,' he said.

'It wouldn't surprise me if there's an ongoing feud between the village watch and the reverend's lost sheep.'

'You could be right,' said Gerry. 'Let's pay the Reverend Selkirk a visit. We can ask her if she knows anything about Patrick North while we're there.'

Gerry's suggestion made sense, but first Wesley made a call to his brother-in-law, Mark, who was the vicar of Belsham, a village on the Morbay side of Neston. As well as Belsham, Mark was responsible for several other parishes in the area, and if anybody knew about the Reverend Becky Selkirk, it would be him.

'I know the vicar responsible for St Helena's church in Nesbarton,' Mark told him. 'But I've never heard of Becky Selkirk. She certainly isn't an Anglican priest, and I know most of the Nonconformist ministers in the area, so she's a bit of a mystery. Hang on, Wes, I think Maritia wants a word ...'

Wesley didn't have time for a chat with his sister, but Mark hadn't given him much choice.

'Day off?' he said when he heard Maritia's voice. She and Mark had met when they were both studying at Oxford, and now she worked as a part-time GP in Neston, always busy balancing work with caring for her son, Dominic, and her duties as a vicar's wife. Wesley wondered why she wanted to speak to him so urgently.

'Have you spoken to Mum and Dad recently?'

Wesley felt a stab of guilt. 'Not for a few days.' In reality, it had been more than a week.

'I called them last night and Mum sounded ... secretive. Then she said she might have some news but she couldn't tell me yet.'

All sorts of possibilities began to flash through Wesley's

mind – most of them bad. His father was so wise and dig-
nified, his mother so full of life. They'd always seemed
immortal, and he couldn't bear the thought of anything
happening to them. Before retirement, his mother had
been a GP and his father a much-respected heart surgeon
who, after reaching the top of his profession, still served
on many committees and used his experience to advise
others in the health service. He wasn't a man who liked
to be idle.

'You don't think one of them might be ill?'

Maritia hesitated. 'It didn't really sound like that. Mum
was more ... how can I describe it? Like a woman who's
pregnant but knows she shouldn't tell anyone until after
her first scan.'

Trust a doctor to use that particular analogy, thought
Wesley. 'What do you think it could be?' he said.
His mother had never been the secretive type, so he
couldn't banish the nag of worry at the back of his mind.
Maritia said she had no idea but she'd try to get to the
bottom of it.

Wesley ended the call, then sat for a few moments staring into space, suddenly shocked at the thought of his
parents' mortality. But his sister had spoken of suppressed
excitement rather than worry, so he told himself he was
probably being too pessimistic.

Gerry was waiting for him, and as they walked to the
village, he told the boss about his conversation with Mark.

'He's never heard of a Reverend Becky Selkirk,' he said.
'He knows all the clergy round here, so he's a bit puzzled.'

'Well, hopefully our little mystery is about to be solved,'
said Gerry with confidence.

When they arrived at the house, the DCI rang the

doorbell and whispered to Wesley that he'd leave him to do the talking. If he let it be known that his brother-in-law was a vicar, the Reverend Becky was bound to be more co-operative. Wesley hoped he was right.

17

The door was opened by a tall woman in her thirties with wild dark hair and glasses. She wore a baggy black dress topped by a clerical collar. Wesley and Gerry showed their ID. The woman had looked mildly curious when she'd first seen them. Now she looked downright hostile, and pulled the door to a little so that they couldn't see the hallway beyond.

'Are you the Reverend Becky Selkirk?' Wesley asked pleasantly, sensing she'd had problems with the police in the past. 'It's nothing to worry about. We're investigating the murder of a man in the grounds of Nesbarton Hall and we'd like to ask you a few questions, that's all. I know an officer's already been round, but we're wondering whether you or anyone else living here saw anything on Saturday evening. Bonfire Night.'

'Just routine, madam,' said Gerry, who was standing at Wesley's shoulder.

She gave him a suspicious look, as though she suspected he was lying.

Wesley felt Gerry nudge his back. He knew the DCI was expecting him to sweet-talk his way in, but he feared that on this occasion, charm alone wouldn't work. He needed to keep her talking, though.

'I wonder if you know my brother-in-law, Mark Fitzgerald. He's the vicar of Belsham.'

This didn't have the desired effect. She shook her head, so he tried again. 'A friend of mine has a farm nearby – Gorfleet Farm. The Haynes family. You'll probably know them.'

'The locals haven't been exactly welcoming.'

'I'm surprised to hear that. I know my friend's family go to the local church. You're not connected with St Helena's?'

'No.'

'Which church *are* you from?'

Her expression remained guarded and suspicious, but Wesley had never before met a member of the clergy who was unwilling to answer such basic enquiries. 'The Church of the Blessed Spirit,' she mumbled. 'Now, I'm rather busy, so—'

'I haven't heard of that one, I'm afraid. Is it an evangelical church?'

She looked surprised that he appeared to be au fait with churches of all denominations. 'It's not a traditionally organised church. I have a mission to help those less fortunate than myself.'

'That's very commendable,' Wesley said, trying to sound sincere. 'I believe you're trying to rehabilitate ex-offenders. That's important work.' He was convinced that this would do the trick. She couldn't possibly object to a sympathetic police officer from an ethnic minority who kept an open mind.

But he was wrong. 'Ever since the busybodies from that so called village watch found out what I'm trying to do, they've been making life awkward for us.'

'They haven't reported you to the police. The local station doesn't even know you exist.'

'They've had no reason to report us because we've done nothing wrong. My guests keep their noses clean.' She folded her arms to emphasise the point.

'How many guests are here at the moment?'

'Just the three.'

'Names?'

'It would be a breach of trust if I told you that.'

'We only want to eliminate them from our enquiries,' Wesley pointed out reasonably.

'You mean if they've done nothing, they have nothing to fear? I've heard that before, Inspector. Nobody here has any reason to trust the police.'

'You can trust us, love,' said Gerry. 'We're good cops, not the other kind.'

She looked sceptical, and Wesley wished the boss had kept silent.

'We've been told that one of your guests might have been near the murder scene on Bonfire Night around the time the victim was killed. We need to speak to him so we can establish his innocence once and for all. Otherwise how are we going to disprove the accusations of the village watch?'

'Vigilantes, I'd call them. They haven't spoken to the police about us because they like to dispense their own justice.'

'That's a serious allegation,' said Gerry. 'Can we speak to your guests?'

She hesitated. 'I'll ask them and let you know.'

Wesley handed her his card. They had no warrant, so all they could do was wait for her to contact them.

As soon as the Reverend Selkirk had closed the door,

Wesley spoke. 'We need to hear Elspeth Bell's side of the story.'

'You're right. Let's go and have a word.'

But as they were heading for the centre of the village, Gerry received a call. They finally had an address for the Gemma who'd been texting Patrick North.

Elspeth Bell and the village watch would have to wait.

April 1787

It is difficult travelling in such close proximity to a companion who does not speak and regards you with as little consideration as he would a flea he found in his wig. In the end, I abandoned all hope of making further enquiries about what would be expected of me once we reached our destination.

The blinds had now been raised so that I could see the passing countryside. My companion read a book as we travelled. Or at least he made a pretence of it, for he seemed to spend an inordinate amount of time perusing each page. I had never felt so lonely as I did in that coach, and I found myself longing for the company of my fellow actors, poor though we were. How I yearned then to laugh with them once more, to fill our empty bellies with ale and hope. I began to be afraid. And in the end, I could bear the silence no longer.

'Pray, sir, do you know where we are?'

The look he gave me seemed punishment enough for my boldness. 'On the way to hell, dear fellow,' he answered in a tone that made me shudder.

Hell was a place I had no ambition to visit, either in this life or the next, so I confess that his words frightened me. How could hell lie in Devonshire? And yet I had learned in London that it can be found in unexpected places – in a low tavern or a vile alley; even in a house of so-called pleasure.

We broke our journey for a second time and rested the night in another inn, where again my companion retired to private quarters and our silent coachman to God knows where. When I asked the pot boy where we were, he told me Dorchester, and the look he gave me suggested he thought me mad. For what man knows not where he is?

We took off after we had broken our fast, having been provided with fresh horses. The coachman drove the beasts hard, and the wheels of the coach thundered over the rutted roads. I asked what time we would arrive at our destination, but Nathaniel Nescote ignored my question as though he hadn't heard it.

It was late in the afternoon when the coach began to slow, and when I looked out of the window, I saw that we were passing between a pair of large gates topped with carved stone pineapples, the symbol of prosperity. There was a fine white lodge beside the gates, but no retainer emerged to greet us. The drive was long, and it seemed an age before the house itself came into view.

I pressed my nose to the coach window to catch my first glimpse of the place where I would work, and saw that it was a handsome white house in the modern style, with pillars at the entrance.

'What is this place?' I asked Nescote, who was lounging in his seat with a bored expression on his face.

'Nesbarton Hall. Home to my cousin. It is him you will be serving.'

As I alighted from the coach, I glanced at our silent

coachman, who was taking our luggage down from the roof.
I thanked him and he opened his mouth. That was when I
saw that he had no tongue.

18

Wesley had promised Ellie that she could be in on the interview with Gemma, but it hadn't worked out that way. Gerry had insisted on going with him, but Wesley resolved to make it up to the capable young DC as soon as he could.

Gemma's address turned out to be a tiny terraced house in a gloomy narrow street near the centre of Dukesbridge, a town some ten miles from Nesbarton. Its white walls needed a fresh coat of paint and its double-glazed windows were misted up. Gerry rapped on the grubby plastic front door, and a few moments later it opened to reveal a young woman with fair curls, large brown eyes, flawless skin and a full mouth. She was tall and slender and wouldn't have looked out of place on a fashion-show catwalk. Wesley glanced at Gerry and guessed that he was thinking the same as him. If this stunning woman was Gemma, Patrick North had been punching above his weight.

With a worried look on her perfectly made-up face, she confirmed that her name was Gemma Latimer and that she knew Patrick North.

'Why are you asking? What's happened?'

Wesley could tell her mind was working overtime, imagining any number of terrible scenarios that might bring the police to her door. Once they were sitting down in the small, shabby living room, he broke the news as gently as he could, wishing that Rachel was with him. She'd acted as family liaison officer so many times, and she always seemed to know the right words to say to bereaved friends and relatives. But in her absence, he'd have to muddle through.

'I heard on the news that a man had been murdered near Neston, but I never connected it with Patrick,' Gemma said.

'His name won't be released to the media until his next of kin have been informed.'

'His family are up in Manchester,' she said. 'Well, it's just his mum and his sister.'

'We know, love,' said Gerry. 'Greater Manchester Police haven't managed to contact them yet. A neighbour said they were away, but they'll keep trying. You're from that way yourself, aren't you? I can tell by your accent.'

She nodded.

'Didn't you wonder why you hadn't heard from him?'

Wesley gave Gerry a look that said: 'Why don't you leave the talking to me?'

But she didn't seem to be upset by the question. 'The people Patrick worked for went away, so he was staying here with me. Then on Saturday he told me he was going back to the hall because he needed time to think.'

'So all wasn't well between you?' Wesley asked gently.

She nodded.

'Why was that?'

She sat in silence for half a minute, as though she was trying to think of the best way to tell them. Eventually she said, 'It was about Jordan.'

'Who's Jordan?'

'Someone I'm seeing. He's a DJ. He's got a job in Ibiza

114

next summer and he wants me to go with him,' she added proudly. She paused for a moment, suddenly solemn. 'You see, I decided to come down here to be near Patrick, because I liked him. But then he kept coming up with excuses not to see me and I wondered if he had someone else. When I met Jordan, I thought, if Patrick's being like that, why shouldn't I enjoy myself. It's his loss. Then on Halloween, Patrick asked if he could stay and I said he could. Jordan knew about Patrick, but I told him we were just friends.'

'He believed you?'

'I thought he did.'

'So you were two-timing both of them, love,' said Gerry.

Gemma looked at him and shrugged. 'Suppose I was really.'

'Tell us about Jordan,' said Wesley.

'Well, he can be a bit possessive and I was getting fed up with him.' She glanced towards the door as though she was expecting the DJ to burst in any moment. 'Patrick was annoyed that he was still around, but when he left my place on Bonfire Night, I texted him asking him to come back. He said he would but he had things to do first. I think he needed to pick up some things from his flat in the hall. Anyway, he said he'd call to let me know when he was setting off, but I never heard from him again. I thought he'd changed his mind and blown me out.'

'And Jordan?'

She hesitated. 'He found out me and Patrick were still seeing each other, and he said Patrick was screwing someone else and he was going to get proof, but I don't know whether he was making that up. He said he was going to have a word with him.' Suddenly she looked worried, as though she'd just realised that she might have incriminated the man. 'But he would never have harmed Patrick,' she said quickly. 'He's not like that.'

Wesley didn't believe her last statement. She'd just claimed that Jordan had said he'd have a word with Patrick, but one man's word was another's threat of violence. He suspected that the possessive Jordan might be a man with a temper.

'What's Jordan's surname?' Wesley asked.

'Green. He's quite well known locally.'

He made a mental note to check whether Jordan Green had a criminal record.

'We believe Patrick was killed sometime on Saturday evening – possibly shortly after he sent you that last text, which is why he never came back here.' He watched Gemma's face and saw that she looked horrified.

'I never knew. Honest.'

'Where were you that evening?'

A look of relief passed across her features. 'I waited in for a while, and when he didn't turn up, I went for a drink with some of the girls – got home about eleven thirty.'

'What about Jordan? Could he have followed Patrick to Nesbarton Hall to have it out with him?'

She shook her head, but she didn't look too sure of herself. 'No. He works on Saturday nights. The Pillar Club. It's a regular gig.'

'We'll have to confirm he was there,' said Gerry. 'Where do *you* work, love?'

'At a salon on the high street. I'm a beautician.'

'So let me get this straight,' said Gerry. 'Patrick was staying here with you from the thirty-first of October because the Smithsons were away, but you had a disagreement so he went back to Nesbarton Hall the following Saturday. Then you made up and he told you he was going to pick up some things from his flat and he'd let you know when he was coming back, only you never heard from him again. And you assumed he'd had second thoughts because of Jordan.'

'That's right.'

'Where did you meet Patrick?' Wesley asked, curious.

'At a club in Manchester. We went out for a while, then he got a job in the Lake District so I decided to look for work up there too. I've always liked the Lake District. My auntie used to have a caravan up there and I went every year with my mum and dad when I was young.' She smiled fondly. 'I found a job at a salon in Keswick and got a flat there. Patrick had to live in at the school, but we saw quite a bit of each other. He wasn't happy there, you know. He said it was full of spoiled brats and they got on his nerves. He was always having to watch what he said in case he told them what he really thought of them. He'd thought it'd be easier working in a school like that, but he said it came with its own problems.'

Her face clouded. 'When he lost that job, it hit him hard. I thought he'd be a lot better once he'd moved away and left it all behind. I told him never to mention that place when he went for the job here. He had good references from schools he'd worked at in Manchester, so I told him to say he'd just taken a year out. That's why the job at Nesbarton Hall was ideal. If it had been a school, they'd have wanted more details and done checks. You don't want something like that following you round, do you? I hoped we'd be able to make a new start, but ... after that girl accused him, he changed. It was as though he couldn't trust anybody any more – even me.'

117

Wesley caught Gerry's eye. 'Did he tell you what happened when the girl made her accusation?'

She took a deep breath and looked from one man to the other before she began to speak. 'He liked that boarding school at first. Said it made a change from the rough comps he'd taught at in Manchester, despite how privileged the kids were. It was a beautiful place and it was great in the first term, but then ... then the trouble started. There was this girl in the sixth form – Lisa – who had the hots for him. She kept asking for extra tuition because she was trying for Oxford and she wanted him to help her with her interviews and all that. She was clever, and at first she was his star pupil. Mind you, he said she was an idle little bitch and the way she took everything for granted annoyed him.'

'But they got too close?'

'No, you've got that wrong. He had a flat in the school that came with the job, and one night she turned up there asking if he could help her with some forms she had to fill in. He told me he tried to keep things professional at first, but he ended up telling her a few home truths then told her to get out.'

Wesley suspected that the words 'he would say that, wouldn't he' were on Gerry's lips, but luckily he stayed silent and waited for her to carry on.

'She turned up in the head's office the following morning claiming that he'd assaulted her. He denied it, of course, but it was his word against hers.'

'Surely the police were called.'

'The girl retracted her accusation soon afterwards, but the head still told Patrick to pack his bags and get out. He came to stay with me, but he was in bits. To be accused like that of something you haven't done ...'

'Do you believe he didn't do it?'

Gemma nodded. 'Absolutely. Patrick wasn't like that at all. He thought this girl had a crush on him and was furious when he rejected her – and he was sure someone had egged her on to make the accusation.'

'Who?'

She shrugged. 'Another of the sixth-formers, I think, but he never said who.'

'How did he find out about the job at Nesbarton Hall?'

'I found the advert online – tutor wanted for home-schooled thirteen-year-old boy. He applied and got the job. They seemed desperate for someone, which should have rung alarm bells, I suppose.' She sighed. 'He thought they'd follow up his references from the schools in Manchester, but he was pretty sure they never did.'

'Didn't he think that was strange?' said Wesley, remembering what Betina Smithson had said about Natalia's faith in her own judgement.

'Yes, but once he'd been there a couple of weeks, he found out why they didn't bother.'

Wesley and Gerry leaned forward, awaiting the revelation.

'The kid, Darius, was a nightmare. But the parents were paying Patrick really well, so he stuck it out.'

'Did the boy have problems?'

She thought for a moment. 'He'd been expelled from a few schools before they decided to teach him at home. He thought he could run rings around Patrick because his parents were paying his wages.'

'So Patrick had a tough time in the months before his death,' said Wesley. 'The assault allegation, then having to deal with a difficult pupil.' He was tempted to add that on

119

top of all this, his girlfriend had been two-timing him, but he stopped himself just in time.

'We'd like to speak to Jordan,' said Gerry. 'Where can we find him?'

Gemma provided Jordan Green's contact details meekly, as though the reality of the situation was starting to sink in. Then Wesley asked another question.

'Does Jordan know how to use a gun?'

'Oh yes. He's in a gun club. But he'd never hurt anybody. Jordan couldn't harm a fly.'

19

Finding Jordan Green had suddenly become a priority. A jealous boyfriend who was a member of a gun club had to be top of their suspect list. Gerry called the incident room as they made their way back. He wanted Green brought in for questioning sooner rather than later.

But before they reached the stable block, Wesley proposed a detour. 'We never spoke to Elspeth Bell.'

'Agreed. And I'd also like to see the Smithsons' daughter, Tatiana.' Gerry checked the time. 'She might not be home from school yet, so let's call on Mrs Bell first.'

Nesbarton was more of a hamlet than a village, Wesley thought as he parked next to the lychgate of the tiny church. The settlement consisted of a couple of rows of houses, bisected by a B road leading to Neston. The church was a relic of the time when the community was a lot larger, and appeared to be Nesbarton's only amenity. There was no village hall or shop, or even a pub. Anybody who needed these facilities had to venture over to Tradington, a mile and a half away.

A fairly constant stream of traffic travelled along the main street to and from Neston, and Wesley noticed an elderly couple standing on a grass verge next to a bus shelter. The woman was holding what appeared to be a hairdryer, which she pointed at any passing vehicle. A speed trap, albeit an unofficial one.

Wesley and Gerry approached the couple, who regarded them warily.

'Afternoon,' said Gerry. 'Catch many?'

The man looked down at the hairdryer and his face reddened. 'Er, it makes 'em think twice about speeding. That's all we're trying to do. You get some people hurtling through here. Won't be long before someone's killed.'

'Quite right,' said Gerry, at his most jovial.

'Those people from the big house tore through the village in that posh motor home of theirs the other day. Doing twenty miles an hour above the speed limit they were.'

'We've heard about that already. I don't suppose you have a record of the exact time?' Wesley asked.

The man consulted the small notebook he'd taken from his pocket. 'First of November at eight fifteen in the morning. Some people think they can get away with murder.'

His companion nodded in agreement. It seemed the Smithsons weren't the most popular residents of Nesbarton.

'Keep up the good work,' said Gerry. 'But mind out for our traffic officers. They'll get jealous – think you're after their jobs.'

He produced his ID and the couple looked at each other.

'We're after an Elspeth Bell of the village watch. Know where we can find her?'

'Elspeth's our co-ordinator. She lives over there. Are you here about the murder?'

'That's right, love.'

The woman looked at her companion and gave him an 'I told you so' look.

'We've all given statements,' she said righteously. 'I hope you've spoken to that so-called vicar woman.'

'Don't worry, love, we won't leave anyone out.'

The man kept silent, and Gerry gave him a sympathetic look as they walked away. Wesley turned his head and saw that the hairdryer was being deployed again.

Mrs Bell lived in the centre of a row of terraced brick cottages whose front doors opened directly onto the road. Her newly varnished oak door opened almost as soon as Wesley had raised the knocker, as though the occupant had been watching their arrival from behind the thick net curtains that hung at every window. She was a small, stout woman with steel-grey curls, a double chin and glasses. She invited them inside with the confidence of a chief constable allowing a pair of subordinates into his well-appointed office.

'I'm glad I haven't been fobbed off with a pair of uniformed constables this time,' she said, looking them up and down. 'I suppose you've come about my call. You'd better sit down.'

She wasn't the sort of woman to be disobeyed. They sat side by side on a floral sofa that seemed too large for the room, while she took her place in an armchair facing them. Wesley looked at the window and noted that he could see outside perfectly, despite the net curtain. An ideal spot for surveillance.

'We've spoken to the Reverend Selkirk.'

'She's no reverend. She rents that place as a safe house for villains.' Mrs Bell spoke with absolute certainty.

'Have you any evidence of that?' Wesley asked.

'She doesn't allow anybody near the place. But I've seen men hanging round. Criminal types. I've seen one of them standing over the road staring at my cottage. I make sure all my doors and windows are locked, I can tell you. And now there's been a murder. That's where you should be looking.'

Wesley met Gerry's eyes. Neither wanted to admit that they'd failed to gain access to the Reverend Selkirk's 'criminal types'. It would be no use explaining that they needed to go through the proper channels.

'Our investigations are continuing, Mrs Bell.'

'But are you about to make an arrest? Nobody here feels safe after what happened.'

'We're following several lines of inquiry,' said Gerry. 'Don't worry, love. I've ordered extra patrols, and my team have set up an incident room in the stables at Nesbarton Hall, so we're not far away.'

She didn't look reassured.

'Do you know the people up at the hall?' Gerry continued.

'I wouldn't say I *know* them, but I've called there a couple of times to see if they're interested in supporting our village watch.' Mrs Bell hesitated, her confidence slipping for the first time. 'The second time, a rather unpleasant child – well, a teenager really – answered the door. He was very rude. I haven't been back since. I hope you've spoken to them as well.'

'They're away at the moment.'

'So I've heard. One of our volunteers at the village watch sometimes helps out with the cleaning, and Ms Carlton told her that her services wouldn't be required until the family got back. Not that they're there all the time. They've got other properties, you know.'

'You've met Ms Carlton?'

'I've seen her on a couple of occasions.'

'What about the son's tutor, Patrick North?'

'Our paths never crossed. But if he has to teach that boy, I feel sorry for him.'

'I believe the daughter's staying with her aunt at the lodge.'

Her expression softened. 'I've seen the aunt. She seems harmless enough, even if she does have purple hair and drives that ridiculous hearse. And the little girl seems quite sweet. Not at all like her brother.'

'I expect the officers from my house-to-house team have already asked you whether you saw anything suspicious on Saturday night?' said Gerry.

'Of course. I know my public duty, Chief Inspector. Even though many don't seem to these days.'

'And you've nothing to add?' said Wesley. 'Nothing you've remembered since?'

'If I had, I would have told you.'

Wesley had an idea. 'Have you seen any strangers hanging around the village recently – apart from the Reverend Selkirk's guests, that is?'

She thought for a moment. 'As a matter of fact, I did see a man sometime last week. He was middle-aged, average height, grey hair, wearing a tweed jacket and an open-necked shirt. He was driving a silver car – a Toyota, I think – and he stopped and walked in the direction of the church as though he was stretching his legs after a long journey. I'm afraid I can't remember which day this was. He looked quite respectable, so I didn't make a note of it.'

They thanked Mrs Bell and left, certain that she'd be in touch if she remembered anything. As they walked to the car, Gerry commented that she would be an asset to any police force.

'She doesn't need a police force. Sounds like she's

organised her own. At least her traffic division confirmed the time the Smithsons left for Scotland, which is useful, I suppose. What about the stranger she saw?'

'Like she said, he might have stopped to stretch his legs.' Gerry checked the time. 'Tatiana Smithson will probably be home from school by now. Let's go and have a word.'

They drove the short distance to the lodge. Wesley wasn't sure when Della was due to take up residence there, but he hoped it would be after their enquiries were finished.

'I'd like to hear what the girl has to say about Patrick North,' he said as he steered the car through the gates. 'He didn't actually teach her, but her brother must have said something.'

This time Betina saw them arrive and came out to meet them, arms folded defensively as though she was afraid they were about to ask her some awkward questions.

'I haven't heard from Silas and Natalia, if that's what you've come to ask.'

'I'm sure you'll let us know as soon as you do,' said Wesley, turning on the charm. 'We'd like a quick word with your niece, if that's OK. I take it she's home from school?'

'She's just got back. You'd better come in. I'm staying while you question her, of course.'

'Naturally,' said Wesley.

She led them to her private living room, where a girl in school uniform was sitting on the sofa watching TV. Wesley recognised her from the photo in Smithson's study. She had a round face and her brown hair was in two long plaits; she looked like an archetypal schoolgirl from the 1950s in her navy-blue gymslip.

Betina took a seat beside her, but the girl's eyes remained fixed on the TV screen.

'These men are policemen, dear. Detectives.'

Tatiana looked up, suddenly interested.

'Hello, Tatiana. We'd like to ask you some questions, if that's OK,' said Wesley with an encouraging smile.

She glanced at her aunt as though she was seeking her approval, then gave a nod.

When they asked her whether she'd had much to do with her brother's tutor, the answer was a definite no. It was Darius who needed a tutor, not her, because he was always in trouble at school. From the self-righteous way she spoke about her brother, it didn't sound as though they got on well. But Wesley and Gerry didn't read too much into this; both knew that although brothers and sisters often fought like cat and dog while they were growing up, they'd usually unite against a common enemy.

She went on to say that it was awful that Mr North was dead but she didn't know anything about it. She'd been with her aunt on Saturday evening. Neither of them had left the house, but she'd seen some fireworks in the distance when she'd looked out of the window. Betina added that her guest, Georgina, had eaten with them and spent the evening at the lodge. Nobody had ventured out that night. It was November after all; hardly the weather for wandering about in the damp air.

Once they were satisfied that the girl had little to tell them that they didn't already know, the two men stood up to leave. But as they reached the car, they were surprised to hear a voice behind them.

Tatiana had rushed out after them, presumably without her aunt's knowledge.

'Can I tell you something?'

'Of course,' said Wesley. 'What is it?'

'I didn't want to tell you when Auntie Betina was there because she'd only worry and say I couldn't get the bus to school any more. She'd insist on driving me to the school gates and that would be so embarrassing.'

'I understand.' Wesley knew that children of that age had a low embarrassment threshold where adults were concerned.

'Last week I was walking home after the school bus dropped me off in the village and I'm sure a man was watching me.'

'Can you describe him, love?' said Gerry, who'd been listening intently.

'He was in a silver car and he had grey hair. He was quite old and he looked as though he wanted to speak to me, but I got scared and ran away because I've always been told never to speak to strangers.'

'Quite right, love,' said Gerry approvingly.

Wesley caught his eye, wondering whether this was the same stranger Elspeth Bell had seen near the church.

'Anyway, I thought I'd lost him at the gates, but when I looked round, he was following me. When I got to the front door, I looked round again and he wasn't there. He'd gone.'

'Were your parents here then?'

'No. It was a couple of days after they left for Scotland. I haven't seen him since, but I thought I'd better tell you.' Wesley saw fear in the girl's eyes as she leaned forward and whispered, 'What if he comes back?'

20

Wesley and Gerry persuaded Tatiana to tell her aunt about the man. But when Wesley suggested that she might help to make a photofit of him, she said she hadn't seen him well enough. When they took her back into the house and shared the news, Betina expressed shock and scolded her niece mildly for not telling her straight away. It was agreed that for the time being, Tatiana was to be met from the school bus. Her safety outweighed any other considerations.

Wesley couldn't forget the threatening note in Silas Smithson's study. The writer had threatened to take Smithson's son, but in the boy's absence, might an abductor have decided to target his daughter instead?

It was coming up to five o'clock when they returned to the incident room, and they were greeted by the news – or lack of it – that the Smithsons still hadn't been located in Scotland. Wesley was surprised that such a high-profile man could go to ground so easily in this day and age, though he also knew that going off grid was possible if you knew where and how to do it. But Gerry reckoned that as the Smithsons had been away when Patrick North was killed, finding them wasn't at the top of their priority list.

There were messages waiting on the DCI's desk. The

Reverend Becky Selkirk had a doctorate obtained by post from an American university, and she was known to have worked in Leeds and Birmingham before settling in Devon the previous spring. The Church of the Blessed Spirit had a website that was vague to the point of being unhelpful; there was a lot of psychobabble about healing and new beginnings but little else. Wesley said he'd ask his brother-in-law to find out what he could; if there was any inter-clergy gossip about the Reverend Selkirk, Mark was the person who would be able to tap into it. While it was at the forefront of his mind, he also asked one of the DCs to contact the police in Leeds and Birmingham to see whether the reverend's activities had ever come to their attention.

Another message was about Lisa Lowe, the girl who'd accused Patrick North of sexual assault then quickly withdrawn her allegation. Lisa's application to study at Oxford had succeeded, and she was now living at Barchester College, one of the university's oldest colleges.

'We could ask the police in Oxford to interview her,' Wesley suggested.

Gerry shook his head. 'I want to speak to her myself. We've got to consider the possibility that her retraction was a lie. And if it was, what if her family found out and traced North to Nesbarton Hall? What parent wouldn't want to take revenge on someone who did that to their daughter?'

'They live in Glastonbury. That's not far away, only a couple of hours' drive.'

'I'll get the local police to check their alibi for the night North was killed.'

The list of people who might wish to harm Patrick North seemed to be growing by the hour. As well as Lisa

Lowe and her family, and Jordan Green, Patrick's rival in love, Wesley couldn't forget the other things that had been going on in the immediate area: the threats to the owner of Nesbarton Hall and the fact that his young daughter claimed that she'd been watched by a stranger. He also had an uncomfortable feeling about the Reverend Selkirk and her ex-offenders. It was understandable that she'd feel protective towards them, but he still wanted to know who they were and what they'd done – and whether any of them had links to Patrick North or Silas Smithson.

'We haven't heard from Forensics about that anonymous letter Ms Carlton found in Smithson's study,' he said.

'I'll get onto them, Wes. Tell them it's urgent. Perhaps whoever sent it didn't know the family were going away, and when they arrived at the hall to carry out their threat, North got in the way.'

'I feel a lot happier now Aunt Betina's keeping a proper eye on the little girl.' Wesley thought for a moment. 'I imagine someone like Silas Smithson receives threats from time to time. Disgruntled ex-employees; random people with grudges against the very rich.'

Gerry smiled. 'At least we'll never fall into that category on a policeman's salary.'

'Trust you to look on the bright side.' Wesley checked the time. 'Any sign of Jordan Green yet?'

'Someone from Dukesbridge nick went round to his address but he wasn't there.'

'If he's a DJ, he'll work in the evenings, so we might have to wait until tomorrow to see what he's got to say for himself.'

Ellie came rushing up to Gerry's desk, an eager look on her face. 'Sir, I rang Leeds like you asked. The sergeant I spoke to remembers the Reverend Selkirk from a couple of years ago. He said she was suspected of harbouring a man wanted for murder, although they couldn't prove anything at the time. She was deliberately obstructive, he said.'

'What do you reckon, Wes? Do we get a warrant for Selkirk's place?'

'It would make sense, although there's been no suggestion yet that Patrick North had any connection with her.'

'Unless he knew one of her ex-cons – or stumbled over something by accident.'

'A planned robbery at Nesbarton Hall, for instance. The place is packed with precious art and antiques, and that's just the bits we've seen.'

'And when better to strike than while the Smithsons are away? OK. We need a warrant for Selkirk's place. And maybe we should send a patrol to make extra checks on the house and warn Ms Carlton to lock up properly.'

While Gerry made the calls, Wesley returned to his desk. He was just wondering what time he'd get home that night when his phone rang.

Neil came straight to the point. 'Have you arranged for me to examine that mannequin you're keeping at the station yet?'

'Sorry, mate, I've had other things on my mind.'

But his words didn't put Neil off. 'The museum's interested in seeing it. It won't take long for you to arrange access for me, surely. Tell them I'll take the thing off their hands. After all, it's in your evidence store under false pretences – it's not connected with any crime.'

Wesley glanced at Gerry, who was talking on the phone, laying down the law to some unfortunate subordinate. 'I'll see what I can do.'

'Thought I'd come round to yours tonight,' Neil continued. 'Keep you company and help you empty your wine rack.'

'I might be here a while.'

'In that case, I'll keep Pam company. If I know her, she'll already have a bottle open. Might see you later.'

When the call ended, Wesley stared at the phone, aware that he'd felt a slight pang of envy at the thought of Pam spending a cosy night in with a bottle of wine and her exboyfriend from university days. But he told himself he was being ridiculous. Pam and Neil had been friends for years and he'd never seen any hint of attraction between them. Perhaps the thought of Jordan Green's jealousy had planted the seed in his mind; if so, he needed to get rid of it.

His phone rang again. It was Gemma Latimer, and she sounded upset.

'Jordan's just left my place. We had a terrible row. He said I care more about my dead ex than I do about him.'

'Hang on, he knew Patrick was dead. Did you tell him?'

There was a long silence. 'Wasn't I meant to?'

'His name hasn't been released to the press yet but it's OK. Tell me exactly what happened.'

'He said Patrick deserved everything he got . . . then he threatened me,' she sobbed. 'He called me a stupid two-timing cow and said he should punch me in the face. He walked out, but I was scared.'

'I'll send a patrol car round now. Do you know where he's gone?'

'He's got another gig at the Pillar Club tonight, but he was in such a state that . . .'

'Has Jordan got a key to your house?'

'No.'

'Don't answer the door to anyone but the police. And dial 999 if he turns up again.'

After telling Gerry what had happened, Wesley gave the order for a car to be sent to check on Gemma – and for Jordan Green to be picked up as soon as possible.

April 1787

That night I slept in the attic of the magnificent house, in a room at the end of a passage. The servants, I was told, slept in another wing, and I saw nobody that evening apart from the sullen maidservant who brought my meal to my room. I attempted to engage her in conversation, but she was as silent as the brute who had driven the coach. I saw fear in her dull eyes and wondered whether she had been mistreated by her master. I confess I was beginning to feel a strange unease.

Earlier I had been led through the house, where I saw signs of great wealth. Neither I nor any of my friends had ever heard of the Nescote family, so it was likely they had no place in London society. However, I surmised that they wielded some influence in the county of Devonshire.

My quarters were humble, though the bed linen was clean and a jug of water had been provided so that I could wash away the dirt of my long journey. But my sleep was disturbed by vivid nightmares. In them I kept seeing the man without a tongue and another man without a face descending on me with a bloody knife. I awoke shaking and covered in sweat. It was too late to alter my decision now, but I found myself yearning for my old life of poverty in London. It seemed my destiny lay in Devonshire, but I had begun to wonder what that destiny might be.

The same maidservant brought me my breakfast. I found this strange, because I had expected to eat with the servants. It seemed I was being kept apart from them, though I could not fathom why. I wondered if the family would invite me to take my meals in the house but dismissed this as mere fantasy. I had given up my status as a gentleman of some education when I left the north for London to follow my ambition to act in the theatre. Poverty had made me accept any paid work that came my way.

My worry increased as I sat in my room, alert to any sound outside in the passage. I wondered then how easy it would be to escape, to sneak past the servants and out into the open countryside. There would be farms where I could offer my services as a labourer, I thought. I was young, and although I was not accustomed to manual work, I would be quick to learn and gain strength. For a few minutes this seemed the ideal solution to my dilemma. But when I remembered the money I had been offered by Nathaniel Nescote, I hesitated. Perhaps I would wait and see what happened.

It seemed like an age before the sullen maidservant knocked on my door and told me I was to go to the drawing room.

As she led me through the house, I noted once again the grandeur around me. Were the Nescotes an old family? I wondered. And if not, where did their wealth originate? I resolved to ask the servants if the opportunity presented itself.

The drawing room was as handsome as the rest of the house, and when I entered, I saw Nathaniel Nescote and

*another richly dressed young man seated by the window.
I stood for a while, conscious of my shabby appearance as
they looked me over.*

*'Well, cousin,' Nathaniel said to the other man. 'Here
is your madman.'*

21

Wesley dropped Gerry off at his home on Tradmouth water-front at ten o'clock that night. The mist had descended like a fleet of ghost ships on the silent river, making it an eerie place where anything might happen. Gerry thanked him and watched him drive off, home to Pam and the domestic chaos of family life. When his own wife Kathy was alive and their children were young, Gerry's house had been like that too. Now things were quieter.

He let himself in and called out to Joyce, but there was no answer. He took off his coat and threw his keys onto the table in the small hallway, then shouted again. This time the door opened and Joyce stood in the doorway, arms folded. She was a plump middle-aged divorcee who worked in the register office in Morbay, and they'd met while he'd been working on a case. At first they'd got on well, but since she'd turned down his recent marriage proposal, things had definitely cooled between them. She'd become sarcastic, as though his little foibles – and he reckoned he had a lot of them – had begun to irritate her. In the past she'd divided her time between Gerry's house and her own flat in Morbay. But recently she'd been spending more and more time at the flat.

'Sorry I'm late, love. It's this case. One of our chief suspects has gone AWOL and we've been trying to find him.'

She rolled her eyes and retreated to the living room. Suddenly he felt like an intruder in his own home.

It came as a relief when his phone rang. He took it from his pocket, hoping it was a message to say that Jordan Green had been picked up and brought in for questioning. But the display told him that the caller was Alison, the daughter who'd been lost to him for so long, and his heart began to beat a little faster.

'Hello, love. How are you? Haven't heard from you for a while.'

Alison's mother was an ex-girlfriend he'd gone out with in his native Liverpool long before he'd met Kathy. She'd kept her pregnancy secret from him when he went away to sea, and he hadn't known he had another daughter until a couple of years ago, when Alison had come to Devon after her mother's death to search for her biological father. She and Gerry had formed an instant bond, and they'd stayed in regular touch after she returned to Liverpool. His other daughter, Rosie, hadn't attempted to hide her resentment of the newcomer to the family, although his son, Sam, more easy-going, had taken the acquisition of a new sibling in his stride. Because of Rosie's attitude, Gerry hadn't seen as much of Alison as he'd have liked, and now he was delighted to hear her voice.

'Dad.' The word gave him a warm glow. 'I've been thinking, do you mind if I come down for Christmas? I was going away with . . . Anyway, we broke up, so I'm—'

'That'd be great, love,' Gerry said without thinking. 'When can you make it?'

'Actually, I've quit my job here and I'm thinking of looking for something down in Devon – near you.'

'That's fantastic,' said Gerry – and he meant it.

'Can I stay with you until I get a place of my own?'

'Of course you can.'

'Er, I hope it won't upset Rosie . . .'

'She'll come round. Leave her to me and Sam,' said Gerry, with a confidence he didn't feel.

'What about Joyce?' In the past, Joyce's manner towards Alison had been guarded, as though she hadn't quite known how to deal with the situation.

'She'll be fine. It'll give her a chance to get to know you better.' Gerry had always been willing to bend the truth a little for an easy domestic life. And he really wanted to see Alison. There had been far too many wasted years when he hadn't even been aware of her existence. 'Look, I'm busy on a murder case at the moment, but come down any time. I'll let Joyce know and we'll get the spare room ready.'

He experienced an excitement he hadn't felt for a long while. Alison was coming back into his life – just in time for Christmas.

As soon as the call ended, his phone rang again. The police in Oxford had contacted Lisa Lowe at Barchester College, and she'd told them she wanted to speak to the officer in charge of the inquiry into Patrick North's murder. She said she wanted to set a few things straight and that she'd catch the train to Exeter tomorrow morning.

Gerry said someone would meet her at St David's station at lunchtime.

All patrols were still looking for Jordan Green. He hadn't turned up as arranged at the Pillar Club that night, and the car stationed outside his flat reported that he hadn't returned home. The management at the club, an

140

insalubrious establishment popular with the youth of Dukesbridge, were asked whether he'd been there the previous Saturday night, and the answer was that he'd only been there for the latter part of the evening, taking over from another DJ at around 10.30.

Finding Green was their main priority, but at the briefing in the incident room the next morning, Gerry also announced that Lisa Lowe was coming to Devon to make a voluntary statement.

'Why would she do that?' asked DC Trish Walton, who'd been listening intently. 'He's dead. It's too late for her to change her story and file an official complaint against him now.'

'I know, Trish, but she might have something relevant to tell us. No doubt all will become clear when we speak to her.'

Wesley thought Gerry seemed to be in a remarkably good mood that morning, and once the briefing was over, the DCI drew him to one side to break the news of Alison's imminent arrival.

'Not good timing,' said Wesley.

'Don't worry, Wes. As soon as we've got Jordan Green in custody, I've a feeling in my water that it won't take long to wrap the case up.'

Wesley wished he could share the boss's certainty. Jordan Green, Patrick North's rival in love and a member of a gun club to boot, was the obvious culprit, but Wesley suspected there might be something strange going on beneath the surface at Nesbarton Hall, and that so far they only had a fraction of the picture.

Gerry's mood remained buoyant even when the results of the anonymous letter to Silas Smithson came back from

141

Forensics. It had been printed on a laser printer and the only fingerprints on it belonged to Karensa Carlton – and someone else whose prints weren't on record.

'I don't reckon it's got anything to do with North's murder,' said Gerry as he handed Wesley the report. 'I think it's just someone with a grudge against a wealthy businessman. It's easy to make threats, harder to carry them out.'

Wesley thought for a moment. 'Do we really know that Darius is safe? Perhaps Smithson's not in Scotland as we've been told. Perhaps he's gone to ground because his son's been abducted and he's afraid of involving the police, in which case he could be anywhere. Perhaps the kidnappers have already got the boy and his father's arranging to pay the ransom.'

'If that's the case, would he leave that letter for Karensa Carlton to find?'

'He might have left in a panic and forgotten it was there. According to the village watch, he was speeding through Nesbarton at eight fifteen on the morning of the first of November. Perhaps he was anxious to get away, to take the lad out of danger.'

Gerry sighed and stared at his phone as though he was willing it to ring with word that Jordan Green had been apprehended. But by eleven o'clock, good news still hadn't arrived.

Gerry sent Paul Johnson to pick up Lisa Lowe from Exeter, with instructions to take her straight to Tradmouth police station. He was to use the comfortable interview room set aside for victims and witnesses and make sure she had lunch and coffee.

At quarter past twelve, Wesley received a call to say she'd arrived. Gerry immediately stood up and reached for his coat.

'Sure you want to come, Gerry? It might be better if I went with Trish. If it turns out Lisa was lying when she retracted her accusation and she really was the victim of an assault, she might feel intimidated if she finds herself being interviewed by two men.'

Gerry sat down again. 'You're absolutely right, Wes. Take Trish.'

Trish Walton seemed a little nervous as Wesley drove to Tradmouth, and he asked her if anything was wrong.

'Not really,' she answered. 'It's just an odd situation. Are we treating this Lisa as a suspect or what?'

'Oxford police checked her alibi for last Saturday. She was out with friends doing normal student stuff. There's no evidence that she came to Devon to kill Patrick North, so we regard her as a witness. I'm just wondering what she'll have to tell us.'

When they entered the interview room, Lisa Lowe was sitting on the edge of a sofa, the remains of a sandwich beside her on a small side table along with an empty coffee mug. She looked up and gave a nervous half-smile. She had an elfin face and fine fair hair tied back in a ponytail, and she was still wearing her padded coat, fastened up as though she didn't intend to stay long.

'Thank you for coming,' said Wesley after they'd introduced themselves. 'It's good of you to travel all this way.'

'It's OK. I have a friend in Exeter I haven't seen for a while and I've arranged to stay the night with her.'

'Good,' he said, glad that she'd have some support after the questioning she was about to face. 'We've been told that you have something to tell us, is that right?'

Lisa stared at her coffee mug for a few moments before speaking. She looked nervously from Wesley to Trish.

'Take your time,' Trish said gently. 'We know this is difficult for you.'

The girl looked her in the eye. 'Do you?' There was a long silence before she spoke again. 'The police who came to see me in Oxford told me that Patrick North is dead. Is that right?'

'Yes,' said Wesley. 'Although his name won't be released to the media until we've informed his next of kin.'

To his surprise, he saw tears forming in her eyes.

'I understand you accused him of assaulting you, then retracted the allegation soon afterwards.'

She bowed her head and sat in silence for a few moments. 'It's all my fault.'

'You mustn't blame yourself,' Trish said angrily. 'It's never the victim's fault. There's only one person who did anything wrong and that's the man who assaulted you.'

Lisa began to shake her head vigorously. 'No, you don't understand. Patrick *didn't* assault me. I lied, and if he killed himself because of what I said about him, then I'm responsible.'

'He didn't kill himself,' said Wesley. 'Somebody murdered him.'

Lisa looked at him in astonishment. 'The police who came to see me just told me he'd died and it was being treated as suspicious. I thought ...'

Trish was about to speak when Wesley signalled her to wait. It was half a minute before Lisa broke her silence.

'I feel so bad about what I did. I was angry, you see. He'd had a real go at me about an essay I wrote. Can I have another coffee?' she said meekly, unzipping her coat and placing it beside her on the settee.

'Of course,' said Wesley. There was a kettle and small

fridge in the room, and he did the honours. Pam had trained him well over the years.

Once the steaming mug had been placed on the table beside her, she began to speak again. Wesley suspected he was about to hear some kind of confession, so he leaned forward, listening intently.

'I went to Patrick's flat that evening. He lived in the staff wing of the school, you see. Anyway, we had a ... disagreement. He said that if I didn't up my game, I'd never make it to Oxford. He was quite brutal – verbally. He called me a lazy, overprivileged little cow and then he started going on about the deprived kids he'd taught in Manchester – how they were worth two of me and if they'd had my advantages in life ... He said I should realise how lucky I was and stop messing him about. He'd always seemed to have a chip on his shoulder, and I suspected he had a problem with the school. I'd thought for a while that he resented us, but that evening it all came flooding out like bile.

'I'd always liked him – had a bit of a crush on him, to tell you the truth. That made it worse somehow, and I thought I'd teach him a lesson, so I told him I was going to make sure he paid for how he'd treated me. He asked me how and I said I'd think of something. He ordered me to get out, but that only made me angrier.'

Wesley waited for her to continue. So far this story matched the one Gemma had told him.

Lisa bowed her head so that he could no longer see the look in her eyes. 'There was a boy in the sixth form, Cosmo,' she began almost in a whisper. 'Thought he was God's gift. When I got back from Patrick's flat, he came to my room and I told him how horrible Patrick had been to me. I was furious, but he seemed to find it amusing. I told him to go, but he locked the door and said that if I wanted to finish off Mr North, he'd give me some real evidence.' She shuddered. 'That was when it happened. Cosmo ... attacked me. When he'd finished, he said he'd done me a favour. I'd get rid of North and nobody would believe what had really happened. If I told anyone what he'd done, he'd just deny it – say that North put pressure on me to lie. He took me to the head's office first thing the next morning and told her that North had assaulted me.'

'Surely you could have told the truth there and then.'

She shook her head, and Wesley saw tears rolling down her cheeks. 'You don't understand. Cosmo insisted on going with me and I was scared of him. He'd threatened to hurt me, to scar my face if I told anyone what had really happened. I went back to the head's office on my own later that day and withdrew the allegation against Patrick, but I was too frightened to tell her about Cosmo. I was afraid of what he'd do.'

'Where is Cosmo now?' At that moment, Wesley wanted to do everything in his power to bring the boy to justice.

'He's at a university in the States. He always said he was untouchable – and he is.'

'He's bound to slip up one day. Maybe he already has.'

'If you mean would I give evidence against him, the answer's no. It would be my word against his. And he never tired of telling everyone that his father was rich enough to buy him out of trouble.'

Her words made Wesley depressed, and one look at Trish told him she felt the same.

'Patrick North was horrible to me that evening, but I feel so guilty when I think of the lies I told about him.

146

I should have been stronger. I shouldn't have let Cosmo intimidate me.'

'It wasn't your fault,' said Trish gently. 'You were under duress. He made threats against you.' She handed Lisa a tissue and watched her wipe her tears away.

'What happens now? Am I going to get in trouble for lying? I never thought it would lead to . . .'

'You tried to put it right when you retracted your accusation,' said Trish, indignant. 'It's Cosmo who should be in trouble.'

'If he ever shows his face round these parts, I'll make sure he comes to our attention,' said Wesley with grim determination. 'Do any of your friends and relatives still believe Patrick North assaulted you?'

She hesitated. 'I never told my parents, and I asked the school not to tell them either. But one of my friends told my brother that I'd reported him. He said he wanted to sort Patrick out, but I told him to forget it. It was over and I wanted to put it behind me.'

'You never told your brother you'd lied?'

She bowed her head. 'Not at first. To tell the truth, I was ashamed. I told him later that my friend had got it all wrong, though I'm not sure whether he believed me.'

'Where can we find your brother?'

'He's at university in Durham.'

Wesley and Trish looked at each other. It seemed there was another person who had a reason to take revenge on Patrick North.

22

Two young constables in a patrol car were waiting out of sight at the bottom of Jordan Green's street and he was apprehended as soon as he returned home. They had orders to take him to Tradmouth police station for interview. They weren't expecting trouble. But trouble was what he gave them.

There was a scuffle as Green made a token show of resisting arrest, but in the end the wanted man gave up the fight because he didn't want to damage the brand-new trainers he was wearing. Eventually he was handcuffed and pushed into the back of the car, and half an hour later he was being led between the swishing automatic doors of Tradmouth police station. But when he was told that he'd been arrested in connection with a murder inquiry, he looked puzzled.

'Murder?' The word came out in a high-pitched squeak. 'I never murdered nobody.'

The arresting officers exchanged a smirk. 'That's what they all say.'

Wesley asked Trish Walton and Ellie Taylor to take Lisa Lowe to her friend's flat in Exeter. He hoped that the company of two young women might encourage further confidences, although he was pretty sure that Lisa had already told them all she knew.

After the formal interview was over, Wesley and Lisa had shared a friendly conversation about student days in general and Trish listened in silence. If Lisa was telling the truth, her brother had been miles away up in Durham at a student party when North was murdered. But they'd still ask someone to confirm his alibi.

As soon as Lisa had left the police station, Wesley called Gerry to tell him he was on his way back to the incident room. When he gave him a brief account of what Lisa had revealed, Gerry made angry noises on the other end of the line. 'Hope that bastard Cosmo gets what's coming to him – rich daddy or no rich daddy.'

'He's in the States.'

'Well, if he tries his tricks over there, they don't mess about. A few decades in a county penitentiary would do him the world of good, in my humble opinion.'

Wesley knew the boss was visualising Cosmo labouring in a chain gang, but he himself wasn't so sure it would come to that. The Cosmos of this world had the wherewithal to wriggle out of sticky situations. It was an uncomfortable fact of life.

The thought of the wealthier classes using their money to evade trouble reminded him of Silas Smithson. There was still no word from the Scottish police, and he'd started to wonder whether the trip north was a smokescreen and the Smithsons had gone somewhere else entirely. Smithson had access to a private plane; if his son was under threat, he might well have lied about his destination. And if he'd kept Karensa Carlton in the dark, so much the better, because nobody would be able to get the truth out of her however hard they tried. Smithson's gleaming yacht was still moored in Tradmouth Marina and his London house had been checked as a matter of routine, but who knew what other accommodation he had access to if necessary.

If the family weren't in the Highlands of Scotland, Gerry wondered whether they might have gone to their house in France, oblivious to the drama that had been played out at their Devon property. Wesley didn't imagine that finding the family to inform them that there'd been a murder on their estate would be much of a priority for the gendarmes in the Avignon area. Lists of ferry and Eurotunnel passengers had been requested, but these things took time.

He was about to start the car when his phone rang and he heard Gerry's voice again. This time he sounded excited.

'Stay where you are, Wes. I'm coming to Tradmouth to join you. Jordan Green's being brought in. I should be with you in half an hour. Rob's driving me over.'

Wesley greeted Jordan Green in the police station foyer. 'Mr Green, we've been looking for you,' he said pleasantly. The man grunted in return. He was tall and wiry, with a man bun, and tattoos peeping from the neck of his pale blue padded jacket. He scowled at Wesley but said nothing as he was led into the grimmest interview room, the one with the furniture bolted to the floor and no natural light.

When Gerry joined them, he looked remarkably cheerful, as though he was satisfied they were about to wrap up the case. He'd just arranged a search warrant for Green's flat, and if there was evidence there, they'd have a reason to detain their suspect. Otherwise their time to question him would be limited.

'We're investigating the death of Patrick North.'

The man looked wary. 'That's got nothing to do with me.'

'I understand you threatened Mr North,' Gerry said after they'd cautioned Green and set the tape running. They'd asked him whether he wanted a solicitor present, but he'd refused. He didn't need a solicitor because he'd done nothing wrong.

'Who told you that? Gemma? She's a lying bitch.'

'You're saying you didn't threaten Mr North?' said Wesley.

There was a long silence before the answer came. 'If you want to know the truth, I went to see him a couple of weeks ago. I texted him on Gemma's phone and asked him to meet me at the gates of that big house where he was staying. He got the shock of his life when he saw me, I can tell you,' he added with a satisfied smirk.

'What happened?'

'I told him not to contact Gemma again. I said she wasn't interested 'cause she was going out with me.'

'What did he say to that?'

'Nothing. I think I got my point across.'

'But your threats didn't work, did they? Patrick moved in with her while the family he worked for were away. She was two-timing you. Bet you weren't pleased about that.' There was a long pause. 'Patrick North was murdered on the evening of Saturday the fifth of November. He was shot.'

Green's eyes widened in panic. 'I never killed nobody. I might have wanted to scare him off, but I never killed him. Honest.'

'Why did you try to get away when the officers told you we wanted a word?'

Jordan cracked his knuckles and said nothing for a few moments. The question had put him on his guard. 'I . . . I thought they were someone else. You hear about people impersonating police officers, don't you? I thought they were after me.'

'Why should anyone be after you?'

He swallowed hard. 'No comment,' he said after a short pause.

Wesley decided not to push it for the moment. 'Where were you last Saturday night?'

'Pillar Club. It's a regular gig.'

'You were only there for part of the evening. The manager said you took over from another DJ around ten thirty. Why was that?'

'Had some business to do, didn't I. But it was nothing to do with North, I swear.'

'What kind of business?'

'Business with people who don't like to be kept waiting.' Green's initial cockiness was gone and he was starting to look downright scared. Wesley guessed that the people he was talking about were considerably more frightening than the police.

'You didn't turn up at the club last night either.'

'Had another job to do.'

'You're pushing it a bit with the manager, aren't you? If he thinks you're unreliable . . .'

'My mate always covers for me. We have an understanding.'

Gerry's phone rang. After a brief conversation he ended the call and looked Green in the eye. 'That was one of the officers searching your flat. They found a quantity of class A drugs hidden in a holdall under the bed.'

Green answered quickly, as though he'd anticipated this and had his explanation ready. 'They were planted. I know how you people operate.'

'We're not the drugs squad, although I'm sure they'll be

152

interested,' said Wesley. 'You're a member of a gun club, I believe.'

'So?'

Gerry spoke next. 'They didn't find a firearm at your place. Where is it?'

'I use the ones at the gun club. It's all legal.'

'Did you borrow a .22 rifle last Saturday?'

Green stood up and Wesley could see fear in his eyes. 'No way. You can't just borrow them, they're kept on the premises, so you can't pin that on me. Anyway, I haven't been to the club for a couple of weeks. Been too busy. Ask anyone.'

'We will. Patrick North was shot with a .22 rifle. And it seems you have a very strong motive.'

Jordan Green opened and closed his mouth, reminding Wesley of a goldfish. 'I swear I never hurt him. I might not be a saint, but murder . . . No way.'

They continued questioning him for another twenty minutes, but he stuck to his story. When the interview was over, they returned to the CID office and Gerry called his counterpart in the drugs squad to inform them of the search team's discovery. The chief inspector he spoke to didn't seem particularly surprised. Green had been on their radar for a while, but they were trying to pin down those higher up in the chain of command. They suspected that Green did the dirty work for others who were far more dangerous than he was.

When the call ended, Gerry turned to Wesley. 'I think I've ruffled a few feathers, Wes. It seems the drugs squad have been keeping an eye on Green hoping he'd lead them to Mr Big. We didn't find any evidence in his flat to connect him with North's murder, so I'm arranging to release him on bail pending further enquiries as long as we know where to find him.'

'Do the drugs squad really use the term Mr Big?' Wesley sounded amused.

Gerry shrugged. 'You know what I mean.'

'If they've been keeping an eye on Green, they might be able to tell us where he was on Saturday night when Patrick North was killed.'

'I thought of that, but it turns out they weren't watching him that closely, more's the pity. He's still at the top of my suspect list, Wes. I've been assured he's unlikely to do a runner, so until we have more evidence . . .'

The phone on Gerry's desk rang, and after a short conversation, the DCI turned to Wesley.

'Jordan Green wants to speak to us again. He says he's got something to tell us.' He rubbed his hands together. 'With any luck, he wants to make a confession. Come on, Wes. Let's get down there before he changes his mind.'

Wesley couldn't share Gerry's optimism as they made their way back to the interview room where Green was waiting. This time the suspect had an eager look on his face, as though what he had to tell them was going to get him out of trouble once and for all.

Wesley and Gerry sat down again.

'We were about to release you,' said Gerry. 'To what do we owe this pleasure?'

'I've got some information for you. Valuable information.'

'Go on,' said Wesley. 'A bit of co-operation never goes amiss.' He couldn't forget that this man had intimidated Gemma, but he knew this wasn't the moment to allow his personal feelings to get in the way.

'If you want to know what that Patrick North was really up to, why don't you ask the woman?'

'What woman?'

'The woman he was with when I went to the big house about three weeks ago. I didn't talk to him that time. I just wanted to know where he lived and what Gemma saw in him.'

Wesley leaned forward. 'Tell us about this woman.'

'It was dead easy to walk in through the gates. Nobody stopped me. Anyway, I'd seen a picture of this North character on Gemma's phone, so I knew what he looked like and that he had a flat in the big house. I went round to the side door and it turned out my luck was in, 'cause I saw him leaving. He was looking round like he was on some secret mission, and I was about to warn him off when this woman appeared and they went into an outbuilding – looked like old stables or something. They were acting as if they shouldn't have been there, if you know what I mean.' He gave Wesley a wink.

'You mean they were having a bit of how's-your-father?' said Gerry bluntly.

Green nodded vigorously, his man bun bouncing on the top of his head. 'Yeah, that's exactly what it looked like. I told Gemma he was screwing someone else, but she never believed me.'

'Can you describe the woman?' Wesley said, wondering if he was about to hear a description of Karensa Carlton – or maybe someone who hadn't yet featured in the inquiry.

'Oh yeah. There were lights in the yard and I had a good view of her from where I was hiding. She was a bloody stunner. Gorgeous. Black hair and one of those moles on her cheek – don't they call them beauty spots? I would

155

have taken a picture to show Gemma what he was up to, but I'd forgotten to charge my phone.' He sounded angry with himself for missing this golden opportunity to put her off his rival once and for all. 'I heard her talking to him. I couldn't hear what she was saying, but she sounded foreign.'

Wesley and Gerry exchanged a glance. They were both certain that the woman he was describing was Natalia Smithson. This was something they hadn't expected.

23

Gerry and Wesley returned to the CID office in silence, taking in the implications of what they'd just been told.

'We should redouble our efforts to find the Smithsons,' Wesley said as he took a seat by the DCI's desk. 'I know they were away when Patrick North was killed, but Smithson might have hired someone to do the job for him. I'm sure he can afford to pay a hit man – keep his own hands clean.'

'But are we sure Jordan Green was telling the truth? He might have been trying to send us off on a wild goose chase.'

'I don't think we can rule anything out at this stage,' said Wesley.

'Natalia Smithson and the tutor, eh? Touch of the Lady Chatterleys?'

'Who knows?'

'Betina might know more than she's saying. So might the kid, Tatiana. In my experience little girls have a nose for these things. Our Rosie knew all our business at that age – always asking questions.' A fond look appeared on the DCI's face. 'I just used to tell her to ask her mother.'

'Tatiana thought a man was watching her. Pity Nesbarton's not bristling with CCTV cameras.'

'It has something even better, Wes. Elspeth Bell and her

village watch. Never underestimate the effectiveness of a net curtain.'

Karensa Carlton felt irritated when she opened Nesbarton Hall's front door and saw Betina standing there.

'Have you heard from Silas and Natalia?' Betina asked anxiously. 'It's just that Tatiana's been asking when her parents are coming back.'

Karensa suspected this was a lie; that it was Betina herself who was curious. She said she'd heard nothing from her employers – but then she hadn't expected to. It was the same the last time they'd decided to retreat from civilisation for a couple of weeks. Peace and quiet was the one thing Silas Smithson's money couldn't buy, but with adequate planning, he was able to find it. And the last thing he wanted was to be disturbed.

She watched Betina walk away down the drive towards the lodge, and as soon as she was out of sight, she retreated to the study. She liked being in there. She liked the old bookshelves that lined the walls. Karensa loved books, an enthusiasm she shared with Silas Smithson. His passion for rare volumes had turned into an obsession over the years, and he had the money to feed it. Often when she entered the study, she found him gloating over his books like a miser over a box of gold. But she understood.

She found the room silent apart from the rhythmic ticking of the clock on the mantelpiece, another precious antique. She stood by the desk, totally at peace. Old books had a certain subtle scent, and she breathed it in, her eyes closed as though in prayer. She'd been putting off this moment since the police arrived to shatter the tranquillity of the empty house, but she wouldn't delay any longer.

The key was kept behind an early edition of *Gulliver's Travels*, and she slid the valuable volume out carefully to retrieve it. Once the desk drawer was open, she stood and looked at the contents. Letters, correspondence. Items she knew she needed to destroy.

Rachel had thought that taking a break from her usual existence as a hard-working detective sergeant would give her the opportunity to play the domestic goddess during Freddie's naps. But the reality had turned out to be quite different. She hadn't been prepared for the amount of work generated by a new baby and the exhaustion created by so many disturbed nights. At times she longed to return to the CID office for a bit of peace, but at least she had Nigel's mum there to lend a hand, and her own mother wasn't far away. She knew she was luckier than most.

While she was up in the night seeing to Freddie, her drowsy thoughts had strayed to Great-Uncle Geoff and her impression that there had been someone else in his cottage. All sorts of possibilities flitted through her head. You heard of county lines drug dealers preying on lonely old people; cuckoos moving in and running their activities from previously innocent premises.

When she'd shared her fears with Nigel, he'd told her she was worrying about nothing. Geoff might be eccentric, but he wasn't a fool. Besides, he wasn't alone; he had family nearby. But Nigel was a farmer; he wasn't a police officer who'd seen things during her working life that made her suspicious of any new and strange situation.

She'd made a casserole for dinner, something easy she could pop in the oven and forget about until it was time to eat. One thing she'd never managed to do was to gauge quantities, so when she finally took it from the oven while Nigel was playing the proud father with Freddie on his knee, she discovered that she'd made far too much.

When they'd finished eating, she left Freddie with Nigel and put on her coat and boots.

'There's so much left over, I thought I'd take it to Uncle Geoff,' she said when she was halfway out of the kitchen door with the casserole dish in her hands wrapped up in a tea towel. 'Won't be long.'

She didn't wait to hear Nigel's reply. Instead she hurried over to Geoff's cottage and knocked on the door.

Geoff opened it a crack, as though he was afraid that his visitor might be unwelcome.

'I've brought you a casserole.' She looked at him expectantly, and after a few seconds' hesitation, he stood aside to let her in. He seemed jumpy, which wasn't like Geoff at all, and she wondered whether it was a delayed reaction to finding Patrick North's body – or something more sinister.

A fire was burning in the little cast-iron grate in his parlour, making the room hot and stuffy. Rachel placed the casserole carefully on the battered pine table and instructed Geoff to put it in the oven to heat it up.

But he didn't appear to be paying attention; he kept glancing nervously towards the parlour door.

'Something wrong, Uncle Geoff?'

As if on cue, the door opened and a man appeared, looming there pale and grey. He shuffled in stiffly and sank onto the old sofa near the fire.

'Who's this, Geoff?' asked Rachel, doing her best to sound calm and unthreatening. At first she took the man for a rough sleeper, but her job had taught her to be observant, and she noted that although his clothes were dirty, they'd once been smart, and his shabby shoes looked expensive, possibly hand-made.

'This is Ben,' Geoff said, looking down at his feet.

'Hello, Ben,' she said warily, her instincts telling her that something wasn't right; that Geoff's naïvety might have led him into a potentially dangerous situation. 'I'm Rachel. I'm Geoff's great-nephew's wife.'

The man stared up at her with bloodshot eyes. He looked ill.

'Ben's lost his memory,' Geoff blurted out. 'I found him wandering in the lane the other day and he doesn't remember how he got there. He doesn't even know who he is.'

'I see,' said Rachel, doing her best to sound calm and casual. 'Ben, I've brought a casserole. Hope you like it.' She was aware that she was smiling, a fixed expression to hide her nerves.

'Thank you,' the man said quietly. 'That's very thoughtful.'

He was well spoken and polite, she thought, and she smiled again, hoping to reassure him before she asked her next question, reminding herself that this wasn't the kind of police interview she was used to conducting. 'Can you remember anything about where you live?'

He shook his head.

Geoff had picked up the casserole and was about to take it into the tiny scullery that served as his kitchen. 'Now, maid, don't you go bothering Ben with your interrogations. He's been through enough.'

'I'm only trying to help,' said Rachel.

Then, to her surprise, Ben lifted up the checked shirt he was wearing so that she could see his pale torso. 'How did I get this, that's what I want to know? It still hurts like hell.'

161

She stared, lost for words. His body was a mass of purple bruises, as though he'd been badly beaten up. He lowered his head, and she saw dried blood matted in his hair.

'Who did this to you, Ben?' she asked softly.

'I can't remember. All I know is that Geoff found me wandering about and brought me back here.' Tears were forming in his eyes now, tears of pain and frustration.

'You really should go to A&E and get those injuries looked at,' said Rachel. 'And we should let the police know. If someone attacked you—'

'No police,' Geoff jumped in. 'Telling them could open a whole can of worms. You should know that, our Rachel. Ben's safe here with me, so let him be. And he don't need no hospital either. He's on the mend, aren't you?'

Ben nodded. 'I'm a lot better than I was when Geoff found me.'

'We need to find out who you are, Ben. You might have family looking for you – people who are worried sick about you.'

'That's enough now. You go home, maid. Ben's fine here with me.' Geoff opened the door to let her out. 'Thank you for the casserole, but you should get back to your little Freddie.'

She hadn't realised how stubborn Geoff could be. He considered Ben to be under his protection and no amount of argument would shift him. But she was reluctant to push the matter just at that moment. She needed to consult Nigel and his parents to see what they thought.

She knew Wesley was busy dealing with the murder in the grounds of Nesbarton Hall, but she wondered whether the attack on Ben – if he had been attacked and not involved in some sort of accident – might be connected in some way to the case. On the other hand, if the killer was armed with a gun and Ben had witnessed something, it was unlikely that he would have survived to tell the tale. Unless . . .

A terrible thought occurred to her. If the victim had been the person who'd beaten Ben up, and if Ben had been in possession of a gun that he'd later discarded, Geoff might be harbouring a murderer.

She had no proof, only a flight of imagination that had led her to an unlikely conclusion. But she knew from experience that unlikely conclusions could occasionally turn out to be correct.

As she made her way back to the farmhouse, she took out her phone and selected Wesley's number.

May 1787

I learned from the maidservant that my new master was called Dionisio Nescote. I remarked on the unusual nature of his Christian name, and she told me that his mother was Italian. Her name was Francesca, but she was known as the Signora. Dionisio's father had met her on his travels and had brought her back as his bride to the grand house he'd had built. There was a handsome portrait of her on the staircase, although it hardly did justice to her beauty.

I asked the girl her own name and she told me it was Dorathea. A gift from God, I said in jest, translating it from the Latin, but she failed to comprehend. She said she was known in the house as Dora.

I then enquired where Dionisio's father had acquired his great wealth, and she looked on me with pity, as though she considered me an innocent. 'Why, he is a privateer, sir. There are several such in the port of Tradmouth, men who go to sea and capture foreign ships. They bring the ships back to port and sell them along with their cargo and amass great riches. They say Captain Samuel Nescote, Master Dionisio's father, has captured more ships than any other master in Tradmouth – and they say he has killed men too.'

I was unable to hide my surprise. I had heard of these

privateers, little more than pirates, and I knew the West Country seethed with them. I had imagined them to be rough sailors and was amazed that such a man lived as a gentleman of means and great taste.

I asked her if she knew why Dionisio and his cousin wished me to play the role of a madman. She looked frightened and said she did not know. Now that she was more talkative, I asked her why our coachman had no tongue. She shuddered and answered that he was once one of Captain Nescote's sailors and she had heard that his tongue was cut out as a punishment. As she spoke, the fear returned to her eyes. It was a fear I was beginning to share.

24

Wesley was on his way home after taking Sherlock for his evening walk when his phone rang and he saw Rachel's name on the caller display.

'I want to ask your advice,' she said before he could ask her how she was. There was a long pause, then she said, 'I'm worried about Uncle Geoff.'

'Why?'

He expected a tale of delayed shock. Finding any dead body could be a traumatic experience, but finding a murder victim ...

Rachel's next words surprised him. 'There's someone staying with him in his cottage. A man called Ben.'

'Is that a problem?'

'Geoff told me he found him wandering about in the lane and took him in. He's badly bruised, as though he's been beaten up, and he's lost his memory. He can't remember a thing.'

'Has he seen a doctor?'

'No. Geoff says he's been looking after him and that he's on the mend.'

'It sounds as though he should be seen by someone.'

'Geoff doesn't want any interference from the authorities.

He can be stubborn and he says it's his Christian duty to look after him.'

'And he's definitely called Ben?'

'That's the name Geoff's given him, but I don't know whether it's his real name. If I give you a description, can you check whether anyone's reported him missing? His clothes are dirty but they seem to be good quality.'

Rachel had always been observant, and he trusted her judgement. 'What are you worried about in particular?'

'We don't know anything about him. He could be a con man, or have convictions for violence. Perhaps he has a reason to be scared of the police. Will you make enquiries?'

Wesley couldn't say no.

Just before nine o'clock the following morning, Gerry entered the incident room like a whirlwind, shouting for quiet and asking whether anything had come in during his absence. Wesley suspected that Alison's imminent arrival was responsible for his cheerful mood.

He hurried to the boss's desk. 'Rachel called me last night.'

'How is she? Still having sleepless nights with young Freddie?' Gerry grinned fondly.

'It wasn't a social call. She's worried about Nigel's great-uncle Geoff.'

'Why? He might have found the body, but I never had him down as a suspect.'

'It's not that. He appears to have taken in a waif and stray. He's letting a man who claims to have amnesia stay in his spare room. The Haynes family don't know anything about this man and Rachel's worried that he might be up to no good. She's afraid he might be taking advantage of Geoff's good nature.'

'And her years in CID have made her suspicious of anything that moves, especially as there's been a murder in the area. You're sure this man hasn't been reported as a missing person?'

'I've checked, and he hasn't. It's his injuries that bother me. Rachel said it looked as though he'd been beaten up. And she's not one to exaggerate, is she?'

Gerry nodded in agreement.

'We need to have a word with him. I know he claims to have lost his memory, but we might learn something. And we can't forget how close Geoff lives to the murder scene. If there was a stranger wandering about . . . I'm also thinking of the man who was watching Tatiana. This man could fit his description.'

'There are lots of middle-aged men with grey hair, but it's worth following up. That man was in a silver car. Rachel's man hasn't got a car, has he?'

'Not as far as she knows.'

'OK, Wes. We'd better make enquiries. But be discreet. We don't want to worry Rachel's in-laws.'

'Am I ever anything else?' said Wesley. He perched on the edge of Gerry's desk. 'There's been a message from Greater Manchester Police. They've finally managed to contact Patrick North's mother and they broke the news to her yesterday. She's coming down today. Should arrive this evening.'

Gerry didn't answer for a few moments, turning a pen over and over in his fingers as though he was deep in thought.

'She's been in Yorkshire with her daughter for a few days

168

visiting friends,' Wesley continued. 'Found the police waiting for them when they got back.'

'Imagine coming home to that,' Gerry muttered, suddenly serious. 'Must have been a hell of a shock. But we'll have to speak to her sooner rather than later.'

Wesley found the prospect daunting. Other people's grief made him feel helpless. However much he wished he could offer comfort, he knew anything he said was inadequate. He'd ask Trish to meet the family and find out what they wanted to do about accommodation. Talking to them about Patrick could come later.

As he gave Trish her instructions, his mind was still on Rachel's call. He couldn't help feeling uneasy about the mysterious visitor who had got his feet well and truly under Geoff's table. Since he had been found wandering in a lane near Nesbarton Hall, they needed to discover more about him.

He returned to Gerry's desk. 'Mind if I go over to Rachel's to try and find out more about Geoff's guest?'

Gerry looked at his desk. 'Good idea. Give Rach my love, won't you? Tell her even the local villains are missing her.'

'I will.' Wesley hesitated for a moment. 'Have we got anything on Cosmo Mearson yet – the man who allegedly assaulted Lisa Lowe?'

'I'll get someone to check. You don't think he's a serious suspect for North's murder, do you? What would be his motive?'

Wesley shook his head. 'Not sure I can think of one at the moment. Besides, according to Lisa, he's at university in the States, so he's got the perfect alibi.'

'You never know, he might have come back home to see his dear old mum or something like that. I'd like to confirm that he's actually where Lisa says he is.'

Wesley gave Rachel a call to warn her of his imminent visit, and as soon as he set off for Gorfleet Farm, the rain started up again. Rachel met him in the cobbled yard in front of the farmhouse wearing a waxed jacket and wellingtons. Wesley zipped up his coat and took his own wellingtons out of the car boot, and together they trudged across the fields, their feet sinking into the earth that had been softened by the recent rain. As they walked, he updated her on the Patrick North case, and he noticed that she looked worried.

'I think someone might have beaten Ben up, and if that person was North's killer, he might come looking for him to finish off the job.' She paused. 'Geoff could become collateral damage. He's an innocent. It would never occur to him to consider his own safety.'

'Or Ben might be North's killer.'

Rachel shook her head as though this was a possibility she didn't want to think about.

'We need to find out exactly what happened to Ben – to eliminate him from our enquiries if nothing else.'

'My father-in-law has tried to persuade Geoff to stay with them until you've cleared up the murder case, but Geoff's refused. Peter, Nigel's dad, calls him a stubborn old bugger.'

'Perhaps we'll get more out of Ben if we speak to him on his own.'

'Good luck with that. Geoff's hovering round him like a mother hen.'

When they arrived at the cottage, Wesley could see a light in the window and smoke rising from the chimney. Geoff answered the door after a single knock. He nodded to Rachel, but when he spotted Wesley standing behind her, a suspicious look appeared on his face.

'What do you want this time? I don't know nothing more about that dead man I found. You're wasting your time.'

'Can we speak to Ben, please, Geoff? There's a chance he saw something that might help us.'

Bessy appeared by Geoff's side, wagging her tail. Rachel stooped to stroke her head. 'Go on, Uncle Geoff. It won't take long. Wesley needs to find out what happened, and if Ben was around that night . . .'

Geoff hesitated, but eventually he stood aside to let them in. When they took their boots off, Wesley was embarrassed to find that he had a hole in one of his socks, but Rachel didn't seem to have noticed.

They found Ben sitting next to the roaring fire in the small parlour. When he tore his eyes away from the flames, it was hard to read his expression. Resignation, perhaps, as though this was something he'd been expecting. But there was fear too.

'Ben,' Wesley began after Rachel had introduced him. 'Is it all right if I call you Ben?' He did his best to sound friendly and unthreatening, but he wasn't sure whether it was working.

The answer was a slight nod.

'Rachel tells me you've been injured. What happened? Did someone attack you?'

After a long silence, Ben said he didn't know. He couldn't remember.

Wesley wasn't sure whether to believe him. 'You really should see a doctor,' he said.

'I'll be all right. I'm feeling better than I did.'

'Even so, I can get someone to take you to A&E. Just for a check-up.'

'That's kind of you, but there's no need. I'm being

well looked after.' Ben shot a grateful glance in Geoff's direction.

'Do you know where you live? How you got here?'

He shook his head. 'I can't remember. All I know is that Geoff found me on the lane and looked after me. Don't know what I would have done without him.'

Wesley noticed that Geoff was listening nervously, as though he feared they might start bullying his guest if he let his guard down.

'Geoff, would you be good enough to show us where you found Ben. Is it far?'

Geoff put his coat and boots on, and Bessy wagged her tail, anticipating a walk. Rachel and Wesley made sure the cottage door was locked behind them. If they were leaving Ben on his own, security was a priority.

Their route led them to a narrow lane with grass growing in the centre. It was an old farm track, barely six feet wide, well hidden and rarely used by modern vehicles. Hedgerows towered either side, making it dark enough for headlights even at this time of the morning.

'Nobody ever uses this lane,' said Rachel. 'It doesn't lead anywhere in particular. I think it's just a short cut to the hall.'

'That's why I come down here,' said Geoff. 'No need to scratch myself on the hedgerow to let blooming cars past.'

'You found Ben here?' Wesley asked.

'Just round this next bend. He looked very shaken, but he was managing to walk.'

Wesley and Rachel exchanged a look.

When they rounded the bend, the hedgerow on the left gave way to a small wood. They walked another fifty yards, and Wesley noticed a set of tyre tracks. A motorist had braved the narrow lane. And whoever that was must have skidded off to the left, because the tyre tracks led into the shadow of the trees.

Without a word, Wesley followed the tracks, with Rachel trailing behind, Uncle Geoff and Bessy bringing up the rear. It wasn't until they were about a hundred feet into the trees that he saw the car: a silver Toyota, crumpled against a tree, windscreen shattered, driver's door hanging open. A silver car like the one belonging to the man Elspeth Bell had seen – the man who'd been watching Tatiana Smithson.

He turned to Geoff, who was staring in disbelief. 'Did you know about this?'

'No. I would have said.'

'I know you would, Uncle Geoff.' Rachel put a reassuring hand on the old man's arm. She tapped Wesley on the shoulder and he turned to face her. 'Think this might explain Ben's injuries?'

Wesley nodded before putting on the crime-scene gloves he always carried in his pocket just in case. He began to investigate the car, discovering two cardboard boxes in the boot. Everything looked undisturbed, and he thought the most likely scenario was that the driver had got lost and suffered an accident in that isolated spot. If Ben had been that driver, he'd been lucky.

The car's number plate was intact, and Wesley called the station to ask for details of the vehicle's owner. With any luck, Ben would soon have a name and address.

'Can you see a phone? A diary?' Rachel asked.

'No. Nothing like that.'

'What's in the boxes?' she said, leaning over to see into the open boot.

'If they're Ben's property, we shouldn't really . . .'

'Go on, Wes. Opening one won't do any harm. And it might help us find out what he was doing here.'

Wesley glanced over his shoulder at Geoff, who was waiting patiently a few yards away, then began to tear at the tape sealing the cardboard box. When the flap was open, he saw a layer of bubble wrap. Whatever was inside was delicate. He pulled the wrap carefully aside, uncovering something dark and rectangular. It was a book. And it looked very old. Spotting a business card, he picked it up.

BENEDICT GRAVES. DEALER IN ANTIQUES
AND ANTIQUARIAN BOOKS.

It seemed the mystery man's name really was Ben after all.

25

Neil was reluctant to sit the naked female mannequin in the passenger seat of his car. If anybody saw it, they might assume it was some sort of sex doll, and he didn't want people to think he was weird. In the end, he decided to put it in the boot, taking care not to damage the fabric limbs, and wrapping the beautifully painted papier-mâché head in bubble wrap for protection.

He'd looked on the internet and found something remarkably similar, but he wanted an expert to confirm his suspicions, so he drove to the museum in Exeter. When he arrived, he asked some of the staff to give him a hand, and once the mannequin was in the curator's office, she examined it carefully before giving her verdict.

'I've seen something like it before,' she said. 'But not in such good condition.'

'Could it be a lay figure?'

The curator, a young woman with bright red hair who favoured long baggy jumpers, nodded earnestly. 'I think you could be right, Neil. Artists used these life-sized figures when they couldn't afford to hire a flesh-and-blood model. They'd use the lay figure dressed in the wealthy sitter's clothes for most of the portrait, then the sitter would only have to pose once while the artist put the finishing touches to the hands and face.' She stood back and looked at the model, which was now sitting upright in one of the office chairs. 'Although in this case, someone's made a beautiful job of painting the head and hands – and she would have had a wig, of course. Where on earth did you find it?'

'In a grotto, would you believe. I think it was built as a folly in the grounds of an eighteenth-century house called Nesbarton Hall, not far from Neston. Unfortunately, the land has been bought by a developer, who plans to build houses there. I hope to persuade him to preserve the grotto.' He paused. 'There are signs that it was used for some sort of rituals.'

'Rituals? You mean black magic?'

'Not necessarily. You must have heard of the Hellfire Club.'

'A load of high-society rakes misbehaving in the eighteenth century.' She smiled.

'Their motto was "Do what thou wilt". I found similar sentiments carved on the wall of the grotto: "We are masters of all and our will is law".'

'Charming,' the curator said under her breath. 'And you think this figure's connected with these rituals?'

'I don't think it had been there long when we found it. If it had been lying there since the eighteenth century, surely it wouldn't be so well preserved.'

'Maybe South Devon's answer to the Hellfire Club is still operating.'

Neil thought of the grotto and a shudder ran through his body. At that moment, his phone rang. It was a number he didn't recognise, but he answered anyway. The man's voice on the other end of the line sounded muffled, as though the caller was trying to disguise it.

'Is that the archaeologist?'

'Yes. Who's that?'

'Just thought you ought to know. Jason Fonsby's sending the bulldozers in soon. He's going to knock down the copse – and that grotto thing.'

Then the line went dead.

Elspeth Bell took her duties very seriously. Word had spread in the district about her traffic calming measures and she was sure that people were now taking more care as they drove through the village.

Elspeth had moved to Devon from the outskirts of London with her husband ten years ago. They'd dreamed of sharing a rural idyll, but he'd passed away shortly after the move. When she first found herself alone, she'd drifted, trying various hobbies to keep herself occupied. She'd become a regular at St Helena's church, although in her opinion church life wasn't the same since they were forced to share a vicar with three other parishes. She'd tried to take up bell ringing, but she'd soon discovered that she had no aptitude for it, and the power of the bells as they swung at the top of that single rope had left her shaking with fear. Flower arranging proved less fearsome, but she felt like an inexperienced amateur amongst the more talented ladies of the parish. More recently, however, the safety of Nesbarton had become her main priority in life.

She'd started the village watch when the Reverend Selkirk set up her hostel for ex-offenders and had had no trouble gaining recruits. The sight of those men hanging around the village smoking, along with knowing the reason they were there, had been enough to instil fear into the tiny community. As far as anyone was aware, they'd caused no actual trouble, but it was as well to be vigilant. She kept a pair of binoculars on her bedroom windowsill behind the thick net curtains. From there she could see Selkirk's premises, and she kept a register of the comings and goings, in case the police needed evidence. She'd been pleased when the two detectives visited her the other day – the well-spoken black one with such nice manners and his scruffier colleague with the marked Liverpool accent. At least their visit meant they were taking her concerns seriously.

After Elspeth had washed up her lunch dishes, she returned to the bedroom to resume her post. Half an hour later, she saw the hostel door open, and a man stepped out wearing what she'd heard was called a hoodie. He had a shaven head, and what she could see of his neck was blue with examples of the tattooist's art. He shut the door behind him, thrust his hands into his pockets, pulled up his hood and walked down the path, looking around as though he was checking he wasn't being watched. But Elspeth was watching. Elspeth would find out exactly what he was up to.

She'd seen the man before, on several occasions, and thought he was watching her cottage. As he walked off down the main road towards the churchyard, there was definitely something familiar about him. He reminded her of someone – a young face fondly remembered from the past. But she knew she had to be mistaken – the person she was thinking of would surely never have anything to do with people like that.

He was heading towards the church. Only a truly evil person would rob a church, but Elspeth would make sure his wicked plans were thwarted. That Selkirk woman had a lot to answer for, bringing that type of person into a nice village like Nesbarton.

She wondered whether to call the police, but decided against it. They were busy in the incident room they'd set up in the stables at Nesbarton Hall, dealing with that terrible murder. The police hadn't given her any details, but she'd heard on the village grapevine that the tutor who taught the billionaire's son up at the hall had been mugged and stabbed. Elspeth would have known if the police had raided Ms Selkirk's premises, but she'd heard nothing, so as far as she was concerned, they were neglecting their duty. She would raise it at the next meeting of the village watch. Perhaps an email to the chief constable would do the trick.

She hurried downstairs and took her thick coat from the hall stand before making sure she had her key and closing the cottage door behind her. She needed to keep an eye on the man, but she would follow at a distance. With any luck, he wouldn't know she was there until she caught him in the act. Then she would dial 999 on her mobile phone.

Her quarry slouched down the lane leading to the ancient church and entered the graveyard through the lychgate. None of Elspeth's ancestors were resting in that particular churchyard, but she still thought of it as hers, a focus of her special care. He was making for the church porch, and she planned to wait a few moments before going in after him to tweak the floral display near the pulpit. She was confident that she could defend herself by the force of her determination. It never occurred to her that she'd be putting herself in danger.

She stood in the shelter of the porch, pretending to read the notices on the board. Then she pushed open the heavy oak door and stepped inside the church. It took her eyes a few seconds to adjust to the gloom. She scanned the familiar scene. The pews; the carved rood screen, painted in faded fifteenth-century pigments, that separated the body of the small church from the chancel and the altar; the tall arched windows with their diamond panes; and the bell ropes tied up out of reach at the foot of the tower to her left. Only one thing was out of place, and that was the man sitting in the front pew, his hood pulled up to hide his shaved head.

Elspeth assumed that he was taking a break from his villainy to count the money he'd just taken from the collection box near the door, and she fingered the phone in her coat pocket.

Then, to her amazement, she saw him fall to his knees onto one of the embroidered kneelers thoughtfully provided by the Mothers' Union to aid the prayers of the devout. She could hear him mumbling, and at first she thought he must be talking into his mobile, probably alerting one of his associates to rich pickings.

But as she crept nearer, she picked up the odd mumbled word. *Please, God. Help.*

She stopped in her tracks. She'd misread the situation badly. The man was actually praying. She was sure he didn't know she was there, so she beat a hasty retreat, closing the door quietly behind her. Perhaps she'd been too swift to rush to judgement on this occasion – but it didn't change the fact that criminals were being harboured in the village.

As she left the church, she saw a figure flitting amongst the headstones. She stopped, but whoever it was disappeared into the trees at the edge of the churchyard.

'Don't go. I want a word with you,' she shouted, almost tripping over an overgrown stone.

But the figure had vanished, and when she turned her head, she saw the man from the church standing in the porch. He was looking straight at her and he called out to her, using her name. Then suddenly she knew who he was.

26

They now had more information about the wrecked car and its owner. It was indeed registered to Benedict Graves, who dealt in antiques and rare books from his premises in Bury St Edmunds. His clients were from the upper end of the market – mainly wealthy collectors. He was unmarried and lived alone in a flat above his exclusive shop. When Wesley rang the number on the business card they'd found, a woman answered. She had the voice of a 1950s BBC announcer – Wesley didn't think they made them like that any more – and said that her name was Julia West.

'Mr Graves is away on business,' she told him with the hauteur of a duchess addressing an undergardener. 'I'm not sure when he'll be back.'

There was an email address on the business card, Wesley asked if he could send over a photograph? He'd taken one of Geoff's guest, careful not to make what he was doing too obvious. Now he emailed the dishevelled image to Suffolk. As soon as she received it, a shocked Julia gave her verdict. 'Yes, that's Mr Graves. But what on earth has happened to him?'

Wesley broke the news that Benedict Graves had been

involved in a car accident. 'He'll probably be indisposed for a while,' he said. 'And I'm afraid he's having problems with his memory, possibly due to concussion sustained in the accident. A local farmer found him a few days ago wandering and confused. He's being taken care of.'

Julia sounded relieved to hear that her employer wasn't in hospital, but when she asked when he'd be returning to Bury St Edmunds, Wesley had to tell her he wasn't sure.

'Do you know who Mr Graves was visiting in Devon?' he asked.

'I'm afraid not,' was the reply. 'I was on holiday when he left – three weeks in Sicily. He wasn't here when I returned, and he'd simply left a note saying he was going to the West Country and that he'd call to tell me when he'd be back. It's a bit of a mystery really.'

Wesley asked her whether she had access to his diary, but the answer was no; nor did she have the keys to his flat or the storage facility where he kept his stock. Her job was to deal with customers and answer email enquiries.

'Are any of Mr Graves's customers based in Devon?'

'He has business contacts all over the country – and even abroad. But I'll check for you.'

After a couple of minutes, she returned with an answer.

'There are a couple of customers in North Devon – Lynmouth and Bideford.'

'Nobody in the south of the county?'

'I'm afraid not.'

'What about Silas Smithson?'

There was another pause while she consulted her records.

'Yes, Mr Graves has sourced a number of valuable books for Mr Smithson's collection. But I have a London address for him, not Devon.'

'Was Mr Graves worried about anything before you left to go on holiday? Did he say anything that might help us?'

There was a lengthy silence. 'I know he'd been having trouble with some late payments, but ... most businesses have similar problems, I suppose.'

'Is there anything else in the file on Silas Smithson?'

'I'm sorry, I can't find anything apart from invoices. He's spent a great deal of money with us over the years. But if Mr Graves spoke to him on the telephone while I was away, I won't have any record of it, of course.'

Wesley thanked her and assured her that he'd ask Graves to contact her once he was well enough.

When the call was ended, he turned to Rachel, who'd been listening in on the conversation. 'That's one mystery solved. He'd been doing business with Silas Smithson in London.'

'But why call at Nesbarton Hall? Smithson's been away since the first of November, so it's unlikely that he'd arrange for Graves to call when he wasn't at home. And I can't see him coming all the way from Suffolk on spec.'

'You're right. He's hardly a door-to-door salesman and I imagine his business is by appointment only.' He looked at the boxes. 'We need to find Ben's phone. Presumably he didn't have it with him when Geoff found him.'

'Perhaps he dropped it somewhere.'

'That's the most likely explanation. And those books could be valuable, so we shouldn't leave them here.'

They took the boxes out of the boot. Graves hadn't actually approached or spoken to Tatiana, and as far as Wesley could tell, no crime had been committed. It had been a road accident. He called Traffic and asked them to retrieve the wrecked car.

'I need to talk to Ben again,' he said to Rachel.

'Maybe that can wait until he remembers more about what happened. I'll break the news about the car. It'll be better coming from me.'

'Agreed. Let's hope his memory returns soon. I think he could be the key to this whole case.'

Neil had never seen himself as particularly heroic, but as he drove to Nesbarton, he imagined himself bravely standing in the way of a fleet of massive bulldozers and bringing them to a halt. The fantasies that formed in his mind made Indiana Jones look like a feeble coward. But by the time he arrived at the field, his courage had receded. He'd do things by the book.

The anonymous caller had got it right. A massive yellow bulldozer was parked at the entrance of the field, and Neil could see another trundling towards the copse. Suddenly his elusive heroic streak returned, and he found himself dashing across the field shouting, 'Stop!'

But his efforts were in vain. Jason Fonsby stepped out in front of him, wearing a hard hat and a wide grin.

'Dr Watson. I tried to get hold of you, but you weren't available.'

Neil knew this was a lie. He'd had his mobile with him all day and there'd been no missed calls from Fonsby.

'The planning permission's come through, so we're making a start; preparing the ground.'

'What about the grotto?'

'What about it?'

'It's historically important.'

'Says who? It's not listed, and the land belongs to me, so there's nothing to stop me demolishing it. You can't stand

185

in the way of progress, Dr Watson. I'm building much-needed homes here. That's more important than keeping a few old rocks.'

Neil knew Fonsby was right. The grotto had no listed status, so the developer could do what he liked with it. But he was prepared to have one last try.

'What if you made the grotto into a feature of the development? It could be a unique selling point. A historical focus. People would love it.'

'You think anyone's going to want to live near a damp cave? The thing's an eyesore, and it's bound to attract undesirables.' Fonsby laughed. The sound wasn't pleasant, and Neil felt his cheeks redden. He'd run out of ammunition. There was nothing he could do now to delay the inevitable. He could hear the buzz of the chainsaws felling the trees in the copse, and watched as they tumbled one by one like skittles. He'd lost the battle.

He couldn't bear to watch the destruction, so he walked back to the car.

Two hours later, he received a phone call from Fonsby, who didn't sound quite so triumphant as he told him that the bulldozers had uncovered something buried near the grotto. Perhaps Dr Watson would like to come back and have a look.

All Elspeth Bell's assumptions had been wrong. The man's attitude of prayer hadn't been a ruse. Since the loss of her husband, she'd learned that people let you down. But the man in the church had the power to change her life completely – and she suddenly realised that this could be a good thing, in spite of how he looked and what he'd become. If things worked out, she might actually be able to help someone, and the prospect felt good.

Her discovery preyed on her mind all afternoon, and she felt excited and nervous in turn. It had almost made her forget about the other person she thought she'd seen in the churchyard. However, she'd told herself that she'd got that wrong. After the surprise she'd had, she couldn't have been thinking straight.

She'd arranged to see him again tomorrow, and she felt impatient. But in the meantime, she had to attend an impromptu village watch meeting at the house of her deputy, Gill Nichols, who lived on the other side of the churchyard. In view of the recent crime wave in Nesbarton, the committee needed to discuss tactics urgently. With a brutal murder and the police taking over the stables at Nesbarton Hall, the meeting was important, she thought as she put her coat on again and left the cottage. Something had to be done.

The nights had drawn in and it was dark as she hurried across the churchyard. Her comfortable shoes meant she could move quickly, but she looked around as she walked to make sure nobody was lurking in the shadows.

She'd almost reached the church when she was aware of soft footsteps behind her. She glanced back, but there was nobody there. She told herself it was her imagination and carried on. The church was in darkness, its squat tower rearing up into the dark sky. There were too many clouds for stars and moonlight, and her foot slipped on the damp leaves that had blown onto the path. The footsteps were there again, echoing her own, and her heart began to pound as she realised she was being followed.

May 1787

It was two days before I was summoned again into the presence of Dionisio Nescote. I had filled the time by walking in the locality, and I found that a village lay nearby. There was a little church with a squat tower dedicated to St Helena and two streets of humble cottages. There was also a small inn frequented by farm labourers, who stared at me as I entered. As I sat alone in the corner, I did not comprehend much of their talk, but I heard the name Nescote uttered in lowered voices and without affection. I remained the focus of curious stares, and when the landlord came over and engaged me in conversation, I told him I was staying at the hall. At this the inn fell silent, and after draining my glass, I chose to depart. I have never stayed where I felt I was not welcome.

The following day Dora knocked on the door of my room. When I opened it, I saw that she looked frightened.

'Master Dionisio says you are to attend him in the library at once,' she said.

'Will you show me the way?'

She nodded, and I allowed myself to be led down the magnificent staircase. As I descended, I noted a portrait of a beautiful woman in a fine blue gown. I asked Dora who she was, and she answered that it was her mistress, painted by *a well-known artist, though she could not recall his name. The master, she said, had argued with the painter, who had fled unpaid, leaving various things behind, even one of the models he used in his work. I felt sorry for him, especially as the portrait, in my opinion, was a particularly fine one.*

As I reached the hall, a servant rushed to open the front door. A big man with a florid complexion strode in, shouting to the servant to remove his boots. His accent was rough, and so was his manner. He reminded me of the ruffians I'd tried to avoid in London, but his clothes suggested he was a gentleman. He saw me and scowled.

'Who the hell is this milksop?' he shouted, taking off his coat and throwing it in my direction. I failed to catch it.

'Charles Burbage at your service, sir,' I said with a bow.

The man looked at me and grunted like a pig. I surmised that this was Dionisio's father, the privateer who had made his fortune by plunder on the sea. To my mind he was little more than a pirate, but his wealth made me beholden to him and his son. Another servant appeared to help his master remove his boots, and he sat on a hall chair, chiding the man for his clumsiness.

'You are here to see me?' he barked.

'No, sir,' I said meekly, my head bowed. 'I was engaged by Master Dionisio and Master Nathaniel.'

'In what capacity?'

'I am not certain, sir.'

At that moment Dionisio burst out of a door to my right, flushed as though he had been caught doing something shameful.

'All is well, Father. This man is to perform a task of great importance for me.'

'Nothing to do with your business in the far field, I hope.

A folly in more ways than one.' The privateer rolled his eyes indulgently, as though he was amused by his son's peccadilloes, and vanished into another room, pursued by the servant who had opened the door for him. The man looked as though he was expecting a blow at any time. From what I had already heard, the pirate captain showed little mercy to those who served under him.

Dionisio signalled for me to enter the library, and I followed him, noting the array of books and wondering whether the house's occupants had ever read them. I thought not. My own late father's library had been poor in comparison, but he had been a man of learning and would have rejoiced to find himself in such a chamber.

Dionisio sat, but I remained standing. He was a well-built fellow with sharp features that reminded me of a rat. There was no sign of his cousin, Nathaniel. He looked me up and down, and I felt uncomfortable under his assessing gaze.

'Ever lived in a cave?' he asked suddenly.

I was taken aback by the question, and it was several moments before I replied. 'No, sir. Never.'

'I have had the men on the estate construct a fine grotto for the entertainment of myself and my friends. Sir Francis Dashwood, I have heard, had such a thing built, and I am of a mind to found a little society of my own to rival his. The country around here lacks diversions, so I must create some for myself. You are a capable actor?'

'I hope so, sir,' I said. 'I understand I am required to play a madman. When is the theatrical presentation to be? And what other actors have you engaged to take part?'

At this he began to laugh as though I had uttered some hilarious joke. The laughter continued for a full half-minute before he dried his eyes with a snowy silk handkerchief. 'Oh sir, you amuse me greatly. It is no play that I would present. Your role as madman is one you must live. You will dwell in the grotto where my friends will assemble for our rites, and you will be their priest.'

He began to laugh again, and I suddenly felt afraid. I had expected to play the role of a madman in a play – not to live the part in reality.

27

Elspeth Bell hadn't turned up for the village watch meeting, and Gill Nichols, her deputy co-ordinator, was worried. Perhaps Mrs Bell was ill, she said to the others when all attempts to ring her failed.

Gill volunteered to call at Elspeth's cottage as soon as the meeting was over, just to make sure she wasn't lying helpless with a broken leg or hip, unable to reach her phone. The others made concerned noises and said they'd leave it to her.

It was then that one of the other ladies said she was sure she'd heard a couple of shots as she was making her way to Gill's house. But no one paid too much attention; this was farming country, and shots were common.

After the meeting, Gill drove to Elspeth's cottage. She had lived in Nesbarton all her life and had always played an active role in the life of the church and village. But even though she knew that walking through the churchyard would have been quicker, she preferred to take the long way round at night, though she'd never have admitted to anybody that she didn't like walking between the graves in the dark.

When she reached the cottage, she saw a light glowing

behind the drawn curtains of the front room. She knew that since the Reverend Selkirk's arrival in the village, Elspeth had left a light on to deter burglars. She knocked on the door and waited, but there was no answer, so she walked round to the back of the little terrace and opened Elspeth's garden gate. There were no net curtains at the back of her house, and when she peered through the kitchen window, she saw no sign of life. She tried knocking on the back door, but again there was no response.

She drove home, still worried. It wasn't at all like Elspeth to miss a meeting without letting her know. But it did seem a little excessive to alert the police so soon.

Her concern about her friend meant that she didn't sleep well, and the following morning she rang all the local hospitals to see whether she had been admitted. When the answer from each was no, she decided to follow the route Elspeth would have used if she'd taken the short cut through the churchyard.

In the daylight, the sleeping dead held no fear for her, and she walked slowly along the path, looking around her carefully. When she felt something crunch beneath her feet, she glanced down and saw that she'd just broken a pair of glasses lying on the path. She recognised them at once. Elspeth Bell had a pair just like them.

It wasn't until the following morning that Neil was allowed onto the building site again. He'd wanted to go over as soon as he'd received Jason Fonsby's call, but he'd been told that they were packing up for the night. Their discovery wasn't going anywhere, and Fonsby had asked the lads to put a tarpaulin over it, adding that he wanted it handled with minimum fuss so that it didn't hold up the work. He also pointed out that he could have kept quiet about it, implying that Neil should be grateful. Neil told him that if he'd kept quiet, he would have been breaking the law. Fonsby had no answer for that.

As Neil drove to Nesbarton, he wished he'd taken Dave along for moral support. But his second in command was busy processing finds from their last excavation, so he was going to have to face Fonsby alone. And if Fonsby's workers had found what they claimed to have found, it would be a job for the police, and the developer couldn't argue with that. He parked in the lane beside the Fonsby Homes sign. Protective fencing had now been erected and the field had turned into a rutted sea of mud. His wellingtons sank into the soft ground as he walked towards the middle of the field, where the trees of the small copse lay felled like dead soldiers.

A group of men in hard hats were standing beside the large heap of stones that had once formed the front section of the grotto. Fonsby was amongst them, hands in pockets, staring at the ground.

Neil put on the hard hat he'd taken from his car boot and joined them, noticing the large yellow dumper truck parked nearby, probably waiting to take the stones away.

'Dr Watson,' Fonsby said. 'Good of you to come.' He was turning on the charm, and Neil wondered whether he'd spent the previous evening looking up the correct procedure to follow when human remains were found.

'You said you'd turned up a skeleton.'

'It's probably been there for years. Centuries,' Fonsby added hopefully. 'If you can confirm that, then surely we don't need to involve the police.'

'Sorry, Mr Fonsby. Whenever human remains are found unexpectedly, we're obliged to inform the police. How can you be sure it isn't a murder victim?' Neil was enjoying the forlorn look on Fonsby's face, but he tried his best not to sound too smug. 'You've demolished half the grotto, I see. It's a pity. It would have provided some context. Made things a lot easier.'

Fonsby looked round at his workers as though he was wondering whether to blame them for being overenthusiastic and conducting the demolition without his permission. But in the end he held his hands up, a gesture of appeasement. 'OK, Dr Watson, maybe we've been a little hasty, but time is money in our business. Besides, we didn't actually find it inside the grotto. It's over there.' He pointed to an area of disturbed ground about twenty feet to the left of where the entrance had once been.

'I'd better have a look,' said Neil.

The group of builders parted to reveal a large tarpaulin stretched across the rutted soil. At a nod from Neil, the tarpaulin was lifted to reveal a skeleton, still mostly buried. The earth had been scraped away by a digger; not one of the small diggers capable of delicate work that Neil often used in his excavations, but a big, clumsy machine. The top of the skull had been smashed, but fortunately the rest seemed intact. Neil squatted down beside the remains and took his trowel from his coat pocket; he never went anywhere without it. He looked at the teeth for evidence of modern dental work, but couldn't see any. Even so, he needed to call some colleagues to help him lift the remains. And he needed to let Wesley know that he had another corpse on his hands.

Gerry listened with interest as Wesley told him about Benedict Graves and the discovery of the car.

'Silas Smithson collects books,' said Wesley. 'If we didn't know Smithson has been away for the past week, I'd suspect that Graves came here to see him. Tatiana saw someone fitting his description hanging around. She thought he was watching her, but what if he just wanted to ask her aunt about Smithson's whereabouts and lost his nerve?'

'Could Graves have been in the area to see someone else?'

'His assistant, Julia West, has no record of any other customers in the district. My bet is that Smithson made an appointment and forgot to cancel it. Which fits with the theory that he decided to go away on the spur of the moment when he received that threat against his son. We need to find out who sent that threatening note.'

Gerry didn't comment. He had more immediate matters on his mind. Patrick North's mother had arrived last night with her ex-husband, and they were staying in a B&B in the centre of Tradmouth. He'd arranged to meet them there at ten o'clock, thinking that they'd appreciate time to settle in and have a leisurely breakfast. After the morning briefing in the incident room, he asked Wesley to drive him back to town. During an unusually silent journey, Wesley volunteered to meet the Norths with him. Gerry thanked him, a look of relief on his face.

Before they'd set off, Wesley had received a call from Neil saying that a skeleton had been found at the site of the now half-demolished grotto. He could hear the disgust in his friend's voice as he told him the developer had jumped the gun and gone ahead with the demolition as soon as he thought he could get away with it, and to make things worse, he planned to flatten the rest of the structure later that day.

Neil admitted that there was no evidence that the human

remains were recent, so Wesley suggested that he call Neston police station if he wanted the matter dealt with swiftly. Neil said he'd prefer to wait for Wesley because he knew what he was doing. There was absolutely no hurry. Wesley didn't know whether to be flattered, but he suspected that Neil was rather enjoying making the developer's life awkward by delaying the inevitable. He said he'd get over there as soon as he was free.

The Norths were waiting for them in the lounge at their B&B, sitting well apart in a room filled with over-stuffed armchairs, a comfortable sanctuary for guests. The heating had been turned to maximum, and the two detectives took their coats off as the proprietor bustled in and asked if they'd like coffee. After consulting the Norths, Wesley thanked her and said it would be very welcome.

'I'm sorry we have to meet in such tragic circumstances,' he began once the coffee was served.

Mrs North was a small woman with a thin face, and brown hair cut in a neat bob. She wore a tweed suit, as though she'd felt she needed to dress formally for the occasion. Mr North, by contrast, was large. He had a neat beard and the bearing of an ex-military man. In spite of their studied politeness, the look in their eyes told Wesley that they were both devastated by grief.

'Yes,' added Gerry. 'I'm very sorry for your loss.'

'I've been away,' said Mrs North in a high-pitched voice, 'staying with friends, so I had no idea. I hadn't heard from Patrick for a week or so, but that was normal. He was young and he had his own life. My daughter wanted to come too, but . . .' she glanced at her former husband, 'she doesn't get on with her father.'

Mr North gave her a withering look, as though he

197

blamed her for the rift. Wesley suspected that the split hadn't been a friendly one.

'Did you have regular contact with your son, Mr North?' Wesley asked. He'd resigned himself to the fact that Gerry was leaving the talking to him.

North shook his head. 'I only heard he was dead when she deigned to phone me. But I wasn't going to stay away. He was my son too.'

It looked as though Mrs North was the one who knew more about Patrick's life, so Wesley addressed his next question to her. 'We're trying to establish the events that led up to his death.'

'You mean it wasn't an accident?' Mr North said accusingly.

'We don't think so, I'm afraid. What did Patrick tell you about his life down here? Do you know if he was worried about anything?'

'He never spoke to me, so I wouldn't know,' North said, folding his arms and looking away.

After a long pause, Mrs North answered. 'He said the child he was teaching was a spoiled brat but they were paying him really well so he was going to stick it out. And he had a girlfriend. Gemma, I think her name is. Have you spoken to her?'

'Yes.'

'Patrick said she'd started seeing someone else and he wasn't happy about that. He said the man was ... involved in drugs and that sort of thing. I told him to watch his step, because you need to be careful with people like that.'

Gerry broke his silence. 'What else did he say about this man?'

Mrs North glanced at her ex-husband. 'Nothing really.'

'Do you know about the incident up in the Lake District?' Wesley asked gently.

'What incident?'

Patrick North clearly hadn't told his mother about Lisa Lowe's accusation. But that was hardly surprising. 'A girl at the school where he taught made an allegation against him. She retracted it soon afterwards, but it was felt that it would have been awkward for him to stay there. That's why he took the job in Devon.'

'He told me he just fancied a change.' North's mother sounded hurt that he hadn't confided in her.

'He thought he was protecting you, love,' said Gerry. 'Did he tell you anything else?' He glanced at Wesley. 'About Mr and Mrs Smithson, his pupil's parents, for instance?'

'He didn't see much of Mr Smithson. But he liked Mrs Smithson – said she was Russian.'

After hearing Jordan Green's statement, this verdict took on a new significance. It was hardly surprising that Patrick would want to keep any sexual relationship with his employer's wife from his mother. There were some things you could share with your parents and some you couldn't. Wesley glanced at Gerry. The Norths had told them nothing they didn't already know, and he was beginning to feel despondent.

'Did Patrick say anything about the Smithsons going away to Scotland?'

'He mentioned something, yes. He said he was going to have some free time while the child was away, and I said he should come home to Manchester for a visit while he had the chance. He said he'd think about it and let me know.' She suddenly frowned. 'He did say something I thought was a bit odd. He said he'd seen someone he wanted to avoid – someone he thought was miles away.'

'Anything else?'

She shook her head. 'No. That's all.' She took a deep breath. 'When can I see him?'

'Any time you're ready,' said Wesley gently.

'I'm ready now.'

After finding the broken glasses, Gill Nichols couldn't banish the shocking thought that something bad had happened to Elspeth Bell en route to the meeting at her house.

She noticed that the unmown grass between a row of gravestones had been disturbed in places, as though something had been dragged over it. Tentatively she began to walk that way, scanning the ground for any further clues. It wasn't long before she spotted a handbag lying on top of an old grave slab. She recognised it at once as Elspeth's: stiff brown leather in the style she'd heard her daughter describe as vintage; the kind of handbag carried by the late Queen on her royal engagements.

She didn't touch it. The crime dramas she enjoyed watching on TV had taught her enough about police procedure over the years to know that it could be valuable evidence. She continued walking, but it wasn't until she reached the trees fringing the churchyard that her worst fears were realised.

Gill Nichols couldn't help herself. She let out an involuntary scream before taking out her phone to call the police.

28

Wesley's appointment with the Norths had taken priority over Neil's newly discovered skeleton, but now he needed to make absolutely sure that the bones didn't belong to a recent murder victim. Gerry needed to call at the police station to bring the Chief Superintendent up to date with their progress and he said he'd get a patrol car to take him back to Nesbarton. Wesley told him he'd go on ahead and call at the building site. The field wasn't far from the incident room, and he promised he wouldn't be long.

When he arrived, he found that the peaceful piece of farmland he'd visited a few days before had now been transformed into a building site, crawling with huge yellow diggers and men in hard hats and high-vis jackets. Particularly shocking was the absence of the little copse in the centre of the field, once a haven for wildlife. The felled trees were being dragged to the edge of the site, and he could see a large pile of stones, with a digger nearby poised to remove them. The grotto was no more. Only a small section at the rear, the inner sanctum, remained standing, exposed to the world. There would be no more secrets.

He could see Neil over by the remains of the structure, talking to a man in a hard hat. From the body language, he guessed that the conversation wasn't friendly. Once he'd changed into appropriate footwear, he marched across the field towards them.

Neil gruffly introduced the other man as Jason Fonsby, the developer, adding that he was in the process of demolishing the grotto. He made no attempt to hide his feelings on the subject, but Wesley noticed that Fonsby looked perfectly calm, like a man who knew he had the law on his side.

'I'd better have a look at the human remains you've found,' said Wesley, unwilling to be drawn into the argument, even though his sympathies lay with Neil.

Neil led the way to a tarpaulin that had been laid over the ground. He removed it carefully as Fonsby looked on, a neutral observer. The skeleton's last resting place was remarkably shallow. Perhaps whoever had buried him or her had been impeded by all the tree roots in that particular spot, an archaeologist's worst enemy.

'I'm getting my team over to lift it properly,' said Neil, shooting Fonsby a meaningful glance. 'They'll be here this afternoon.'

'Good,' said Wesley. He looked at Fonsby. 'Until we have some evidence of when this individual was buried, we can't rule out a recent interment. If it was within the past seventy years or so, we're obliged to open an investigation and this location will have to be cordoned off as a crime scene.'

The look of triumph on Neil's face contrasted with Fonsby's barely concealed irritation.

'I'm sorry, Mr Fonsby. This needs further investigation and Dr Watson's team are the best people to conduct the initial excavation. They have the necessary experience in the preservation of evidence.'

'Do what the hell you like,' Fonsby muttered before marching away, signalling to his digger driver to stand off.

'Thanks for that, mate,' said Neil.

'Just doing my job,' said Wesley, trying to keep from smiling. 'Everything I told him was true, as you know. We won't know for certain that this isn't a recent murder until you've done your stuff. The skull's damaged and the pelvis hasn't been uncovered yet, so we don't even know whether it's a man or a woman at the moment. Good luck.'

'Pam OK?'

'She's fine apart from the possibility of an inspection at her school. Why?'

'It looks as though I'll be busy here for a few days, so I'm staying at my usual B&B in Tradmouth tonight. They're glad of the custom at this time of year. I might call in at yours later if that's OK.'

'Always glad to see you, Neil, you know that.'

'How's your investigation going?'

'We're following several lines of inquiry. Just hoping one of them leads to the killer. Looks like our victim led a complicated life.'

'Unlike a humble archaeologist,' said Neil.

Wesley trudged back over the field, aware of Fonsby's men watching him with undisguised curiosity. As he reached the car, a call came through from the incident room. Could Inspector Peterson get to Nesbarton church as soon as possible. There was a body in the churchyard.

It was at the back of Wesley's mind that someone might be playing a practical joke. 'There's a body in the church-yard' ranked in calls to the police alongside sending a new recruit to go for 'a long stand' or 'a tin of tartan paint'. But as soon as he arrived at Nesbarton church, he realised that this was no hoax.

The crime-scene team were already there, and he could see Gerry Heffernan wearing what he always called his snowman suit, the white overall stretched across his chubby midriff. The officer guarding the outer cordon handed Wesley a suit of his own, and he struggled into it before joining Gerry at the hub of the action.

'Well?'

Gerry turned to face him, his expression solemn. 'Looks like another shooting, Wes. And this time we've met the victim. Elspeth Bell. Head of the village watch.'

Wesley stood silently for a few moments while he took in the information. He remembered the woman well, and the news came as a shock. Then Gerry stepped to one side so he could see the body, surrounded by photographers and CSIs.

'We're waiting for Colin. He's busy doing a post-mortem but he'll be here as soon as he can.' A satisfied look appeared on the DCI's face. 'Mind you, I reckon we can pin down the time of death. She was found by a lady called Gill Nichols, who's her deputy in the village watch. Elspeth was due to attend a meeting at her house at seven thirty last night, but she didn't turn up. Apparently she was in the habit of walking through the churchyard to get there. Ms Nichols went to Elspeth's cottage after the meeting because she was worried that she might be ill, but when she arrived there was no answer, so she went home. When she was walking through the churchyard this morning, she found the victim's glasses and handbag, and signs that something had been dragged between the gravestones. She followed the signs of disturbance, found the body and called it in. I've already spoken to her and sent her home. I know there's an old theory that whoever finds the body has to be chief suspect, but in this case, I think we can rule Ms Nichols out.'

'So Elspeth was probably attacked on her way to last night's meeting. Unless Colin finds something to contradict it, we can put the time of death at between seven and seven thirty. I'll arrange for a house-to-house team to go through the village. And this time I'll get a search warrant for the Reverend Selkirk's premises.'

'My thoughts exactly. We need to know exactly where her merry men were at the time of the murder,' said Gerry with a grim smile. 'Patrick North was shot in the chest, but it looks as though Mrs Bell was shot in the head at fairly close range, and according to the CSIs, she was probably facing her killer. They think she died near the path and then was dragged to the edge of the churchyard to delay discovery and give the killer time to distance himself from the scene.'

'You say "himself". It might be a woman.'

'You're absolutely right, Wes. I really must stop indulging in gender stereotypes.'

They made their way to where the body lay and Wesley peered down at the earthly remains of Elspeth Bell. She lay on her back, her limbs straight, as though somebody had arranged her neatly. There was a small hole in the centre of her forehead, and her wide, startled eyes gazed up at the bare trees surrounding the churchyard. She looked more surprised than terrified.

When Wesley had seen enough, he began to walk away. Gerry followed.

'We should have been able to prevent this,' said Wesley.

'Don't see how, Wes. Jordan Green was our best suspect, but he was definitely at the Pillar Club all last night. Lots of witnesses. Someone's already checked, so he's in the clear for this one. What's the news on Neil's skeleton? Hope it's nothing we need to worry about.'

'Not sure yet, I'm afraid. Neil's getting a team over to lift the bones and excavate the surrounding area this afternoon, so we'll know more once they've finished. Let's keep our fingers crossed that it's a medieval monk or the victim of a highwayman.'

'Amen to that.'

'Are you OK to hang on here until Colin arrives? I want to speak to Ms Carlton up at the hall and find out whether Graves called there before his accident.'

Colin Bowman chose that moment to appear, carrying a large bag containing the tools of his trade and calling out a hearty greeting. 'I believe you have another one for me, Gerry. Hello, Wesley. Nice to see you again.'

'And you, Colin,' Wesley replied. 'Looks like another shooting. And before you ask, it's definitely not a shotgun. In fact, it looks very similar to our previous victim. But of course we'll await your verdict with bated breath. We have a pretty reliable window for the time of death, you'll be pleased to know. She was on her way to a meeting at seven thirty last night and we think she was killed en route.'

'Good to know,' Colin said with a twinkle in his eyes.

Wesley left them to it and walked back to Nesbarton Hall. He decided to knock at the front door rather than use the tradesman's entrance, and it was a while before there was an answer. As soon as she saw him, Ms Carlton's mask of calm efficiency slipped for a split second to reveal a hint of irritation.

'What can I do for you this time, Inspector? I've told the police everything I know, and I haven't heard from Mr and

Mrs Smithson since we spoke last. I think I said I'd let you know as soon as I did.'

'That's right, Ms Carlton, you did. But that's not why I'm here. I wonder if you recognise this man.'

He showed her the picture of Ben he had on his phone. The man in the photograph had unkempt hair and a week's beard growth, and his clothes looked shabby. Julia West from his shop in Suffolk had recognised him, but then she obviously knew him better than a woman who might only have spoken to him at the door.

'He looks like a vagrant,' Ms Carlton said with a sniff.

'Imagine him smartly dressed and clean-shaven. He's a dealer in antiques and antiquarian books and he's done business with Mr Smithson in London. Did he call here? His name's Benedict Graves. Does that ring a bell?'

'When do you say he called?'

'Over a week ago – possibly shortly after the family left for Scotland.'

'There's certainly no appointment in the diary, although sometimes Mr Smithson makes private arrangements without letting me know. But why would this man turn up when Mr Smithson wasn't here? What's he said? If he told you he came here, I really don't remember seeing him.'

'Mr Graves hasn't been able to help us because he's suffering from amnesia. Would you be good enough to check whether there's any correspondence from him in Mr Smithson's study?' It was chilly, and Wesley hoped he'd be invited in.

Karensa Carlton hesitated before stepping aside and instructing him to wait in the hall. After ten minutes, she emerged from Smithson's study holding a file.

'Yes, Mr Smithson has used Graves to source rare books

for him on a number of occasions. But the most recent correspondence was back in February and there's been nothing since. If Mr Graves was in the area, he must have been seeing another client. I can't help you, I'm afraid.' She handed him the file, which contained correspondence relating to the purchase of a number of first editions Graves had managed to track down for Smithson. All the details were there, including Graves's generous commission. But as Ms Carlton had said, there was nothing dated after February that year.

Wesley had another question. 'Were you aware of a relationship between Patrick North and Mrs Smithson?'

Karensa Carlton raised her eyebrows. 'No, I wasn't.' Her expression told Wesley that the possibility didn't come as a surprise. 'If that's all, I'm rather busy.'

Wesley knew she wasn't going to say any more, so he headed for the incident room to pick up his car. It was time to drive to Gorfleet Farm.

Since the discovery of Elspeth Bell's body, a warrant had been obtained to enter the house rented by the Reverend Becky Selkirk. It seemed there had been bad feeling between the latest victim and the reverend, so Acting DS Paul Johnson, along with DC Rob Carter and three uniformed constables, had gone to make a search of the house and interview the occupants. According to Gill Nichols, Mrs Bell had been very concerned about the hostel, and the reverend's previous refusal to co-operate with the investigation into Patrick North's death had sounded alarm bells. Paul had always been a great believer in the old maxim 'if you have nothing to hide, you have nothing to fear'. He was, at heart, an honest and straightforward man and some of his colleagues thought he could be a little too trusting at times.

The Reverend Selkirk greeted them at the door, although greeted was hardly the word Paul would have used. She opened the door halfway and scowled as soon as she spotted the uniforms. When Paul presented the warrant, the scowl turned to fury and she stood blocking their way with her arms folded like a mother defending her young. But when he explained patiently that the warrant meant they could search the property, with or without her permission, she stood aside, resigned to defeat.

Inside, they found two men seated at the kitchen table smoking roll-ups and drinking tea. When the police entered, Paul saw panic in their eyes, then suspicion, which changed rapidly to acceptance.

He asked his uniformed colleagues to take everyone's statements before he went upstairs with Rob to search the bedrooms.

The search yielded very little. The men had few possessions and there was no sign of anything incriminating; no obviously stolen goods, nothing connected with Patrick North or Elspeth Bell and certainly no firearm. Paul was starting to think they were wasting their time.

The largest bedroom contained two single beds and stank of cigarette smoke. The furniture was cheap chipboard and the carpet was old and worn, with some unpleasant-looking stains. Paul walked over to the window and looked out over the overgrown back garden.

A movement in the bushes caught his eye. At first he thought it was an animal, but when the creature broke cover, he saw it was a man in a grey hoodie. He hadn't been in the kitchen with the others, so Paul assumed he'd seen the police arriving and had decided to make his escape – which suggested that he had something to hide.

Paul shouted to Rob, who was searching the adjoining room, and they both hurtled down the stairs and out of the open back door. Paul's experience as a runner gave him the advantage. The man had slipped out of the back gate into the lane, but it didn't take long for Paul to catch up, and he was quite proud of the rugby tackle that brought him down.

Rob watched as Paul helped the man to his feet. Luckily the fight had gone out of their prisoner, and he stood with his head bowed.

'Why did you run?' Paul asked, trying to sound calm and sympathetic, copying Inspector Peterson's technique. He usually got results.

'I knew you'd pin it on me, that's why.'

'What's your name?'

'John Bell.'

Paul was intrigued. The man's neutral accent belied his appearance, and now that they were talking, there was no sign of hostility. He glanced at Rob. At one time he would have been butting in, keen to notch up another arrest. Now it was almost as though he'd lost interest.

'What brought you here to Nesbarton?' Paul asked.

'I came to look for someone. A mate told me about the rev having a place here.'

'And did you find the person you were looking for?'

'Yes, but . . .'

Paul waited for him to continue.

'In the end, she found me,' he said quietly.

'What's her name?'

'Elspeth. Elspeth Bell. She was my auntie.'

29

Neil felt pleased with himself. He'd managed to persuade Jason Fonsby not to complete the demolition of the grotto until his team had taken a closer look at it and recorded their findings. A few subtle words about one of his fellow archaeologists having a girlfriend who worked for the local press seemed to work wonders. It would be such a shame, he told Jason, if Fonsby Homes were to acquire a reputation for playing fast and loose with the county's historical heritage. Almost as bad as it being revealed that they were destroying the habitat of some threatened species of cute animal. After this, the developer appeared to come round to Neil's point of view, and told him he could have another few days to complete his investigations.

As for the skeleton, the CSI team were glad of Neil's help to lift the remains from their resting place. The bones turned out to belong to a woman who as far as Neil could tell was in her late teens or early twenties and had never given birth. Despite the damage done to the skull by the digger, the jaw was intact, so he could see that she had three teeth missing and there was no evidence of modern dental work. There were no rusty zips, plastic buttons or half-rotted man-made fibres with the remains. Nothing, in fact, to suggest the woman had died less than a hundred years ago.

The proximity to the grotto with its signs of occult activity made him feel uneasy. Had the woman been some kind of sacrifice? He was an archaeologist, a man of science who judged things by the available evidence, but what he'd discovered in that field made him uncomfortable. He certainly wouldn't fancy buying a house there – even if he could have afforded it.

The bones were placed in a box provided by the CSIs, leaving Neil and Dave to investigate the grave. They worked methodically and came across a few bone buttons, a half-rusted shoe buckle and a silver coin dating to the reign of King George III. Then, directly beneath where the bones had lain, Neil spotted a glint of gold. Another coin – a sovereign, again bearing the profile of George III; then another, and another. He wondered whether the coins had been placed in the grave deliberately by whoever had buried her. Surely if they'd fallen from her killer's pocket they would have been missed and retrieved.

In the end, Neil and the CSIs arrived at the same conclusion. The burial was of more concern to an archaeologist than the police. Once a bone specialist had had a look and the contents of the grave had been analysed more closely, Neil would be able to tell Wesley the good news. It was nothing for him to worry about.

When Wesley and Gerry received the news that the search of the Reverend Selkirk's premises had turned up a relative of their latest victim, Gerry sat for a few moments taking it in. Their visit to Gorfleet Farm would have to wait.

'I've told Paul to take John Bell to Tradmouth, although

Becky Selkirk's kicking up a fuss and talking about police brutality,' Wesley said with a roll of his eyes. 'I said we'd be there shortly to speak to him. Colin said he'll do Elspeth Bell's post-mortem at five o'clock.'

'That'll give us time to question this Bell character and be at the mortuary in time for Colin's excellent tea,' said Gerry. 'John Bell, eh? Wonder what his story is.'

'Hopefully we'll soon find out.'

'Funny if this whole thing turns out to be about a will or something. Dodgy nephew does in rich auntie for his inheritance.'

'And Patrick North?'

'Maybe he was collateral damage. Perhaps he stumbled on something.'

'How?'

'Let's not worry about little details like that yet, Wes.' Gerry grinned. He was in a remarkably good mood considering they had two unsolved murders on their hands.

Wesley's phone rang, and after a short conversation he turned to Gerry. 'Good news. That was Neil. He says that skeleton in the developer's field almost definitely isn't our problem.'

Gerry beamed as though he'd just been told he'd won the lottery. 'That's one less thing to worry about. Let's go over what we've got.'

Wesley took a seat next to his boss's desk, ignoring the buzz of activity going on around them in the incident room. He reached for a piece of paper and began to make a list.

'Our first victim was Patrick North, tutor to Darius Smithson, the son of a billionaire businessman who collects rare books. Said businessman, his wife and Darius go off to Scotland, and a few days later, in their absence, the tutor returns to the hall and gets himself shot. The question is why. We've been working on the theory that his murder was personal, but after Elspeth Bell . . .'

'All the licensed firearms in the area have been checked out,' said Gerry. 'Mind you, .22 rifles are pretty common round here – people out after rabbits and that sort of thing. At one time they were available without a licence, so there are bound to be some around that we don't know about. Even so, I think we can probably rule out the criminal underworld.'

'Does the criminal underworld include Gemma's jealous boyfriend, Jordan Green? He's involved in drug dealing.'

'He's small fry; low down in the criminal pecking order. However, he's a member of a gun club, so he knows how to shoot.'

'Along with a lot of kids in rural areas.'

'I take your point, Wes. But jealousy is a classic motive for murder. He might have an alibi for Elspeth Bell's murder, but he doesn't have one for Patrick North.'

'What about Green's claim that he saw North with Natalia Smithson? A man with Smithson's wealth and connections doesn't have to pull the trigger himself.'

'A hit man?'

'It's not beyond the realms of possibility, although a .22 rifle isn't usually a hired assassin's weapon of choice.'

'Maybe we should have another word with Smithson's sister, Betina,' Gerry suggested. 'She might have her suspicions about her sister-in-law's love life.'

Wesley made a note. 'Then there's Benedict Graves, the dealer in antiquarian books. It seems he's done business with Silas Smithson in London in the past. But I can't think why he'd turn up here while Smithson was away.'

'Unless Smithson made the appointment and forgot to let Graves know that he'd changed his plans. Presumably he's a busy man. And if he went unexpectedly to get his son away from a potential kidnapper ...'

'It's a feasible explanation, I suppose. We haven't found Graves's missing phone or a diary, though he could have dropped them anywhere after his accident. Was he the man who was watching Tatiana?'

Gerry's face clouded. 'He fits the description. On the other hand, that could have been a local pervert who hasn't appeared on our radar yet.'

Wesley had to concede that Gerry could be right. But he had a daughter around Tatiana's age, so he felt uncomfortable about the DCI's last suggestion. He thought for a few moments. 'Are we absolutely sure Elspeth Bell's death is linked to Patrick North's?'

'We won't know for sure until ballistics come up with the verdict on the weapon used. Mind you, surely there can't be two gunmen on the loose. Although I can't think what Patrick and Elspeth had in common. We don't even know if they ever met.'

'Elspeth kept her eye on all the comings and goings in Nesbarton, so she might have seen something she shouldn't.'

'You could be right, Wes.' Gerry suddenly looked solemn. 'But if ballistics say the same weapon was used and we can't find any connection, we might have to face the uncomfortable possibility that there's a maniac going round shooting random people who are out on their own after dark.'

Wesley checked the time. 'Let's get over to Tradmouth and speak to John Bell. We should be finished in time for the post-mortem.'

They were about to reach for their coats when Ellie hurried over to Gerry's desk. She looked worried.

'Sir, I've just discovered something. Cosmo Mearson, the boy Lisa Lowe claimed assaulted her.'

'What about him?'

'He did go to the States, but a month ago a woman accused him of inappropriate behaviour at the university where he was studying. He caught a plane home before the authorities could become involved. He fled the country.'

'So presumably he's back in England now,' said Gerry quietly. 'This is all we need.'

May 1787

I was taken to the grotto and discovered that it was hidden in the midst of a copse of trees some way from the house. It was built of local stone and had two chambers. Inside the inner chamber was something that resembled an altar, and there were strange carvings on the walls. I was told that my food would be brought to me and that I could light a fire in the outer chamber for warmth if the weather grew cold.

The clothing for my role was to be provided. Rags and animal skins. I had to look the part. And act the part too. If anybody approached, I was to pretend to have lost my wits. I agreed, but I couldn't but think of the poor beings I had once seen in Bedlam when my friends persuaded me to visit that terrible place. I felt some discomfort about imitating those wretches' behaviour for the entertainment of Nescote and his silly friends. Then I thought of the fortune I had been offered and said nothing.

I was told that I was to begin my strange duties the following day, as my employer was expecting visitors to arrive from Exeter. That night I slept ill, for my heart was crying out that this strange enterprise might be beyond my capabilities as an actor. As I lay awake, I was sorely tempted to flee, to throw myself on the mercy of my brothers and play the repentant prodigal. But to do so would be to admit that I had failed in my theatrical ambitions, and any pride I had once possessed would be forfeit. I thought of their mockery and resolved to stay at Nesbarton Hall.

The next morning, I was summoned to Master Dionisio's chamber, where the rags and skins I was to wear were laid out for me. Dionisio and Nathaniel watched me with some amusement as I dressed.

'You are a madman to the life,' Nathaniel said with delight. 'Come, Dionisio, we must take our wild king to his realm.'

They led me through the house with some glee, each looking out in case I was seen. We did not take the back stairs because the servants were up and about, so they led me down the main staircase and through the hall with its fine chequerboard floor and watching portraits. As we reached the front door, a richly dressed lady emerged from the drawing room, a maidservant walking in her wake. The lady was dark of complexion and her hair was black.

My companions stopped and bowed.

'Mama. I wish you good morning,' said Dionisio.

I bowed too. This was Dionisio's mother, the Italian lady, and I wondered how much she knew of her son's plans. My curiosity was soon to be satisfied.

'This is Charles, a friend from London, Mama. We are trying on clothes for a fancy dress ball. Charles is a wild man. His costume is most amusing, do you not think?'

The lady stared at me for a few moments. 'Most amusing, my dear,' she said. She did not sound amused.

She turned and swept up the staircase, leaving me bowing with the others. Francesca Nescote, the beautiful signora, had seen me in that strange garb and I felt embarrassed.

The walk to the grotto seemed very long that morning,

and when I arrived, flanked by my two companions like a prisoner between his guards, I was told I was to stay there and not visit the house again until I was given permission.

The first rite, I was told, was to take place the following evening. I was to prepare for my role. The wild man was to be master for the night.

30

Gerry had ordered Cosmo Mearson's whereabouts to be traced, but so far they'd had no luck. In the meantime, they needed to speak to John Bell.

Wesley wanted him to feel relaxed. He'd just lost his aunt, and no firearms had been found on the Reverend Becky Selkirk's premises. Until they knew otherwise, Bell should be treated as a witness rather than a suspect, in the hope that this approach would encourage him to talk.

He had been taken to the comfortable interview room where they'd spoken to Lisa Lowe. Wesley and Gerry found him waiting for them, fidgeting with an empty paper cup that had once contained coffee from the machine in the corridor. Gerry was fond of pointing out that making suspects drink that particular beverage should count as part of their sentence.

'Mr Bell, sorry to keep you waiting,' said Wesley as they took their seats.

The man scratched his shaved head, and Wesley watched him, fascinated by the creatures etched in blue and red ink that crawled on his scalp and neck. Dragons, unicorns and other mythical beasts.

'I believe Elspeth Bell was your aunt?' he began, doing his best to sound sympathetic.

'That's right. I spent a lot of time with Auntie Elspeth and Uncle George when I was little. We even went on holiday with them. Then they moved down to Devon and we lost touch, although I heard Uncle George passed away soon afterwards.' He bowed his head. 'My dad died when I was fifteen and my mum never really took to Elspeth, so she stopped seeing that side of the family. She used to call her a snob and a nosy parker.'

'But you liked her?'

'I did when I was young. Then Mum died a few years ago and I had no one.'

Wesley waited, knowing there was more to come. 'I got into drugs and ended up in prison. Someone told me about the Reverend Becky, and when I turned up, she took me in, no questions asked. But I had an ulterior motive for coming to Nesbarton. I'd found out that was where Auntie Elspeth had moved to, and I hoped . . .'

'You wanted to find your aunt?'

'I recognised her, but I didn't dare speak to her at first because I knew she wouldn't approve of me. Auntie Elspeth never liked anything or anyone . . . dodgy. I first saw her soon after I'd arrived, and I followed her to find out where she lived, but she seemed so . . . unapproachable. She'd changed since Uncle George died, become this . . .'

'Head of the village watch,' said Gerry.

'That's right. The Reverend Becky used to go on about how awful she was and how she was always making trouble for the Sanctuary. Auntie Elspeth started up petitions and spied on us, reporting any little thing to the authorities.

How could I turn up on her doorstep when I was one of the very people she hated?'

'I see your problem,' said Wesley, feeling some sympathy. From what he had gleaned about Elspeth Bell, this young man's appearance alone would have given her a fit of the vapours, and he wasn't sure whether even revealing that he was her long-lost nephew would have improved the situation.

'For a while, I wasn't sure how to play things. I watched her house, but I didn't know how she'd react if I told her who I was. You see, last time she'd met me, I was in my teens, destined for university, with my life all mapped out.' Bell looked up and gave Wesley a bitter smile. 'I was quite academic at one time, would you believe. Then, like I said, I lost my dad, and then my mum got ill and died a couple of years later. I was eighteen by then. Too old to go into the care system and too young to fend for myself. My mum had remortgaged the house when my dad died and got into a load of debt, so I didn't even have any inheritance to fall back on. There was no chance of university because I failed my GCSEs and abandoned any hope of A levels when Mum got ill. I had no qualifications and no home, so I lived on the streets for a while; got into drugs and turned to crime to feed my habit.'

Wesley listened intently, feeling deeply sorry for the man, who appeared to have been the victim of circumstances beyond his control. One glance at Gerry told him he was thinking the same. But had desperation driven Bell to murder? He waited for him to continue his story.

'One day I went to the church. The Reverend Becky was always telling us that it helped to share our troubles with God, and that prayer was the answer to all our problems. Some of the others laughed about it, but I'd been brought up going to church and . . . well, I thought it was worth a try. Anyway, while I was there, she came in – Auntie Elspeth.' He looked Wesley in the eye. 'When she left I didn't think it was any use going after her, because I thought she wouldn't recognise me – not like this. I was going to ask the reverend's advice about what to do next. But as it happened, I didn't need to.'

'What do you mean?' Gerry asked.

'When I got out of the church, she was standing there in the churchyard. At first I thought she'd reported me to the police and was waiting for them to arrive. But I told myself I had nothing to lose, so I called out to her. "Auntie Elspeth," I said. "It's me – John. Sorry if I frightened you." She turned and stared at me as though she'd seen a ghost.'

'She recognised you?' said Gerry.

John shook his head. 'I don't think she did at first. She looked confused. Then I called out to her again and she said something like "John, is it really you?". We were there talking for ages, and when I told her what had happened to me she was really sympathetic, which wasn't what I'd expected at all. She told me I had to get out of that place, meaning the Sanctuary, because it was full of criminals. A den of thieves, she called it. She even gave me the spare key to her house and said I should come and stay in her spare room until I got back on my feet. Once she knew who I was, her attitude changed completely and she kept going on about the holidays we had when I was a kid. I thought that if I stayed with her I could make a new start – and maybe persuade her to stop her campaign against the reverend. Make her understand what she was trying to do.'

'If all this is true, I don't understand why you ran away from the police,' said Wesley.

223

John hesitated, as though he was trying to find the right words. 'I've got so used to everyone thinking the worst of me that when I heard Auntie Elspeth had been killed, I knew I'd get the blame. That's why I'm here, isn't it? You want to pin it on me, but I swear I had nothing to do with it. Why on earth would I kill my own aunt when she'd offered to take me in and give me a fresh start? Like I said, she even gave me the key to her cottage. She said I could move in any time I liked.'

'We've only your word for that,' said Gerry. 'You might have taken the key when you killed her.'

'I'm not lying. I didn't kill her. Why would I?' Bell slumped back in his seat, as though he was resigned to being accused of crimes he hadn't committed. Wesley saw tears welling in the young man's eyes, and he wondered whether they were tears of grief for the aunt whose kindness he remembered from childhood, or of despair that the police had caught up with him and he was facing the hell of a long prison sentence.

The Reverend Becky hadn't allowed her guests to be interviewed after Patrick North's murder out of a misguided desire to protect them. But now that he had one of those guests here in front of him, Wesley seized the opportunity to ask some questions.

'Did you ever meet the man who was killed in the grounds of Nesbarton Hall at the weekend? His name was Patrick North and he was tutor to Silas Smithson's son.'

'As far as I know, I've never met anyone from the hall. They don't mix with the people in the village. I certainly didn't know the tutor.'

'You said that when you left the church, your aunt looked confused. Do you know why?'

Bell shook his head.

'Did you see anyone else in the churchyard?'

He frowned as though he was trying to retrieve some elusive memory. 'Now I come to think about it, I'm sure I saw somebody disappearing into the trees, but I didn't see who it was. Auntie Elspeth was staring in that direction and she looked really puzzled, but then we started talking. Sorry, that's all I can tell you.' There was a long pause before he asked, 'How was she killed?'

'She was shot,' said Gerry, watching Bell closely.

A look of relief appeared on the young man's face. 'In that case, I'm in the clear, and so is everyone else at the Sanctuary. The reverend doesn't allow guns. It's in the rules. No guns, drugs or knives.'

'And you all stick to the rules?'

'Absolutely right. Nobody argues with the Reverend Becky.' He took a deep breath. 'Look, I didn't kill my auntie. She was offering me hope. I had no reason to want her dead.'

Wesley glanced at Gerry and saw him nod in agreement.

31

John Bell was released without charge on condition that
he stay at the Sanctuary for the time being so they'd know
where to find him.

Wesley was intrigued by what he had told them near the
end of the interview – that Elspeth Bell might have recognised somebody who had vanished into the trees around
the churchyard. But why would the woman renowned for
digging out the wrongdoings of Nesbarton and calling
the police on a regular basis keep quiet about something
untoward? Unless finding her long-lost nephew had made
her forget about whatever it was. In which case, it might not
have been that important.

He pondered this question as he walked down the water-
front to the hospital with Gerry. The churning river was an
uninviting dark grey in the gathering darkness, but at least
it wasn't raining. He could see the lights of Queenswear on
the opposite bank, but there were few vessels on the water;
only working boats like the ferries and fishing boats that
were forced to brave the cold and damp.

The marina was filled with yachts laid up until the spring,
and Silas Smithson's gin palace was amongst them, resting
for the winter at its expensive mooring. Wesley wondered

why Smithson had chosen cold, wet Scotland for his off-grid break, rather than sailing the yacht down to the south of France, where the weather was bound to be better. But what did he know about maritime matters? He left that sort of thing to Gerry. Besides, the trip to Scotland suggested that Smithson favoured challenge over luxury. Wesley and Pam would have preferred a yacht in the Mediterranean, but each to his own.

When they reached the hospital mortuary, Colin was ready for them. Wesley averted his eyes as the first incision was made into Elspeth Bell's chubby flesh. There was one thing in particular that Wesley wanted to know: was the bullet that had killed Elspeth fired from the same gun that killed Patrick North?

Of course, he should have known that he could trust Colin to provide the answer. The bullets had been retrieved, and as far as the pathologist could tell, they were identical, although his findings needed to be confirmed by Ballistics. The only difference was that North had been shot twice in the chest and Elspeth had been shot twice in the forehead. Both had been facing their killer, and both had been shot at fairly close range. There were many .22 rifles around in the country, not all of them licensed, so the weapon wouldn't be easy to pin down, but they needed to find it as soon as possible.

Wesley left Gerry enjoying tea and biscuits in Colin's office. The DCI, he noticed, didn't seem in much of a hurry to get home these days, and he sensed a distinct coolness whenever Joyce was mentioned, in stark contrast to the light in his eyes when he mentioned his long-lost daughter, Alison.

Before heading home, Wesley called in to the incident

room to see whether anything new had come in, but no one there had anything to report. There was still no word on the Smithsons. Trish told him that Patrick North's parents intended to stay in Tradmouth for a few days. They'd asked to see the flat in Nesbarton Hall where their son had spent the last days of his life, and Trish had told them she'd see what she could do. She'd call at the house and speak to Karensa Carlton at the first opportunity. Surely the woman couldn't refuse such a request from the bereaved family.

By the time Wesley arrived home, it was 7.30. Pam met him in the hall with the news that Neil was in the living room helping Michael with his homework, adding that his friend had something he wanted to show him. Ever since his conversation with Maritia a couple of days ago, Wesley had been intending to call his parents, but it seemed his best intentions were to be thwarted again.

As soon as he walked into the living room, Neil greeted him with the question 'How's your murder going? Got him yet?'

'Murders plural. There've been two.'

Michael's eyes lit up at the mention of violent death. 'Tell us all about them, Dad. It said on the news that it was a shooting. Is it terrorists, or gangland?'

The last thing Wesley fancied at that moment was to describe the deaths of Patrick North and Elspeth Bell to a sensation-hungry teenager. 'Sorry. I can't give away any details at the moment. It's hush-hush.'

This seemed to satisfy the boy, who looked at his father knowingly. 'But you'll tell me all about it when you've caught the killer?'

'We'll see,' Wesley said, which was parent code for *I*

doubt it. 'Pam said you have something to show me, Neil.' He hoped this would distract Michael from his enquiries.

Neil delved in his pocket and pulled out three small plastic bags. 'Coins found with that skeleton. Margaret, my tame bone specialist, says she thinks the bones are old, possibly contemporary with the coins we found in the grave. Late eighteenth century. George III. The field was part of the Nesbarton Hall estate in those days, and I'm wondering whether the burial is linked to the grotto, but I can safely say it's not your responsibility. I've managed to stop Jason Fonsby demolishing any more of it, by the way.'

'How did you do that?' Wesley slumped down in an armchair, preparing to listen to Neil's tale of triumph.

'I pointed out that he didn't want to get a reputation for riding roughshod over the county's heritage. He agreed that we could conduct further investigations before he carried on with the demolition. He said he's been planning to start construction elsewhere in the field, but I think that was just to save face.' He passed the coins to Wesley.

'Gold sovereigns. Big money in those days.'

'My thoughts exactly. They might belong to her murderer.'

'Was Margaret able to give you a cause of death?'

'She said there was a small nick on one of the ribs near the heart consistent with a knife wound. The bones belonged to a young woman, and I'm working on the theory that she was stabbed, then bundled into a shallow grave.' He paused. 'As for the coins, I've no idea.'

'Can I see the bones?' asked Michael eagerly.

'We'll see,' said Neil, giving Wesley a knowing grin.

A phone call at 11.30 at night usually heralded an emergency. Wesley answered at once, because he didn't want to disturb Pam, and crept out onto the landing before speaking. He didn't recognise the caller's number, but he assumed it would be someone from the station. He crossed his fingers, hoping it wasn't news of another murder.

Although the voice on the other end of the line was familiar, it had nothing to do with the investigation.

'I didn't get you out of bed, did I?'

'Hello, Della. What can I do for you?' he said with studied patience. His mother-in-law often chose awkward times to make contact, but this beat the lot. 'Pam's in bed. She's got work in the morning – as have I.'

'Just thought you'd like to know that I've been doing your job for you.'

'What do you mean?'

'I suppose Pam's told you I booked to go to the writing retreat at Nesbarton Lodge? Well, I arrived there this morning. I'm there now. That woman Betina's very good.'

'Pleased to hear it.' Wesley wished she'd come to the point. He was tired.

'She told me about the police investigation, but she's determined that things should carry on as normal. Anyway, my fellow scribe, Georgina, has been working on her novel for four years and—'

'I've met her. What did you want to tell me?'

'After the session this afternoon, I was walking back to my room with Georgina. She dropped some papers and I picked them up. I wasn't being nosy, but I couldn't help catching a glimpse of them.'

'Of course you couldn't,' said Wesley, wishing she'd get on with it.

'I thought they'd be pages from her novel, but they weren't. They were drafts of letters.'

Suddenly Della had his full attention. He'd thought there was something a little out of place about Georgina Selby. She seemed to know too much about Silas Smithson's affairs.

'Who were these letters addressed to, and what did they say?'

'I'm coming to that. They were in capitals – that's always a bad sign. And the one I saw said that he was an evil man and if the money wasn't in her bank account by the end of the month, he'd regret it.'

'Do you know who these letters were addressed to?'

Della paused for dramatic effect. 'Didn't I say? They were addressed to Silas Smithson.'

32

After Della's phone call, Wesley had lain awake going over the case in his head. There were too many possible suspects, but nobody who stood out, apart from Jordan Green, North's love rival, although he had a solid alibi for the shooting of Elspeth Bell. And then there was Cosmo Mearson, who was back in the country but hadn't yet been found.

The men staying at the Sanctuary had been interviewed and the Reverend Becky had vouched for them all, but would she go to any lengths to defend them against the police? And what if Betina Smithson had found out about Patrick North's affair with Natalia, her brother's wife? She was obviously devoted to her niece, Tatiana, so if she feared the family was about to be broken up, might she have decided to remove the cause? Although from what Wesley had seen of her, he really couldn't imagine her killing Elspeth Bell in cold blood.

Now there was Della's fellow aspiring writer, Georgina, who clearly had some mysterious connection with Silas Smithson, Patrick North's employer. Could North's killing have been a case of mistaken identity? In his experience, stranger things had happened.

The following morning was Remembrance Sunday, but for the team it was a working day. Wesley arrived in the incident room with possibilities swirling around his head, including one he'd been reluctant to share with Rachel. Benedict Graves had come all the way from Suffolk. Had he had problems with Silas Smithson, possibly because he was owed money? Did his discovery that Smithson wasn't at home make him so desperate that he'd ended up killing the wrong person? If he'd been fleeing the scene of the murder, it would explain why his car had gone off the road. He couldn't be ruled out as a suspect, although there'd been no sign of a weapon either in or near the wrecked car. But he too had an alibi for the murder of Elspeth Bell, because someone had checked and he'd definitely been with Geoff at the time.

When Gerry arrived looking harassed, Wesley could tell that something was wrong. Unlike the CID office at Tradmouth police station, the incident room in the stables lacked a secluded space where the two of them could talk in private. It wasn't raining, and the weak November sun had deigned to show itself after a long period of hiding shyly behind the grey clouds, so Wesley suggested they take a walk. They had a lot to discuss.

He began by telling Gerry about Della's call the previous night.

'I hope that mother-in-law of yours won't get in the way of our investigation,' said Gerry.

'So do I. But what she told me last night could be useful. Could Georgina Selby be responsible for that threatening letter to Smithson?'

'We should speak to her. There's been a threat against the boy, so she could be at Betina's in order to keep tabs on the Smithson family's whereabouts. In which case, we might have a would-be kidnapper on our hands. And if Patrick North stumbled over what she was up to . . .'

'What about Elspeth Bell?'

'She was the village nosy parker, so she might have discovered something too. I wouldn't put it past her to think she could deal with it herself. I'll send a team to search Georgina's room at the lodge. And her home address. Where did she say she lived?'

'London.'

'We can give that job to the Met.' Gerry smiled. 'If we weren't so busy, I'd get you to go – give you a chance to drop in on your mum and dad.'

His words reminded Wesley that he still hadn't called his parents. But there was no time to think of that now.

'I'll get the ball rolling with the Met, but first we need to question this Georgina Selby.' Gerry hesitated. 'Are you quite certain Della isn't imagining things?'

'I admit she's flaky, but she seemed pretty sure of her facts.' Wesley looked at his boss. There were dark rings under his eyes. Normally he claimed to sleep like one of Colin Bowman's patients in the mortuary; not the most tasteful way of putting it, but Wesley knew what he meant. 'Anything the matter, Gerry?'

Gerry came to a sudden halt and turned to him. 'I think me and Joyce are finished, Wes. When I told her Alison was coming for Christmas, she went mad – said didn't I realise how much I was upsetting Rosie and why was I making such a fuss of my child who'd been born on the wrong side of the blanket.'

Wesley couldn't help smiling. 'It's a long time since I've heard that phrase.'

'She said she wouldn't share the house with Alison if she moves down here. I told her it was my house. She didn't like that.'

'Doesn't she realise that you and Alison have got a lot of time to make up?'

'Apparently not. What should I do, Wes?'

Wesley had never been thrust into the role of agony uncle before, and he wasn't quite sure what to say. 'What do you feel you should do?'

Gerry sighed. 'Alison has to be my prime concern. If she's coming down to live here ... Her mum didn't tell her about me until she was on her death bed so we've lost so many years, Wes. She's my own flesh and blood. I know Rosie's my daughter too, but she's settled in Morbay with her teaching job and her boyfriend. And our Sam's keen on getting to know Alison better.'

'Then you've answered your own question.'

When they reached the lodge, Betina Smithson herself answered the door.

Before asking to see Georgina Selby, Wesley broke the news about the second murder, and Betina put on a show of being shocked, although as she told them, she'd only met Elspeth Bell once, when she came round recruiting for the village watch. She'd given her a leaflet, but these village things weren't really her scene, she said, adding that Mrs Bell had seemed – she chose her words carefully, not wishing to speak ill of the dead – like an efficient sort of woman and passionate about keeping the village free of crime. Wesley knew this was a tactful way of saying she'd been a busybody and Betina had wanted nothing to do with her.

Then he asked another question. 'Were you aware of

a relationship between your sister-in-law, Natalia, and Patrick North?'

Betina didn't speak for a few moments, twirling a strand of hair in her fingers. 'No, but it wouldn't surprise me. Natalia's ... well, I believe she makes a habit of that sort of thing.'

'But she and your brother stay together.'

'My brother's no saint,' was the simple reply. 'Six of one and half a dozen of the other. I think they have what's known as an open marriage. But don't ask me who else is involved, because they don't confide in me.'

It seemed the subject was exhausted, so Gerry asked after Tatiana and was told that she'd been dropped off at school earlier. The stranger the girl had seen might have been Ben Graves. On the other hand, it might have been someone linked to Georgina Selby. And there was only one way to find out.

They found Georgina in her room, typing away on her laptop. When they entered, she turned and frowned. They'd disturbed the muse.

Wesley explained why they were there, careful to leave Della's name out of it. An anonymous letter had been found at Nesbarton Hall; a letter that included a kidnap threat to Silas Smithson's son. Did she know anything about it? He added that some officers were coming to search Betina's premises and would be arriving in the next half an hour.

'I never threatened Smithson's son. I wouldn't do anything like that.' She sounded affronted; a woman who was upset at being misjudged.

'But you have written to Silas Smithson making demands?'

She gazed out of the window for a few moments before

she answered. 'It was just a draft. I wanted Smithson to realise how much damage he'd done.'

'You were demanding money.'

'All I want is for him to pay me what he owes.'

'What does he owe you?'

For a long time she didn't speak, just stared at her laptop as though she was seeking inspiration. Then she turned to face them.

'Silas Smithson wrecked my business. He makes out he's a philanthropist, but there's no philanthropy in the way he treats people who supply his companies. I had a successful florist's business in London and Smithson's headquarters became my main client. I provided plants and flowers for his premises, and the demands became so great that I let all my other clients slip away. It was fantastic at first, then ...' She fell silent, as though the subject was too painful to discuss.

'What happened?' said Gerry.

'The payments became later and later, but my suppliers still needed to be paid. In the end, Smithson stopped paying at all. By that time all my former clients had taken their business elsewhere and I had no other source of income, so I had to declare myself bankrupt. Thanks to Smithson, I'd lost a thriving business, and I know he's done the same to other people. I came here hoping to make him aware of the consequences of his actions, but by the time I plucked up the courage to confront him, I discovered that he'd gone away.' She nodded towards her laptop. 'I'm writing a book, so I thought I'd stay anyway and use the time productively. Besides, the yoga Betina teaches is helpful to the whole creative process.'

'Smithson's daughter is staying here while her parents and brother are away. Were you planning to kidnap her now her brother's out of reach? Was that how you were going to exact your revenge?'

She looked hurt. 'Tatiana's a sweet girl, considering who her father is, and I swear I'd never do anything to harm her. And I didn't write that anonymous letter you mentioned. I never made any kidnap threats. That wasn't me.'

'How do you get on with Betina?' Gerry asked, suddenly curious.

'She's nice. You wouldn't think she and Smithson were related.'

'What were you planning to do with the letter you wrote?'

She looked embarrassed. 'I was going to drop it through the front door of the hall, but I lost my nerve. I needed time to get the wording right.'

'When exactly did you arrive?' Wesley asked.

'The thirtieth of October. It made me furious to see where Smithson lived. It's people like me who've paid for Nesbarton Hall, you know.'

'That must have been before the Smithsons went away?'

'Yes. The next evening, the thirty-first, I walked up to the house – just out of curiosity – and there were a lot of lights on and I heard shouting. It sounded like an almighty row, but I couldn't understand anything the woman was saying. I think it was Smithson's wife, because she was speaking Russian. At least it sounded like Russian.'

'A row?'

'Yes. I didn't hang around. I ran back down the drive to the lodge. It was dark, so nobody saw me. I intended to return but, as it turned out, I'd missed my chance.'

'According to Smithson's PA, he went away with his wife and son the following morning,' said Wesley.

Georgina gave a bitter smile. 'Perhaps he spotted me out

238

of the window. Perhaps he knew I'd make trouble for him if I got the chance and I scared him off.' She sighed. 'On the other hand, that's highly unlikely. To him I was a nobody. He tramples over little people like me.'

'Do you know anything about a man who was watching Tatiana?' said Gerry. 'Is that something you arranged?'

Georgina looked alarmed and shook her head. 'Certainly not. I admit I'm angry with Smithson, but I'd never do anything like that.'

'How long are you intending to stay here?' Wesley asked.

'I've almost finished the first draft of my book. It should take another week or so, and Betina says there's no hurry.'

'You say Smithson ruined you financially. How are you paying for all this?' Gerry said bluntly.

Georgina gave him a sad smile. 'I had a nice win on the premium bonds. Coming here to work on my novel and do some yoga was a present to myself. And with the possibility of getting through to Smithson and securing what I'm owed, I hoped it might be an investment as well. My last throw of the dice. Maybe if I'm still here when he gets back . . .'

'If we want to speak to you again, we know where to find you.' Gerry's words sounded to Wesley like a threat.

May 1787

Dionisio told me I was to prepare for that evening's revels. His eyes shone with anticipation – and something else. Something malevolent, perhaps. But I dismissed such thoughts. I was there to perform a role. Nothing more. This was merely the folly of gentlemen with too much money and too many opportunities for idleness. And I was being paid well.

In the daylight, my fears dwindled to nothing, but as darkness fell and I found myself alone in the grotto in candlelight, a creeping fear entered my mind. Two sullen servants came with tankards and supplies of wine for the night's revels. They also brought me food and ale and a mattress upon which I could sleep, but when they departed, I could not ignore the noises of the night; the screech of owls sounded like souls in torment, and in my solitude the snuffling of night creatures in the surrounding woods became the approach of predatory demons. I waited, filled with trepidation and unsure what would happen when Dionisio and his companions arrived.

After a while, I saw figures looming through the trees, hooded in robes such as monks wear and bearing blazing torches. In the flickering light the trees looked like monsters, and I stood at the grotto entrance, planning my first act.

I decided to begin my performance at once, jumping

forward, eyes wild and arms flailing. 'What means this? Who comes to disturb my peace?'

'Poor monks of the Order of St Dionisio,' said a booming voice. 'We seek a wild man to lead us in our revels.'

'I am he,' I said proudly, getting into the role. Flagons of drink were produced and we danced wildly. I confess that I enjoyed my part, making up crazy forfeits for my little congregation. We drank deeply until my fellows collapsed on the ground. This was the easiest money I had ever earned, I thought. But I had little inkling of what was to come.

33

Even though it was Sunday, the building work continued. Neil had agreed to meet Jason Fonsby in the site office, newly erected near the entrance to the field. He knew Fonsby had been informed that the human remains were old and of no concern to the police, which meant he could no longer use that to delay the work. But he'd try to appeal to the man's better nature – if he had one.

The previous day Neil had spent some time on the phone to Annabel, his contact in the Exeter archives, and she'd come up with further interesting information about the former owners of Nesbarton Hall to add to what he'd discovered from Edward Hawk. The man who'd had the hall built in the 1760s, Samuel Nescote, had indeed begun life as a humble sailor on various Tradmouth ships involved in the lucrative wine trade with France and Spain. He must have shown considerable talent, because after a few years he had worked his way up to captain his own ship, the *Tradmouth Lady*. This was where his story became interesting. A change in the law in 1740 meant that privateers, who were little more than legalised pirates, could keep all the ships and goods they captured rather than giving a percentage to the Crown. Samuel went about the business of piracy in earnest, capturing Spanish, French and Dutch ships, and made a fortune out of selling both the vessels and their valuable cargos. Nesbarton Hall was built on piracy, which to Neil's mind made it all the more fascinating.

The story became even more dramatic when Samuel and his Italian-born wife, Francesca, were brutally murdered in 1787. A servant was convicted of their murder and hanged at Exeter. The estate passed to Samuel's son, Dionisio, and then to Dionisio's nephew, after which it was handed down from father to son until the Nescote family ran out of money in the twentieth century, selling off farms and fields first before the house itself was put on the market. Considering their humble beginnings, they had had a good run for their dubiously acquired money.

Neil hoped to use this story to beguile Fonsby into letting him investigate what remained of the grotto in more depth. Surely nobody could resist a tale of pirates and murder.

He entered the site office full of optimism, but his worst fears were soon confirmed: Fonsby's sole interest lay in the bottom line rather than romantic tales from the past. He refused to extend the deadline further. Neil and his team had a few days to complete their investigations, and after that, the remains of the grotto would be flattened. That was all. And they should count themselves lucky.

Dave and the others were waiting for him outside the site office, already wearing hard hats and high-vis jackets. Neil gave a thumbs-down signal as he descended the small flight of steps. Dave shrugged and said that with any luck they'd find another skeleton, which would put a proverbial spanner in Fonsby's works. Neil harboured a sneaking hope that he was right.

The once green field was now a sea of mud where the earth had been churned by massive wheels, and as they approached the grotto, Neil saw that the remaining trees had been felled and the half-demolished stone structure stood alone like a single pimple on unblemished flesh. Fortunately the entire inner chamber was still intact, and he squeezed through the entrance, ignoring Dave's anxious question: 'Are you sure it's safe?'

Now that the outer room had gone, daylight flooded in and the place didn't seem as sinister as it had on his first visit. The altar was still there, and he wondered again who had put the lay figure there and where it had come from. He feared it was a puzzle that might never be solved. The motto carved above the entrance still made him uneasy. *We are masters of all and our will is law.* Did that will include the murder of the young woman they'd found buried outside the grotto?

'Let's make sure everything's photographed and recorded,' he said. 'And I'd like to sink a few test pits too, just to make sure there won't be any surprises when Fonsby starts work. If there's anything to find, I'd like to find it *in situ.*'

'You mean more bones?' said one of the PhD students, an earnest young woman who'd worked with him before.

'Exactly. I'm going to start in front of the altar. Anyone got a mattock?'

Wesley and Gerry returned to the incident room to find that someone had already driven into Neston to fetch the sandwich order, and had left theirs on their desks. Gerry beamed around the room and thanked whoever had run the errand; it turned out to be Ellie. Gerry's was cheese and

Wesley's tuna, their usual choices, and Gerry told her she'd done well to remember.

DC Rob Carter was speaking on the phone when they walked in. He was making notes and didn't look up. After the long conversation was over, he stood and approached Wesley's desk.

'Hi, Rob. Anything new come in?' Wesley said as he breached the packaging on his sandwich.

'I've been talking to Cosmo Mearson's local station in Formby near Liverpool. They sent someone to his address and his mother said he's staying with his stepfather in Devon at the moment. According to the officer who visited, the mother had been drinking – a lot.'

Rob now had Wesley's full attention. 'Cosmo's in Devon at the moment ? That feels like a big coincidence. Whereabouts exactly?'

'She wasn't sure, but his stepfather's working here temporarily.'

'Do we have an address for Mr Mearson?'

Rob hesitated. 'It's not Mr Mearson. Cosmo uses his real father's surname; his mother's first husband. The stepfather has a large building company. His name's Jason Fonsby.'

Gerry seemed more than usually excited by the news about Cosmo Mearson. He patted Rob on the back and said he'd done a good job, but Rob's only reaction was a sad half-smile. The old Rob would have been crowing over such praise for days.

'I think something's definitely up with Rob,' Wesley said to Gerry as they walked across the stable yard to the car. He didn't like to think of anyone on the team suffering in silence. 'Have you noticed a change in him over the past few weeks?'

'Now you mention it, he's not been his usual enthusiastic self.'

'I saw him when I was walking the dog one evening last week. He was with a man who really didn't look well – a relative maybe. He didn't see me and I haven't mentioned it.'

'He never talks about his personal life, but if something's wrong, I'd like to know. Why don't you have a word? You're better at that sort of thing than I am.'

Wesley knew the boss was right, but he suspected he'd lose sleep trying to think of the right words to use. 'OK. I'll say something as soon as I get the chance.'

Neither man spoke again until they arrived at the building site.

'Isn't that Neil's car?' said Gerry, pointing at a filthy vehicle parked some way off down the lane.

'Yes. But I promise I won't allow myself to be distracted,' Wesley replied with a grin.

He could see that a temporary site office had now been erected. The developers were wasting no time.

'I think Cosmo Mearson being down here is a coincidence too far, don't you, Gerry?' he said as they climbed out of the car. 'He sounds like an unpleasant little shit, but surely he wouldn't kill his former teacher just for fun. Could he have a motive for getting rid of North that we haven't discovered yet?'

Gerry's eyebrows shot up in astonishment. 'Not like you to use such language, Wes.'

'I think it's justified in this case. I don't like entitled men who do what Cosmo did to Lisa Lowe.'

They found Jason Fonsby in the site hut, poring over plans with another man in mud-caked working clothes. The two detectives stood in the open doorway, waiting until Fonsby's conversation was finished. Their business was better discussed in private. Fonsby began to roll up the plans and the other man left, pushing past them as though he was eager to get back to work.

'Mr Fonsby. Can we have a word?'

Fonsby swung round. He hadn't seen them and he looked startled. 'If it's about that skeleton . . .'

'It's not about the skeleton. We've had confirmation that those remains are of more interest to archaeologists than the police, so we're not opening an inquiry.'

'I'm relieved to hear it. I said they could carry on in that grotto place for another couple of days. Then it goes whether they've finished there or not.' He sounded impatient. 'What do you want? We've had police round already talking to the men about the murder in the village, but nobody knows anything. I hope this won't cause more disruption.' Clearly he put the police in the same category as Neil's team of archaeologists: a minor nuisance, like a buzzing fly at a picnic.

'Not if you co-operate, sir,' said Wesley, suspecting that his next question was going to come as a surprise. 'Where are you staying?'

'I told the constable who came to take everyone's statements. Don't you people talk to each other? If I ran my business like that . . .'

Gerry took out his notebook. 'When you were interviewed about the murder in the grounds of Nesbarton Hall, you said you were renting a flat in Neston for a month so you could supervise the start of the build.'

There was no mistaking the irritation on Fonsby's face. 'If you know that, why are you asking?'

'You didn't mention that someone was staying with you.'

Fonsby's face reddened. 'I was never asked.'

'You have a stepson called Cosmo Mearson.'

'Is that a crime?'

'Earlier today we sent someone to the address you gave and they were told that you moved out a couple of weeks ago because you needed somewhere with two bedrooms. You provided our officer with the wrong address.'

Fonsby put his hand to his forehead. 'I had a lot on my mind at the time. The start of the build and those bloody archaeologists. I hold my hands up. It was my mistake. But I can't see what it has to do with you.'

'Your stepson knew Patrick North, the man who was shot on the Nesbarton Hall estate. Does Cosmo own a gun?'

Wesley could see Fonsby weighing up his options. Did he cover up for the boy or tell the truth? In the end, he made the decision.

'Cosmo's done some shooting, yes.'

'What kind of shooting? Clay pigeon shooting? Target shooting?'

'Target shooting mainly, although he did do some clay pigeon shooting during his school holidays when he was younger.'

'What kind of rifle does he use?' Wesley asked, trying to sound casual.

'A .22. He has a licence, so it's all quite legal. It's little more than a toy really.'

'A toy that can kill at close range,' said Gerry. 'Where can we find Cosmo?'

Fonsby's mouth fell open, as though he'd just realised

the implications of what he'd said. As he mumbled the address, Wesley guessed that he was wondering how he was going to explain the situation to his wife, Cosmo's mother.

They thanked him and left.

34

Jason Fonsby was renting a flat overlooking the river in Tradmouth. In the summer months, the flats provided accommodation for holidaymakers, but in the winter, the landlord was glad to let them out on a more long-term basis to anyone who had work in the area. Wesley and Gerry decided to conduct the visit themselves rather than leaving it to one of the team. Cosmo Mearson was a suspect – and a good one.

They found the main streets blocked off for the annual Remembrance parade, a major event in the town, so they parked at the station and walked. The bells of St Margaret's were already ringing, half muffled in mourning; each note followed by an eerie echo. Gerry muttered that he should have been attending the service, but at that moment, catching the killer took priority.

When they knocked on the flat door, they had a lengthy wait before it opened a crack. They couldn't see the person on the other side, and Gerry thrust his warrant card through the gap.

'Cosmo Mearson? Police. Can we come in?'

The door closed an inch, and Wesley feared that whoever it was would try to shut it on Gerry's arm, so he pushed at it hard. It swung open to reveal a handsome young man with fair hair and a full, arrogant mouth. His muscular physique suggested that he excelled at sport, but today, with tousled hair and dressed in the shorts and T-shirt he'd obviously slept in, Cosmo Mearson wasn't looking his best. Wesley noticed fading bruises on his face and a healing cut on his cheek. He'd either been in an accident or a fight.

They stepped into the flat, ignoring Cosmo's peevish mutterings about police states and solicitors. Wesley suspected that Jason Fonsby wouldn't make any great effort to back up his stepson's threats, and he knew Gerry was determined that the boy wouldn't get the better of them.

'This is harassment,' Cosmo shouted.

'This is a murder inquiry,' Wesley said firmly. 'We can do this down at the police station or we can have a chat here. It's your choice.'

Cosmo rolled his eyes and led them into a spacious lounge with a large window giving a spectacular view of the choppy grey river.

Wesley and Gerry sat down, but Cosmo hesitated before sinking into a leather armchair facing the window. He was trying to feign confidence, but his wary expression gave him away. He looked like someone who'd just realised his past was about to catch up with him but was still trying to brazen it out.

'You've been in the wars,' said Gerry. 'How did you get those bruises?'

'None of your bloody business. I don't even know why you're here. I haven't done anything wrong.'

'We're investigating the murder of Patrick North. He used to teach at Falsham Place, the boarding school you attended.'

Cosmo gave Wesley a look of contempt. 'I don't have to answer your questions, you know. I have the right to remain silent – isn't that what they say?'

'If you want a solicitor present, we can go to the station. It's only a short walk away,' said Wesley pleasantly, resisting the temptation to lose his habitual cool.

'I told you before, I haven't done anything.'

'In that case, you won't mind answering our questions.'

'I do mind. North was a pathetic loser, but I never shot him.'

Wesley and Gerry looked at each other.

'How did you know he was shot? We haven't released that information to the press.'

'Jason told me. He's working round there, so he must have heard.'

Wesley left the room and made a phone call. When he returned, he saw that Cosmo was scrolling through messages on his phone, looking bored.

He looked up. 'You can't pin anything on me, you know,' he said. 'I haven't seen North since he was kicked out of Falsham Place, and you can't prove otherwise. I've been in the States.'

'Thrown out of the States, you mean,' said Gerry.

Wesley bent and whispered in his ear, and Gerry gave Cosmo a dangerous grin a crocodile would have envied. 'Inspector Peterson here has just spoken to your stepdad. He denies telling you that Patrick North was shot – says he's never discussed it with you.'

Cosmo remained calm. 'I must have got it from someone else then.'

Gerry stood up and recited the familiar words of the caution. 'We're taking you to the police station for questioning.

Call your solicitor if you like. I'm sure your stepdad has a tame one.'

The colour drained from Cosmo Mearson's face. It looked as though his luck had run out.

Wesley called Jason Fonsby to inform him of his stepson's arrest. The builder didn't sound particularly concerned, and when Wesley asked if he wanted to send a solicitor, Jason said he'd rather not bother his usual man. Wesley suspected that relations between stepson and stepfather weren't exactly rosy.

When Wesley said that Cosmo would have to make do with the duty solicitor at the police station, Fonsby relented and said he'd call his man, although he didn't sound pleased about it.

They decided to leave Cosmo to stew in their most unwelcoming interview room until Fonsby's solicitor arrived. In the meantime, they went upstairs to Gerry's glass-fronted office and he made tea with the kettle he kept on top of his filing cabinet.

No sooner had they settled down for their break than one of the civilian investigators who helped out in the department knocked on the open door. She was a middle-aged woman who'd retired from the force a couple of years ago and, according to Gerry, couldn't keep away. Wesley could tell she had news.

'Excuse me, sir, but this has just come in from Forensics. The incident room said you were in Tradmouth, so they sent it over here.'

She handed Wesley a sheet of paper – a report from the vehicle investigators – and returned to her desk. As soon as he'd read it, he passed it to Gerry.

'Well, this is a turn-up,' the DCI said. 'The brake pipes on the silver Toyota had been cut.'

'I must admit, it's the last thing I expected,' said Wesley. 'Who on earth would want to do that?'

'Someone who wanted Benedict Graves dead. But who'd want to harm him? Unless it was someone's idea of a joke.'

'I can't imagine anyone cutting someone's brake pipes for fun. I think you were right first time, Gerry. Somebody wanted Graves dead. But why? He's a dealer in rare books from Suffolk, for heaven's sake, not a Mafia don. This means we should provide some protection for him and Geoff Haynes. I don't like to think of them being in that isolated cottage on their own. They're vulnerable – and that sheepdog of Geoff's isn't much of a guard dog.'

'You're right. She's more likely to lick an intruder to death.' Gerry made a note on a scrap of paper in front of him. 'I'll see to it. And I'll ask Rach to have a word with them about security. I think this puts Ben out of the frame for Patrick North's murder, don't you? And Geoff's given him a solid alibi for Elspeth Bell.'

'I never saw him as a likely suspect anyway, but he might have witnessed something on the night North was killed.'

'Then if the killer finds out where he is, he'll be in danger.'

Gerry's phone rang. It was the incident room. Something had just come in. As soon as the Norths had identified their son's body, his name and photograph had been released to the media. Gerry had been hoping this would bring in more witnesses, and now it seemed it was his lucky day.

The landlord of a pub in Tradington, the nearest hostelry to Nesbarton, which sadly had lost its only pub in the 1980s, had called the incident room to say that he recognised

North as one of the men he'd had to throw out just before 6.30 on the night the tutor met his death. He remembered the incident particularly because it was Bonfire Night and he'd been hosting a firework party in the pub garden. The evening had been going well until North and another man started fighting. The landlord and a couple of the bar staff broke it up and asked them to leave.

Wesley sat on the edge of his seat waiting for the punchline.

'He gave a good description of the man North had a scrap with,' said Gerry, his eyes gleaming with triumph. 'We've got him down in the interview room.'

35

Neil's test pits had contained nothing apart from the remains of a dagger, half rusted away. It was in such a state of decay that it was difficult to tell what it had originally looked like, but he knew the lab could work miracles with corroded metal.

His next job was to dismantle the altar to take it to a safe place, and when he suggested to Dave that they try to move it, Dave agreed, adding that some of the builders might be able to help.

Neil muttered, 'In our dreams' before making a tentative attempt to shift the structure to see how heavy it was. He slid his hand into a small hollow space round the back and his exploring fingers came into contact with something soft. As they reached in further, the object moved. Something was hidden in there, and he intended to find out what it was.

Rachel called at Geoff's cottage, carrying little Freddie on her hip. Benedict Graves found it hard to imagine her as a police officer – a detective sergeant. He thought of her as a maternal farmer's wife because that was the only role he'd ever seen her playing. Although at times he'd noticed that her manner was sharp, as though she was accustomed to asking awkward questions.

She'd brought surprising news about his damaged car; news that had upset Ben so much that at first he refused to believe it. He still couldn't recall much about his past, but surely he'd remember if he had the sort of enemies who'd want him dead.

'I know you've been asked this before, but can you remember who you were visiting? Please try. Was it Nesbarton Hall? There were books in your car.'

'Are they safe?'

'Yes, they're at the police station. The police have been told that you've done business with Silas Smithson in London. Were you here to visit him or somebody else?'

Ben shook his head. Smithson's name was familiar, but the memories were still elusive. Rachel left, promising to return, and adding that as soon as he remembered anything, the police would want another word.

'She's a good 'un,' said Geoff as she shut the front door of his cottage behind her. 'When our Nigel said he was marrying a policewoman, I wondered what the family were getting, but she's all right is our Rachel. Are you sure you don't remember anything?'

Ben didn't answer. Instead he told Geoff that he was going to lie down because he had another headache. Geoff had been against him seeking medical attention, saying the old country ways were still the best, but Rachel and her husband had persuaded him to go to A&E first thing that morning, despite his insistence that Geoff's regime of rest, care, compresses and herbal mixtures was working wonders. Nigel had driven him to Tradmouth Hospital, where, after a scan, an overworked doctor had assured him that he could detect no lasting damage.

However, Rachel's shocking news that his brake pipes had been tampered with and the police were treating it as a crime made him feel quite sick. She'd asked him whether he had any enemies, and his answer had been no. Definitely not. Then she'd asked whether there was anyone who would benefit from his death. A relative, for instance? Again the answer was no. When he told her that as far as he knew, he was alone in the world, she'd given him a pitying look.

She'd revealed that the police were wondering whether there was any connection between his accident and the murder of Patrick North. But all Ben knew for certain was that he hadn't killed North or anyone else for that matter. Why would he?

He hadn't known whether to tell Rachel that his memory had begun to return in short bursts, like a pitch-dark room illuminated for a few seconds by a flash of lightning. He wasn't sure whether the trauma of the accident was causing his mind to play tricks on him, so he didn't mention that he had a vague memory of calling at a big house and being sent away. After that, everything was blank. He also kept having brief visions of a sedan chair, with its richly dressed passenger, a Georgian lady in a wig and satin gown, waiting to be taken ... he didn't know where. He remembered her dull, dead eyes staring at him, and when he closed his own eyes, he saw her again, as though she was determined to haunt him.

Cosmo Mearson's chair was bolted to the floor. It was a chair that had been sat in by countless criminals, violent and not so violent.

The solicitor provided by his stepfather was a small, dapper man with a neat beard and an expensive suit. Wesley guessed his advice was expensive too. The man looked alert, as though he was preparing to pounce if they overstepped the mark in any way. He was a professional, but even so, Cosmo didn't seem particularly happy about him being there.

He was even less happy when Gerry asked his next question.

'You were drinking in the Crown and Anchor in Tradington when they had their fireworks party last Saturday.'

'There's no law against it.' Cosmo smirked at the solicitor, who shot him a warning look.

'What time were you there?' Wesley asked.

'I went about five to see the fireworks. Left around six thirty.'

'Left or was chucked out?' said Gerry.

Cosmo turned to the solicitor. 'You can't let him ask that. It's not relevant.'

The solicitor gave a slight shake of his head. 'It's a reasonable question, so it might be best if you answered.'

'Fat lot of help you are. OK, that little Hitler of a landlord threw me out.'

'Because?' Wesley tilted his head enquiringly.

'Had a bit of a disagreement with one of the locals. Nothing heavy.'

'Is that where you got those bruises?' Gerry asked.

Cosmo shrugged.

'We have reason to believe the man you had the disagreement with was Patrick North. You knew him when he was teaching at Falsham Place, the school you attended. Why were you and North fighting?'

'He recognised me. Started giving me a hard time. Asked me why I wasn't in America. I told him it was none of his bloody business what I did. He was getting on my nerves, so I punched him. He fought back, but I got the better of him. You should have seen his face,' he added with an unpleasant smirk. 'That man was a complete loser.'

'Patrick North died later that night. He was shot.' Wesley calmly opened the file in front of him and took out a sheet of paper. 'Officers have made a search of the flat you're sharing with your stepfather. They found a firearm in your wardrobe, which is against the firearms regulations – it should have been in a secure cabinet.'

Mearson gave another bored shrug. 'So charge me.'

'It was a .22 rifle. Mr North was killed with a .22 rifle and yours has been sent off for testing at our ballistics lab.'

Cosmo froze and sat expressionless for a few moments. 'For your information, I was back at the flat by half seven and I spent the rest of that evening with Jason. He'll tell you.' He turned to his solicitor. 'I've had enough of this crap. When can I go?'

'We've been told that you were responsible for a serious sexual assault against a young woman called Lisa Lowe.'

The solicitor whispered something to him. Mearson replied, 'No comment.'

'I have to warn you that the incident might be investigated, resulting in charges being brought.'

Cosmo turned to his solicitor. 'Can they do that?'

The man didn't reply.

Tatiana was fed up of staying with Auntie Betina and the two old women who were trying to be writers. The one called Della kept talking to her, telling her about all the things she'd done, and how writing was good for her soul and helped to balance her chakras, whatever they were. Della's long hair was turning grey, and she wore bright long dresses. She really fancied herself and Darius would have found her hilarious. But then her brother laughed at a lot of things, even things that weren't funny. The other woman was called Georgina and she was intense and a little scary. Tatiana didn't particularly like either of them, and she felt sorry for her auntie having to put up with people like them for money.

Since she'd told her aunt that she thought a man had been watching her, Betina had met her from the school bus every evening in that embarrassing purple hearse. Some of the other girls had seen it and had started teasing her and saying hurtful things. She wished she'd never mentioned the man, but today she intended to thwart Betina's plans. School had finished early because of a broken boiler, so she planned to walk home from the bus stop on her own.

She got off the bus in the village and headed down the lane. There'd been another murder – an old woman from the village had been found dead in the churchyard, which was really exciting. Boring, boastful Della had mentioned that the black policeman who'd come to speak to her was her daughter's husband. She'd quite liked Inspector Peterson. He was nicer than the others and she wondered what he thought of Della. But most of all she wondered whether he had any idea who'd killed Mr North and the woman in the churchyard. Auntie Betina said it might have been one of the criminals from the hostel in the village, but Tatiana was sure she was wrong.

She was free for once and she felt daring, reckless. So daring that she fancied venturing into the woods to see where Mr North had been found. She'd never seen a crime scene before and she wondered whether there were any clues left there. She'd heard her auntie saying that the police had finished searching and that they were now concentrating on the churchyard, so she wouldn't be disturbed. Her heart was beating fast as she left the lane leading to the lodge and made her way across the fields.

But when she got to the woods, her courage started to fail her. What had seemed exciting in the safety of the school bus now felt scary. She saw the trees towering in front of her, cutting out the fading light, and the crows calling from the treetops sounded like mocking demons, daring her to enter their dark domain.

She'd go in just a little way and then she'd hurry home to the safety of Auntie Betina's lodge. She took a step into the gloom. Then another, and another. Eventually she stopped at the tattered barrier of blue and white tape, certain that she could feel the ghost of the dead man behind her, breathing down her neck. She heard a twig crack, and muffled laughter. The ghost was mocking her fear.

She thought her heart would burst from her chest as she ran towards the lane, her feet heavy with terror.

A week later, the servant who brought my victuals told me that the monks were to assemble again that night. I did not know their identities, but I surmised that they were rich young men of the neighbourhood, perhaps even the sons of Samuel Nescote's fellow privateers.

As I readied the grotto for my guests, I found that I was looking forward to another night of folly. I had greatly enjoyed that first occasion, and the thought that I would be paid handsomely for my pains lifted my spirits.

Darkness fell, but by now I was used to the sounds of the night. Soon there would be more sounds, drunken singing and revelry.

It was late in the evening when I saw the blazing torches approaching, and as they drew near, I saw that there was one amongst them who did not wear a robe. The young woman was carried by one of the monks, her body limp and her head lolling back. She had either fallen in a faint or she was dead. My heart sank. This wasn't what I had anticipated.

The leader of the little procession pushed back his cowl, and I recognised Dionisio at once. He was grinning. 'Fellow monks of the Order of St Dionisio,' he began. 'Behold, our high priest – the wild man.' He turned to the others. *'Bring in the sacrifice.'*

I watched with horror as they carried the insensible girl into the grotto and then into the inner chamber. She was laid upon the altar and I was handed a blade.

The silence seemed to crackle in the flickering torchlight. To my horror, I realised that I was meant to end this girl's life; to commit the dreadful act of murder. She was half naked, her clothes torn and her skirt, or what was left of it, raised. She was bleeding. I was not so innocent in the ways of lust that I did not understand what had befallen her.

I wanted no part of this. I had imagined foolishness, not this evil. I took the blade and held it above her, ordering the others to retreat. I'd once had to pretend to stab one of my fellow actors in a play, and I would repeat that performance now. I shifted her arm a little and glanced round, ensuring that they could not see my deception. I held the dagger up in both hands and embarked on an incantation in a strange language of my own invention, dancing around a little until my body was shielding the girl's. Then I plunged the dagger downwards, uttering a great cry.

I turned to the assembled company. *'The sacrifice has been made. The soul is offered and accepted.'* There was blood on the girl's legs, and I smeared some on my hands, which I held up to the heavens, gibbering like the wild man I was pretending to be.

'Let the revels commence,' I shouted, hoping the girl wouldn't stir. I had plunged the dagger between her arm and her armpit, just as I had with my fellow actor. I needed to get rid of Dionisio and his companions if I was to preserve her life.

They were filling their tankards when I bent and whispered

in the girl's ear. 'Do not move. Play dead and you will be safe. Keep perfectly still.' I prayed that she had heard me.

In my role of high priest, I was able to lead the monks outside into the clearing, where we danced and drank. I took Dionisio to one side and whispered that I would deal with our victim if a servant would bring me a spade. He laughed, and I realised to my great relief that he was far too drunk to realise my deception. But I only pretended to drink the wine. I needed to keep my wits about me.

36

Another phone call to Jason Fonsby was enough to confirm that their suspect had lied to them. Wesley and Gerry returned to the interview room. Cosmo's solicitor was looking restless, as though he'd rather be somewhere else. Wesley couldn't blame him.

'Your stepdad says you weren't at home on the night of the fifth. You said you were back at the flat by seven thirty, but he told us you didn't get back until midnight. We know you had a fight with Patrick North in the pub, but what did you do after that?' Gerry leaned forward, his eyes focused on the suspect's face, alert for any slight change in expression that might indicate he was lying.

Cosmo sat back in his chair and shrugged, avoiding Gerry's gaze. 'OK. I admit I was a bit economical with the truth, but I didn't want to get the person I was with into trouble.'

'Why should they be in trouble?' Wesley asked.

'No comment.'

'We need a name. If we don't get one, you have no alibi for the murder of Patrick North.'

Cosmo Mearson's expression of studied boredom hadn't changed, but Wesley thought he saw a glimmer of something akin to doubt in the young man's eyes; as though he was weighing up his options. The solicitor asked if he could have a word with his client in private, and the two detectives stood up to leave, announcing their departure for the benefit of the tape and switching off the recording machine.

'What do you think, Wes?' Gerry asked outside the interview room.

'He isn't as cocky as he was before Jason Fonsby refused to back up his alibi.'

'Agreed. But did he do it?'

'He assaulted Lisa Lowe, and he punched Patrick North in the pub. He can't control his impulses, so I think hunting North down with his rifle is very much in character, don't you?'

Gerry nodded. 'What about Elspeth Bell?'

'She probably witnessed something and Mearson found out somehow.'

'Then why didn't she tell us when she spoke to us?'

'That's the one thing that doesn't make sense. I can't imagine her covering up for anyone, and I certainly don't see her as a blackmailer.' Wesley thought for a moment. 'Of course, there's another possibility. She might not have realised the significance of what she saw until later.'

'Or maybe Mearson found out he enjoyed killing and decided to use her as target practice. I wouldn't put that past him.'

'You could be right.' Wesley looked at his watch. 'I think his solicitor's had enough time now, don't you?'

When they entered the interview room for round two, Cosmo seemed more subdued. And the solicitor was looking more confident.

'My client has decided to provide the information you asked for,' he said. 'He went straight from the pub to Dukesbridge, where he met a drug dealer. He purchased a quantity of illegal substances and spent the rest of the evening there.'

'We'll need the name of the dealer,' said Gerry, his pen poised over his notebook.

It was the solicitor who answered. 'Apparently he's quite well known in the Dukesbridge area. His name's Jordan Green.'

Neil's hand came into contact with something that felt like rotting wood, which crumbled under his touch. He guessed it was some kind of container that had disintegrated over the years, and he needed to take care if he wasn't going to damage the contents. But the more he wriggled his fingers in an attempt to get hold of it, the more it seemed to slide from his grasp. They needed to move the altar further out – which might be easier said than done.

In Jason Fonsby's absence, he managed to persuade a couple of the builders to come and lend a hand, and with their help, it didn't take long to shift the altar so that he could access the concealed space in the back. He had a finds tray ready to receive the remains of what turned out to be a wooden box. It had once been richly carved with what might have been a hunting scene. It was a foot long and eight inches high, and the front had completely rotted to reveal something soft within. The hinges had long since rusted away and the wood was spongy to the touch, but he managed to lift the lid in one piece.

Inside was an ancient piece of oilcloth that looked as though it had once protected something inside, but it had clearly been disturbed and whatever the box had once contained had been removed – possibly recently. Even so, he handled the box carefully as he placed it in the tray. He'd examine it more closely in the lab. In the meantime, he needed to be patient.

But the proximity of the skeleton and all those coins told him he was on to something important.

Jordan Green was nowhere to be found. He wasn't in his flat, and nobody at the Pillar Club knew where he was either. He was still a suspect for Patrick North's murder, and now another suspect was using him as an alibi. They needed to find him as a matter of urgency.

They hadn't had enough evidence to hold Green in custody, and the budget hadn't allowed for round-the-clock surveillance, but Wesley knew that blustering about the situation made Gerry feel better. Wesley contacted the drugs squad to find out whether they had any idea where Green might be, but they said they didn't know.

It wasn't until six o'clock that evening that the news came in. Jordan Green had been found in an alley in Morbay suffering from stab wounds and had been taken to hospital. It was touch and go.

Tatiana had been unusually quiet since Betina had told her off the previous night. She'd shouted at the girl, more in worry than anger, because she'd been imagining all sorts of terrible scenarios while she'd been out looking for her niece. It turned out that Tatiana had been sent home from school early, but instead of letting her know, she'd taken the bus and walked home by herself; then, to make matters worse, when she'd arrived at the lodge she'd refused to say why she was late or where she'd been. When Betina had demanded an explanation, Tatiana had clammed up. Betina's main fear was that the girl's silence might have something to do with the man who'd been watching her.

But there was another possibility. Perhaps Tatiana had been late because she'd called at the hall for some reason. Perhaps Karensa Carlton had upset her and that was why she was refusing to talk. Karensa had always seemed to regard Tatiana as a nuisance, favouring Darius. Betina suspected she knew the reason, but that didn't mean it was right. Betina loved her niece, and she wouldn't tolerate anybody upsetting her.

Betina left Tatiana doing her homework. Della and Georgina had finished work for the day, and they'd agreed to keep an eye on the girl for her. Since Georgina had told her about her dealings with Silas, the two women had struck up a new rapport. Betina had never had anything to do with her brother's questionable business methods, but even so, she couldn't help feeling a little responsible. Silas was her own flesh and blood, and if he was ruining people's lives, he had to make amends.

Betina had suggested to Georgina that she write a letter to Silas as she'd planned, detailing all the problems she'd encountered since she'd started to do business with him, and that the tone should be calm and unemotional, just setting out the facts. She'd even offered to deliver it to the hall in person so that her brother would find it on his return. To ensure that it received his personal attention, she would write a covering note and address the envelope herself so that Silas would recognise her writing; then she'd leave it in a prominent position on the desk in his study marked *Private and Confidential*, for his eyes only.

270

Delivering Georgina's letter was important to her. Her brother's behaviour had been disgraceful – and it had grown worse over recent years. If Betina could help to put things right, she would.

She put on her coat against the brewing November storm and set off down the drive.

37

As Betina reached the front door of Nesbarton Hall, she struggled against an icy gust of wind. On one occasion Karensa Carlton had sent her round to the servants' entrance, but she wouldn't get away with that this time. She might be the poor relation, but she was family, which was more than the stuck-up Carlton woman was, however many years she'd acted as Silas's indispensable assistant.

She felt in her pocket for the key Silas had given her after the last incident with Ms Carlton. He'd agreed with her that the PA had gone too far on that occasion, but Betina didn't know whether he'd ever tackled her about it. Silas seemed to be afraid of offending Karensa Carlton. As for Natalia, she had other interests, and those didn't include her daughter.

She opened the front door and stepped into the hall, glancing up at the elegant staircase. All was quiet; no sign of life. Perhaps the Carlton woman was out, although Betina couldn't think where she might be. She squatted there in Nesbarton Hall like some great spider in the middle of her web, and for some reason Silas didn't seem able to do without her. She'd heard him call her his 'rock'.

Betina thought it was an appropriate name, because she was as hard as one.

Summoning all her courage, she strode towards her brother's study, taking Georgina's letter from her pocket. It was dark outside, but she didn't switch on the light because she could find her way well enough in the dim moonlight that trickled in through the tall windows.

She deposited the letter in the centre of the desk, placing a paperweight on top of it so nobody could use the excuse that it had been blown off when the door opened. Once she'd completed her mission, she went out into the hall again and was about to open the front door when she heard a voice.

'What do you think you're doing?'

She swung round and saw Karensa Carlton descending the staircase. She was dressed all in black, but her face was red with anger.

'Why shouldn't I look in from time to time while my brother's away?' Betina did her best to sound defiant.

Karensa didn't answer. Instead she walked across and put her face close to Betina's.

'You've got no business here. Silas only lets you have the lodge because Natalia feels sorry for you, but things are going to change. You're a parasite, and it's time you stood on your own two feet.'

The words were uttered with such hatred that Betina took a step back as though she'd been struck. 'You can't talk to me like that,' was the only thing she could think of to say. 'Who do you think you are?'

'Someone who looks after Silas's interests. He can't go on supporting dead wood like you. You're a waste of space, Betina.'

'We'll see about that. Just wait until they get back. You'll be out on your ear.'

'I don't think so,' Karensa said in a hiss.

Wesley woke early on Monday morning. Pam was still asleep, but he could hear Sherlock whining in the kitchen to be let out for his morning call of nature. He climbed out of bed and made his way downstairs.

The previous evening they'd received a visit from an excited Neil, who'd shown him the old box he'd discovered in the grotto. It contained an oilcloth wrapping intended to protect whatever was inside from potential damage – only those contents had been removed by somebody, possibly not too long ago. It was a mystery, but Wesley had been too tired to share his friend's excitement, and one look at Pam's closing eyes told him she felt the same. They'd both been relieved when Neil left at 9.30, taking his treasure with him. Once the case was over, Wesley promised himself that he'd make an effort to share Neil's enthusiasm. He hoped they'd be able to make an arrest soon. All the signs were good. It was just a matter of assembling the evidence.

Cosmo Mearson was still in custody but hadn't yet been charged. They were waiting for permission from the hospital to interview Jordan Green. But even if Green provided Cosmo with an alibi, Wesley wasn't sure how reliable his testimony would be.

When he arrived at the incident room, Trish greeted him with the news that the Norths had decided to return home to Manchester and that she'd promised to let them know as soon as their son's body was released for burial. He thanked her and made for his desk, where there was a message from Forensics waiting for him. Fingerprints had been found around the severed brake pipes on Benedict Graves's car, but unfortunately, they weren't on record. Struck by a sudden idea, he put in a request for them to be compared to the prints of Jordan Green as well as those of the young man they were holding for questioning – Cosmo Mearson. It was worth a try.

He called Ballistics, but they still hadn't got the results of the tests carried out on the rifle found in Cosmo's wardrobe at his stepfather's rented flat. He broke the news to Gerry before his briefing, which put him in a bad mood. There were no jokes that morning, and when the briefing was over, Wesley reminded the boss of the old saying, 'It's always darkest before dawn'. Gerry let out a snort. 'If we get enough to charge that little toerag Mearson, I'll be a happy man.'

'When's Alison arriving?'

'Next weekend. Let's hope this case is wrapped up by then.' There was a long pause. 'Joyce has moved out. Says she doesn't want to get in the way when Alison's here.'

Wesley thought it was unfair of Joyce to make Gerry choose between herself and his daughter, but he decided not to share his opinion. 'I'm sorry, Gerry.'

The DCI sighed. Like many men of his generation, he wasn't good at sharing his emotions, and he pulled himself up straight. Down to business.

'Right, Wes. We've got our prime suspect, Mearson. What else?'

'I think we can rule out anyone from the Reverend Becky's hostel, especially John Bell. If he's telling the truth – and I think he is – there was no animosity between him and his aunt; quite the reverse. She was offering him a fresh start, so I can't see him wanting to kill her. And there's no evidence that he had any dealings with Patrick North.'

'What about Elspeth's will? Could that give Bell a motive?'

'It hasn't been found yet. And he denies knowing its contents. It's worth bearing in mind, although I can't see it myself.'

'Jordan Green's still in the frame for Patrick's murder, don't forget. But why would he kill Elspeth Bell? Although he knows how to shoot and he had access to firearms.'

'He's a petty drug dealer. But I agree, I can't see him taking much interest in Elspeth.'

'Unless she got in his way. Don't forget he threatened Gemma.'

'I didn't say he was a saint. Just that I can't see him shooting Elspeth.'

Gerry took a deep breath. 'I think Cosmo Mearson's our man. He had a grudge against North and I wouldn't put it past him to shoot the village busybody just for the hell of it.'

'What about Benedict Graves's brake pipes?'

'Who knows? Graves might have had a disagreement with Mearson. Road rage. According to Jason Fonsby, Cosmo's been in the habit of borrowing his car.'

'I haven't had a chance to tell you. A message from Forensics was waiting for me when I arrived. They've found fingerprints around the brake pipe on Benedict Graves's crashed car. I asked them to compare the prints with Green's and Mearson's and I'm awaiting the results. On the other hand, they could belong to some innocent garage mechanic who worked on the car in the past.'

'Any evidence we can get against Cosmo Mearson will be more than welcome.'

There was a note of determination in Gerry's voice. He seemed to be certain that Mearson was their killer, and

Wesley knew he could well be right. But he still harboured a sliver of doubt. His gut instinct told him that there might be more to the case than an act of bloody revenge that had then spilled out to anybody who might have witnessed it.

He needed to know more.

38

Wesley's phone rang. After a short conversation he hurried over to Gerry's desk and the boss looked up hopefully.

'There's been a sighting in Scotland of a mobile home the same make and model as Smithson's. The traffic police are trying to trace it, but if it turns out to be a false alarm, I'd be inclined to think they've gone somewhere else.'

'The rich are a different breed from the rest of us, Wes. He might have been so paranoid after receiving that anonymous letter that he lied about where they were going.'

'Even to Karensa Carlton?'

'If nobody knows, then nobody can let the information out accidentally.'

Wesley's phone rang again, and this time it was good news. Jordan Green was now well enough to be interviewed, if they didn't stay too long. He assumed Gerry would want to go with him, but the DCI shook his head, clearly disappointed. He had to report to the chief superintendent to bring her up to date on developments, so he suggested that Wesley take Rob instead. And once they'd finished in Morbay, Wesley could join him at the station to resume the interview with Cosmo Mearson. Hopefully Green would refuse to back up his alibi. Gerry said he'd keep his fingers crossed.

Wesley let Rob drive. Normally his companion would have been chatting about the case, putting forward theories, but instead he stared ahead, concentrating on the road.

As they reached the outskirts of Morbay, Wesley couldn't bear the silence any longer. 'Is anything the matter, Rob? Is something worrying you?' he said gently. He came from a family of doctors and liked to think he'd absorbed some of their bedside manner during his formative years.

To his surprise, Rob pulled the car into a lay-by. After a lengthy silence, he took a deep breath. 'I've never mentioned my private life at work because I've always preferred it to stay . . . well, private.'

'I can understand that,' said Wesley.

'My partner, Harry – he's not well. Cancer. The doctors haven't given him long.'

Wesley sat in stunned silence, shocked by the revelation and feeling a pang of guilt that he hadn't realised the enormity of what the colleague he saw day in and day out had been going through. He searched for the right words, something that would express his sympathy and wouldn't sound trite. 'Oh Rob, I'm so sorry. If you need time off to be with him, I'm sure we can arrange something.'

Rob shook his head vigorously. 'I'd rather keep working, thanks. It helps to take my mind off it.'

Wesley looked at the young detective constable, wishing he could do or say more. He recalled seeing him a few days before. The man he'd been with had looked very ill, but he hadn't put two and two together. Fine detective he was.

'I wish you hadn't kept this to yourself.'

'Well I've told you now,' said Rob, staring ahead bravely. 'Will you tell the boss?'

'I think he needs to know, don't you? He'll want to help.'

'I've never told anyone at work about Harry.'

'You should have done.'

Rob took another deep breath. 'Let's get to the hospital,' he said before starting the car.

He remained silent for the rest of the journey, and Wesley hoped he wasn't regretting taking him into his confidence. Rob might value his privacy, but in his opinion, nobody should face something like a partner's serious illness alone.

At the hospital, they found Jordan Green in a room on his own, propped up against his pillows with tubes attached to bleeping machines. When he saw the two detectives, he shut his eyes.

'Mr Green,' Wesley began. 'I believe you're feeling well enough to speak to us.'

Green opened his eyes and Wesley saw they were blood-shot. 'I've already had a couple of your lot here to take my statement. I told them I didn't see who attacked me.'

Wesley guessed he was lying – and he wasn't good at it. According to the drugs squad officer he'd spoken to earlier, the attack was related to his career as a drug dealer. But this didn't interest Wesley.

'A young man called Cosmo Mearson has given your name as an alibi. He claims he met you on the evening of Saturday the fifth of November to buy drugs.' He produced a photograph of their suspect and held it in front of Green's face. 'Recognise him?'

'Arrogant little bastard. Thinks he's streetwise, but he's the type who goes running to Daddy as soon as he runs out of cash.'

'That sounds about right,' said Rob. 'Did you see him that night?'

Green closed his eyes again, as though he was making

a great effort to remember. 'Yeah,' he said after a while. 'I did. He was an obnoxious little shit – wanted a discount. We had words.'

'What time was this?'

'Must have been about seven thirty. It wasn't the first time we'd done business. He treated me as though I was his private dealer, at his beck and call. But I soon put him right. He wasn't pleased about that.'

'What about the rest of the evening?'

Green glanced sideways at Wesley. 'He went into the Pillar Club. I saw him giving the doorman a bit of lip, but they allowed him in.'

'What about you?'

'Doing business, wasn't I. But no names. I'm not a grass.'

'I understand it was a business rival who put you in here.'

'No comment.' He closed his eyes again. 'It's time you left – or do I have to call the nurse? I never killed that Patrick North. You should be asking that woman I saw him with.'

Wesley knew he was referring to Natalia Smithson. He wished he *could* ask her, but the Smithsons were being as elusive as ever.

As they left the hospital, Wesley did a swift calculation in his head. Taking into account the time it would have taken to get to and from Dukesbridge, it was looking increasingly unlikely that Cosmo Mearson was their killer. And this seemed to be confirmed twenty minutes later. They were on the road to Neston when he received the call from Ballistics he'd been waiting for. Cosmo's rifle wasn't the murder weapon. All the weapons at Jordan Green's gun club had been examined too, and no match had been found. They were back to square one.

'Looks as though Green and Mearson have alibied each other anyway,' said Rob as they arrived at the incident room.

'Yes. Much as it pains me to say it, we'll have to let Cosmo Mearson go.'

Wesley wasn't happy about the prospect of releasing the boy. But unless Lisa Lowe wanted to press charges for sexual assault, there was little they could do about it.

As he made for the door of the stables, Jordan Green's words echoed in his head. *You should be asking that woman.* But they had to find Natalia Smithson first.

May 1787

Our revels ended when Dionisio's monks became too drunk to stand. They left the clearing noisily, supporting one another as they staggered away.

Once they'd left, I hurried back into the grotto and found the girl still lying on the altar, although she had shifted a little and was groaning. I lifted her and placed her on my mattress, holding a cup of wine to her mouth and praying she would return to life.

During the night she recovered a little but was in great distress. I comforted her as best I could, saying over and over again that I had rescued her and I meant her no harm, for such was her fear of men after her terrible ordeal that at first she was afraid. I found some food and gave it to her along with more wine and ale, and she ate and drank hungrily. 'They will not return,' I promised, hoping it was the truth.

I asked her for her name and enquired where she lived, and she told me she was called Annie and she lived with her mother in a cottage on the estate. She was only sixteen and she worked as a milkmaid on the home farm. Master Dionisio and his friends had accosted her on her way home and she had been unable to escape. She wept as she recited her story and I vowed to return her to her mother. But my clothes were at the hall, so I would have to venture out as a wild man.

When I stepped outside the grotto, I saw a spade leaning against a tree. The sight of it shocked me, for I knew I was meant to bury Annie with it.

At that moment, I told myself that I had to escape and return to London.

I walked part of the way with Annie, then urged her to run back to her family and to keep away from Dionisio and his cousin. As for what they had done to her, I knew there would be no justice. Until that night, I had imagined the grotto and the monks of the Order of St Dionisio to be the foolish jape of rich young men seeking to fill their idle hours. Now I knew there was evil behind their folly.

For the next two weeks I dwelled in that grotto, my needs catered for by servants from the house. So that my masters would think I had obeyed their orders, I dug a shallow grave, then filled in the empty hole. If I was questioned, I would say that Annie rested there, but I had no further visits from Dionisio, so I hoped the terrible incident had been forgotten. I was sorely tempted to seek Annie out to discover what had become of her after her ordeal, but I knew this was unwise. Besides, as my proper clothes were at the house, I was trapped in my role of a wild man.

The grotto was more comfortable than I had feared, and as the nights were warm, I had no need to light a fire. Yet I longed to get away, and I resolved to leave as soon as Dionisio had paid me what he had promised. As soon as I had the money in my hands, I would make my way back to London, for I had no desire to involve myself further in his wicked antics.

Then, on the fourteenth night, word was sent that I was to play my role once more.

284

39

Ben was gaining in strength, little by little. His bruises had gone through all the colours of the rainbow, but now they were fading and he felt up to going out; just for a short walk to help trigger some recollection of what had actually happened. He put on the old coat and wellingtons Geoff had lent him and left the cottage.

He'd learned from Rachel that the precious books in the boot of his car had been taken to the police station, so at least they were safe. But why had they been there? He'd been told that he definitely had one client in the area – Silas Smithson, who owned an estate nearby. But as far as he remembered, he'd only done business with Smithson at his London address, so why would he have journeyed all the way to Devon? He'd hardly have made such a long trip unless he had an appointment, and he'd been told that Smithson had been away since the beginning of the month. What if he'd made a mistake and got the date wrong? He usually kept his diary in his pocket, but it wasn't there when he'd been found, and he'd heard that the police hadn't discovered a diary or a phone in the wreckage of his car. Perhaps somebody had taken them for some reason, although he couldn't think why.

Geoff seemed to be happy to look after him, and until he regained his memory fully, Ben felt he was in the best place. He'd been told that his assistant, Julia, whom he only remembered vaguely, was holding the fort back in Suffolk, and besides, he didn't feel up to making the long journey just yet.

He'd walked almost a mile before he reached the lodge. The building seemed vaguely familiar, and he carried on up the drive. Eventually he rounded a bend and saw Nesbarton Hall in front of him, and he suddenly realised that he'd been there before.

When he wandered round the side of the house, he was faced with a number of police cars parked in the stable yard. People were going in and out of the stables, some in uniform, others in plain clothes.

As he watched them, the image of the woman in the sedan chair returned, more vivid than ever. He was sure he'd seen her somewhere near here. Perhaps she was a ghost from the hall's past, and yet in his mind she'd seemed very real.

The memories started to flood into his head, playing through his mind like a film. Calling at the hall and being turned away. Then seeing her – the woman in blue satin.

The police officers ignored him, but then someone familiar emerged from the stable entrance. He remembered that the man's name was Inspector Peterson, and that he appeared to have an interest in antiquities. He saw Peterson approach him, a look of concern on his face.

'Can I help you, Mr Graves? Is there something you want to tell us?'

Ben grabbed the inspector's arm, hardly aware of what he was doing. 'I think I came here before the accident; I told a woman I had an appointment, but she said I'd come at the wrong time. I remember being angry when she sent me away. I think it was something to do with money . . . but I can't be sure.'

Wesley listened intently, making no attempt to move his arm. 'Why don't you come and sit down. I'll get someone to fetch you a cup of tea.'

As Ben allowed himself to be led into the busy incident room, he caught sight of a large noticeboard filled with photographs. His own photograph was up there beside a picture of his wrecked car. Did that mean he was a witness? Or a suspect?

He suddenly felt scared. Had he been so angry and desperate that he'd done something terrible? Could he be the man the police were looking for?

A few minutes later, Benedict Graves was sitting at Wesley's desk with a mug of tea in front of him. Once he'd taken a few sips, he started to speak again.

'You're going to think I'm mad, Inspector. I must have sustained head injuries in the crash, but now I think I've started to remember things. Only I don't know what's real and what's in my imagination.'

'Tell me everything you remember.' Wesley leaned forward, hoping he was about to hear something that would crack the case wide open; that Ben would be the witness they'd been waiting for.

'I keep getting what I can only describe as visions of a woman in eighteenth-century costume: a blue satin gown and a powdered wig. She's sitting in a sedan chair – you know, those contraptions that were carried through the streets by two servants.'

'I know,' said Wesley. 'Where did you see this sedan chair?'

Graves closed his eyes tight, reminding Wesley of a clairvoyant at a seance, trying to see into another dimension. When he opened them again, he looked round, confused. 'It might have been in the house, but I'm not sure.'

Wesley stood up and called for silence, looking at the empty desk next to him. Gerry still hadn't returned from his appointment with the chief super in Tradmouth, and Wesley wished he'd hurry up and get back, because he wanted him to hear what Ben had to say.

A hush fell over the room and Wesley began speaking. 'Does anybody remember seeing a sedan chair in the main house when Patrick North's flat was being searched?'

One of the uniformed constables put up a nervous hand. 'I think I saw something like that in the old wash house on the other side of the courtyard.' He looked round at his colleagues. 'Some of us were going to try sitting in it,' he said, looking embarrassed that such frivolity had been considered during a murder inquiry, 'but Ellie said it was really old and we might damage it.'

Wesley gave the young detective constable an approving smile. 'Quite right, Ellie. Is it still in the wash house?'

'As far as I know, sir,' she said. 'Do you want me to take a look?'

'Please. Was there anything in it?' he asked, thinking of Ben's woman in blue.

'No. Nothing,' Ellie said before hurrying out of the building. She returned a few minutes later. 'It's still there if you want to see it, sir.'

Wesley asked Ben to follow him, and they walked out into the damp afternoon air, led by Ellie, who was looking hopeful that she was about to play a part in finding

288

an important breakthrough. The stable yard was already gloomy; the days were shortening fast and it wouldn't be too long before darkness fell. She opened the door of an outhouse near the courtyard entrance and stepped inside.

The sedan chair stood in the middle of the stone-flagged floor, out of place amongst the ancient washing equipment: the tubs and washboards, sinks and boilers. Wesley examined it and concluded that it was original, with an interior padded in worn leather and faded paintwork on the exterior. He turned and saw Ben staring at it, mesmerised.

'There was blood on her gown,' he said. 'Just below her left breast – near her heart.'

Wesley carefully opened the door at the front of the sedan chair, grateful that the hinges held. When he peered inside, he could see dark stains on the flaky leather. They looked recent – and they could have been blood, although it would take tests to confirm it. He turned to Ellie.

'Ellie, will you call the CSIs. I'd like this examined as soon as possible.'

As they left the wash house, Ben leaned towards him. 'So I'm not going mad? I did see the woman?'

'We'll know more when the CSIs have done their bit,' said Wesley, giving the man a comforting pat on the shoulder. If his suspicions were correct, this changed everything.

40

The previous evening, Georgina had thanked Betina pro-
fusely for offering to deliver her letter to Silas Smithson's
desk. Her sincere hope was that reading it would prick his
conscience and make him pay her what he owed her. But
she wasn't sure when he'd be back – or whether her efforts
would work. And she couldn't stay at the lodge indefinitely.

'You look worried. Why have you got your coat on?'

She hadn't heard Della entering the room. She tried to
smile, but didn't quite manage it.

'Where's Betina?' Della asked.

'I don't know.'

'She wasn't at breakfast this morning and she's supposed
to be doing a yoga session with us later.'

'I know. And there's no sign of the little girl either. She's
usually back from school by now.'

'I saw you talking to Betina yesterday,' Della said
accusingly.

Georgina suddenly felt she had to confide in somebody,
and Della happened to be there. 'She offered to take a
letter up to the hall for me last night. It was to her brother –
Silas Smithson.'

'You never said you knew Silas Smithson.'

'I did business with him. That's why I chose to come here. He owes me a lot of money, and I thought if I could get near him, speak to him . . .' She looked at Della. 'I'm getting worried. Two people have already been murdered.' She paused, looking round as though she imagined an assassin hiding in a cupboard or behind the full-length curtains. She wished she was home in London. Maybe she'd go back soon, but in the meantime, she had Betina's absence to deal with. It crossed her mind that Betina and her niece might be in trouble. And if that was the case, they needed help.

The answer to Wesley's question came back remarkably quickly. The stains on the sedan chair were indeed human blood. Ben might not have been hallucinating; there might well have been a dead or injured woman in the chair, perhaps a woman wearing a powdered wig and a blue satin gown. When he called Gerry with the news, the DCI sounded excited and said he was on his way back to Nesbarton.

Wesley took pity on Ben and offered him another cup of tea before calling Rachel to ask her to take him back to the cottage, adding that Gerry had ordered regular checks to be made of the premises and making it plain that Geoff was to ring the police if he saw anything suspicious. It now seemed likely that whoever had hurt this unknown woman had also cut Ben's brake pipes in an attempt to eliminate a witness. And if that someone was still around, Ben might be in danger.

There was one thing Wesley couldn't understand: why had the woman been dressed in the way Ben described? There had been no talk of a fancy dress party at Nesbarton Hall, but there was one way to find out, and

291

that was to ask Karensa Carlton. Gerry was due back any moment, and he reckoned it would be better if they spoke to her together.

Rachel arrived just as Ben was finishing his tea, and Wesley watched the two of them set off, wondering whether he should have given such responsibility to an officer who was still on leave. In the end, he asked Rob to catch them up and make sure they were all right. Rob looked grateful for the distraction.

When Wesley's phone rang, he looked at the caller display and saw Della's name.

'Betina Smithson's missing and so is the little girl, Tatiana. Georgina and I are worried. Wasn't there a Russian princess called Tatiana?'

He ignored her last question. He needed her to focus on the matter in hand. 'How long have they been missing?'

'We haven't seen either of them since last night. Betina went up to the hall to deliver a letter for Georgina at about nine o'clock. She'd promised to leave it on Silas Smithson's desk so that he'd find it as soon as he got back. Did you know that Smithson ruined Georgina's business? Anyway, Betina offered to help because she doesn't approve of her brother's business methods, though I suppose that's how the rich get rich.'

Wesley cut her off before she could launch into a rant about the evils of capitalism. 'Did Tatiana go with her aunt to the hall?'

Della had to admit that she didn't know.

'And nobody's seen either of them since then?'

'That's right. If Betina stayed at the hall for some reason, surely she would have let us know. We're paying for this retreat after all.'

'There might be an innocent explanation. Tatiana might have fancied going back to her own room. You know what girls of that age are like. Betina might have stayed with her, thinking you and Georgina could manage on your own for a few hours.'

'But she promised us a yoga session this afternoon.'

'Perhaps she had other things on her mind. Anyway, Gerry and I are going over to the hall soon, so we'll ask if they're there.'

'I might have more luck than a couple of policemen. Some people don't like the police.' As far as Wesley knew, Della had never committed a crime, but she expressed contempt for her son-in-law's profession whenever the opportunity arose.

'No, Della. Leave it to us. I'll let you know if we discover anything.'

He heard her issue a dismissive grunt. 'I thought you'd be glad of the offer. It'll save you a job.'

The line went dead.

It was another twenty minutes before Gerry returned from Tradmouth. The DCI didn't bother taking off his coat. They made straight for the front door of Nesbarton Hall.

John Bell had told the Reverend Becky Selkirk that he intended to move out of the Sanctuary. He had somewhere else to go and it wasn't fair of him to take up a place somebody else might need.

The police had searched Elspeth's cottage, but as far as he knew, they'd found no clue to the identity of her killer. But that didn't mean he couldn't conduct his own search – just to make sure. Elspeth had given him a key before she'd died, and there might be a clue to her murder somewhere amongst her belongings; something the police hadn't thought significant.

When he opened her bureau, he found everything neatly filed, and was pleased to see that the police hadn't made too much mess. As he was about to lower the top of the bureau, he heard a knock on the door. For a few moments he froze, hoping it wasn't somebody from the village watch; someone who was bound to accuse him of breaking in.

He decided to brave it and answer the door, only to find a middle-aged woman standing there staring at him in astonishment.

'I've a right to be here,' he said before she had a chance to speak. 'Auntie Elspeth gave me a key.'

The woman nodded. 'I know. She told me.' He held out her hand. 'Gill Nichols. I was your aunt's deputy co-ordinator. May I come in?'

John stepped aside, pleasantly surprised at the woman's reaction. 'I was about to start going through her papers and that,' he said. 'The police have already looked, but I thought there might be something they missed.'

Gill sat down. She was clearly used to making herself at home, and John guessed that she and Elspeth had been friends. 'Your aunt came to see me after she spoke to you in the churchyard. She told me she'd asked you to move in with her because she didn't like the thought of you staying in that hostel.' She hesitated. 'And she said she was worried about something.'

'About me?'

'No, not about you. I did ask,' she added apologetically. 'She said she'd been in the churchyard and she'd seen someone who shouldn't have been there, although she didn't say who it was. She said she'd tried to find out whether she was right but she had been assured that she'd made a mistake. Then we started talking about something else and I forgot all about it . . . until now. Did she say anything to you?'

'No.' He thought for a moment. He thought he'd glimpsed a figure in the shadow of the trees when he'd spoken to his aunt, but he couldn't be sure, so he decided not to mention it.

Gill took a small notebook from her handbag. 'I found this under my sofa. It's in her handwriting, so I suppose it must have fallen from her pocket when she took her coat off. I've taken the liberty of reading it, and there's one rather strange entry. I didn't think it was important at first, but now . . . well, I suppose I ought to show it to the police.'

John flicked through the book. Auntie Elspeth's surveillance of the village had been thorough, with the residents of the reverend's Sanctuary, including himself, featuring prominently. She'd been observing his comings and goings, noting the fact that he'd been watching her cottage but totally unaware at that time of his true identity. His appearance alone would have made her suspicious. Perhaps he'd change it one day and grow his hair – although the tattoos wouldn't be easy to hide.

'There. Look.'

Gill had stood up and was leaning over his shoulder, pointing at a certain page. 'Do you think that's who she meant?'

John shrugged. 'I don't know. Perhaps you're right, you should let the police see it.'

He returned the book to Gill. He didn't fancy going to the police himself, but his new-found ally would be able to do the job for him.

41

There was no sign of life at the hall.

'I would have expected to find Karensa Carlton here,' said Gerry. 'Perhaps she's gone somewhere with Betina and the girl.'

I had a look in the garage,' said Wesley. 'All the cars are there, so they can't have gone far.'

'It's a huge estate. They could be anywhere.'

'Well according to Della, they're not at the lodge. What do you want to do?'

Before Gerry could answer, a van drew up. The dog unit they'd requested had arrived. If a body was hidden anywhere around here, the dogs would sniff it out. Since welcoming Sherlock into the Peterson household, Wesley had gained a whole new respect for the canine species.

The officers jumped out of the van and released their charges from the back. They would be given a sniff of the bloodstains on the sedan chair, then it would be a matter of waiting while they completed their part of the investigation. Wesley and Gerry watched the dogs disappear round the side of the hall with their handlers.

An hour later, darkness had fallen but they were still waiting patiently. They could hear voices in the distance. And barking.

There was something Wesley needed, and that was a proper map of the extensive Nesbarton Hall estate. One of the team produced a modern Ordnance Survey map of the area which just showed the hall as a small rectangle in the middle of an area of countryside. He needed something older and more detailed. He called Neil, who was puzzled at first but said he had a map of Nesbarton village and the estate dating from 1910 in his office – was that any good? Half an hour later, he had scanned the appropriate section of the map and emailed it to Wesley. There were a few faint features, barely visible to the naked eye, that looked as though they might have been barns and outbuildings at one time, including one on the far edge of the estate, about a mile from the house and not far from the grotto. On the later map they didn't appear at all, suggesting that whatever was there had long ago been demolished or fallen into disuse. The police hadn't come across anything during their search, but that had only covered a half a mile radius from where Patrick North's body was found.

He was still examining the map when Gerry's phone rang. Something had been found.

The sniffer dogs had located a tumbledown barn on the edge of the estate. It was masked by trees and the roof was gone, leaving only skeletal rafters behind. The ivy-covered walls blended with the green landscape, so it was very easy to miss. When Wesley and Gerry arrived, the double doors, fragile and half rotted away, stood open and the crime-scene team were standing around in their protective suits.

The two detectives stepped inside and saw a large mobile home parked in the middle of the cavernous space; a luxurious and spacious new model, gleaming white and as out of place in the ruined surroundings as a spaceship on an ancient village green.

They left it to the CSIs to open the doors at the back of the vehicle, and a few seconds later they had their answer.

'Not a nice sight, sir,' said one of the men. 'I'd cover your noses if I were you.'

'Colin Bowman swears by eucalyptus,' Gerry muttered, taking a handkerchief from his pocket and putting it to his face. They made their way towards the vehicle, where the floodlights were being set up. The smell made Wesley gag, and he pulled a couple of clean tissues from his pocket.

'They must have been here a while,' said a CSI who'd started photographing the scene.

Wesley's eyes were drawn to two figures lying in the back of the luxurious interior. A man and a woman, their flesh discoloured, and observable insect activity. The female corpse was wearing a blue satin gown in a style popular with well-to-do eighteenth-century ladies, the rich fabric now stained by unspeakable fluids. In the floodlights he could see that she had a mole on her cheek, like a patch that would once have adorned the face of a lady of fashion – only the dead woman's was real. The powdered wig on her head had slipped to a jaunty angle to reveal dark hair beneath.

The man beside her was more conventionally dressed in a sweater, chinos and snow-white trainers. His hair was grey and well cut and his clothing had the deceptively simple look that went with a large price tag.

Wesley had seen photographs of Silas and Natalia Smithson at Nesbarton Hall, and in spite of the state of the bodies, he knew it was them. The sighting of the mobile home being driven away from the village at speed had been either a mistake or a decoy. The Scottish police hadn't been able to find them because they'd never left Devon.

Colin Bowman had just arrived, smearing something under his nose to combat the smell. 'Two of them, eh? You're keeping me busy, Gerry.'

'Not me,' Gerry replied. 'I think we've got a flaming serial killer on our hands.'

Wesley and Gerry watched in silence as Colin carried out his initial examination of the two bodies.

'Cause of death?' Wesley asked hopefully.

'Pretty obvious. You might have noticed the gunshot wounds to the chest.'

'We think she was sitting in a sedan chair when she was killed, or soon after,' said Wesley. 'We found bloodstains on the seat.'

'Sedan chair? That's a first. Well, I can't give you an exact time of death, but I can tell you they haven't been here since the eighteenth century, in spite of the lady's attire. A couple of weeks, I'd say. Post-mortems tomorrow all right for you?'

'Fine,' said Gerry before turning to Wesley. 'Where's the boy, Wes? What's the killer done with him? Is this a kidnap attempt gone wrong?'

Wesley didn't have an answer to that question. Not yet.

'According to Della, Betina and Tatiana are missing, and we don't know where Karensa Carlton is either. If they're not at the hall . . .'

'Then where the hell are they?'

Gill Nichols had offered to take Elspeth's notebook to the police, but once she'd gone, John wondered whether they'd both read too much into his aunt's account of the comings and goings of Nesbarton village. He'd found binoculars in her bedroom upstairs. She'd certainly been the eyes and ears of the village. Perhaps, he thought, if he'd made himself known to her earlier, he might have been able to control her obsessive spying on others. Maybe if he'd acted sooner, she might still be alive.

He'd heard police car sirens heading in the direction of the hall, and he couldn't resist trying to find out what was happening. Gill had agreed with him that what Elspeth suspected was highly unlikely. But he told himself there was no harm in attempting to solve his aunt's little mystery. It was something he could do for her – something he was sure she would have wanted.

He took the short cut across the fields to the hall, walking near the woods where the tutor's body had been found. After a few minutes trudging over the damp grass, he reached the lodge. He'd heard the owner's sister lived there, and thought she might be a good person to ask. But as he approached the building, he heard a sound behind him and swung round.

'What are you doing here?' a voice asked.

'I could ask you the same thing,' John answered, emboldened by Gill's support and the knowledge that he was now on the right side of the law. He could see a lot of activity in the distance and the blue flashing lights of police vehicles. But they were at least half a mile away – and the danger was close.

He hadn't expected to see the rifle that was pointing at him. 'No,' he said, putting his arms up to defend himself before collapsing to the ground.

Della and Georgina were in the porch at the lodge when they heard something that sounded like a gunshot. But they thought nothing of it; it was sure to be some farmer slaughtering an innocent fox or rabbit.

Della had a terrible feeling that Betina and Tatiana might have come to harm; almost like a premonition. She liked Betina and felt sorry for the little girl who'd been dumped on her aunt while her parents and brother went gallivanting off in their luxury mobile home. She suspected they'd used school as an excuse and they simply hadn't wanted Tatiana with them. Parents having a favourite child was bad news, she thought, suddenly grateful that her Pam had been an only child so she'd never had to experience that particular temptation.

Wesley had ordered them to stay at the lodge and leave everything to the police. But Della didn't like doing as she was told, particularly by her daughter's husband, so she interpreted the order loosely as 'don't stray too far from the lodge', which meant she could still venture outside to see what was happening. And there seemed to be a lot going on in the distance: police vehicles, flashing lights and distant figures in white crime-scene suits. She was tempted to walk over and find out what all the excitement was about, and as Georgina had offered to stay in case Betina and the little girl returned, she decided to give in to her curiosity.

She left with Georgina's warnings to be careful ringing in her ears, fastening her coat against the chill air. She wanted to discover what was going on, but she knew Wesley wouldn't tell her. *If you want something doing, do it yourself.* That was what her own mother used to say. And she'd been right.

She opened the gate and started to walk down the drive. As she rounded the first bend, she had a better view of what was going on. The activity seemed to be focused on a

301

location some way from the hall, and she could hear dogs barking in the distance. She carried on walking. But when she was fifty yards away from the lodge, she spotted something lying beside the drive. At first she took it for a heap of clothes. Then she realised it was a man.

She took out her phone and dialled Wesley's number.

'What is it, Della? We're busy.'

'I haven't called for a chat, Wesley. I've found a man lying at the side of the drive. He's not moving. I think he might be dead.'

Her son-in-law didn't answer for a few seconds. 'Are you sure?'

'Absolutely.'

'Don't touch anything. Where are you exactly?'

'On the drive. I'm scared.'

'Don't hang about. Get back to the lodge. Go now, and lock all the doors.'

She heard a sound and sensed a movement in the bushes lining the drive. And she ran.

May 1787

I was afraid, more fearful than I had ever been before in my life. There were five monks in total, all strong young men. Even if I attempted to halt the proceedings, they outnumbered me, and I feared that I could not appeal to their better natures. I knew that a repeat of last time's events would lead to a death – either mine or that of some innocent village girl. I had not seen Annie since that night, but I prayed she was safe with her family.

As night fell, I waited for the monks to join me, and near midnight I heard the sound of cruel laughter approaching through the trees. My heart beat faster and I yearned to flee. But if they had some innocent girl with them, then maybe I was her only hope of escaping their evil machinations.

They appeared bearing flaming torches as before. Dionisio was carrying something, and as they drew near, I saw it was Annie lying in his arms, limp and senseless. I had been found out.

'Look what I discovered at the home farm, wild man.' Dionisio's scoffing voice made my blood run cold. 'It seems you spared her. And now you will rectify your error.'

I could no more murder a blameless girl in cold blood than I could fly. I knew I had to defy him, whatever the consequences. 'No,' I said. 'This is wickedness. Let her go and we will speak no more of it.' I tried to address him with authority, calling upon all the skills I had learned on the stage. But Dionisio and his companions merely laughed.

'Would you spoil our revels, wild man? If you will not perform your duties, then I must make you. Or I will perform them for you and you will not be paid what I promised.'

At that moment, I did not care about the large sum of money. I wanted to escape, and take Annie with me.

They carried her into the inner sanctum. 'Now we test your loyalty to our brotherhood, wild man. And no trickery this time.'

I had known poverty. When I left the north to venture to London, hunger and rejection had become familiar companions. But I was no murderer.

They had placed the helpless young woman upon their stone altar, and Dionisio thrust a knife into my hand. 'As the high priest of our brotherhood, you must make the sacrifice before our revels begin,' he announced, pushing me forward.

'No,' I cried. 'You exceed the bounds of behaviour, sir. Release the girl at once.'

His evil leer chilled my very blood. 'If you will not do it, it must be done by others.'

I could tell that he had already drunk deep, as had his companions. One of them sank to the ground as I tried to make them see reason.

'Surely a libation of wine is sufficient. There is no need to commit the greatest sin. Think of your eternal souls.' I raised my voice and held up my arms in benediction. 'As your high priest, I spare the woman's life and demand a sacrifice of your best claret poured upon the altar.'

Dionisio leered again. 'And as abbot of this order, I say

this is not sufficient. St Dionisio, god of our festivities, demands blood.'

He pushed past me, and I stumbled, unable to stop him. He had snatched the dagger I had dropped, and to my horror, I saw him standing before Annie's prone body upon the altar, blade raised. He plunged it down, again and again, and I must have cried out for him to stop, but I cannot remember, as my mind has blocked out the horror I witnessed.

I recall the shocked silence that fell upon the company when it was over, as though the others had awoken from a nightmare and found themselves paralysed with terror.

One by one, the monks fled; even the man who had passed out was roused by his friend and dragged out of that dreadful place. Last time, when I'd pretended to kill Annie, Dionisio believed I had done the deed, although I wondered whether his friends had guessed that I was play-acting. But now this was real; the lifeless corpse was lying on the altar, her torn garments covered in blood. Dionisio Nescote had committed murder, and he stood staring at his handiwork, breathing heavily as though killing had been a great effort – and a greater pleasure.

I recall saying something about fetching the constable from the village, but he turned to me, his eyes glinting in the candlelight.

'You will open the grave and bury her as you were meant to do before. There is no need to rouse the village. No guilty man draws attention to himself in such a way.'

'But I am not guilty of her death.'

He took a bulging purse from his pocket and thrust it into my hands. I saw that his own hands were stained with blood, and now mine were too. 'If she is discovered, you will face the gallows. I have witnesses who will swear you murdered

305

her, all fine gentlemen whose word the constable will believe above yours. Besides, I am paying you well for your silence. And now that you bear the mark of Cain, there is another task for you to perform.'

The horror I felt had made me bold. 'I will do nothing more for you. I am leaving, for it is you who are the madman, not I.'

He ignored my words and carried on speaking. 'There are two people I would have removed from this earth – a brute and a whore. And once my father and mother are gone, I will be a rich man.'

I covered my ears. I would listen to his ravings no longer.

When he departed, saying I would receive my instructions in due course, I buried Dionisio's fine dagger in the floor of the grotto before opening the grave I had dug. Then I buried Annie with a solemn little ceremony, uttering prayers and scattering woodland flowers upon her poor body. Before I laid her in the earth, I threw in Dionisio's purse full of gold coins. It was blood money and I wanted none of it.

42

Neil Watson's report wouldn't get written that day. He'd intended to do it, but Wesley's enquiry about the map had stopped him. He still had the mysterious box in his office, ready to take to the lab for conservation. It was fragile, but he'd searched it very carefully for clues, finding nothing apart from a scrap of brittle paper caught up in the oilcloth. But by good fortune, that scrap bore a name in faded ink.

It was dark outside. And he suddenly realised he was hungry. It was time to return to his flat and make something to eat. Beans on toast probably. Or alternatively he could send out for a pizza. Earlier that year he'd stayed with Wesley and Pam after he'd been injured in an attack, and he still missed the lively atmosphere of the Peterson household. With two children, and Wesley and Pam both working, things sometimes became chaotic, but he'd relished the company. His Exeter flat seemed silent now. And lonely, especially out of the digging season, when most of his work was office-based.

He decided to make a call. Annabel, who worked in the county archives, was an old friend and he had something to ask her. And after he'd asked his question, he would ask her another. Did she fancy coming round to share a takeaway?

As soon as she answered her phone, he asked his first question. 'Can you have a look in the archives tomorrow and see whether you can find anything about a Charles Burbage?'

She said that was no problem, and if she found anything, she'd let him know. Then he asked his second question, and the answer came back immediately.

'Yes. That'd be great.'

Wesley ended the call and turned to Gerry. 'That was Della. Sounds like she might be in trouble.'

'So what's new?'

'I'm being serious. She said she found a man lying on the drive and she thinks he might be dead.'

'Where is she?'

'I told her to go back to the lodge and lock the doors.'

'Quite right. I hope she made it. We'd better find this man – and fast.'

'I heard a gunshot earlier. Better lock down the whole area and call Armed Response.'

Gerry made the call before rounding up some officers to search the drive between the lodge and the house, warning them to take care. Wesley called Della back. To his relief, she'd made it safely back to the lodge. She sounded terrified, all her usual defiance gone.

The wait seemed endless, but it was only ten minutes before the report came in. A man had been found lying beside the drive, injured but alive; he was on his way to hospital.

'How serious are his injuries?' Wesley asked.

'He took a bullet in the abdomen and it's touch and go.'

'Any ID?'

'Still waiting.'

'It's time we cleared this up once and for all,' said Gerry. 'We've got four dead, one injured, three missing and a boy who's possibly been kidnapped. And let's not forget the attempt on the life of Benedict Graves. Where are the ARU?'

'I've been told there's been an accident on the A38 so it might take them a while to get here. While we're waiting, I want the hall searched thoroughly. The owner and his wife are dead, so we don't need a warrant.'

'I've already sorted it, Wes,' said Gerry. 'While you were on the blower to Della, I ordered a CSI team to go up there. Told them to break in if necessary. What's the betting the Smithsons were killed at the hall and the killer thought that disused barn was a good place to hide the vehicle and the bodies? Which means he has an intimate knowledge of the estate. Karensa Carlton, Betina Smithson and both Silas Smithson's kids are missing. If the kidnapper took them away by car or van, they could be anywhere by now.'

'The area's been locked down and there've been police vehicles around all day. No non-police car has left the estate. Ms Carlton's car is still there and Betina Smithson's vehicle is still at the lodge, along with Della's and Georgina's.' Wesley took his phone out again.

'What are you doing?'

'I'm calling Rachel. Gorfleet Farm belonged to Nesbarton Hall in the olden days, before the Haynes family bought it from the Nescotes. It's a long shot, but I wondered whether her in-laws or Great-Uncle Geoff could think where the missing people might be. Geoff Haynes has been wandering round the estate for years, so he probably knows the place like the back of his hand. I'll take another look at Neil's map too.'

'It's worth a try.'

When Rachel answered, she sounded glad to hear Wesley's voice and said she'd go to Geoff's cottage to ask him if he knew anything. But Wesley told her to stay where she was. There was a gunman in the area, so she wasn't to put herself in danger. The same went for the rest of the Haynes family. He asked her to keep trying Geoff's number. He needed to be warned.

An hour later, news came back that Nesbarton Hall was being thoroughly searched by a large team, but so far they'd found no signs of violence or murder. If anything had happened in the hall itself, somebody had cleaned up well.

'And we know who's responsible for the housekeeping, don't we, Wes,' said Gerry. 'I've got a feeling in my water that Karensa Carlton's involved in this up to her neck. Who better to do away with her boss and abduct his kids?'

'But she can't have done it on her own. She must have had help to move the bodies. And no weapon was found in or near the hall. Anyway, why would she do it? What's her motive?'

Before Gerry could answer, Wesley received a call from Rachel. 'Geoff's come up to the house. He's worried about Ben. He went out for a walk an hour ago, saying he wouldn't be long, and he hasn't come back.'

Wesley's heart sank. This was all they needed. 'Tell Geoff to stay with you and I'll order all patrols to keep a lookout for Ben. Did you ask Geoff about places on the estate where someone could be hiding out?'

'He says the only place he can think of is a ruined cottage

near the field where they're building the houses. He used to play there as a kid, but nobody knows it exists because it's in a hollow surrounded by woodland so it's impossible to see. He said he mentioned it to Ben yesterday when they were talking about his memories of the estate while he was growing up.'

She paused. 'Freddie's asleep, so I can leave him with Nigel's mum and give Geoff a hand looking for Ben. We won't go far. Promise.'

'Stay where you are, Rach. The danger's not over yet. Leave it to the patrols.'

She promised she'd be careful, but the half-hearted way she said it made him uncomfortable.

The ruined cottage wasn't on the recent Ordnance Survey map featuring the Nesbarton estate. All they had were Geoff's vague childhood reminiscences and an almost invisible mark on the old map of the estate Neil had provided. Wesley brought up that map on his computer screen again and enlarged the section near the grotto field, scanning it for the tiny faint square that might indicate a building. There was something there all right, and he suddenly felt cold with fear.

What if Ben had ventured out and encountered the person who'd tried to kill him before? If he came to any harm, Wesley would never forgive himself. He tried Rachel's number again, but there was no answer, so there was little he could do – apart from hoping the ARU would arrive quickly.

Gerry had given orders that the entire estate was to be searched, and Wesley called the search team to ask them to concentrate on the area near the grotto field. Surely a building, however dilapidated and hidden by trees, wouldn't be hard to find.

'Rachel sounded very worried about Ben. I'm afraid she might have gone looking for him,' he said, putting his fears into words.

'She won't put herself at risk, Wes,' said Gerry. 'She's not daft.'

Wesley stood up. 'If no vehicle has left the estate, then those missing people must be holed up nearby. I want to have a look for this derelict cottage myself. I'll take the car. It'll be quicker. And safer.'

'I'm coming with you,' said Gerry.

Five minutes later, they drew up by the Fonsby Homes sign. The field that had been buzzing with purposeful activity during the hours of daylight was now silent and littered with building materials and machinery that had been abandoned for the night. Wesley did a quick calculation and concluded that the land to the left belonged to Nesbarton Hall, but he couldn't see beyond the tall hedgerow that marked the boundary. He hurried down the lane with Gerry following breathlessly, and eventually found a gate leading into the neighbouring field. He took out his phone and called Rachel's mobile, but there was no answer. Then he called the farm, but it was Nigel Haynes who answered.

'Is Rachel there?' Wesley asked.

'You've just missed her. Geoff was panicking, so she's gone out to help him look for Ben. She said she wouldn't be long.'

'I've tried her mobile but there's no reply.'

'She'll have it on silent because of Freddie. Probably forgot to put the volume up.'

Wesley had never been angry with Rachel before, but he was now. He'd told her to stay put, but she'd left the farm with a gunman at large. He tried to stay calm. 'Did Geoff say anything to you about a ruined cottage?'

'Yes. He said it was at the top of the field next to the building site. There's an area of woodland on the brow of the hill and it's behind that, where the land dips right down again. He says it can't be seen from the road end of the field. To be honest, I knew nothing about it. But then I've never tended to go trespassing on hall land. It might not even be there any more.'

Wesley thanked him and signalled to Gerry to follow him up the steep field.

Gerry was lagging behind, trying to catch his breath. 'How do we know that Rach has gone there?'

'We don't. But Geoff mentioned it and she's afraid Ben might have gone exploring. Besides, this is the only part of the estate that isn't already crawling with police. I told the search team to get over here, but according to Nigel, the place is hard to find. Even he didn't know about it and he's lived here all his life.'

Wesley reached a small copse of trees that reminded him of the one in the next field where the grotto had lain hidden for centuries. He climbed the slope, and as he emerged from the shelter of the trees, he suddenly saw a small tumbledown brick building nestled in the green hollow below. The roof appeared to be fairly intact, but the windows were mostly boarded up. It looked uninhabited – then he spotted a plume of smoke rising from the chimney.

He waited for Gerry to catch up, panting with the effort. When this was over, Wesley would advise him to improve

313

his fitness. In the meantime, they had more urgent things to think about – particularly as a figure had just emerged from the open front door carrying a rifle.

43

Wesley recognised him from the photographs he'd seen in Silas Smithson's study. He was pudgier in the flesh – and taller, like a fully grown man but with the half-formed look of an adolescent; a work in progress. There was a fine down of fluff on his chin, but his eyes were old and merciless, as if they'd witnessed terrible things and enjoyed the experience.

'Who are you?' he said, raising the rifle so that it was pointing straight at Wesley's chest.

Wesley felt in his inside pocket for his ID and held it up like a shield. Surely Darius Smithson wouldn't be stupid enough to threaten a pair of senior police officers at gunpoint. But then Wesley suspected the boy wasn't quite sane; that the problems he'd heard about weren't mere adolescent difficulties but something more; something time and maturity might never heal.

Sure enough, the warrant cards Wesley and Gerry showed him might as well have been supermarket loyalty cards for all the effect they had. The boy smirked unpleasantly and jerked the rifle. 'Get inside. I'm having a little party.'

It was never wise to argue with somebody carrying a gun, so they did as they were told, hoping back-up would arrive soon. When Wesley glanced in Gerry's direction, he saw that the DCI had his hand in the pocket where he kept his phone. Wesley kept his eyes fixed on the boy's, hoping he wouldn't notice what Gerry was doing, but the tactic didn't work. With the rifle still aimed, Darius leaned forward and thrust his hand into Gerry's pocket, taking out the phone and throwing it on the ground before stamping on it.

'Let's have yours too,' he said to Wesley.

He didn't have any choice. He took out his own phone and threw it on the ground, where it received the same treatment as Gerry's.

'What are you hoping to achieve by this?' Wesley said calmly, straining his ears for the sound of sirens.

Darius didn't answer. Instead he prodded Wesley with the rifle, forcing him towards the open doorway. He'd mentioned a party, and Wesley wondered who else was there – and why they hadn't attempted to escape when Darius left them alone.

His first question was soon answered. Inside the cottage, a feeble fire was burning in the grate, filling the room with wood smoke. Wesley's eyes started to water, and it took him a few moments to adjust to the dim moonlight trickling in through a single unboarded window, opaque with years of filth and mould. He could make out a figure on the floor in the far corner, sitting propped up against the wall, but it took him a few seconds to realise that it was Betina Smithson. He heard a whimper of pain. Then he realised that the sound wasn't coming from Betina but from Tatiana, who was leaning against her aunt as though seeking protection.

Darius ordered the two detectives to sit on the opposite

side of the room to Betina. They had no choice but to do as they were told.

Wesley guessed that Darius had shot his parents as well as his tutor and Elspeth Bell. And the man Della had found was on his way to hospital with possibly fatal injuries. He wondered what had gone through the boy's mind as he'd pulled the trigger. But he knew one thing for sure – Darius Smithson was dangerous.

He addressed Betina. 'Are you all right, Ms Smithson?'

There was no answer.

'Tatiana. Are you hurt?'

Tatiana whimpered again, but before she could reply, Darius shouted, 'Shut your mouth. If you make a sound, you know what you'll get.' He jerked the rifle towards the terrified girl to emphasise his point.

Wesley was sure he'd learned the threat from the movies. He sounded as though he was enjoying himself; enjoying the power he had over them. He could see Gerry sitting very still, controlling his natural urge to say something. They'd have to play this carefully.

All of a sudden, the flames in the fireplace flickered brightly, illuminating the room for a few moments. To his horror, Wesley saw that Betina's eyes were closed and her head was bowed; it was clear that she was unconscious. Tatiana huddled closer to her, her frightened eyes never leaving her brother.

Darius produced a roll of duct tape from his pocket, and there was a sharp rip as he pulled a strip out.

'Put your hands behind your back.'

Both men did as they were told, and Wesley felt his wrists being bound roughly. He sent up a silent prayer that Rachel had already found Ben and taken him back to the farm or Geoff's cottage; that she wouldn't wander into danger. He felt the DCI nudge his arm, and after a few seconds he heard a sound. Somebody else was in the building, probably in the adjoining room. The rotting door to the far side of the fireplace was closed, and Wesley was struck by the terrible possibility that Rachel was already a prisoner in there.

He explored the wall behind him with his fingers, trying to find some means of releasing himself. Darius was pacing up and down the room, poking his rifle in his prisoners' faces from time to time and smirking unpleasantly as though he was enjoying himself immensely. Wesley feared he'd lost touch with reality.

'At least let your sister go,' he said, keeping his voice calm and reasonable. 'Tatiana's only a child. She can't have done you any harm.'

'Just shows what you know,' Darius replied petulantly.

'You can't possibly get away with this, but we can get you help.'

Darius laughed as though Wesley had just told a hilarious joke. 'I'm holding a couple of trespassers. You're on my land, so I've every right.'

Wesley saw that Gerry had opened his mouth, about to put the boy right on the legal situation. But he caught his eye and the DCI bowed his head. He'd got the message.

'I'm worried about your aunt,' Wesley said softly, nodding towards Betina, who still hadn't moved. 'She doesn't look well.'

'She drank something that disagreed with her, that's all.'

The possibility that Betina had been drugged hadn't occurred to Wesley. It was a marked change of MO, but perhaps Darius hadn't wanted to harm his aunt, just put her out of action for a while. This unexpected act of mercy gave him a faint glimmer of hope.

'Why don't you tell us what happened?' he asked. 'What did Patrick North do to make you shoot him?'

Darius's grin twisted his face into an unpleasant mask. 'He got on my nerves. I told Silas and Natalia I wanted to kill him, but they said not to be silly. They treated me like a kid.'

'You killed them too?'

'They were a waste of space. All Silas cared about was money and Natalia was embarrassing. She was even screwing my tutor – how gross is that?' He sounded truly disgusted – and something else; hurt perhaps. 'I wanted to go away to school again but they wouldn't let me. They said I had to put up with that pathetic tutor. It wasn't fair.'

Whenever Wesley's offspring came out with that phrase, he usually pointed out that life *wasn't* fair. He wasn't tempted to utter that particular cliché now.

'We found Natalia in an eighteenth-century costume. Why was that?'

'She wanted us to dress up for Halloween. I told her it was lame, but she took the dress and wig off that stupid dummy thing in the sedan chair and put it on and made ghost noises, saying she was the blue lady who haunts the hall. She thought it was funny, but I soon stopped her laughing.' His fingers tightened on the rifle and he raised the barrel a little as though he was reliving the memory. 'You should have seen her face when she saw the gun pointing at her.' He began to laugh again; wild, uncontrolled laughter that filled Wesley's heart with dread.

'Why aren't you laughing?' he said, prodding Wesley with the gun. 'It was really funny. Her in that blue dress and then I . . . She wanted to be a ghost, so I made her one.'

319

Gerry was unable to stay silent any longer. 'She was your mum. How could you do that to your own mum and dad?'

Darius's finger hovered on the trigger. 'Shut your mouth. You don't know anything.'

The door at the side of the fireplace began to open, the rotting wood scraping on the stone-flagged floor, and Wesley held his breath.

It was Karensa Carlton who stepped into the room, looking surprisingly calm.

'Bloody police sniffing around,' Darius said, his eyes still fixed on Wesley. 'I'll have to deal with them.'

'That's not a good idea,' said Karensa.

Darius swung round to face her. 'You can't tell me what to do. I've got the gun. I'm in charge.'

'I'm just saying it's not a good idea to threaten a couple of policemen. And I've every right to tell you what to do, Darius. I'm your mother.'

44

Rob Carter had been trying to call Wesley's phone, but there was no reply, and when he tried the DCI's, the same thing happened. They'd both gone off after speaking to DS Rachel Tracey, who lived on a farm nearby. Rob hadn't been told what the call was about, but they had been gone for a while and he was starting to worry. There were a lot of police about; some around the barn and others at the place near the drive where the man had been found injured. But it was a massive estate, and darkness was falling fast.

The ARU were on their way and the CSIs were searching the big house. Judging by the number of officers involved, they were doing a thorough job, but if Rob had had his way, they would have searched the place a long time ago, and that search wouldn't have been confined to the murdered tutor's quarters. He suspected the chief super hadn't wanted to risk offending Silas Smithson and his billions, but now that Smithson was dead, all that had changed and every nook and cranny of Nesbarton Hall would be poked into. Even the rich had no privacy in death.

Rob had stayed in the incident room helping to co-ordinate the investigation, and he felt restless. He needed to keep busy to take his mind off the situation at home.

His phone rang and he heard Rachel speaking in a hushed voice. His first thought was that she'd just got her baby to sleep and she didn't want to wake it. But he was soon to learn that he was wrong.

'Rob,' she said in an urgent whisper, 'I'm outside a derelict cottage on the edge of the estate, not far from the building site, and I think Wesley and Gerry are in trouble. When the firearms unit arrive, tell them to get over here fast, and to be discreet. I suspect we might have a hostage situation, so it wouldn't be wise to go in mob-handed. We might need to call a specialist negotiator,' she added, before giving him directions.

'Maybe you shouldn't be there, Sarge. You're on maternity leave.'

Rachel didn't reply.

Wesley stared at Karensa Carlton, wondering whether he'd heard correctly. If she was Darius's mother, that meant he wasn't Natalia's son as the police had always been led to believe. Suddenly certain things made sense. If Darius was Karensa's son, it wasn't surprising that she'd go to any lengths to protect him, whatever he'd done. A mother defending her young was always dangerous. It was the same throughout the animal kingdom.

'If you're Darius's mother, why did you keep it a secret?'

Karensa glanced at her son. 'I had my reasons.'

'Why don't I tell them everything, Mum?'

'Stop talking, Darius,' Karensa snapped.

'Why? They can't snitch on us when they're dead, can they?'

'You won't get away with this, Darius,' said Gerry quietly.

'Why not? We'll say my kidnappers did it before I

managed to make a miraculous escape.' He grinned. 'Or maybe we should say that Auntie Betina killed everyone because she was madly jealous of her brother. She's always been a bit crazy anyway, with her hippy writers' retreat and that purple hearse. No wonder Silas kept her short of money.'

'Darius, be quiet.' Karensa sounded exasperated. 'Stick to the kidnap story. It's what we agreed.'

Wesley looked at Betina, who was still unconscious. Tatiana was staring ahead with tears glistening in her eyes, and Wesley wondered whether she'd been drugged too. Then he saw her turn her head slowly and give her brother a pleading look.

'Please, Darius,' she whispered. 'Let us go.'

May 1787

I had surmised that Dionisio's father, the privateer, was a man of great influence in the town of Tradmouth and its surrounding area. I wondered if he was a murderer like his son. Knowing his trade, I thought it most likely.

I slept ill that night, planning how I would flee the county. I had ventured out in the darkness, but I could find no way into the house to retrieve my possessions and I could not wander the countryside as a wild man. I would be thrown into some village lock-up as soon as I showed myself. I needed to be inconspicuous if I was to make my way back to London.

I broke my fast that morning with some bread and cheese brought to me by the servant with no tongue. From the way he regarded me, I suspected he had been told that I had harmed the girl. Perhaps Dionisio had lied and claimed that he'd tried to stop me. It is a servant's place to believe his master.

When he had gone, I knelt by Annie's grave with tears welling in my eyes. If what happened became known, I was sure I would be blamed. I had to get away. And that meant entering the hall without being seen by masters or servants. It was a matter I needed to ponder, as it would not be easy.

After my time by the grave, I returned to the grotto and brooded upon my situation. But I was not alone for long.

I heard a cheerful voice calling, 'Wild man. I would speak with you.'

Dionisio was approaching and I felt afraid. He had talked of two people he wished to remove from the earth. Whatever riches he might offer me, I knew I would not do it. It occurred to me that if I found him sober, I might be able to reason with him. But when he arrived at the grotto, I realised that I hoped in vain.

'The matter we discussed last night,' he began as though he was talking about some everyday business transaction. 'You will do it tonight and be paid handsomely for your trouble.'

45

Darius looked at Tatiana. 'Sorry, Tatty. That's not part of the plan.'

The rifle had been pointing at Wesley and Gerry, but he suddenly swung it round and aimed it at his sister, who gave a little yelp of horror.

One look at Karensa Carlton told Wesley that she hadn't expected this. She darted forward to grab the gun, but in the struggle that followed it went off, shattering the filthy remains of the window glass above where Betina was lying, oblivious to what was happening.

The door burst open and Darius swung round, still holding the rifle he'd grappled from his mother's grasp. But before he had a chance to fire, Rob Carter hurtled in, taking Darius by surprise. He lunged at the boy, and after a brief struggle, his superior strength prevailed and he managed to wrest the weapon from his hands. Wesley saw Rachel hovering outside the open doorway, watching Rob as though she was longing to join in the fight. As soon as Rob had snapped handcuffs on his struggling prisoner, she rushed to Wesley and Gerry to release them from their bonds.

While her attention was focused on her task, Wesley saw

Karensa Carlton sidle into the adjoining room, and Tatiana began to cry loudly. He shouted over the girl's howls of anguish, 'Don't let her get away!'

With perfect timing that in Wesley's experience didn't happen very often, the ARU arrived, bursting into the room, overwhelming the small space with their body armour and weapons. Wesley, Gerry, Rob and Rachel identified themselves before hitting the floor as ordered. Darius, already handcuffed, sat on the dusty ground glaring defiantly at the newcomers, while the rifle Rob had kicked away lay out of reach in the corner of the room.

Wesley watched Karensa Carlton being grabbed and handcuffed with ruthless efficiency. Gerry pointed out that someone needed to call an ambulance for Betina, but Wesley also needed to take care of Tatiana until she could be interviewed in the presence of an appropriate adult. He wasn't sure how deeply she would be affected by witnessing her brother's murderous plot. If he was indeed her brother – Wesley still wasn't absolutely certain about the precise family relationships in the Smithson household.

'I need them taken back to Tradmouth police station to make statements,' Gerry said, mustering all his authority as he addressed the officers of the firearms unit. He went on to caution the suspects, while Rob helped Tatiana to her feet, whispering that the ambulance would be there soon and her aunt would be in good hands. Wesley had never seen the young man behave in such a sensitive way before. He was impressed.

He heard a voice behind him. 'I'd better get back. Nigel will be wondering where I am.' He turned and saw Rachel at the cottage doorway.

'What about Ben? Is he still missing?'

Rachel checked her phone. 'I've just had a message from Nigel. He's found his way back to Geoff's, thank God. I thought . . .'

'Get home to Freddie,' he said quietly. 'One of the patrol cars can give you a lift. You really shouldn't have been wandering around in the dark with a gunman about.'

She took a few steps towards him and kissed him on the cheek. 'Nice of you to be concerned, Wes, but you should have trusted me not to do anything stupid.'

Gerry was watching, a wide grin on his face. 'Hurry back, Rach. We miss you.'

As she left the cottage, she looked over her shoulder at Wesley and smiled.

The man found unconscious near the drive had been identified from a letter from the probation service found in his pocket as John Bell and the following day there was news from Morbay hospital. He had undergone surgery the previous night and was still in the intensive care unit, but the medical staff were optimistic that he'd make a full recovery. As for Betina Smithson, the doctors concluded that she'd been drugged with barbiturates, but she was recovering well and was up to being interviewed. Gerry sent Trish Walton and Paul Johnson over to speak to her. Tatiana was being looked after in a foster home arranged by Social Services until her aunt came out of hospital. Wesley had some questions for her too, but they could wait. First they needed to interview Darius Smithson and Karensa Carlton.

'Who do we start with?' said Gerry as he walked down the corridor to the interview rooms with Wesley by his side.

'Darius – I want to get it over with.'

'Someone from Social Services has just arrived to act

as his appropriate adult. Let's hope whoever they've sent realises that Darius Smithson isn't your average thirteen-year-old. I wouldn't put it past him to act the innocent victim. He might be evil, but I don't think he's stupid.'

Wesley didn't answer. He'd been thinking the same himself. Even after knowing what Darius had done, he was finding it hard to come to terms with the fact that the boy was the same age as his own son, Michael, who was a good-hearted lad preoccupied by school work, football, friends, computer games and, most recently, taking an interest in his Uncle Neil's digs. He told himself that Darius and Michael's life experiences had been totally different, but was that enough to explain everything? He wasn't sure.

Darius was waiting for them in the comfortable interview room with the social worker in attendance. He had a cherubic look on his face, the picture of innocence, and the woman, in her twenties, with long fair hair and a bulging briefcase, looked at him protectively. He was putting on a good act and Wesley suspected she'd leap to his defence if the questioning became too heavy.

Wesley and Gerry sat down on the sofa facing the suspect's armchair.

'Would you like to tell us your side of the story?' Wesley began, assuming his best sympathetic expression.

'No comment,' said Darius. He glanced at the social worker confidently. But Wesley saw something in her eyes, doubt perhaps. Maybe he'd misjudged her.

'You murdered Silas and Natalia Smithson. Then you shot your tutor, Patrick North, and a woman from the village, Elspeth Bell. Not only that, you shot and injured Elspeth's nephew, John Bell. You also drugged your aunt, Betina Smithson. What have you got to say?'

'Same as before. No comment. It's up to you to prove it.' The boy sounded cocky, as though he was sure he was going to get away with it. 'I'm not going to help you.'

The social worker dropped her pen. She looked astonished. Perhaps it was the first time she'd encountered such malevolence, and Wesley could tell she couldn't wait to be out of there.

He knew they'd get nothing more out of the boy for the moment. But Karensa Carlton was waiting in the interview room downstairs. She was their best hope.

46

They spoke to Karensa Carlton in the sparsely furnished room with no windows. It smelled of sweat and fear and it was the most intimidating place available. A very young duty solicitor sat by Karensa's side. He was wearing a cheap suit and a nervous expression. Silas Smithson was no longer around to provide her with the best legal representation money could buy.

'Darius Smithson called you "Mum". You're his biological mother,' Wesley began after the formalities had been completed.

She sat up straight, looking directly ahead. She wore the expression of a noble martyr. 'I've worked for Silas for fifteen years. We became close and I got pregnant.'

'Was he married at that time?'

'Yes, to his first wife, but she was ill.'

'What about Natalia?'

'He met her shortly after his first wife died and they didn't waste any time getting married – or rather she didn't. I suspect his money was the main attraction.' She sniffed. 'She was very beautiful, and the beautiful can get away with most things, don't you find?'

'You must have resented her,' said Gerry. 'He made you

331

pregnant then he went and married someone else as soon as he was free.'

She didn't answer.

'But he did acknowledge Darius as his son,' said Wesley. He needed to get the whole story; the wounds and resentments that had led to murder.

'That was part of the deal. As far as the world was concerned, Darius was his son by his first wife. I was given a home and a job, but I would never be acknowledged as Darius's mother. Silas trod on little people like me. I'd been one of his employees – a humble admin assistant in his London office – but when I became pregnant, I was promoted to his PA and put in charge of Nesbarton Hall. He had another PA in London, the one who did the serious work while I stayed near my son. I'd been in love with Silas and I couldn't support a child on my own, so I signed over custody to his father.' She paused, staring down at the stained surface of the table. 'I was ... vulnerable at the time, and he convinced me it was a good deal. The arrangement worked for a few years.'

'And then?'

'When Darius discovered who he really was, he began to hate his father.'

'You must have hated Silas too.'

A smile played on her lips. 'He thought the money and position he gave me was adequate compensation for the fact that he'd rejected me and deprived me of being a real mother to my own child. Yes, my love for him soon turned to hate, although I managed to hide it well.'

'I don't understand,' said Gerry. 'You could have brought all this out into the open any time. Why did you continue to play along with Silas's demands?'

She looked at him with pity in her eyes. 'The very rich aren't like you and me, Chief Inspector. Their wealth gives them power over people's lives. He forced me to sign a confidentiality agreement, and it was made quite clear that if I caused trouble, he'd arrange it so I'd never see Darius again and it would be impossible for me to find other employment. I lived a life of pretence, and in the end he came to trust me. He called me his right-hand woman.' She gave a bitter little laugh. 'If only he'd known what was really in my mind. If only he'd known the things I filled his son's head with.'

'You poisoned Darius against his father?' Wesley glanced at Gerry, who was listening with fascinated horror.

'Eventually I told him who I really was and what his father had done to me. How was I to know that the truth would make my son hate his father enough to kill him? You've got to believe that I didn't plan this. I just protected my son like any mother would.'

'Tell us what happened,' said Wesley, leaning forward like a priest preparing to hear confession.

'Darius had the rifle Silas had bought him for target practice. Silas didn't know the thing could be lethal – or maybe he didn't particularly care. He never bothered getting a licence for the thing; Silas made up his own rules and Darius could have anything he wanted. Darius hated Natalia, with her fancy clothes and her lovers, and at Halloween she was really getting on his nerves, flouncing about in that old dress and talking about being the ghost of the blue lady who haunted Nesbarton Hall. He shot her first, then he went to Silas's study and . . . You've got to believe that I was horrified by what he'd done. But he's only a child. I couldn't let him spend the rest of his life in prison.'

'Even when he started killing innocent people like Patrick North and Elspeth Bell?'

Karensa looked away.

'Whose idea was it to put the bodies in the motor home?'

'Silas and Natalia had been planning to go away in it the day after, taking Darius with them. It was something they'd done before. Silas had this romantic idea of leaving civilisation behind; pretending he wanted to be close to nature, although that vehicle had every modern convenience. He said it would be good for the boy to get away from all his electronic gadgets, and Darius went along with it.'

'But instead he was planning to kill them?'

'I didn't know what he was going to do, I swear.'

'What about the barn?' asked Gerry.

'It was abandoned years ago and I don't think anybody knew it was there. But I've come to know the estate pretty well over the years. Every nook and cranny.'

'You helped Darius hide the bodies.'

'What else could I have done? I'm his mother.'

'We found traces of blood on the sedan chair in the stables,' said Wesley. 'Tell us about it.'

'When Silas bought the hall, we found the sedan chair under the main staircase. Natalia discovered the mannequin and the clothes in the attic. The dress was the one from that portrait at the top of the stairs – the blue lady – and she had the idea of dressing the model and sitting it in the sedan chair. I never ceased to be surprised at the things she found amusing. At Halloween she was wearing the dress and wig, and after he killed her, Darius thought it was a huge joke to put her body in the sedan chair.' She smiled fondly. 'Later we discovered that it was stained with blood, so we moved it to one of the outhouses.'

'We found the mannequin in the grotto in the field where the construction work is taking place.'

'That was Darius's idea. He used that place as a den sometimes.'

'What about Tatiana?'

'She was asleep in her room when they were killed, so she didn't know what had happened. Silas and Natalia had arranged for her to stay with her aunt while they were away in Scotland, so I took her to the lodge first thing in the morning as though nothing had happened. We needed to convince everyone they'd gone away, so I drove the motor home through the village at speed, hoping it would be noticed by those nosy villagers, and then returned to the estate using the back lanes. Whenever people were around, Darius either hid in the cellars or went to the little cottage where you found us. It was awkward when Betina let you use the stables as an incident room, but there are plenty of places in the hall and estate where you won't be found if you don't want to be.'

'You turned Darius against his father,' said Gerry. 'You used him – worked on him until he was ready to murder for you.'

Karensa leaned forward, her eyes ablaze with righteous anger. 'I didn't use him, I protected him from that man. I saw what Silas was capable of – how he treated his suppliers and business rivals, even tiny operations that were never any threat to him. Many people would say that Silas Smithson deserved everything he got.'

'And Natalia?'

'She was a bitch. The original wicked stepmother. Darius loathed her. Even her own daughter preferred her aunt to her mother.'

'Tell us what happened when Darius killed Patrick North,' Wesley asked.

'Patrick thought the Smithsons were going away, so he took time off to stay with his girlfriend in Dukesbridge. But he came back unexpectedly and found Natalia's body. Darius left her sitting in that sedan chair for a few days, you see. He even posed his dead father sitting next to it on one of the hall chairs and took photos on his phone. Patrick found Natalia and Silas sitting there and ran off. He would have gone to the police, so Darius went after him with the gun. In the end, the bodies began to . . .' she wrinkled her nose, 'so we put them in the motor home and I drove it to the barn.'

'Surely you weren't planning to leave them in there indefinitely?' said Wesley.

'Oh no, I was going to drive the motor home to an isolated spot on Dartmoor and set fire to it. I wrote that kidnap threat, and ransom notes would have followed; then when the police eventually found the bodies, Darius was going to tell them that he'd been kidnapped. He'd say he'd managed to escape but the kidnappers killed his parents. Knowing Darius, he would have been very convincing.'

'I'm sure he would,' said Gerry.

'You've got to realise that if Patrick had reported finding the bodies, it would have been the end of everything. We would have put his body in the van too, but a trespasser found him before we had the chance. It was regrettable, but Patrick North was collateral damage.'

Her words made Wesley angry. But he needed to hide his feelings if they were to learn the whole story. 'What about Benedict Graves, the book dealer?'

'He turned up out of the blue demanding payment.

Silas owed him thousands; he was quite fanatical about his book collection, you know. The man pushed his way in and demanded to see Silas, and when I said he was away touring Scotland, he said he'd stay in the area until he got back. He wasn't leaving until he'd spoken to him, because the debt was ruining his business. Not that Silas would have cared in the least; as I said, he didn't bother about what he called "little people". He never paid anyone until the solicitors' letters started to arrive – and maybe not even then.

'Anyway, Graves saw Natalia's body in the sedan chair and Darius came downstairs and realised what was going on. He'd left his gun at the cottage, but he managed to sneak out to cut the brake pipes on the man's car. Graves stormed out and drove off in a terrible panic. Darius said he was bound to come to grief on one of the narrow lanes around here and it would appear to be an accident. Later, he fetched his rifle and went out to look for the car. He found it, but there was no sign of Graves, although he managed to take his phone and diary from the wreckage in case they held evidence of where he'd been.'

'Benedict Graves survived,' Gerry said, unwilling to give the woman the satisfaction of knowing he'd lost his memory. 'What about Elspeth Bell? What did she do to deserve being murdered?'

She frowned for a second, as though the name was unfamiliar to her.

'She was the organiser of the village watch and she was shot with Darius's gun. I presume he was responsible,' said Gerry, leaning forward until his face was close to hers.

Wesley saw her cheeks redden. 'I told Darius not to leave the estate, but he was getting bored. He told me that some nosy old bag from the village had seen him in the churchyard. She recognised him and assumed the Smithsons were back from their travels, so she marched up to the hall to complain about something, I'm not sure what. I answered the door and told her that she was mistaken; that the family were still away. But Darius said we couldn't take the risk of her talking. You know what these village gossips are like. Everyone thought that Darius and his parents were in Scotland but if she told the police that was a lie ...'

'Did Betina know that Silas and Natalia were dead?' Wesley asked, wanting to get a clearer picture of who'd been involved.

'She had no idea. There was no love lost between her and her brother, so she hardly ever visited the hall. And if she did, I let her know she wasn't welcome. As far as Betina was concerned, they were all in Scotland enjoying the scenery of the Highlands.'

Wesley felt relieved; he liked Betina. He leaned forward again and looked Karensa in the eye. 'When you encouraged Darius to hate his father, you created a monster, and the trouble with creating a monster is that one day you can no longer control it,' he said. 'I don't expect you planned for him to embark on a killing spree; to start shooting anyone he thought was standing in his way. Innocent people like Elspeth. The hospital said that his aunt was given barbiturates. Was that your idea or his?'

'The pills were Natalia's,' said Karensa, matter-of-factly. Then she frowned. 'Betina came up to the hall and I was afraid that Darius would ... harm her, so I thought of the pills. I put them in a cup of tea. I'm sure he wouldn't have wanted to hurt Tatiana.'

'How do you know?' said Gerry. 'Like my colleague said, you created a monster.'

Karensa Carlton put her face in her hands and began to cry. Her young solicitor looked on as though he had no idea what to say.

47

Three weeks after the interview with Karensa, the case was over bar completing the paperwork for the CPS. Darius Smithson was being held in a secure unit, and his half-sister, Tatiana, was back with her aunt. Karensa Carlton had been remanded in custody. There had been no question of bail.

Wesley called Rachel to tell her the outcome. Whether Gerry liked it or not, she'd become involved in the investigation because of Benedict Graves's connection with Nigel's great-uncle Geoff. Graves was still staying at Geoff's cottage and was slowly regaining his memory. His convalescence would take time, but his business in Bury St Edmunds was being looked after by his assistant, who was working tirelessly to try and sort out her boss's financial affairs, even persuading Betina to cover some of her late brother's debts.

There was nobody to look after Ben in Suffolk – he was a bachelor who lived alone – so he was happy to remain with Geoff until his recovery was complete. According to Rachel, Geoff enjoyed having someone to look after, and the two men were often seen out walking together, deep in conversation. Ben had become a fixture in Geoff's life, and the older man was bound to miss him when he eventually returned to Suffolk.

After Betina was released from hospital, she moved into Nesbarton Hall temporarily to attempt to sort things out. She told Wesley when he called to see her that she planned to sell the hall and the estate. He'd wanted to check that she was all right. Her life had been shattered too.

'Once I've gone through everything, I'll find somewhere else,' she said. 'Somewhere that doesn't hold so many terrible memories for poor Tatiana. I really need to get her away from here. We both need to make a new start.'

They were sitting in the hall's impressive drawing room, expensively decorated in Natalia's opulent taste, with tasselled drapes at the window, brocade sofas and golden chandeliers. Betina made tea for them both, a surprisingly mundane thing to do in the circumstances.

'Will you carry on with your writers' retreat?' Wesley asked.

'Oh yes. If anything, this has made me more determined. I've been looking at a place on Dartmoor – bigger and better.'

'My mother-in-law said she was enjoying it immensely until her stay was cut short.'

'That's very kind of her to say so, Inspector.'

'Call me Wesley, please.'

'Wesley then.' She smiled. 'Della has real talent . . . You look surprised.'

'I confess that I am a bit.'

'She should carry on with her novel. It would be a shame if she allowed what happened here to put her off writing.'

'Knowing Della, nothing will stop her.' He was telling the truth. Once Della had an idea in her head, she didn't give up easily. She'd been regaling Pam with the ins and outs of her plot, so much so that Pam had started to dread every phone call. When Wesley pointed out that it was good for Della to have a new interest, Pam hadn't looked convinced.

Betina took a deep breath. 'The police made a thorough search of the house, as you probably know,' she said. 'They took Darius's room apart, looking for evidence, I expect, but I don't know what they found.' Wesley saw tears welling in her eyes. 'Tatty's always been a sweet child, but I was never fond of Darius – he was always difficult. Even so, I still can't believe . . .'

'I think Karensa filled his head with all sorts of ideas, and they festered in his mind.'

'Do you think there's any hope for him, Wesley?'

'That'll depend on whether he's considered to be a danger to society.' Wesley felt he had to be honest. Darius's future would be decided by someone else – and he was glad the decision wasn't his responsibility.

There was a long silence while they drank their tea. Then Betina said something unexpected.

'When the police left, I had a look through Darius's things myself. I suppose I was looking for some clue to why he did what he did. He was always a strange child, even when he was little.' She hesitated. 'He had a goldfish once and . . . he took it out of the water and watched it thrashing around until it died. He thought it was funny. He used to crush insects very slowly and watch them die. He wanted a puppy once, but Silas wouldn't buy one for him. He said pets were too much trouble, but I don't think that was the reason. I think even then he was frightened about what Darius would do.'

'Parents often know instinctively, even if they can't admit it to themselves,' said Wesley.

'But Karensa defended him. She helped him; covered for him.'

'Mothers protect their young, even when those young do terrible things.'

Betina nodded. 'When I was going through his room, I found something hidden under his bed; I think it's some sort of diary. It looks very old. The police didn't take it. They probably didn't think it was connected to what happened.'

She rose from her seat slowly, as though standing up was a great effort. She left the room and returned a few minutes later with a thin leather-bound volume. The leather was darkened by time and handling. It looked ancient, and as she handed it to Wesley, he wondered what it contained.

'I've read it,' she said. 'I don't know where Darius found it, but it appears to have been written by a young actor who was employed by someone called Dionisio Nescote to live in the grotto and act the part of a wild man. It seems a crazy idea, but when I looked it up on the computer, I discovered that it was quite a fashionable thing to do in the eighteenth century. The diary mentions the grotto and what went on in there; the story it tells is very dark. After I read it, I did some research on the internet and found out that the actor in question was hanged for the murder of Dionisio's parents. I think you should read it for yourself.' She paused. 'Darius used to use that grotto as a den, so he might have found the book in there, and I've been wondering whether it gave him the idea for killing his own parents. Perhaps he was under the impression that once they were dead, he'd inherit the hall. Be master of all he surveyed and all that.'

Wesley flicked through the pages carefully. They were brown and delicate and covered with writing, an educated hand from centuries ago. Some of the entries were headed by a date: 1787, the reign of King George III.

'Take it with you,' Betina said. 'It upsets me to see it. It reminds me too much of Darius and what he did. You can keep it.'

Wesley thanked her and put the book in his coat pocket. If it concerned the grotto, Neil was bound to be interested.

Neil was back in the office, wrestling with reports on the various digs he'd been in charge of that year. It was coming up to Christmas. Decorations had been up in houses since the beginning of the month, and Christmas songs were blaring out in every shop, driving the staff to distraction. The weather had turned a lot colder, and the days were short. The grotto near Nesbarton had been his last archaeological investigation of the year, and now the site had been flattened; all trace of the strange man-made cavern gone, soon to be replaced with executive homes. Jason Fonsby and his bulldozers had moved fast. Time was money.

He'd agreed to drive to Wesley's that Friday evening for a meal, and Pam had invited him to stay over in their spare room so he wouldn't have to worry about having a drink. Michael had expressed an interest in taking part in a dig next season, and Wesley wanted to discuss the arrangements, as it would have to fit in with school. He had also told Neil that he'd found something interesting; something to do with the grotto that might provide the solution to a few unsolved mysteries about the place.

Neil drove out of Exeter after rush hour was over and arrived at Wesley's house an hour later. Pam greeted him with a glass of wine, and as he entered the living room, he saw that the Petersons' Christmas tree was already up and covered with twinkling lights. Wesley stood up to greet him. He looked relaxed. His major murder inquiry was over and crime in the area had receded to its usual routine level: burglaries, drunken assaults, vandalism. For Wesley and his CID team, it was a time of comparative peace. And he was hoping it would stay that way.

After Neil had chatted with Michael about his plans for a community dig in the spring that would coincide nicely with the school Easter holidays, the boy retired upstairs to get on with his homework. Amelia, who had been listening with what Neil suspected was a touch of envy, went to her room too. Amelia was welcome at the dig too, he pointed out to Pam, who replied that she might be a bit young but they'd decide nearer the time.

Once the children were gone, he was unable to contain his curiosity any longer. 'You said you'd found something, Wes. Something about that grotto Jason Fonsby destroyed?'

Wesley opened a drawer in the sideboard and took out a sheaf of papers held together with a staple. He handed it to Neil. 'I'm wondering whether it was originally in that box you found in the grotto. There was a scrap of paper with a name, wasn't there?'

'Yes. Charles Burbage.'

Wesley nodded. 'That fits. We've had to keep the original, but I've made this copy for you. Gerry thinks we might be able to produce it as evidence if the case against Patrick North's killer doesn't go our way.'

Neil tilted his head, puzzled.

'Charles Burbage wrote this account of what happened in 1787 – his version of events. He was an actor employed to play the part of a wild man at the grotto. The owner of Nesbarton Hall at that time was Captain Samuel Nescote, a notorious privateer who made his fortune by capturing foreign ships. His son, Dionisio, formed a nasty sort of secret society with its headquarters at the grotto – hence the carvings and altar. According to the journal, Dionisio and his friends killed a local girl. It was her body you found. It all fits with what Burbage wrote. The vicar of St Helena's church has given her a Christian burial, by the way.'

'I discovered that Charles Burbage was hanged in Exeter for a double murder.'

'That's true. But according to this diary, Burbage was innocent. Dionisio ordered him to kill his parents, but when Burbage refused, Dionisio did it himself so he could inherit the estate. Burbage was framed. It was a gross miscarriage of justice.'

'Wow,' was all Neil could think of to say as he eyed the sheaf of papers greedily. 'And you're going to use it as evidence in your case?'

'If necessary. The original was found in the suspect's room.' Wesley paused. 'I think it's what gave him the idea.'

'Of killing his parents? That's . . .'

'Disturbed,' said Pam softly.

'Trouble is, Dionisio got away with it because he had a handy scapegoat.'

'I hope your suspect doesn't share Dionisio's luck,' said Neil.

'I don't think there's much chance of that. Do you know what happened to Dionisio after his parents were killed?'

Neil grinned. 'I've been doing some research, and I'm pleased to say justice caught up with him eventually. He inherited the hall and lived in some style until he was in his early thirties, then one night he was attacked and killed on the way home from evicting a local tenant farmer for being late with his rent. His nephew inherited, and by all accounts he was a decent man who lived to a ripe old age. The tenant farmer overcame his temporary financial embarrassment and kept his farm.' He paused, as though he was about to impart momentous news. 'You might be interested to know that farmer's name. It was Haynes. Rachel's husband's ancestor.'

'Small world.'

'The farmer came under suspicion for Dionisio's murder, but in the end they arrested someone else – a labourer with a reputation for getting into fights. Makes you think, though. What if it *was* Farmer Haynes? What if Rachel's married to the descendant of a murderer?'

Suddenly Wesley wanted to change the subject. 'Let's eat,' he said.

May 1787

I heard nothing more from Dionisio that day, and as night fell, I began to wonder whether my objections had made him change his mind. I expected him to turn up at the grotto when darkness fell, but there was no sign of him.

It seemed I might have a temporary reprieve, but I still had to try to rescue my possessions. I could think of no other way if I was to make my escape. I needed clothes and money to return to my former life in London. I would never be able to forget Annie, but her death was none of my doing, and at least I had afforded her some respect. Perhaps her poor body will never be found, but I said prayers for her. It was all I could do.

I made the decision to venture to the house that night when all the household was asleep. Surely there would be a window where I could sneak inside. I prayed that fortune would favour me in my escape from Dionisio and his friends, and if my efforts failed, I planned to throw myself upon the mercy of Dionisio's father, the privateer – or even his mother, the beautiful Italian lady. I would offer to leave without any fuss, to absent myself as though I had never crossed the threshold of Nesbarton Hall. I was nothing to them, so why should my departure concern them?

That night the moon was almost full, casting a silvery light on the fields, woods and hills. I walked in the direction of the hall, wondering whether I would meet Dionisio on the way. After all, he had said that the deed was to take place tonight. Perhaps I would be able to prevent it. But there are times when I fear the devil endows his followers with extra strength. In any case I will make my escape and I have hidden in my sleeve this account I have made of the events. When I am free I will look back upon what I have written and ponder upon my foolishness.

The house appeared to be in darkness as I crept towards the entrance. There was no sign of life and I surmised that the family and servants had retired for the night. To my surprise, I saw that the front door was ajar, and I felt a sudden thrill of fear. Surely no servant would leave the house so vulnerable to robbers, especially when their master was such a formidable man; a man who had punished one under his command by the loss of his tongue.

I crept up the steps and pushed the door open. There was still no sound from within.

Then I heard a faint cry from above, from one of the bed-chambers. I gathered my courage and began to ascend the wide oak staircase, stopping when it creaked a little beneath my weight, as I had no wish to alert anyone to my presence. I heard the cry again, the muffled sound of someone in distress. I reached the landing and saw an open door. Dionisio was inside the chamber, standing there with a bloody dagger clutched in his hand. I looked beyond him into the room and saw two bodies on the floor. He turned slowly to face me, a gloating smile on his lips.

'Come see what has happened,' he said in a hiss.

I stepped into the room, and immediately he grabbed me,

wrestling me to the ground. I was quite unprepared, shocked as I was by the sight of the two lifeless corpses before me, drenched in blood, with glazed, staring eyes. I recognised them as Captain Nescote and his beautiful wife, robbed of her loveliness by violent death. Dionisio was standing over the bodies of his parents.

I felt the dagger being thrust into my hand and another pair of hands holding me down. The man with no tongue had come to Dionisio's aid. In the struggle, my own hand brushed against the signora's face, and I felt the iciness of her flesh, as though she had been dead some time.

Dionisio bent and spoke in my ear. 'I have sent word to the constable,' he said. 'I said to tell him that our wild man has run amok and slaughtered the master and mistress. He and his men will be here presently. You are for the gallows, my friend.'

They have taken me to the grotto and chained me to the altar to await my fate. I am continuing my true account of what has occurred here and I will hide it in a secret place I have discovered behind the altar in the earnest hope that one day the truth about Dionisio's evil deeds will be known to all.

I am an innocent man, so surely they cannot prove I am a murderer. I will not dangle from the gallows like a common felon.

48

Christmas came and went in the usual blur of food, drink and social activity. Wesley's parents spent Christmas in Devon, staying with Mark and Maritia, who had plenty of spare room in their large, draughty vicarage. They seemed cheerful – on good form, as Maritia put it.

On Christmas Day itself, Della joined them for dinner at the vicarage. She talked of little else than her work in progress. According to the budding author, it was going to be the greatest contribution to British literature since Dickens. Wesley and Pam exchanged glances, but said nothing.

Neil had been invited to the feast, but had declined, saying he was spending the day with Annabel. Pam had been fond of his former partner, Lucy, but now it looked as though she was history. He had known Annabel for many years through his forays into her archives in Exeter, and she'd split up with her partner a while ago. Wesley wished him luck. Pam, however, said nothing.

When they returned to work on twenty-eighth of December, Wesley found Gerry in a cheerful mood. Their case was wrapped up, the area's criminals seemed to have taken a well-earned festive break and the DCI had had a good Christmas with Alison. Rosie had even been civil to her long-lost half-sister. Joyce hadn't been there, he added. Perhaps that had made things easier where Rosie was concerned. She'd never particularly liked Joyce, the woman she imagined was trying to take her late mother's place.

But when Wesley wandered into the DCI's office the following morning, he saw that Gerry was looking deadly serious. He noticed that one desk in the main CID office was unoccupied; the desk by the window, the one with the best view over the river, that Rob Carter had bagged for himself.

'Where's Rob?'

'He rang first thing. His partner's in a hospice. Looks like he hasn't got long.'

Wesley nodded solemnly, feeling a deep sorrow for Rob and regretting all the times he'd found his overconfidence irritating.

'I told him to take as much time off as he needs. That's all we can do really.'

The boss was right. There was nothing else they could do. Pam had been diagnosed with breast cancer a few years ago, and Wesley could easily imagine himself in Rob's position. She'd been cured, but the spectre still haunted him.

He returned to his desk just as his phone began to ring. When he picked up the receiver, he was surprised to hear Betina Smithson's voice. She'd moved to her new premises on Dartmoor with Tatiana just before Christmas. Della had kept in touch with them and told Wesley that everything seemed to be going well and that the little girl was happy in her new home. However, Betina's voice on the other end of the line sounded breathless and worried. 'Inspector, I need to speak to you urgently. Something's happened.'

An hour later, after driving through sleet and wind,

avoiding wandering sheep and ponies on the winding Dartmoor roads, Wesley and Gerry arrived at a long, low stone house. There were no guests there yet because Betina had put the writers' retreat on hold until she'd fully settled in.

She led them into a dark living room where a wood-burning stove was glowing merrily in a huge inglenook fireplace. She had started to make the place homely, with bright cushions and throws and a richly patterned rug on the flagstone floor. But the unpacked cardboard boxes in the corner suggested that it was still a work in progress. The wooden coffee table was empty apart from an ordinary school exercise book. Once she'd invited her guests to sit, she picked the book up by the corner as though it was contaminated and passed it to Wesley.

'Tatiana found it when she was unpacking some old school books she'd kept in her wardrobe at the hall. She thinks her brother must have hidden it there so it wouldn't be found.' Wesley saw tears in her eyes.

When he opened the book, he saw drawings on every page. The violent and graphic depictions of murder were the work of a talented artist. He recognised Patrick North in one of them, reeling backwards while Darius pointed a rifle. There were others: Natalia Smithson in eighteenth-century costume slumped in the sedan chair with staring eyes and a terrible wound to her abdomen. Darius had written beside it: *We are masters of all and our will is law.*

Sickened, Wesley passed the book to Gerry, who uttered an expletive.

'This is proof, isn't it?' Betina said. 'When it comes to trial, he can't lay the blame on Karensa. He'll lie and put on a good act, but please make sure they lock him away for ever. For Tatiana's sake.'

Gerry put the exercise book in an evidence bag and said they'd do their best.

The trial of Karensa Carlton and Darius Smithson would be held in a few months' time, and it was expected that Karensa would be jailed for life and Darius sent to a secure institution. Darius's exercise book would be enough to prove his guilt, although Wesley thought it likely that the judge would rule the journal of Charles Burbage inadmissible. Evidence from the eighteenth century could hardly be relevant to a modern jury.

Darius was in a safe place for now, but Wesley feared that one day he would fool the experts into thinking he was no danger, something he suspected might never be true. He found himself wondering whether some people were born wicked; individuals who in the past would have been called children of the devil. And yet his church upbringing had taught him that nobody was beyond redemption.

As he was getting ready to leave the CID office on New Year's Eve, he received a call from Maritia, who had just returned from spending a few days with their parents in London, taking advantage of the lull after Mark's busy Christmas, the most hectic time of a vicar's year. She had news. And she sounded excited.

'You know I said Mum and Dad were keeping something from us?'

'That's right. But they seemed fine at Christmas; really cheerful.'

'I've just found out why. You're not going to believe this, Wes.' She paused. From her voice, he could tell it was something exciting; something good. 'They knew about it in November, but they weren't allowed to say anything until now. Dad's been mentioned in the New Year honours list. The King's given him a knighthood for services to medicine. He's now Sir Joshua Peterson FRCS and all those other letters after his name; I lose track of how many he's got. Mum's going to ring you tonight – or should I call her Lady Peterson?'

Wesley laughed, suddenly joyful, as though all the burdens of the past couple of months had been lifted from his shoulders. 'Does that mean we're members of the aristocracy?'

'Probably not. But it's not bad for a lad who came from Trinidad as a poor medical student.'

Gerry was most impressed when Wesley broke the news, and he couldn't wait to tell Pam. But as he made his way home that night, he kept seeing Darius Smithson's face, twisted with hatred and something else – pure evil. However, when he reached home and Sherlock greeted him like a long-lost friend, he was reminded of the old saying that every man was a hero to his dog, and for the first time since the murder of Patrick North, he felt that the world was a good place.

That evening, as he was getting ready to celebrate the New Year and his father's good news with Pam and a bottle of champagne, his phone rang and his spirits sank. He'd hoped that the criminals of Tradmouth and district would be taking a break for just a few days. He was relieved to hear Rachel's voice, and once seasonal and family news had been exchanged, she said she had something to tell him. Something surprising.

'I thought you'd like to know that Ben's going home to Suffolk.'

'Good. As long as he feels well enough.'

'That's not all, Wes. Geoff's decided to go with him. It's a big move, and Nigel and my in-laws reckon he should take a while to think it over, but Geoff says it's time he started a new life. He's moving in with Ben – says they're going to look after each other.'

'New year, new start. Good luck to him.'

'Happy New Year,' she said softly. 'See you soon.'

As soon as he ended the call, Wesley opened the champagne.

Author's Note

I am often asked where I get my ideas from, and my usual answer is that ideas can come from anywhere. The inspiration for this book came from two sources, the first being the discovery that November was once known as Blood Month. It was the time when animals were slaughtered before the winter set in, and second of November is All Souls' Day, traditionally the day when the dead are remembered. Later, of course, it became a time for remembering the war dead. It has always been a month associated with death.

My second source of inspiration was a visit to Packwood House in Warwickshire (I love visiting historic houses). There I spotted a sedan chair with what looked like a woman in eighteenth-century costume sitting inside. On closer inspection, this was a life-size (and very realistic) model, a 'lay figure' used by artists as a model so that the aristocratic subject would only have to pose for a short time in order for the artist to paint her hands and head. As soon as I saw this model, I knew I had to include her in a book.

The eighteenth century was noted for its tasteful architecture and, amongst the wealthy, its crazy fashions and excess. Ornamental follies and grottos were the height of fashion, and some rich people employed a garden hermit to live in the grounds of their magnificent houses. These characters were meant to be at one with wild nature, and functioned as living garden ornaments whose services were rewarded with pay and board. Often limitations were placed on their lives for the duration of their employment. One such hermit lasted three weeks before he was dismissed for the crime of going to the local pub.

In some cases this excess led to dark deeds. This was an era of secret clubs, frequented by high society. The most famous of these was the Hellfire Club (motto *'Fais ce que voudras'* – 'Do what thou wilt'), founded by Francis Dashwood around 1749 and known as the Order of the Friars of St Francis of Wycombe. Their ceremonies were obscene parodies of religious rites, and the 'persons of quality' met in caves decorated with phallic symbols in West Wycombe Hill. Members addressed each other as 'brother', and the attendant 'nuns' were prostitutes. The caves where the club met are now a tourist site known as the Hellfire Caves. Dashwood's club inspired many similar sex and drinking clubs, and Dionisio Nescote's society in his ornamental grotto would hardly have been unique in that particular era.

Another aspect of this story that wasn't uncommon in the eighteenth century was the source of the Nescotes' wealth. After 1740, privateers flourished because the state no longer claimed a percentage of profits from ships captured as prizes. In the part of the West Country where my books are set – Dartmouth in Devon – the gentry often invested in ships involved in privateering and made huge profits. Captured merchant ships (often French, Dutch or Spanish) were brought into Dartmouth and 'sold by the candle' (a form of auction that was only completed when a candle had burned down) at the Castle Inn (now the Royal Castle Hotel) and at Mrs Hatton's Coffee House at the end of the Butterwalk. During the American War of Independence, no fewer than fifty-eight privateers were fitted out, and the *Exeter Flying Post* recorded that almost every month a prize ship was captured and brought into Dartmouth.

To come forward over two hundred years to the present day, I read that recently there has been a surge in demand for 'residential tutors' to live in the family home to teach the children of the super-rich. I hope any teacher tempted by this prospect fares better than my fictional Patrick North.

I'd like to thank my wonderful editor, Hannah Wann, my agent, Euan Thorneycroft, my publicist, Beth Wright, my copy editor, Jane Selley and everyone else who helps to get Wesley Peterson's investigations to my readers. I'd also like to thank Gary Stratmann for his advice on firearms; my son Olly for sharing his archaeological and historical expertise; my son Tom for creating my website; and my husband, Roger, for all his invaluable technological help. And finally I'd like to say a particularly big thank you to Gill Nichols, who allowed her name to be used in aid of Young Lives vs Cancer.

Discover Kate Ellis's next mystery in the
DI Wesley Peterson series

COFFIN
ISLAND

Read on for a sneak peek of *Coffin Island*

1

St Rumon's Island, South Devon

The storm on Monday night was more violent than usual. It battered St Rumon's Island relentlessly for several hours and the wild wind snatched the flagpole from the church tower and dislodged a couple of stone tiles from the roof of Coffin Hall before dying down in the early hours. However, the lighthouse, now automated, survived unscathed.

By ten o'clock on Tuesday morning, everything appeared to be more or less back to normal, as though the storm had never happened, and the sea was calm when the Reverend Charlotte Jennings, known to the worshippers in the five parishes under her care as the Reverend Charlie, crossed from the mainland in the little motorboat she'd been lent by a generous parishioner. In her former life in an inner-city Leeds parish she'd had nothing to do with boats, and at first the short journey had terrified her. After some expert instruction in handling the boat, her confidence had increased, but given the choice, she still preferred to walk to the island along the causeway that emerged at low tide.

The crossing took less than five minutes, and as Charlie headed for the jetty on the church side of the island, she noticed that the storm had brought a small section of cliff down onto the shingle beach below, exposing tree roots and fallen rocks. She cut the engine and let the boat drift while she shaded her eyes to peer at the damage. The stone wall marking the boundary of the churchyard lay a few yards away from the cliff edge, and she sent up a swift prayer of thanks that it seemed to be undamaged. She'd often feared that the erosion of that particular piece of coastline would worsen one day and send coffins and their sleeping occupants tumbling onto the shore and into the fierce waves.

She was about to resume her short journey when she spotted something flapping at the foot of the cliff: a piece of purple cloth caught by the breeze. She fired up the engine and steered the boat towards the island, and when she came as close as she dared, she dropped the anchor and removed her shoes to wade to the shore, hoisting her skirt out of reach of the lapping waves. As soon as she reached the beach, she scrambled towards the scrap of garish cloth, which stood out incongruously against the rock and earth dislodged by the storm.

She could see yellowing bones amongst the fallen mess – and two skulls: grinning death's heads with bared teeth. Her fears that human remains would one day fall from the top of the cliff had been realised, but she needed to stay calm. This had to be reported and dealt with in a respect-ful, prayerful manner.

She was about to return to the boat when the breeze shifted the purple material to one side, revealing some-thing beneath. She edged towards it. Surely nothing could be worse than the shattered bones and grinning skulls she'd already seen.

But she was wrong. The half-rotted face of the corpse wrapped in the purple floral shroud would be imprinted on her memory for years to come.

2

DCI Gerry Heffernan enjoyed the short voyage to the island on the deck of the police launch as the clouds scudded across the spring sky. The sea was a little choppy, but he stood on the prow in the sharp breeze like a ship's figurehead, breathing in the salty air.

He turned to his colleague, who was sitting quietly with his eyes shut.

'You all right, Wes?'

'I'm fine,' DI Wesley Peterson said bravely. Unlike the DCI, who'd once served in the Merchant Navy and now filled his leisure time with outings on the thirty-foot yacht he'd restored after the death of his wife, Wesley wasn't keen on boat trips, and he couldn't wait to set foot on dry land.

'Soon be there.' There was a hint of sympathy in the DCI's voice, as though he understood.

Over the years, Wesley had seen suspects underestimate Gerry, mistaking the overweight, scruffy man with the thick Liverpool accent for a fool. Wesley himself always dressed smartly and spoke with a public school accent – or dead posh, as Gerry put it – although he had similarly experienced suspects misjudging him because of the colour of his skin. Despite their apparent differences, even the chief super admitted they made a good team.

Once the launch docked at the jetty, Gerry leapt off the rocking boat first and held out his hand to steady Wesley, who grasped it gratefully as he stepped off. They wasted no time in making their way along the shore to the place where part of the cliff had tumbled onto the narrow strip of shingle. A couple of officers were there already, looking as though they were waiting for guidance.

'No CSIs yet?' Gerry said as they neared the site.

'They're on their way, sir,' one of the uniformed constables said sheepishly, as though he was afraid the DCI would blame him personally for the delay.

It was Wesley who stepped forward, assessing the situation.

'I always thought nylon sheets were the work of the devil,' said Gerry as he joined Wesley gazing down at the corpse. 'Especially purple ones.'

Wesley nodded in agreement. He was too young to remember the days when such bedding was ubiquitous, but he was an intelligent man with a good imagination.

'Should we wait for the CSIs and the doctor, or shall we take a peek?' said Gerry.

Wesley shook his head. 'I don't think we need to worry about disturbing a crime scene. The body obviously came down with those other bones when the cliff collapsed. They'll have to be dealt with as well, but it looks as though they might have come from the churchyard.'

He glanced at the sheet, imagining what it contained. All they could see at the moment was a head that reminded him of an unwrapped Egyptian mummy: discoloured flesh, dusty brown hair still clinging to the skull and teeth bared in the semblance of a growl.

Gerry put on his crime-scene gloves and squatted down, flipping the sheet aside to expose part of the corpse's left side. 'The clothing's pretty much intact, which should help with the ID – and there's a ring,' he said.

'The sheet and the state of decomposition suggest that this isn't a historic burial. But those others definitely look old.' Wesley pointed to the yellowed bones nearby. The fall had separated skulls from femurs, pelvises from ribs. It was a tangled mess. 'I think it might be best to get Neil to have a look at them.'

'Good idea,' said Gerry. He'd come to know Wesley's old university friend well over the years, and he had to admit that Neil's expertise had often come in useful when the services of a reliable forensic archaeologist were required.

'He's digging on the site of a new housing estate near Dukesbridge, so he's not a million miles away. I'll give him a call.'

Neil answered quickly and Wesley told him he needed someone to have a look at some old human remains. He asked him to get over to St Rumon's Island as soon as he could. When he ended the call, he saw that Gerry had flicked the sheet back into place so they wouldn't have to look at the corpse any longer.

'Let's wait for the team,' the DCI said. 'In the meantime, I'd like a word with the woman who called it in.'

'The Reverend Charlie. I've heard my brother-in-law talk about her,' Wesley said. His sister's husband, Mark Fitzgerald, was the vicar of Belsham near Neston but he also had responsibility for several neighbouring parishes. 'According to Mark, she's quite a force of nature.'

'With any luck she'll be able to give us a name for our dead body.'

'Not sure about that. As far as I know, she's only been in the job six months. Besides, I don't think this is a conventional interment. Sheet from the second half of the twentieth century. No coffin. I think we've got a suspicious death on our hands. Either that or it's an illegal burial.'

The sun had just emerged from behind a large grey cloud, and Wesley shielded his eyes, scanning the mainland for the arrival of the team. Sure enough, a couple of patrol cars and a van had drawn up on the strip of concrete behind the sandy beach thoughtfully provided by the Heritage Trust to serve as a car park.

'Here's the cavalry,' said Gerry. 'Let's go and have a word with the Reverend Charlie. I take it she's at the church.'

'That's where she said she'd be.'

'Do we know much about this island then?' Gerry asked as they made their way along the shore towards a set of stone steps leading up to the top of the cliff, fortunately still intact after the storm. 'Strange, but I've lived in south Devon for years and I've never been here before.'

'The inhabitants must be very law-abiding,' said Wesley with a smile.

'Well, it's about fifteen miles from Tradmouth, and it isn't as famous as Monk's Island five miles further up the coast, with its posh art deco hotel, so tourists probably give it a miss. Also, it's only accessible via a causeway at low tide, so the rest of the time you have to get here by boat. No picturesque sea tractor like Monk's Island.'

'I looked at the Ordnance Survey map before we set out. I know it's called St Rumon's Island, but when I spoke to Neil just now, he said the locals sometimes call it Coffin Island.'

3

Gerry raised his eyebrows. 'You're joking?'

'I'm not. I noticed on the map that it's shaped a bit like a coffin; I'm guessing that's the reason for the alternative name.'

'Is there much here?' Gerry asked, looking round.

'The map shows a church, a pub, the ruins of a priory, a large house, ten cottages and an unmanned lighthouse. I've done a bit of research.'

'Good. What did you find out?'

'The pub's called the Hanging Monk, and only four of the cottages are occupied all year round. The rest, including the former lighthouse keeper's accommodation, are used as holiday lets. As for the big house, it's owned by an author called Quentin Search – he's quite well known, I believe. The church, St Rumon's, used to belong to the priory and is still used by people from the village of Midton, just across the water. I looked up St Rumon. He's a Devon saint.'

'You *have* done your homework.'

'I was a Boy Scout in my younger days,' said Wesley with a self-effacing grin. 'I like to be prepared. Seriously, I can't claim all the credit. When we got the call to come here, I asked Ellie in the CID office to find out all she could about the place.'

'That was quick.'

'She's good,' Wesley said, appreciating their recent recruit's efficiency. 'Also when I spoke to Neil, he told me he'd been contacted by an amateur archaeology group from Millicombe. They asked for his advice because they want to investigate the site of the priory. Apparently all that's left of it above ground is the church, a few ruined walls, parts of the pub, and the house where the prior used to live before the place was shut down by Henry VIII.'

'Is Neil going to be digging here?'

'No. He's tied up at Dukesbridge, so he'll have to leave St Rumon's Island to the archaeological society. He thinks it might prove to be more interesting than the Dukesbridge dig, but the developers are paying, and money talks.' Wesley checked his watch. 'He said he'd be here soon to have a look at those bones, though.'

'There's never an archaeologist around when you want one.'

They climbed the steps, Wesley leading the way, and once at the top they found themselves at the edge of a churchyard filled with lichen-covered headstones. The number of graves suggested that there had once been a thriving community on the island. But life must have been tough for the fisherfolk who used to live there, particularly in the winter months.

It was promising to be a pleasant spring day, and it was hard to believe the previous night had witnessed a violent storm. However, as they walked, Wesley saw that the weather had left its mark in the form of fallen branches and a flagpole blown down into the churchyard. The church itself, a sizeable stone building with a stubby tower, appeared undamaged, but it must have survived many storms over the centuries and witnessed many a maritime disaster on the rocks beyond. He could see telltale signs that it had once been considerably larger; scars of demolition had been left on the ancient stones where sections of the building had been removed, possibly by the islanders in need of building materials.

As they walked Wesley halted every now and then to read the inscriptions on the headstones beside the path. Some were illegible, weathered by time, but amongst the few he could read were memorials to drowned sailors. The old inhabitants of St Rumon's Island had made themselves responsible for burying dead strangers who had come to grief on the sea; their act of Christian charity.

Gerry led the way to the church porch, where they found the weathered oak door unlocked. The interior of the building surprised the two detectives. They had expected it to be bleak and neglected, but instead the aisle was carpeted in red and the old pews and brass memorials were gleaming. Sunlight streamed in through stained-glass windows, casting colourful patterns on the scene, and there was a faint whiff of wax polish in the air.

The Reverend Charlie was standing with a group of people of varying ages. Wesley counted nine in all. She was a small, stocky woman wearing a knee-length skirt and a bright red jumper with a dog collar peeping from the neck. Her brown hair was curly and untamed and there was a benign but determined look on her round freckled face.

She detached herself from the group and walked over, her hand outstretched in greeting. 'You'll be the police.'

'Is it that obvious?' said Gerry.

She laughed. 'No. I was expecting you.' She studied Wesley for a few seconds. 'You wouldn't be Mark Fitzgerald's brother-in-law, would you?'

'Guilty as charged.' It was hardly surprising the local clergy knew each other's business – and the fact that the vicar of Belsham's wife, Maritia, a doctor of Caribbean descent, had a brother who was a DI in Tradmouth CID was probably common knowledge.

She gave him a beaming smile. 'Mark told me you used to be an archaeologist back in the day.'

'I studied the subject at university. Archaeology has a lot in common with detective work. Piecing together the clues.'

'Which goes to prove what I've always thought – nothing is ever wasted,' said Charlie. 'Millicombe Archaeological Society are keen to do some digging here. They're interested in what's left of our priory.'

'Yes, they contacted a friend of mine, Neil Watson. He's got some fancy title now, but he's what used to be known as the county archaeologist.'

'Well, if he wants to come here, he's welcome to have access to the church whenever he likes,' she said as though she meant it. She turned to look at the assembled group, who were listening in with interest. 'Let me introduce you to my champing guests and their colleagues. They're all bell-ringers.'

'Champing?' Gerry sounded puzzled.

'Short for church camping. It's very popular. Matt and Julia are champing here in the church and the others are renting a couple of holiday cottages on the island. They're all from up north, apart from Jack, who's local.'

'Up north?' said Gerry eagerly, as though he was hoping to find some fellow Liverpudlians.

'North Cheshire. They arrived yesterday to tackle five peals on our bells.'

'Peals?' He frowned.

'A peal involves ringing for three hours non-stop. I'm told it's something only expert ringers do, but I'm a little vague about the details. We have eight bells here in good condition, so I was delighted when Matt contacted me.' She lowered her voice. 'We have a few faithful ring-ers who come over from the mainland to ring for our Sunday-morning service. They do their best, bless them, but they're hardly experts. Jack is the only one who rings locally – by locally, I mean at St Luke's, Cranton, just along the coast.' She nodded towards one of the ringers, a lanky man in his fifties with thinning hair. 'I'm looking forward to hearing some really impressive ringing sound-ing out over the island again. Although not everyone approves.'

'I wouldn't have thought the bells would disturb many people round here,' said Wesley.

Charlie looked as though she was trying to come up with the most tactful way to answer. 'There is one person on the island who doesn't approve of the church making itself known.'

'Really?'

'I think I've said enough, Inspector. I've only been here for six months, and you learn which battles to fight and which to leave well alone.'

'So you don't know anything about the burial you came across?'

'There haven't been any burials in this churchyard for decades, as far as I know. And besides, burials nowadays are all in decent wooden coffins – or those lovely willow baskets that have become popular lately. I've never seen anyone buried in a purple floral shroud.'

Satisfied that the vicar couldn't provide them with any helpful information, Wesley and Gerry turned their attention to the bell-ringers, who were standing round awkwardly in the chancel. The northern group had only arrived the previous day, but even so, during an inquiry into a death that might be suspicious, everyone had to be interviewed and eliminated.

Wesley studied the ringers: an athletic-looking pair in their forties who looked as though they might be in charge, a fresh-faced young couple who were holding hands, and a tubby man with faded red hair flanked by two strapping teenage boys, probably his sons judging from the family likeness. The man Charlie had pointed out as Jack, the only local ringer, stood a little apart from the others next to a woman of around his own age. Neither of them looked as though they quite belonged.

'When did you all arrive on the island?' he began.

'Late yesterday,' the man in charge said. He was tall, with a shaved head and a concerned expression. 'I'm Matt Evans, by the way, tower captain of St Olaf's in north Cheshire, and this is my wife, Julia – Julia Partridge. This outing to Devon was my brainchild. It was me who contacted the Reverend Charlie.' His words sounded like a confession. 'The prospect of ringing five peals on an island appealed to our band, so here we are.'

'You're actually sleeping here in the church?' said Wesley pleasantly, wanting to put the man at his ease. 'It was pretty stormy last night.'

'Matt and I are the only ones staying here,' said Julia. She was slim, with long ash-blonde hair and tight denim jeans.

'It's surprisingly cosy.' She looked at the others. 'Eddie and Ruth are renting one of the cottages on the island, and Simon and his two lads are renting another.' She smiled at her husband. 'Matt and I thought champing would be fun.'

Matt nodded enthusiastically, and Simon's teenage sons looked a little envious, as though they wished their father had opted for more adventurous accommodation. From the keen expressions on their faces, Wesley guessed that they were enjoying the excitement of being involved, however tentatively, in a police investigation.

It was time for the others to introduce themselves properly. There was Eddie Culpepper, a tall man in his twenties with dark wavy hair, his small, pretty fiancée, Ruth Selby, together with Simon Good and his two student sons, James and Andrew. They were all fellow ringers from Matt's tower in north Cheshire, and it was clear the seven knew each other well.

The last to make his introductions was the local man, Jack Beattie, who was there with his wife. Maggie Beattie was blonde, with the prematurely lined features of someone who spent too much time on sunbeds. She wore a short leather skirt and looked a little out of place amongst the keen visiting ringers in their jeans and matching sky-blue polo shirts with the words *St Olaf's Ringers* printed on the back. The Beatties were both in their fifties and lived in Cranton on the mainland. Jack, as Charlie had mentioned, was a regular ringer at his local church, although he seemed eager to point out that Maggie had never touched a bell rope in her life.

He was the more chatty of the pair, and he revealed that when someone from the northern group had dropped out because of illness, Matt Evans had put out an appeal to local towers via the bell-ringers' grapevine for someone to make up the numbers. Maggie had decided to come along to keep her husband company amongst the northern strangers. The Beatties seemed to be an unremarkable couple, but Wesley kept an open mind as usual.

'We're planning to attempt our first peal today,' said Matt. 'We're aiming for five in all – one a day. Norwich today. Bristol tomorrow. Then London and maybe Glasgow the day after, finishing off with Cambridge if all goes well.' He saw that Wesley and Gerry were looking puzzled at the mention of these geographically diverse cities. 'They're different methods. An interesting variety of changes. Completing a peal is the ringers' equivalent to running a marathon,' he added by way of explanation, before changing the subject. 'So what exactly is going on here?'

'The recent storm caused a landslip, which brought some bones down from the graveyard. But it also brought down a burial that appears to be recent; an unexplained death.' Wesley deliberately didn't use the word 'murder'. 'I take it none of you know anything about it?'

The ringers shook their heads as expected. Gerry thanked them all for their time and wished them luck with their peals before turning to go. But Wesley made no move to follow. 'Has anyone been to the pub here?'

'The Hanging Monk,' Matt said quickly. 'We went there last night after we arrived. All of us apart from Jack and Maggie, that is.'

'We might go again tonight,' said Eddie Culpepper. 'Celebrate our first peal . . . if we manage to get it.'

Matt suddenly looked worried. 'It is OK for us to go ahead with our ringing, isn't it? We've come a long way.'

The DCI said he didn't see why not, and Wesley noticed

an expression of sheer relief on Matt Evans' face. None of the group seemed concerned with anything other than achieving their bell-ringing goals. Wesley knew true passion when he saw it. Only Maggie Beattie didn't appear to share the general enthusiasm. Wesley saw her glance in the direction of the door, as though she longed to be somewhere else, and he couldn't help wondering why she'd decided to come.

As they walked outside into the spring sunshine, Gerry checked his phone. 'Better get down to the beach. Colin and the CSI team have arrived.'